THE STAR OF SIERRA LEONE

PAUL DAVIS MD

ISBN: 978-0-9969287-0-0
October 23, 2015

Blewitt Pass Publishing
Seattle, WA

This book is dedicated to my Mother who taught me an appreciation for writing at a very early age. Also to all the friends, co-workers & passengers I have worked with on cruise ships over the years.

The Star of Sierra Leone

The 968.9-carat Star of Sierra Leone diamond was discovered by miners on February 14, 1972 in the Diminco alluvial mines in the Koidu area of Sierra Leone. It ranks as the third-largest gem-quality diamond and the largest alluvial diamond ever discovered. On October 3, 1972, Sierra Leone's then-President, Siaka Stevens, announced that Harry Winston, the New York City jeweler, had purchased the Star of Sierra Leone for under $2.5 million. The stone was initially cut into an emerald shaped stone weighing 143.2 carats, but was later re-cut due to an internal flaw, eventually resulting in 17 separate finished diamonds, of which 13 were deemed to be flawless. The largest single finished stone was a 53.96-carat flawless pear-shaped diamond. Six of the diamonds cut from the original rough were later set by Harry Winston into the "Star of Sierra Leone" brooch.

Ref: http://www.embeediatech.ca/the-star-of-sierra-leone/

CHAPTER ONE

Betty Palmer

THE LADY WHO WAS CLIMBING the gangway was not elderly but she was not young either. Her brown hair was expertly coiffed, and her designer summer dress had obviously not been bought at the local market, it was exquisite in its simplicity and elegance. She made it to the platform where she was met by Ms. Babette, the famous French playwright.

"Truly, Babette, I don't know why they don't hoist people like me in a basket to the top deck," Betty Palmer said, tittering. "It would be much simpler. Besides, the unacceptable passengers could be dumped on the spot, wouldn't you say?"

Laughing now, Babette said, "I have to agree with you, Betty, these gangways are not the most practical things in the world. But you've made it and that's marvelous." Babette turned to the couple stepping beside her friend. "And who might you be?" She shot a curious glance at the lady and then her eyes traveled the height of the man beside her.

"Let me make the introduction," Betty said, "This is my assistant and secretary, Adele Muesli, and her companion is Gregory Ashton." She giggled, "Gregory can't do enough for me. Short of massaging my feet – truly he would if I let him – he finds the things I need whenever

I need them."

"Like a *"garçon de course"*," Babette remarked, throwing a quizzical glance at the young man.

"Very much like that, yes," Betty agreed, "But both have been most helpful."

"I'm certain they are," Babette added. "Pleased to meet you, I'm sure."

Betty looked around her and noticed, as if for the first time, the chief purser waiting for the three newcomers to register with him. "Let's check-in, shall we?"

The young man smiled when he said, "I'm Armand Guillaume, the chief purser here on *The Contessa*, Mrs. Palmer. If you'd like to go to the reception desk at the back of the foyer, you and your companions will be given your embarkation packets and cabin keys."

"Thank you, Mr. Guillaume. I think we can manage from here."

As she accompanied her friend to the reception desk, Babette's gaze seemed to be lost in some other dream-like vision. She let the three of them register and waited in one of the mini salons furnishing the elegantly decorated foyer. As she sat down on the sofa, out of earshot from any of the passengers standing about the room, she murmured: "Edmund, would you mind trying to find out who the two with Betty are?" She didn't have to wait for a reply; she knew her ghostly friend had heard her request and was on his way already, to try finding out an answer to her question.

When Betty joined Babette in the salon, she told her that she was going up to her suite to freshen up. "I'll see you later today, Babette. Maybe we can have some tea at one of the cafés upstairs this afternoon?"

"Sounds like a plan," Babette replied. "If you give me your suite number, I'll call you later to set up a time."

"Perfect," Betty replied, turning to Adele and Gregory. "Come on, you two, we've got things to do and plans to make."

Ms. Babette was a well-to-do woman in her sixties now. Although she belonged to a noble family in Europe, she detested being reminded of the fact. She had always preferred the accolades and applauses she received for the writing of many splendid Broadway and London plays. More than that, she didn't want or need. At the end of the previous cruise, which took her to Antarctica and South America, she had mentioned in passing that she would love to return to Tenerife in the Canaries and Africa. Lo and behold, a couple of weeks later she received a letter from the cruise line company saying that the management had already been organizing a voyage along the West Coast of Africa, as soon as *The Contessa* returned from her trip around the Mediterranean. Babette couldn't have been more pleased. She had not been to the Canary Islands in nearly forty years and was looking forward to the visit. On the other hand, she had been a little afraid to visit other places on Africa's west coast so soon after the Ebola epidemic had ravaged the population of so many countries. Yet, there was no stopping Babette's adventuresome character. "If my friend, Dr. Alan Mayhew, says it's okay, I don't see why I should miss such a wonderful opportunity," she had said to her producer. The latter was now in charge of staging her next play, which would regale the audience of the Parisian theaters the following winter.

Babette returned to her suite and waited for Dr. Edmund Netter to come back. Talking about Edmund; he was Dr. Alan Mayhew's great-grandfather. Perhaps a little explanation would be a propos here. Dr. Mayhew found his great-grandfather's photograph in an old museum in South East Asia. He was not only absolutely delighted with the find, but terribly puzzled. The reason being that, as soon as he handled the picture frame, Dr. Edmund Netter literally came out of the photograph, to begin haunting his great-grandson with his delightful presence. But that wasn't all. During his lifetime, Dr. Netter had the pleasure of being acquainted with a young lady by the name of Miss Babette. Nearly a hundred and fifty years ago, Miss Babette delighted the Parisian audiences of stage and variety shows. She was the current Ms. Babette's great-grandmother.

When Edmund "met" the 21st century's Ms. Babette, it was

"friendship at first sight." The two of them now traveled together as much as possible or as often as Alan was traveling on a cruise of Babette's choice.

When Edmund came back to Babette's suite, he found his friend reading the latest news in the local newspaper while sipping on her morning coffee.

"Now, milady," Edmund began, hovering over a seat across from Babette, "at first glance, the two people accompanying your friend Betty seem alright. Of course, I would have to spend a little more time with them…"

"But did they say why they're here?" Babette interrupted, putting the paper down on the coffee table.

"No. They only talked about the camel drive in Mauritania. They seem very intrigued by the prospect of traveling on a camel's back across the Sahara. I can't see the attraction in doing such a thing myself. My brother recounted the many tedious hours he spent on camel back in the service of the French Foreign Legion. I guess one might try everything once, while one can," Edmund remarked pensively.

"What about Betty? Do you think she'll be okay?"

"Why are you asking, dear lady? She didn't seem ill or suffering from any ailments, as far as I could tell anyway."

"No, Edmund, it's not her health I am worried about, it's her mental condition."

Edmund raised a questioning eyebrow. "Do you think there's something wrong with her brain?"

Babette had to smile. "That's a crude way of putting it…. But no, I only meant; does she look worried about something?"

"No, not that she showed during the few minutes I was in her suite." Edmund paused. "Interestingly, I did notice her pensively looking at the photograph of a young woman holding a baby in her arms…"

"Do you think that was Betty herself in the picture?"

"I could not tell you, Babette. The woman held some

resemblance with Ms. Palmer, but the photograph is at least thirty or forty years old. People do change in that time."

"Yes, yes, of course. I'm afraid I am letting my imagination run away with me. You see, Edmund, there was something unsettling about Adele Muesli. Perhaps it was the way she was dressed, with the scarf around her head and the many pieces of jewelry adorning every part of her exposed skin that disturbed me. I frankly don't know what to make of her. She certainly didn't look like any secretary I know."

"Maybe you should remember that Betty and her companions are on holidays and a more formal frock for this young woman would have been out of place."

"Not as out of place as the gypsy-looking costume she was wearing on a six star cruise," Babette remarked, getting to her feet. "I think I will call her and see when she's free this afternoon. We'll soon see what these two are all about."

Dr. Alan Mayhew, the medical officer aboard *The Contessa* was whistling when he entered the medical center. He loved to be working on this particular vessel. Perhaps it was because he had assisted in the design and construction of the center some years back, or maybe it was because *The Contessa* was a relatively small cruise ship with only two hundred passengers and the same number of crew. The passengers owned condos on this ship and were regular travelers, which made it easy to make friends and to know your patients. Besides, since *The Contessa* only catered to the very rich and not so famous people on earth, the crew, staff and officers were "top of their class." This meant a lot less work for Alan and his nurse, Olga Nureyev.

Olga, besides being a qualified registered nurse with many years' experience aboard cruise ships, was a polyglot. She had a talent for learning and speaking a foreign language to perfection in a matter of weeks. Currently she spoke practically all major languages spoken in Europe and was working on her Mandarin. *The Contessa* hosted so many passengers speaking different languages; Olga was often called upon to interpret some conversation or other when needed. Alan didn't mind Olga's extra-curricular activities one bit. He was actually proud of her accomplishments. As far as nursing was concerned, Olga had just served as an inoculation nurse in Liberia and Sierra Leone. This was just after the Ebola vaccines had been delivered to the West Coast countries that had been most affected by the deadly Ebola virus.

For this particular cruise, Alan had ordered the delivery of a very secure vaccine refrigerator to be placed in the medical center. This would hold canisters and vials of the Ebola vaccine he would use on passengers intending to travel inland during the cruise. The vaccines and refrigerator cost a fortune, but were both an expense the company could not avoid.

There was another aspect of this trip that was very attractive to Alan. Ms. Betty Palmer was making an enormous donation to the main hospital in Dakar to ensure the construction of a wing that would host victims of contagious diseases. From AIDS to Cholera and Ebola, the "Betty Palmer Wing" would serve as the central and pivotal infectious disease hospital on the African West Coast. From there, Betty intended to open satellite facilities in every country, from Senegal to Ghana, which would be connected via Internet to the hospital in Dakar.

Of course, Alan could never have hoped for such a plan to be put into motion so soon. Yet, it seemed that Betty Palmer was not only a woman of great means, but also one of force of character and determination. Nothing usually stopped her. In her younger days, she was a businesswoman whose endeavors and fortune making on Wall Street had astonished many a trader.

Alan's happy disposition this morning was also due to the fact that "his favorite lady" was to travel with him on this cruise. Tiffany Sylvan was a very able and experienced entertainment director. She was somewhat younger than Alan, but there was something between the two of them that could not be broken. They had sealed their union silently some two years ago. There was no marriage, no church or civil ceremony or even a certificate attesting of their desire to live and enjoy the rest of their lives together. But there was a seal, an allegiance between them that seemed endless. Perhaps it would be remiss not to mention that Tiffany was gorgeous. Her shoulder-length natural blond hair and her superb facial features had attracted more than a glance or two.

While everyone was getting ready for *The Contessa*'s departure later that night, Mr. Isaac Atkinson was coming aboard. A small man in stature, he was gentleness personified. His thinning hair attested to his age and his shallow cheeks were remnants of the man's latest illness. Dressed in a cream linen suit and white shirt, his face was nonetheless radiant. He looked like a man who was about to have the time of his life. He was carrying a black steel case, which had been sealed with a metal stamp at his shop in New York. The case had been the subject of a thorough examination at customs upon his arrival in Gibraltar. It contained the largest and most precious alluvial diamond on earth. The Star of Sierra Leone and its lugubrious legend were to accompany everyone on this cruise.

CHAPTER TWO

Gibraltar in the distance

AS *THE CONTESSA* SET SAIL through the passage that separates Europe from Africa, Babette was looking out into the distance at *The Rock*. During World War II, a similar natural fortress hosted forty guns – known as *The Guns of Navarone*. Many a man lost their life during the battle of the Isle of Leros. It lasted no less than fifty days. Gibraltar was defying the enemy invasion, much like Leros, defied the allies' many assaults.

"Very pensive aren't we, my dear?" Edmund said to Babette as he floated down to stand close to her against the ships' railing.

Babette turned her lovely face to him. The softness of her aging but still lovely features was only made more attractive in the setting sunlight. "Yes, Edmund. I was thinking of my first trip to the Canaries. It was a time for the frivolities of my youth. I was carefree and only thought of the pleasures a vacation from Paris would offer. I had the opportunity, at the time, to visit the Isle of Ibiza. It was there that I met a young man who literally swept me off my feet and invited me to sail to the Canaries with him and his family. And before you put any wrong ideas into your head, there was no romance between Yves and me. We enjoyed what life had to offer. We wrote plays and sketches for the hungry audiences of Europe. They were starving for amusement regarding the issue of World War II. We thought of nothing else but putting a smile on those faces that had seen much too much of the miseries of war."

"How long did you stay in Tenerife?"

"As long as Yves and his family had time to spend. Two weeks, as I recall. Afterward, we sailed up the coast of Spain and landed in Monaco where their boat had a mooring. We said goodbye there. Yves and I never saw each other again."

"That's sad. Have you ever tried finding him?"

Babette nodded. "Yes. On quite a few occasions I would have liked to have heard his critique of my plays. I would have loved to have seen his face in the front row of the theater, but it never happened. As I said, there wasn't any romance between us. What we had was a friendship that isn't found very often."

"Do you think he knows that you've become famous?"

"I don't know, Edmund. I only wished he had found the time and desire in his heart to contact me. But he never did."

"Well, don't let sadness invade your heart, dear Babette, we're en route to where you found joy and fun in the sun, so let's enjoy the return to it."

Finally a smile broke on Babette's lips. "But tell me, why have you come to join me here this evening? Have you found out anything new about Ms. Muesli and Mr. Ashton?"

"No, I'm not sure what they're doing here, but they seem to be attending to your friend's every need. In any case, what I came to tell you is that I just met, I mean visited, a man who's quite famous…"

"Oh, and who might that be?"

"Mr. Isaac Atkinson. Does his name ring a bell?"

Babette held a blank, quizzical look in her eyes. "Not a clue."

"He's the person who bought the Star of Sierra Leone in 1972 after its discovery…"

"And what is "The Star of Sierra Leone?" Is that a precious stone or carving?"

"Yes indeed, milady. It's the largest alluvial diamond in the world."

"How large is it?"

"968-carats."

Babette's eyes grew wide with amazement. "And this man bought it?"

"Oh yes, for 2.5 million dollars."

"How come you know all that? Have you read something about him?"

"Not exactly, milady, but I heard him talking to the chief purser just after he came aboard tonight. When Mr. Guillaume asked him if the case he was carrying contained the Star of Sierra Leone, Mr. Atkinson was only too pleased to tell him, yes! He then went on to describe it as the most beautiful diamond in the world and that it was now aboard *The Contessa,* and handed the steel case to Mr. Guillaume. When Mr. Atkinson left the foyer, one of the young ladies at the desk asked what the chief purser had been referring to. And that's when I heard the full story of the diamond."

"But what would he be doing with such a valuable stone aboard a cruise ship do you think?" Babette asked, still a bit baffled.

"I think he wants to return it to Sierra Leone, for some reason or other."

"How very odd! Why would he want to return the stone to its original place after all these years?"

"Far from me to speculate, milady, but such diamonds all have some sort of legend attached to them, don't they?"

"Not all of them, Edmund. Some are ascribed with a curse to their existence to deter anyone from stealing them. 'If you touch it, you'll be struck by lightning' or some such warning to deter most from even approaching the precious item." Babette turned to look at the sun setting on the western horizon again. The purple and orange color streams aloft seemed to herald a most beautiful twilight.

"It looks like we're going to have some wind and heavy swells tonight," Edmund declared pensively as he looked at the sky.

"Do you think we should brace ourselves for a storm?"

"I do not know, dear Babette, but I would recommend you have dinner early before the ship starts rocking too much."

"Aren't you the party-pooper?" Babette said, turning away from the railing and starting to walk in the direction of the nearest elevator.

"Just trying to be helpful, milady," Edmund said before disappearing from sight.

Babette returned to her suite, and when she opened the door, she was surprised to find an enormous bouquet of flowers standing in a gorgeous crystal vase in the middle of the coffee table. She looked around her to see if Edmund was there. He appeared in front of her, a broad grin on his lips.

"Do you know anything about this?" Babette demanded, pointing at the flowers.

"Not a clue, milady. I only know the steward brought it in when I was about to go out to meet you on the promenade." He pointed to the small envelope nestled amid the flowers. "Perhaps reading the note would give you the clue you're looking for?"

Babette shrugged and returned the smile. "I'm getting too old for this sort of game, Edmund." She opened the envelope, pulled out the card and stared at it for a moment before showing it to Edmund.

> *To the most talented*
> *playwright on*
> *Broadway ~*
> *Your admirer,*
> *Isaac Atkinson*

"Wow! I never thought the man would know who you are," Edmund remarked. "How did he know your suite number? And why is he sending flowers today? Have you ever received gifts from this man before?"

"Not that I recall, Edmund. Besides, he lives in New York and most of the time I am staying in the flat in Paris. But you're right, why now? Maybe it has something to do with that diamond of his."

"Are you going to send him a thank you note?" Edmund asked.

"Well Edmund, I don't know his suite number and I'm sure the chief purser is not about to tell me where Mr. Atkinson resides without good reason."

"Well, the next thing you could do is ask Alan for the passengers list."

"I told you, I am too old to play that game, Edmund. I rather go to the restaurant and ask the Maitre d' to point him out to me, if he's dining there tonight."

"By the way, how was your afternoon tea with Ms. Palmer?"

"Just as expected, Edmund. She is thrilled with her assistants and can't say enough good things about them. But one interesting fact came out of our little chat..."

"Oh, what's that?"

"Remember the photograph you saw in her suite?"

"Yes; a woman and child..."

"Exactly. That's a picture of her sister with her nephew. Betty's nephew I mean. Apparently, her sister gave the baby up for adoption soon after birth. A couple of missionaries adopted the infant and moved to Africa. Betty now wants to find him. She intends to find out as much as she can about the boy, who's obviously a grown man now, and see if he would be a suitable candidate to manage her fortune when she passes away."

"But, milady, Africa is one of the largest continents on earth, how does she expect to find him? Does she have any idea where the missionaries worked?"

"Only that they traveled extensively through the French-speaking countries, which means West Africa."

"And is that why Ms. Palmer took this cruise – to find her nephew?"

"Yes, that's the general idea. Apart from that, she wants to make a large endowment in Dakar to organize the construction of a wing to be added to the Dakar General Hospital. The wing will be dedicated to the treatment of contagious diseases..."

"That's what I call a worthwhile endowment, milady. I should have a chat with my great-grandson about it. I am sure he could help. So, will Ms. Betty stay in Dakar when we reach that port?"

"I don't think so. From what she said, most of the paperwork was handled by a firm of lawyers in the States. She has set the money aside, but it won't be allocated to anything until all the planning and permits have been verified."

"That means a lot of palms will have to be greased before anything can be started." Edmund sounded a little sad.

"Why would you say that? It's not like we're talking about a profitable enterprise. It's only a large donation as I understand it."

"Well, milady, I would hate to disappoint you in that regard, but in Africa, as it is in Asia, nothing is accomplished without paying the multiple middle men their cut for their efforts."

"And we're talking about a few hundred or thousands of dollars?"

"Most likely, hundreds of thousands, Babette. But I'm sure Ms. Palmer will keep an eye on the money and its distribution. Reaching her goal will be difficult but certainly not impossible. She'll just need the right guidance and know-how."

A while later, Babette entered the restaurant dressed in a gorgeous black cocktail gown. She looked radiant. Before the maître d' led her to her table, she asked him if Mr. Atkinson had already arrived.

"Hum, yes, Ms. Babette, he is having a glass of champagne before his meal."

"Would you point him out to me without making it obvious, Charles? I must thank him for the flowers he sent to my suite this afternoon."

"Of course, Ms. Babette. He's the gentleman in a white smoking jacket, sitting by the window. Would you like me to introduce you?"

"That would be wonderful, Charles, if you wouldn't mind?"

"Not at all, Ms. Babette. Follow me."

As the two of them walked in the direction of Atkinson's table, heads turned to admire the lovely lady. Most passengers knew who Ms. Babette was. She was extremely well known in Europe.

"Mr. Atkinson, sir, I am very sorry to interrupt you…"

"No matter, Charles," Atkinson interposed, getting to his feet. "Ms. Babette, if I am not mistaken?"

"Indeed I am, Mr. Atkinson. It's a pleasure making your acquaintance," Babette said.

"The pleasure is all mine, dear lady. Would you like to join me for dinner?" Atkinson asked.

"I wouldn't want to impose…"

"No imposition at all. I would love the company."

"Very well then, thank you." Babette then sat down in the chair that the maître d' had pulled out for her.

As soon as Babette was sitting down, she thanked the man for the lovely flowers and asked him why he did not contact her while she was in New York – the last time being that past winter.

"Well, you see, Ms. Babette, my health has been of some concern to me lately and last winter was the worst."

"Oh, I'm very sorry to hear that, Mr. Atkinson…"

"Call me Isaac, please. I leave the "Mr. Atkinson" at the office when I travel for pleasure."

Babette had to titter at the rejoinder. "I'm still sorry to hear that you were ill, though," she said, a lilt of laughter in her voice. "And now you're better I hope?"

"Oh yes. The minute I decided to return the Star of Sierra Leone to its original place, where it was found forty-three years ago now, I seemed to regain my strength day by day."

"You mean the stone made you sick?"

"I have to believe it did, dear lady. I have suffered from one ailment or another every year since I bought the diamond."

"But wasn't it cut?"

"Well, the truth of it is that many people tried to have it cut, but every time the stone was to be delivered, the jeweler suffered one accident or another and either died or was unable to do the work."

"Are you saying that the diamond is cursed?"

"I cannot bring myself to believe it, but yes, that appears to be the case. You see, in forty-three years, no one has been able to cut the stone. Doesn't that tell you something?"

CHAPTER THREE

Laughter is the best medicine

WHEN ALAN SAW MR. ATKINSON enter the medical center, he thought he recognized him from Babette's description of the man. Olga led him into the office and made the introduction.

"Please, have a seat, Mr. Atkinson," Alan offered, pointing to one of the visitors' chairs across from his desk.

Both men sat down. It took a moment for Isaac Atkinson to do so. Alan recognized the symptoms from his 'streetcar diagnosis'. The poor fellow probably suffered from some back problems.

"Thank you, Doctor," Atkinson said at long last. "I'm sorry to be taking your time when there is actually nothing wrong with me ... at the moment."

Alan frowned. "Are you expecting to be sick sometime in the near future, sir?"

"No, not really, Doctor. However, I am carrying a gemstone, which I have to believe is cursed, and until I see it returned to its original bedrock, I won't rest easily."

"You are talking about the Star of Sierra Leone, aren't you?"

"I gather you've heard of it then?"

"Yes. Ms. Babette mentioned that she made your acquaintance last night."

"Ah, of course. The dear woman has put a smile on my lips many a time, I can assure you."

The two men fell silent for a moment.

Then Alan said, "So, you are looking for my help in keeping eventual diseases away until we reach Sierra Leone, is that the reason you're here?"

"Well, I won't bore you with all my medical woes right now, but perhaps you could help me stay healthy until we reach that destination, yes."

"You know, this reminds me of a little story. One of my more difficult patients was telling me about all of his medical problems shortly after he came aboard. He also mentioned that as we get older we sometimes begin to doubt our ability to make a difference in the world."

"Very true indeed," Atkinson agreed, cracking a tentative smile.

Alan went on, "My patient then added, "It is at these times that our hopes are boosted by the remarkable achievements of other 'seniors' who have found the courage to take on challenges that would make many of us wither." He said that "I've often been asked, 'What do you old folks do, now that you're retired?' Well... I'm fortunate to have a chemical engineering background and one of the things I enjoy most is converting beer, wine and whisky into urine. I do it every day and I really enjoy it."

Atkinson was laughing out loud now.

"Very good, Mr. Atkinson," Alan told him between chuckles. "Keep on enjoying yourself during the cruise. Laughing is the best preventive medicine I could prescribe for you. Don't think of why you're here; rather think of what activities you are going to do from one port to the next."

That morning, after Mr. Atkinson left the center, Alan and Olga were going to have a vaccination session with some of the crew and a procedural practice for an Ebola exposure. Getting dressed for such an 'event' had Olga in stitches! Once Alan had donned the required personal protective equipment and had fitted on his hood and mask, he truly looked like a 'space man'. The World Health Organization guys were on hand, dressed in the same outfits as Alan and Olga, when Simon Albertson, the sanitation engineer, otherwise known as 'The Potty Man', made his entrance. He stopped dead at the sight of the 'space men and woman'. He turned around and exited the center. He walked in again a few minutes later, only clad in red underpants, a feather in his headband, imitating a Sioux War Dancer with an axe (presumably in place of a tomahawk) in one hand.

The three WHO physicians, together with Alan and Olga could not stop laughing. When Alan finally stopped laughing, he asked Simon what this was all about.

"Well, see, Doc, we're at war with an invader – that one we call Ebola. And it's only fitting that all the warriors of our Sioux tribe on this ship show you and the 'suits' here the way to victory."

"Alright, Simon, that's very good of you, but do you think the passengers will appreciate being accosted by a pseudo Sioux Indian brandishing an axe?"

"Never mind the axe, Doc, I'll use anything – even a feather – if it convinces them to be careful around our enemy."

"Yes, I think a feather would be more appropriate," one of the WHO fellows said. "Perhaps we could give a feather or some such thing to every crew and passenger that has been inoculated. What do you think?"

"Like a badge of honor, you mean?" Olga asked.

"Something like that, yes," the WHO fellow – a man by the name of Jean Hawkins – replied, as he looked around him for his colleagues' approval.

"I don't think we would have enough feathers as would be required to distribute to everyone, " Alan interposed. "But giving something to the careful and inoculated passengers as a reward for being cautious might be a good idea."

"Well, glad to have been of some assistance, fellows," Simon began to say while walking backward toward the door. "But I think I better get back to my tanks…"

"Oh no, you don't," Olga said, stepping up to him and grabbing him by the arm. "You're going to get the needle, like it or not, Simon." Olga then pulled the axe out of Simon's clenched hand. "And this tomahawk of yours better stay where it belongs."

"Yes, ma'am," Simon said somewhat resignedly. "I'm only trying to help."

"Yes, we know you are, Simon, but we need you to be what you intended to be in the first place – an example for everyone to follow." Olga was doing a great job. Alan could clearly see why she was being assigned to the front line of the vaccination effort. She was firm and yet patient.

"Okay, okay, let's have it then," Simon said. "Does it hurt?" He looked up at Jean Hawkins who had already pulled a syringe out of its packet and was preparing to draw up the vaccine dose into it.

"Not at all," Alan told him. "You might feel a bit feverish for a couple of days, but other than that, you should be okay."

An hour or so later, most of the engineering crew had been vaccinated. It was then time to take a break for lunch. The WHO crew was quite satisfied with the way the morning had gone. Alan and Olga were pleased with the turnout as well. Simon had been a good leader, once again, and without a tomahawk or a feather.

After the session Alan made sure the cabinet containing the vaccines was locked up securely and the temperature regulator set properly. He didn't want anything to happen to these vaccines. They were truly going to save lives throughout the cruise. But, if mishandled, the content of these little vials could soon become deadly themselves.

After the WHO guys had left the center for lunch, Alan, too, walked out, leaving Olga holding the fort for a while. He made his way to the café and met with his favorite lady for, perhaps a salad. He was hungry and very thirsty for some reason. When he sat down, he noticed the large bottle of mineral water standing in the middle of the table.

"Are you thirsty too?" he asked Tiffany.

She was munching on a mouthful of salad and only nodded. When she swallowed, she said, "Yeah. I can't believe it. I feel like a camel at the trough. I would drink a bathtub full if there was one in my office." She frowned. "Why are you asking?"

"Because I feel the same way," Alan replied. "Anyway, I'll ask the guys from WHO. They've been here more often and stayed much longer than either of us has. Maybe they'll have an answer for us."

As they were finishing their meal, they saw Betty Palmer walk into the café, her two assistants in tow. They sat down, and as soon as they did, Ms. Muesli got up again and went to fetch three one-liter bottles of mineral water from the open fridge beside the self-service counter.

"I guess we're not the only ones suffering from thirst," Alan remarked. "Perhaps it's the proximity to the Sahara...?"

Jean Hawkins was passing by their table just at that moment. He said, "Yes, Doctor, that's exactly the reason why you're getting thirstier than usual. The easterlies manage to dry the air to such an extent that you can physically feel the heat and, of course, your thirst increases exponentially." He paused. "May I sit down?"

"Oh, of course, Jean," Alan said. "Sorry." He nodded to Tiffany. "This is Ms. Tiffany Sylvan, our Entertainment Director."

"Pleased to meet you, Ms. Sylvan. I am Jean Hawkins, one of the guys from the World Health Organization."

"Nice meeting the man behind the needles," Tiffany replied a lilt of laughter in her voice.

"And we're all looking forward to your presentations. I've been told you always manage to put on some great shows."

"Only trying to do my best, Dr. Hawkins..."

"Please call me Jean. Dr. Hawkins sounds too much like the man himself – you know the one I mean."

"Yes, of course," Tiffany said, still tittering. "I bet you get a lot of that, don't you?"

"Sometimes, yes." Jean turned to Alan and smiled.

The latter asked, "Have you had your lunch already?"

"Yes, just some fish and salad. Nothing too heavy for me. Can't stand it." He laughed. "That's why I never gain weight. I am not a meat and potatoes man. Never could finish my plate, when I was a boy, to my mother's great dismay, I must admit."

"So, we're to expect an increase in dehydration cases; is that what you're inferring?"

"Well, not too many cases when we're at sea I expect, but once we get to Mauritania and the camel drive, that's when people will need to be aware of the danger of exposing their skin to the air and sun. It's deadly. No tanning sessions for anyone!"

"Yes, I've read something about it, actually," Alan rejoined. "And that's presumably why the Bedouins wear heavy linen and woolen clothes even in temperatures above a hundred-and-twenty degrees Fahrenheit."

Jean nodded. "Not only to protect them from losing their skin moisture but to be warm during the night when the temperatures can easily drop to 50 degrees.

"You mean we'll need a parka at night?" Tiffany inquired, obviously amazed.

"Oh yes, Ms. Sylvan. The nights in the desert are awfully cold as opposed to the days which are extremely hot."

"I don't know if anyone has packed anything warm. I sure didn't," Tiffany said, throwing an inquiring glance at Alan.

"We can always buy a djellaba or two on the way and plenty of blankets if you like?" Alan wasn't joking, but he saw Tiffany's frown recede into quiet laughter soon enough.

"Can you imagine us dressed as Bedouins? That would be so funny."

"Do you know, Ms. Sylvan…"

"If you want me to call you Jean, you'll have to call me Tiffany, otherwise it'll be Dr. Hawkins all the way to Ghana."

"Alright, alright, Tiffany it is. As I was about to say, being dressed as a Bedouin or with other long garments, would be the best thing you could do on the camel drive."

"Okay then. I'll have to see what I can find when we get to Mauritania. Maybe they'll have something for us." She looked at Alan again.

The latter said, "Don't look at me, Tiffany. I don't think the staff captain would allow us to ignore the dress code, even if it's in time of need. Off the ship, we will *go native.*"

As the trio laughed at the thought of seeing everyone dressed as Bedouins, Babette entered the café from the promenade attired in a gorgeous afghan.

"There is a woman who knows how to dress for the circumstances," Jean exclaimed as he got up to walk toward the playwright.

"Is he always that outgoing?" Tiffany asked quietly, when Jean had his back turned to her. Alan nodded.

CHAPTER FOUR

A thirst is hard to quench

"WHAT'S WITH EVERYBODY and what's with the bottles of water?" Babette inquired as she and Jean Hawkins rejoined Alan and Tiffany at their table.

"Ah yes," Alan said, "Jean here was telling us about the reason for our increasing thirst. It is important to drink at least three liters of water a day. The water from the tap is perfectly pure, thanks to our sanitation engineer. Otherwise you can drink the mineral water in your cabin. Have you any?"

"Yes, yes, Alan, I have. Thanks for asking," Babette replied and then returned her attention to the gregarious Jean Hawkins. "Jean was complimenting me on the afghan I'm wearing…"

"I sure did. And I was saying that it's the perfect apparel for this part of Africa." Jean smiled at Babette. "Where did you get yours?"

"When I was in Tenerife, many years ago, I saw an old woman weaving some silk ones. I think I spent most of my travel money on two of them. Afterward, I look for them every time I travel to Asia or the Middle East. But I'm told I'll need something a little different when we get to Mauritania, right?"

"Maybe, but your afghan is a great start."

"What about the countries south of Mauritania; do they have similar climate?"

"Not really, Tiffany. From Senegal to North Guinea you're

looking at a sub-Saharan climatic region called *The Sahel*. Depending on where you live, it can be as dry and hot as in the Sahara or as humid and jungle-like as Cameroon. In Timbuktu…"

"Are we really going to visit that place?" Babette interrupted. "I've always wanted to go there."

"No, dear lady," Jean answered, "Timbuktu is located in Mali, hundreds of miles from the coast."

"But if you'd like to visit it," Tiffany interposed, "I'm sure we could arrange for a private aircraft to take you there during the couple of days we're in port in Dakar."

"That would be absolutely wonderful, Tiffany," Babette said so enthusiastically that Alan thought he saw a tear pearling at the rim of her eye.

"I'll see what I can do. I'm sure there are charter flights in Dakar, aren't there?" Tiffany directed her query to Jean.

"Yes, I am sure there will be some available by the time we get there."

"You don't sound too sure," Alan inquired.

"No-no, I'm sure there are private aircrafts available, but there are two things to consider: First, not all pilots want to fly inland these days. The people at the other end are so afraid of catching the disease; they won't let the pilot land. Secondly, many of the planes have been requisitioned by our organization to carry out vaccination missions in more remote areas." He turned to Babette and took her hand. "But there's always a way to accomplish one's dream or desire, dear lady. I'll see what I can do the next time I talk to my colleagues on site."

Babette pulled her hand out of Jean's. "No, Jean, please don't do anything. I don't want to be seen as the woman who prevented some family from receiving the vaccine when they needed it, just because I wanted to go to Timbuktu."

"We'll see," Jean said, looking down at his lap.

When Alan returned to the center, he phoned Gregoire Albert, the chief of security aboard *The Contessa* on this cruise.

Gregoire was a young Frenchman who had served in the French army in Algiers for a few years. Following a tour of duty in the Middle East, he wanted to visit the world before settling down in his village in Lardeche, south of France. Thanks to his impeccable army record and his helpful attitude, it wasn't long before he made it to the cruise line's security department. He spoke English fluently and was the handsomest guy on the vessel according to the female crew. Unmarried, Gregoire didn't shy away from flirting with the ladies aboard. He hadn't been reprimanded for his frivolous conduct yet, since the staff captain was a good friend of his and needed his help regularly.

"Yes, Doctor, what can I do for you?" Gregoire answered as soon as he picked up the receiver.

"Why don't you come down to the center, Gregoire, I would like to have a chat with you about a few things."

"Sure thing, Doctor. I'll be right down," the chief replied before hanging up.

Alan shook his head. He knew this cruise was going to be different in many aspects, in particular in regards to the crew's attitude. These European people were not relaxed enough for him. He would have preferred a more laid back attitude than the one displayed by most members of crew.

"Yes, Doctor, how can I be of assistance," Gregoire said as he rushed into the doc's office and sat down in one of the visitors' seats.

Alan smiled and reclined in his chair. "First, I wanted to make sure that you get your vaccination before we get to the Canaries tomorrow. Maybe this afternoon would be as good a time as any."

Gregoire's face paled. "Do I have to get the vaccine? I am not intending to go anywhere…"

"Don't, Gregoire. You will need to be vaccinated before most of the crew. You're the one who's going to look after the vaccines that will go to the various clinics near the ports we visit. So, will this afternoon be okay with you?"

"I suppose so. I just don't like being vaccinated for anything. The thought of being injected with that disease so that my body can fight it and build its own antibodies is ludicrous to me."

"It may be ludicrous to you, but I think it might be a lot more ridiculous for you not to be vaccinated and then having to be sent home in a coffin. I don't think your parents would appreciate it, do you?"

"Okay, okay, Doctor. I knew I would have to go through this nightmare when I accepted this assignment, but I thought I could dodge the bullet for a while."

"Well, you can't, Gregoire. Besides, think of it this way: you'll be free to roam where ever you please and carry on with your flirting without fear of catching the virus."

"I don't think I'd want to flirt around the places we're going to visit, Doctor. I've got a girlfriend in Paris that wouldn't like my gallivanting during the cruise or bringing her back syphilis or other diseases."

"Oh? And what have you been doing thus far? What do you call that?"

"I know, I know, Doctor, but the ladies love me. What can I do?"

"Is that what you're going to say to your girlfriend when you go back? You couldn't do anything because they found you irresistible?" Gregoire shook his head. "Anyway, as long as you don't flirt with the passengers and you are discreet, I guess you'll be fine."

Gregoire was about to get up when Alan said, "Don't go yet, I'm not done with you. As you know we're carrying two sets of vaccines. One set is strictly to be used on the passengers and crew traveling on *The Contessa*. The other set belongs to the World Health Organization. These canisters, those containing the vials, are to be transported to the clinics at each port of call. I know you've alerted the local police and Interpol to give the WHO physicians appropriate protection. However, I'm very concerned about the canisters themselves. Do you see what I'm getting at?"

"Not really. I know they're precious cargo, and they'll be heavily guarded, but I haven't been told anything else about the operation, no."

"Well, let me get you up to date then. The WHO canisters will not all contain the vaccine vials – some will be filled with vials of water."

"You mean you want to fool any potential thieves?"

"Exactly. One of my colleagues ran a similar operation when he traveled with the organization. It's a very simple procedure. We have several empty canisters and cases in the storage room, which we will use to transport the false vaccine. The others, as you know, are in the fridge."

"But how will the doctors know which is which once they arrive at the clinics?"

"Once the cases are loaded and sealed, the WHO guys will not tell anyone, not even my nurse or me, which is the real canister. They'll open the canisters at the clinics and inform the doctors on site themselves. So each time we go ashore, you'll be protecting three or four steel cases, instead of one."

"But, Doctor, won't I need to know which is which?"

"Why would you want to know? Your task will be the same, whether you're protecting one or three cases, placebo or vaccine, won't it?"

"I guess so." Gregoire didn't sound convinced. He rose to his feet, seemingly determined to leave now.

"Alright then," Alan said, getting up too. "Let's get you inoculated, shall we?"

Gregoire burst out laughing. "And here I thought I could escape. But didn't you say you'd see me this afternoon?"

"Yes, but I changed my mind. There's no time like the present." Alan smiled and nodded imperceptibly to his nurse standing at the door.

When Gregoire turned around to exit the office, Olga was on hand, with a needle ready to prick a terrified Gregoire.

When Gregoire left the center, Olga began giggling by herself.

Curious, Alan asked her what made her laugh.

Olga then replied, "All this, the vaccinations and us traveling to the most dangerous places on Earth right now, oddly enough reminded me of a joke I heard not too long ago."

"Really? Did you find time or occasion to laugh during your latest assignment in Sierra Leone?"

"Oh yes, Doc, we needed to laugh at ourselves. The nightmare was too great to be faced without that release valve."

"So what's the joke?"

"Well, imagine this: Three nurses died at the same time and went to heaven where they were met at the Pearly Gates by St. Peter. To the first, he asked, "What did you do on Earth and why should you go to heaven?"

"I was a nurse in an inner city hospital," she replied. "I worked to bring healing and peace to the poor suffering city children."

"Very noble," said St. Peter. "You may enter." And in through the gates she went.

"To the next, he asked the same question, "So what did you do on Earth?"

"I was a nurse at a missionary hospital in Africa," she replied. "For many years, I worked with a skeleton crew of doctors and nurses who tried to reach out to as many people and tribes with a hand of healing and with a message of God's love."

"How touching," said St. Peter. "You too may enter." And in she went.

"To the last nurse, he asked, "So, what did you do back on Earth?" After some hesitation, she explained, "I was just a nurse at an H.M.O."

"St. Peter pondered this for a moment, and then said, "Okay, you may enter also."

"Whew!" said the nurse. "For a moment there, I thought you weren't going to let me in."

"Oh, you can come in," said St. Peter, "but you can only stay for three days..."

"You're right," Alan said after he stopped chuckling. "Precisely what we will need in the next few weeks, appropriate humor. And I must say something else, Olga, I'm very glad you're aboard on this assignment. I don't think many nurses could have been more suited for this cruise."

As soon as Gregoire returned to his office, he looked to see if anyone was around. Fortunately, most of the security staff had gone on their rounds. He then opened one of his desk's drawers and pulled out a satellite-phone. He punched the digits necessary to get him in touch with his acolyte in France.

"Hey, Francis," Gregoire said as soon as the line was opened. "There's going to be a change of plan." He listened for a fraction of a second before saying, "I'll tell you what's going on, if you just shut up and listen for a minute. They're going to move three cases at a time, instead of one, at each port. So, you guys better make some adjustments to your plans. Understood?" When Gregoire heard his contact's reply, he hung up abruptly and replaced the phone in the drawer.

CHAPTER FIVE

A clove or two won't make any difference

ALAN WAS WRITING HIS REPORTS that afternoon when the door to the medical center opened and a whiff of mixed scents teased his nostrils unexpectedly. He didn't know if he was going to cough or throw up, or try identifying each of the odors before he would say something.

Olga put a hand to her mouth and nose before she greeted the couple. Obviously the woman was the one wearing what must have been an entire bottle of perfume on her person. The man reeked of garlic and three-days of body odor. It reminded Alan of a cartoon he had seen a long time ago. The coyote had fallen into a tub of manure and when he exited he was covered by the offensive, malodorous steam. Alan got up from his seat and strode out of his office to meet the couple.

"Ah, Doctor," said the man, "I come to have a check-up. My doctor said I must have a check-up every month."

"Yes, yes, of course," Alan replied, "but why don't you give me your name first so that I can start a chart for you?"

"Ah yes, of course. My name, Abdullah Dumas and this is my wife, Alameda."

"Please come through," Alan said, extending an arm toward the examination room.

The cost of a deodorant stick or some deodorant crystals is really minimal when compared to the benefit it can bring one and to the people around you. As the physician who is forced to be in close contact with patients in a typically small cruise ship's medical exam room, the issue of using or not using deodorant becomes quite important. There are groups of people who vehemently refuse to use deodorant because it is "not natural." Using ammonium alum deodorant crystals (a form of salt) is, of course, totally natural. In a traditional medical exam room you often have good ventilation and often a window to open. On a cruise ship, that luxury is seldom available. There have been times that Alan wished he did not have any sense of smell. On the medical center's waiting room wall, there was a friendly reminder about body hygiene and how it can keep your body healthy. But, in this instance, Abdullah and Alameda obviously had not read it nor taken notice of it.

When a ship goes through certain areas of the world, the cruise company will make generous offers to locals for a mini-cruise to fill empty cabins. For the local passengers and visitors, they find the ship a convenient way to go to their next destination. It was not the case for *The Contessa* at this point since she was full to the brim on this cruise. If any of the North African ladies had been allowed on board, one would have noticed that they generally cloaked themselves with their black or sometimes colorful djellaba and burqa and made sure that they had all their gold jewelry drooping from their bodies. Unfortunately they would have failed, in many instances, to spend the $1.52 to buy a deodorant stick. Even though they were not "instant passengers," Alameda and her husband fit the above description to a tee. Her "grandbou-bou," as her djellaba is called in West Africa, was threaded with gold embroidery, her gold earrings, which adorned not only her ear lobes but also the rims of the outer ears, must have cost thousands judging from their weight. She also had an immense gold filigree pendant that hung proudly over her ample bosoms. And the rather expensive perfume she was wearing did nothing to cover the fact that she probably bathed only once a week, as is customary in that part of the world.

As for Abdullah, he was concerned about his heart. He was truly obsessed with his cardiovascular system. It is said that garlic is good for one's blood pressure. However, such as with anything in life, moderation is the key to better health. And moderation didn't seem to have been part of Abdullah's vocabulary when it came to garlic consumption. He had been told by one of his friends that if he took one clove a day, he could avoid taking the pills that his doctor had prescribed for him.

Olga checked his blood pressure a couple of times and it was within normal range. When Alan re-entered the exam room he nearly fell over. The offensive odor of garlic, body perspiration mixed with perfume truly overwhelmed his senses. When he asked Abdullah what he had eaten today, he explained that instead of taking one clove a day, he had been taking one bulb a day. He felt that if he consumed more, it would be better. Since fresh garlic was easily accessible in the kitchen, he helped himself to anywhere between 4 or 5 bulbs a day. Needless to say even deodorant wouldn't have helped. He had wondered why everyone gave him a wide berth in the restaurants or any of the public areas. Alan had the dubious honor of telling him.

"So, you are saying that I should consume everything, including garlic, moderately, is that it?" Abdullah queried, obviously incredulous.

"Yes, Mr. Dumas. Moreover, I would suggest that you and Mrs. Dumas give some thought to bathing regularly."

"Why would that be?" Alameda interrupted, "We follow our teachings…"

"Hush, Woman," Abdullah cut-in, "Let the doctor explain."

"Well, I just want you to understand that your body carries millions of bacteria, germs that can cause a number of nasty diseases. These bacteria and germs fester in your armpits and in every other crack or pleat of your body. If you don't clean them every day with soap and water, and if you don't use deodorants, these bacteria will ultimately eat your skin."

"I have never heard of such thing, Doctor," Abdullah objected. "How is it possible when both my wife and I spray our bodies with perfume? Perfume contains alcohol…"

"Which evaporates quickly and is not effective," Alan interrupted. "I could culture the bacteria that live right now under your arms if you like. I have a microscope…"

"No-no, Doctor, that will not be necessary. We will do as you say," Abdullah agreed. "What about the medication my doctor gave me; do I have to take them still?"

"It would be better for you to follow your doctor's instructions, yes. And, please, leave the garlic alone for a while."

In the meantime, Adele Muesli and Gregory Ashton were busy discussing their future plans. They needed to be the first ones to locate Betty's nephew. Thus far, they only found out the name he was given at birth: Lionel Archer, which was not the adoptive couple's last name. Betty did not know the couple's last name either.

"I guess this is his father's name," Adele suggested, "unless Betty's sister gave him a name that had nothing to do with her family."

"Who knows what that woman did? Giving her son away for adoption to make sure she'd never see him again is typical of a heartless, ignorant *bitch*, if you want my opinion." Gregory sounded truly offended. He, himself, had been the subject of beatings from a brute of a father. He had also been the object of his mother's alcoholic woes. He didn't have any pity for an "unfit" or "unwilling" mother.

"Well, whatever the sister did is none of our business. She's six feet under now anyway," Adele said, shrugging her shoulders. "What we need to look at is the year the boy was given away and where."

"But didn't Betty say that the couple who adopted him traveled as missionaries throughout Africa?"

"Yes, that's the only thing Betty has found out. But I now believe there was no couple, no adoption of any sort. I think Betty's sister gave her boy away to a missionary while she was in France." Adele paused and frowned at her laptop screen. "We just need to find out which mission that monk came from."

"How do you expect to find that out? It's been nearly five decades since it happened; things have changed, especially in these countries. They change despots and tyrants every second year and they're never satisfied with what they've got."

"My, my, aren't we sore this afternoon. What's the matter, Gregory? Have you forgotten about the reward?"

"No, my dear, I have not forgotten anything. I'm just blowing off some steam before I have to face the old bitty again. As soon as we arrive in Tenerife, she wants me to go and buy some Afghans like her friend wears."

"You mean Ms. Babette, do you?"

"Yeah, that's her. She's another one of these rich, old women…"

"I suggest you stop hating and biting the hands that are liable to feed you, Gregory. We've got to find that nephew and when we do we'll be sure to be included in Betty's will. A million bucks to locate the nephew is nothing to sneeze at and it will do us nicely enough until our old bitty, as you call her, kicks the bucket."

"Okay, okay, I know what we've got to do. No need to remind me. I'm just getting a little antsy. I hope it's not going to take another ten years before we see the first cent of that prize or I'm liable to do something we'll both regret I'm sure."

"Alright, enough!" Adele said, obviously fed-up with her partner's ranting. "I've got a historical record of the missions that have existed or were operating throughout West Africa in the sixties and seventies."

"You do?" Gregory sounded astonished. "Where did you get that?"

"Before we left Gibraltar, I was searching the Internet for missions from Senegal to Ghana and since I found an address for the archdiocese in Dakar, I sent them an email and I got an answer from a nice missionary working somewhere in Mali…"

"But, Adele dear," Gregory interjected, "Mali is a land-locked country, or..."

"Don't be such an arse, Gregory. The missionary works in Mali but that doesn't mean Betty's nephew is there. The white monk (as they're called over there apparently) is just a source of information, that's all."

"And what did this nice missionary tell you?"

"He said that each village had a church or chapel. He said that most of the boys who lived in the missions would work in these churches or chapels for their meals and lodging. Most of them would become missionaries themselves..."

"You mean that idiot nephew is a monk now?"

"Listen, Gregory," Adele uttered, sounding frustrated, "I am getting tired of your lip, you know that? It seems that I'm the only one around here making any progress toward finding the boy – the man I mean. I've not seen you lift a finger or give some thought to the problem."

"Well, since you're doing so well, why should I do anything?"

"Okay; if that's the way you feel, I think I'll keep the findings to myself and tell Betty what she wants to know when I find Lionel. Of course, since you wouldn't have seen the need to help, I will not see any need to share the prize money with you either."

Sitting side by side on the small sofa in their suite, Gregory passed an arm around Adele's shoulders. "I'm sorry, Addy, I know I'm just all talk and no action sometimes, but I'll be right beside you whenever you need me. You know

that, don't you?"

"Alright. Yes, I know you've got the brain of an ant and it's not your fault..."

"You miserable little pest..." Gregory burst out, before erupting in loud laughter.

When he regained a smidgen of composure, Adele went on, "Do you want to hear what my "nice missionary" said, or not?"

"Of course I do. What's his name by the way? Or do we call him

"Nice Missionary"?"

"His name is Père Gilbert – that's how he signs his emails anyway."

"Okay, and what did Père Gilbert tell you about our missing Lionel?"

"He said that he, himself, never had a white boy working in any of the churches or chapels in his region. He did know another monk from eastern Senegal who mentioned a young white boy who grew up in the monastery. He seems to recall the name being Lionel. But he doesn't think he ever heard his last name spoken."

"But that's fantastic news, Addy. Do you think we should tell Betty?"

"Absolutely not," Adele flared. "We're nowhere near finding the nephew. If anything, we need to see if we can get Père Gilbert to come to Dakar when we get there. By that time, he might have found out something else about the monastery where Lionel grew up."

"Okay, I see what you mean. But do you know, from that historical record you got, if the monastery still exists?"

"Père Gilbert said that yes, the Monastery of Tambacounda is still standing, but it's only run by a few monks these days. Apparently it's a very difficult region to handle. There are a lot of Muslims living in the area – the majority of people are Muslims actually – and a catholic monastery seems to be a pain in the local Imam's backside."

Gregory erupted in renewed chuckles. "Anyway, I agree. I think it's best for you to keep digging and for me to keep our *old bitty* entertained. What do you think?"

"Yes. Until I've got something more concrete from the archdiocese or from Père Gilbert, I think we better keep my findings under wraps."

CHAPTER SIX

Con artists par excellence

LEO SUMMERVILLE AND HIS WIFE LINDA were having a drink at the bar facing the promenade on the upper deck. Leon and Linda were rich. Any, which way you looked at it, the Summervilles, had money, or so it appeared. Linda was a pretty, petite lady in her late forties. Her cosmetic surgeon must have earned his keep with the various corrective surgeries that now maintained her face in a permanent, frozen mask of perfection. Was she forty or thirty? No one would have sworn to either. As for Leon, he was tall, handsome and quite elegant in his linen suit. His light blue shirt, opened at the neck, only enhanced the tan of his face and the white of his hair. In his mid-fifties now, the plantation owner was aloofness personified. He would have taken the lollipop out of the mouth of babes if it suited his purpose and swelled his wallet with a few more greenbacks.

As they were savoring their drinks, a scotch for Leon and a martini for Linda, a younger man joined them.

"Sorry to interrupt, Leon," the younger fellow said familiarly, taking a seat beside him at the couple's table, but I thought you'd like to know that your Harley has arrived at the plantation. Jim just called me to give me the news."

"That's excellent news, Gaston," Leon replied. "Finally I'm going to be able to roar along the highway like I used to in the old days." He looked satisfied and took another sip of his scotch before he lifted his gaze to Linda. "What do you think of that?"

"I think – no, I hope – it's got a passenger seat," Linda said, cracking a smile, "because if you think you're going to roar down the highway or through town without me, you've got it wrong!"

"I knew that would happen," Leon said, "that's why I've ordered you your own bike, dear. Yours is a white one. I thought I'd leave it as a surprise for when we got home, but since you're mentioning traveling with me, I can't keep the secret from you any longer."

"Okay. That's better." She turned to Gaston. "Has it been delivered as well?"

"Yes, ma'am. You two will have a ball when you get back." Gaston lowered his eyes. He knew these two probably better than many. He knew they were here, on this cruise, to dip their fingers into someone else's fortune. He had worked with them too long not to notice the games they played. They had never been caught because they never forced anyone to sign on the dotted line. Nevertheless, they divested quite a few people of their savings, investments and wealth. They were con artists par excellence.

As for Gaston, he didn't care what these two did. He was an executive secretary – that's all – the man behind the paperwork that kept the IRS and any of the other federal agencies from digging into the Summerville's affairs. When he returned from Afghanistan, he was broke. His fiancée had left him and life seemed grim at best and not worth living at worst. So, he went through the ritual of applying for jobs that closely resembled what he had done in the military and landed himself a position at the Summerville's estate. Soon after being hired, Gaston realized Leon and Linda were not all of what they appeared to be. They were thieves, but not felons per se. They convinced people to give or invest money in their various ventures. The ventures were only a front for a grand scheme of thievery. These ventures never existed, yet they each had a veritable network of investors and employees all visible on the Internet, but never in reality. In short these people were "virtual" thieves.

"Go get yourself a celebratory drink, boy," Leon suggested, "and bring us some pretzels or something to snack on, okay?"

"Sure," Gaston said, getting to his feet. "Do you want another drink," he asked Linda, seeing that her martini glass was nearly empty.

"Yes, why not," she replied, throwing him a gentle smile, "especially if you're bringing back a snack."

While Gaston was getting the drinks, Gregory Ashton slipped into the vacant chair and put his beer on the table. "Sorry, folks, but I couldn't help overhear what Gaston told you…. I'm Gregory, Gregory Ashton, by the way…"

"And I don't think I invited you to our table, Mr. Ashton," Leon said, the acerbity in his voice palpable. "What do you want?"

"Hold on, sir," Gregory said, "I'm just getting acquainted here. No harm meant. I've just overheard that you guys are getting a couple of Harleys to "roar" down the highway…"

"So what? What do you want?" Clearly Leon was not impressed.

Linda patted his hand from across the table. "Come now, Leon, don't be rude to a fellow passenger. Let's hear what Gregory has to say about our Harley's. Maybe he's a fellow rider."

"That I am, ma'am. That I am. And when I overheard you speak of the delightful beasts, I couldn't help but recall a joke my father told me when I brought home my first Harley. It was a mess I tell you…"

"So, what's the joke," Leon demanded, getting more impatient by the minute now.

"Okay, here it goes: The inventor Arthur Davidson, of the Harley Davidson Motorcycle Corporation, died and went to heaven. At the gates, St. Peter told Arthur, "Since you've been such a good man and your Motorcycles have changed the world, your reward is that you can hang out with anyone you want in Heaven." Arthur thought about it for a minute and then said, "I want to hang out with God." St. Peter took Arthur to the Throne Room, and introduced him to God. Arthur then asked God, "Hey, aren't you the inventor of women?"

God said, "Ah, yes." "Well," said Arthur, "professional to professional, you have some major design flaws in your invention." God was somewhat taken aback, and when He asked what the flaws might be, Arthur Davidson produced a list for Him to read.

1. There's too much inconsistency in the front-end protrusions.

2. It chatters constantly at high speeds.

3. Most of the rear ends are too soft and wobble too much.

4. The intake is placed way to close to the exhaust and finally,

5. The maintenance costs are outrageous.

"Hmmmm, you may have some good points there and it may be true that My invention is flawed," God said to Arthur. "But the last time that I checked, more men are riding My invention than yours."

Leon was laughing so loudly that everyone in the bar turned and started chuckling too.

Even Linda had to laugh. "What did I tell you, Leon," she said between giggles, "passengers are sometimes worthwhile knowing."

"Yeah, yeah," Leon admitted as he stopped chortling. "And where do you come from, Mr. Ashton?"

"Call me Gregory, please. Ashton is the name of my family, a family that didn't really care for me, so Gregory it is."

"And where do you come from?" Leon repeated as Gaston came back to the table with a cheese plate and two glasses; a scotch for him and another martini for Linda.

Gregory introduced himself and didn't wait to be asked to take a piece of cheese and cracker from the plate. He then turned to Leon again. "Hum, yes, we're from the States. I mean my boss, Betty Palmer is from the States and my fiancée and I are traveling with her. We're sort of doing the chores like Gaston does for you guys."

"And what does Betty Palmer do?" Linda inquired.

"Oh, she's taken over her husband's business when he died and now she's taking time off from the stress of handling all the responsibilities and demands on her time." Obviously Gregory was well trained in the art of saying a lot while divulging nothing. He was not about to disclose his scheme to these two – if anything, he'd want to fleece them before this cruise was over. He rose from his chair. "And that's all folks," he said, chuckling. "Sorry, but I have to get back to my dear Adele, my fiancée, otherwise there's going to be unrest in heaven." And with these words, Gregory left the Summerville table.

Leon, Linda and Gaston exchanged a glance. "Do we know who this Betty Palmer is?" Leon asked Gaston.

He shook his head. "No, not really. She's a friend of a famous playwright – the one who's traveling on this cruise – a Ms. Babette."

"Is that right?" Leon said, munching on a pretzel and a piece of Gruyere. "I've heard of Ms. Babette. She's really top of the Broadway list." He shook his head. "But unapproachable. Too visible and too well protected, I'd say. We don't need that kind of publicity."

"But that Betty Palmer sounds better, doesn't she?" Linda inquired.

"Definitely," Leon answered. "We'll just have to see if she could be a valuable mark." He turned to Gaston. The latter knew what was coming. "Would you run a discreet check on her finances for us?"

"Absolutely," Gaston agreed, nodding, "But I think there's someone else aboard that should really interest you."

"Oh yeah, and who might that be?"

"I only met him at the café yesterday – just in passing mind you – but I've since learned the man is a multi-billionaire on his way to Sierra Leone to put the largest alluvial diamond on the planet back in its original site. It's cursed apparently. But besides that, he's a jeweler with investments and assets all over the world. Fingers in many pies, as it were."

"As you say, boy, that's an interesting target. And he probably wouldn't mind sharing a piece of pie with the likes of us, would he now?"

Alan, in the meantime, was bringing Olga up to speed on the division of labor. She had heard a rumor that the medical department might have to be part of the hotel department on these smaller vessels. Alan would not even want to contemplate such a possibility and the disasters it could engender. He was thus explaining to Olga what happened to him in years past.

"Room stewards and stewardesses are a division of the hotel department; usually the largest employer on the ship. Sometimes the hotel department is split up and has some of its divisions under others. This keeps one from having one fellow who is all-powerful in the scheme of corporate ladders. Sometimes the least competent is advanced. This DOES happen in the hotel department of cruise ships. Fortunately it does not happen in the deck and engine department where the captain and senior officers are divisional staff. Medical also usually comes under deck and engine. Only once did it fall under hotel department, and it was a total disaster. The hotel director thought he was a doctor and tried to manage the department, which he was legally allowed to do in their corporate structure. Earnst, a good solid Aryan German fellow, was friendly on the surface. We all questioned his sexual orientation with his longish hair and beautiful jewelry, but the rumor mill never picked up any specific liaisons, so we dubbed him the eunuch. Earnst was just useless. He would spend hours reviewing reports and never come up with any useful recommendations or changes. He would spend hours looking over the shoulder of various well-experienced chefs, housekeepers, and food and beverage directors. Not in a practical way to help them cope with a certain problem or anything, just to intimidate by being there breathing down their necks. In any event, besides trying to practice medicine, he would hang out in the medical center. He would have us get him free medicine to beautify his skin, of course charged to our budget. Then he would yell and scream that the medical department was spending too much money and, of course, did not generate money like the casino. Enough said: he was a disaster in a uniform.

"Room Stewards and stewardesses are one of the biggest divisions of the hotel department on the large ships. They clean rooms. On a large ship, that is a lot of rooms. For the passengers, the room stewards can be the passengers' link to all the little extras that make a cruise a memorable adventure and a comfortable one. They make animal shapes out of towels on the turn down. They place the chocolate in the beak of the towel's mouth. They remember where things are and how one likes things placed. On a long cruise they become real buddies. On many ships, they garner big tips too. I remember one room stewardess from Romania who was given a Christmas tip of $10,000 by a wealthy passenger that thought that she was "so nice … why not?" No doctor ever got a tip like that! Even after saving some one's life. Most of the tipping on the larger ships is included or strongly suggested or automatically added to a room account at the rate of 10 or 15% or a fixed dollar amount per day. This is much fairer in that then the whole amount is divided among all the persons in that division."

"Wow! I had no idea of the implications related to becoming part of the hotel department," Olga remarked after Alan's long explanation. "To me, it would be just a matter of filling out different paperwork."

"Well, now you know. Small ships like *The Contessa* are the jewels of a cruise company. Believe me, Olga, they bring in more money sometimes than a two-thousand-passenger vessel. Fifty to two-hundred thousand dollars a ticket is not uncommon, depending on the suite, the cruise's itinerary and the length of it, of course."

"I truly had no idea," Olga concluded, rising to her feet. "I'm going to the café. Do you want something?"

"Not for me right now, thanks."

CHAPTER SEVEN

Someone else must have done it!

THE MORNING OF THE CONTESSA'S ARRIVAL in the port of Santa Cruz of Tenerife was quite memorable. The island itself seemed to be surmounted by an eternal cloud over its volcano, Pico del Teide standing about thirty-two hundred meters above sea level. Although deemed extinct, it looms over the land surrounding it. The port is a hubbub of commercial and tourist activities. The 'crowded' harbor could have been one way of describing the cafés lining every inch of the nearby marina, the fishermen's market, and the usual tourist stores. The *populous*, a veritable mass of bodies more or less dressed in anything from bathing suits to elegant attire or floral beach gowns, added to the crowded feeling.

Santa Cruz, the Canaries' twin capital (with Las Palmas) is a vibrant city. Its energy friendly tramway whose rails are laid on grass in the middle of the streets along the twelve kilometers of its course, is as colorful as its inhabitants.

"This is not the way I remember it," Babette remarked when she and Betty Palmer arrived in town. "Mind you, the last time I was here, it was still a natural, mostly artistic island."

"And why didn't you come back until now?" Betty asked.

"Never thought about it. When I could not reconnect with my

school friend, I guess I let it go as another thing to be filed under memorable events."

"Do you ever regret not having children?"

"But I do have hundreds of kids," Babette countered, giggling. "Every child I rear, teach in Sunday school or treat to a few days with me becomes and remains my child forever."

"I wish in some ways I had had the courage to marry or to elope with the young man I once loved. I wanted so much to have a family." Betty's ruefulness was unmistakable. The woman was sad. "But when I saw what happened to my sister and the way she ended up giving her child away, I could not go through with it. In the end I had to marry the man my parents chose for me."

"It does take great courage to go against one's parents' wishes, and I often had the opportunity to see first-hand the damage intolerance can do to a child's emotional wellbeing. It's never easy to witness the downfall of a child when you know it's not his or her fault."

"Oh I can imagine the impact it would have on me, Babette, if I were to discover that my nephew turned out to be a criminal of some sort."

As the little tour bus stopped in front of the Castle of St. Andres, Babette had to admire its circular tower made of strange reddish stones. It was impressive not only because the tower was perfectly circular but also because each stone seemed to have been chosen so as to fit a puzzle.

"These are pyroclastic stones," the guide replied to Babette's query regarding the kind of rocks these were. "They're volcanic and they originally "bubble" out of the ground into foam, which, when it cools, gives you the impression of being in the presence of an immense beehive."

"Is that typical of the volcanoes in this region then?" Betty inquired. "I don't recall having seen such things on the flank of other volcanoes."

"Yes, Mrs. Palmer. The volcanoes of this area – all around

Madeira actually – have all been characterized by these pyroclastic events."

"Well, that was most interesting," Babette concluded as the two women made their way up the stairs leading to the castle's tower.

In the meantime, Alan was getting ready to disembark later that morning, hopefully with Tiffany, when one of the passengers came in the medical center. Alan recognized the old fellow immediately. He was a man in his eighties, in the best of health for his age and always happy to talk about his numerous seductive prowesses with the ladies that populated his love life. Alan had not expected to see him for another few days, not until they were in sight of Nouakchott in Mauritania.

As soon as he came into Alan's office, as usual, sporting an elegant linen suit with a beautiful cane hooked on his right forearm, and a mustache that would have made Hercule Poirot jealous, Isidor Russell sat down and affixed a broad grin on his lips.

"Mr. Russell; very glad to see you," Alan told him, "But you're not due for your check-up for several days yet. How are you feeling?"

"I've never been better!" Isidor replied. "I've got a thirty-year-old bride who's pregnant with my child! What do you think about that?"

Alan had to think about this for a minute. He knew Isidor Russell was on this cruise with Helen Russell, but he never imagined Isidor could impregnate anyone at this stage. Alan then said, "Well, before I congratulate the both of you, let me tell you a story. I know a guy who's an avid hunter. He never misses a season. But one day he was in a bit of a hurry and he accidentally grabbed his umbrella instead of his gun. So, he was walking in the woods near a creek and suddenly he spotted a beaver in some brush in front of him! He raised his umbrella, pointed it at the beaver and squeezed the handle. "BAM," the beaver dropped dead in front of him."

"But that's impossible!" Isidor exclaimed, "Someone else must have shot that beaver."

"Exactly," said Alan to a goggle-eyed Isidor.

A moment passed before Mr. Russell exploded in loud laughter. "I see what you mean, Doctor. It must have been my neighbor, Arthur. He's always running after Helen!"

This time it was Alan's turn to erupt in chuckles.

"And now that I got you laughing, Doctor Mayhew, let me bid you a very good day."

As Isidor walked out of the medical center, Alan had to admit, Isidor had put a broad smile on his face and joy in his heart.

Several decks above the medical center, Joe and Mack were having a beer with an early lunch at the Panorama Bar. Joe was clearly unhappy. Mack asked him what was going on with him, "Why the long face; what's happening?"

Joe took a long swig of his beer and replied, "It's Jocelyn. She's been cheating on me all these years."

"How can you be so sure about that? You've got six children with her, how could you say she's cheated on you?"

"It's because the other night, just before we came on the cruise actually, we were out at a party with some friends…"

"So? Did someone put his paws on her?"

Joe shook his head. "No, nothing like that. It's because I'm so proud of her that I call her, "Mother of Six" all the time. And I introduced her to everyone as "Mother of Six"…"

Mack had his nose in his beer. He didn't want to say anything but he thought that calling one's wife by the number of kids they have together was a bit insensitive. "And then what happened?" he asked Joe.

"Well, the evening went fine but when I asked her if she was ready to go home, she replied, "Yes, "Father of Four," right behind you, dear!"

"Wow!" Mack exclaimed, laughing his head off. "She got you there, didn't she?"

"What do you mean?" Joe flared.

"Hey, calm down, buddy," I just meant that calling Jocelyn

"Mother of Six" was kind of insensitive, don't you think?"

"But what am I supposed to make of that "Father of Four" bit then? Am I supposed to believe two of my kids are not really mine?"

"I don't think so, Joe," Mack answered, "I think Jocelyn was trying to teach you a lesson – don't call her "Mother of Six" anymore."

"And you don't think she's cheating on me then?"

"No, Joe, she's not that kind of woman, I'm sure."

As for the Summervilles, Leon had rented a car to travel around the island. He had no patience for the organized tours. Linda, for her part, chose to go shopping with Gaston. She wanted to find some afghans, some sort of sarong or beach wraps and sandals. Nothing in the States could ever compare to what the couturiers and European dressmakers would put out in their summer collection. They went to a couple of stores, to a market downtown and then Linda decided she wanted to take a break. Gaston offered to have lunch at one of the marina's cafés and then perhaps take a stroll to one of the hotels in town.

Linda burst out in loud giggles. "I thought you'd never ask. It's been a few days since we've had a couple of hours on our own, hasn't it?" She grabbed Gaston's hand as they were fraying themselves a passage in between the tables of the Marina's Santa Cruz Café.

"You took the words out of my mouth," Gaston replied, squeezing Linda's hand.

Meanwhile, Leon was having a bit of a break of his own. He loved his wife, always did, but he needed some "fresh" adventure once in a while. Soon after leaving Santa Cruz, he stopped at one of the resort hotels and called the room of one of his "lady friends." She had come down from New York to Tenerife especially to meet him and spend some "vacation time" with him in bed.

When Alan and Tiffany were finally able to get away, the afternoon sun was nearly blinding them as they came off the ship. Tiffany was glad to get on shore for a few hours. She would not be able to stay away for very long since she had engaged some local dancers to do an exhibition dance for the passengers that night. Gladly, her assistant, Michele, was a capable person on which Tiffany could count. She definitely spoke better Spanish than Tiffany did and she knew how to handle hot-blooded Spaniards.

As they arrived in town, Tiffany rushed to take the tramway. She thought this was the neatest thing she had ever seen since traveling aboard the San Francisco cable cars.

She started running to the stop when she saw the tram come down the street. Alan ran after her and realized, not for the first time either, how much spunk and how impulsive his "lovely lady" was. He knew it was no use reasoning with her and trying to inject some sense of decorum into her veins, she wouldn't have it. But wasn't that part of her attraction? Wasn't that why Alan loved her so much? He had to agree with his conscience, all those things she did, made him love her all the more.

The ride aboard the tram took them through town as they went from one surprising sight to another. Alan never imagined they would have such an impressive skyscraper dominating the city skyline; a fantastic cathedral and botanic gardens that could equal the best in the world.

As they made their way back to the ship, Alan couldn't get over the fact that Tenerife was very different than what he had imagined.

With arms full of packages, most of them containing Afghans that Dr. Hawkins had recommended for the ladies to buy, Tiffany made her way back to her cabin. She knew she would probably wear these outfits once or twice while working on a cruise, but when she would go on holidays with Alan, she'd be sure to don the gorgeous gowns. She only bought two of them since Jean had also mentioned to wait until they were in Dakar to buy those famous Grand-Bou-Bous the Muslim men and women wear in West Africa. Alan had pointed Alameda Dumas to her: *That gown was gorgeous,* Tiffany thought at the time. So, two Afghans would do her until she got to Dakar for sure.

CHAPTER EIGHT

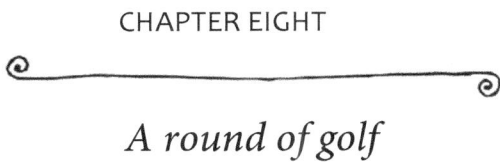

A round of golf

AS MACK AND JOE WERE on their way back to the clubhouse, after a very nice round of golf, Joe erupted in loud chuckles. Mack wondered if Joe had seen something funny, which warranted such an outburst. Joe shook his head, stopped laughing and said, "Maybe I should get my wife to come and play a round with me."

"And that makes you laugh?" Mack asked, befuddled by now.

"Yeah, actually, it's the story of Steve and Sorrelle, friends of ours, that has me in stitches every time I think about it."

"Okay, what you just said doesn't make much sense to me, but let's have it: what's the story?"

"Steve and his wife, Sorrelle were out playing golf. Everything was going fairly well for Steve until the 7th hole. He sliced his tee shot a mile to the right so he and his wife had to go looking for the ball. Eventually they came across a shed with the door slightly ajar, and surprisingly enough the golf ball was slap bang in the center of the floor. And so, not wanting to drop a shot, Steve decided to play on instead of taking a penalty by dropping the ball. Sorrelle, noticing that if Steve played a good shot he could get his ball on the green, offered to hold the door open while her husband played the shot. After a lengthy period of sizing up his shot, Steve hit the ball, but struck his wife in the temple with it. She slumped down dead, instantly. Fast forward five years, Steve found himself on the same golf course, on the same hole, this time with his friend, Jim. So, coincidently, Steve's tee shot took the same path as it did five years ago, and the ball found itself, again, slap bang in the center of the shed. As Steve thought seriously what to do with his shot, Jim offered to hold the door of the shed open so he could take his shot. But with a look of shock on his face, Steve replied instantly, "Hell No! The last time I tried that, it took me seven shots to get on the green."

Mack stared at Joe for a fraction of a second before he cracked up laughing too. "Good one, Joe. But why are you so hung up on Jocelyn these days. She's a great woman. I am starting to wonder if you're not a bit jealous. Are you?"

"Of course I am! I've been with her for nearly twenty years and never once did she give me reason to distrust her. But, as I told you, ever since she gave me that "Father of Four" bit, I've had my doubts about her."

"You're a real fool, you know that?" Mack said in all seriousness. "Jocelyn is devoted to you and the kids. You just have to look at her. I'm sure, even today I bet she'll bring you back something from town…"

"Okay, okay, I'll try to get back on course, okay?"

"Okay. But talking about "course", and this being a golf "course"; and since I've won this round, you owe me a drink tonight."

"Alright. I admit defeat, but I'll put it down to my being distracted."

"Okay, let's get back to the ship. There are a few hours before they've got that exhibition dance tonight."

"And you're going?" Joe asked, somewhat surprised.

"Of course I am. I want to see these guys. I've seen photos of them and they make me think of these Maori people in New Zealand…"

"You mean the ones that stick their tongues out to welcome you?"

"Yeah, those are the ones. But these look like they're a bit more civilized. Anyway, you and Annie should join Jenny and me for the show."

"Sure, why not, there's not much else to do anyway."

"Good grief, buddy, you really have to get off that sad train of yours. It's getting boring."

"Maybe you're right. I should shake all these nasty thoughts off my mind and get back to having fun."

When Leon Summerville got back to the ship, Linda was waiting for him. She knew he had been seeing some girl or other. She didn't really mind. In fact, she didn't mind his philandering at all. Every time he came home afterward, he would treat her to a fantastic dinner or buy her an expensive present or even make love to her until dawn.

"Did you have fun?" Linda asked, as she turned to him when he opened the door of their suite.

"Sure did. The island is fantastic. Gorgeous place. We should think of buying a house and spend our holidays around here. What do you think?"

Linda stepped up to him, locked her arms around his neck and kissed him, before saying, "Grand idea, Lover. I would love to laze about this place. Let's get Gaston to arrange for a realtor to show us some of the properties that might be available."

"Yeah, but before we make a decision, we might have to divest someone on this ship from their money to pay for the house, wouldn't you say?"

"I agree," Linda said, unlocking her arms from around Leon's neck. "I think that Betty Palmer is probably our best choice – *bet* – as it were." She laughed. "She's got several billion to her name and I'm sure she wouldn't mind sparing a couple for us."

"What about Mr. Atkinson? He's got that diamond. We could get at least a few million for it on the black market," Leon suggested.

Linda shook her head. "As you recall he wants to put it back – or should I say return it to the country of origin. And I don't particularly relish the idea of being chased through an Ebola-infested country for a diamond that might only be worth a couple million."

Leon went to sit beside Linda on the sofa. "Well then, I've heard of two other marks that might be of interest…"

Linda turned her face to him. "Oh? And who are they?" She swung in her seat. "But before you tell me who these people are; tell me where you got your information from?"

"Always the cautious one, aren't you?" Leon replied, grinning. "Well, while I was at the resort on the coast this afternoon, I met with someone who looks after their investment portfolios…"

"And you just happened to meet this guy by sheer coincidence, on Tenerife Island, in North Africa. Is that what I'm supposed to believe?"

"Now, Lover, don't jump on your high horse. No need for that. The guy is a girl actually. She's vacationing here with her hubby. I've met her in New Orleans a couple of times. And yes, it was a coincidence to find her here. One of her investors recommended Tenerife to her." He paused. "This guy is a French entrepreneur with millions in the wine business. And believe it or not, he happens to supply the wines for some of the cruise ships in the Mediterranean, like *The Contessa*."

"And don't tell me, he's on this cruise?" Linda sounded as incredulous as she was.

Leon nodded and chuckled. "I told you, this is worth the trip – I mean worth the cruise! The guy is going to be lecturing two days from now. He's going to tell his story…, look"—Leon got up, went to the desk and returned with a pamphlet that he handed to Linda— "this is him. I'm not fibbing."

"Well okay, I'll buy that. And who's the other one, you're lady financial analyst"—Linda's voice was scornful—"told you about? Is he another wine king?"

"No, not at all. This one is a Russian real estate magnate who was building a multitude of poorly constructed condos in downtown Toronto and bribing officials, like that fat, cocaine snorting mayor, to get the building permits passed."

Linda shook her head. "I want nothing to do with those slobs. I told you that before, Leon. These sorts of people truly nauseate me.

Besides they're like flies, you can't get rid of them unless you swat them dead. And I have no intention of spending the rest of my life in prison for murder. Emptying the pockets of some rich guy or gal is one thing, but getting involved with Russian brutes or an idiot diamond dealer who's afraid of his own shadow, no thank you."

"Alright, it's settled then. We'll go after the Palmer lady and the wine tycoon, right?"

Linda nodded and got up. "That's right." She went to the liquor cabinet. "Do you want a drink?"

"Yeah, why not; it must be five o'clock somewhere in the world, as they say."

When Betty and Babette returned to the ship, arms laden with tote bags, Adele Muesli was on hand to help.

"Ms. Palmer; what have you done? Have you bought the entire market?"

"No-no, my dear, just a few of these robes for our camel trip. I really don't want to look out of place or like an idiot tourist and burn every exposed part of my body during the ride." Betty turned to Babette. "Why don't we meet for drinks in an hour?" she added as she stepped off the gangway platform and into the hallway.

"I think that's great, yes," Babette agreed. "I need to put my feet up. Maybe I'll go to the spa and have a short massage before I join you for that drink. Say six o'clock, would that be okay with you?"

Betty nodded. "No problem. Maybe I'll have a swim in the upper deck pool. I need some restoring exercise."

The ladies exchanged a few more words before each going to their suites.

When Babette reached her cabin, she could hardly wait to open the door, drop her packages on the floor and plop down on the sofa. She took her shoes off and stretched her legs on the coffee table.

Edmund floated down from his perch atop the liquor cabinet and chuckled. "It looks like you've had an excellent shopping day, haven't you?" he said, sitting himself down in the chair facing the sofa. "It's too bad that I can't give you the massage you so deserve, but I'm thinking of a way I could help those sore feet of yours."

"No need to concern yourself with that, Edmund. I'm going to have a shower and take myself to the spa. They'll give me the massage I want. As for my feet, they're okay. I learned a long time ago that flat supportive shoes are the only things they'll tolerate when I'm intending to put them through hours of shopping."

She got up from her seat and turned in the direction of the bathroom. Before she reached the door, Edmund said, "I think you better return to your seat, dear lady. I've learned something that you might be interested to hear."

"Oh? And what would that be? Have you been listening at someone's door again?" Babette said, returning to her seat on the sofa.

"Yes. However, I did not listen at the door, I was inside the couple's cabin when I attended their conversation in silence."

"Who are they?"

"They're the Summerville's. They're plantation owners from Louisiana. I was interested in their movements when I saw Linda Summerville take off with their young secretary, Gaston. I believe they had a flirtatious day on the island…"

"Are you saying you snooped on these two?"

Edmund shook his head and looked somewhat indignant at the suggestion. "No, dear woman, I wouldn't dare do such a thing. I'll only intrude on my great-grandson's nights with Tiffany in case of real emergencies…"

"Alright, Edmund, sorry. Do go on, please."

"Yes…, well, when Linda Summerville came back from shopping on the island, like you did, her husband, Leon returned to the ship a half-an-hour later. The thing that attracted my attention was the fact that they began talking about Mr. Atkinson."

"You mean the man with the big diamond?"

"The very same. But that's not the name that really froze me in space – if that were ever possible – it's when Linda mentioned the name Betty Palmer that I started listening to what the two of them had to say."

"And what was that?"

"Well, I don't want to bore you with the whole conversation, suffice to say, however, that these two are targeting your friend. I believe they're intending to fleece her of some of her billions, as the modern expression goes."

"You mean they're thieves or some sort of fraudsters, is that what you're saying?"

"Yes, milady. It looks very much like they are, yes."

"And do we know anything else about these people, apart from what you know?"

"Not really. But I think I could probably find out a little more if I stay with the couple for a while…"

"What about this Gaston fellow; what do you know about him?"

"Apart from the fact that he's sweet on Linda Summerville and that he's the couple's secretary, I don't know anything else."

"Okay," Babette said, getting up again. "I'll have that shower now and then go to the spa. After that, I'll have a word with Betty. I hope she won't drag her two assistants along. They are the ones that truly bother me.

CHAPTER NINE

French chivalry is not dead

WHEN BABETTE REACHED THE Panorama lounge on the upper deck, she spotted Betty right away. Dressed in one of her new Afghans, she looked absolutely radiant. Babette was glad to see that Betty was sitting at a small table and that her assistants were not with her.

"How was your massage?" Betty asked, sipping on her pina-colada.

"Restoring is the word for it. The woman has angel hands, I'm sure." Babette looked around for the waiter. He came rushing to their table. "I'll have the same," she told him, pointing to Betty's glass.

"Another pina-colada coming up, Ms. Babette," the young man replied, already swinging on his heels.

"Everyone knows you on the ship, it seems," Betty remarked, smiling. "Why is that?"

"That's because, as I've told you, when time permits and I'm not embroiled in endless discussions with some demanding producer, I spend my time cruising around the world. I have seen the most interesting places and met the most intriguing people. And if I am ever tired of the people around me, I can always stop somewhere for a week or so and rejoin the cruise at its next port-of-call."

"You must have a fantastic life," Betty said, "I envy you. Me; I'm always behind a desk, trying to keep my businesses in one piece or make sure the pieces don't fall off." She laughed mournfully.

"Listen, Betty, there's something I've got to tell you…," Babette began as the waiter came back with her drink. She thanked him and sent him on his way with a gentle smile. She was sure he understood that she didn't want to be disturbed further.

"This sounds serious," Betty said, "what is it?"

"Well, it is very serious in fact. As you noted just a moment ago, I know a lot of people aboard the ship. And one person I would trust with my life has told me that he overheard someone talking about you."

"About me? What on Earth for?" Betty sounded as surprised as she was.

"Because you are, or will be shortly I should say, the target of a fraud. Someone aboard *The Contessa* is definitely after some of your money."

"Who is that person? Do you know him, or her?"

"Him *and* her," Babette corrected.

"You mean, it's a couple?"

"Yes. You might have met them. Or maybe your assistants have met them. They call themselves Leon and Linda Summerville. They're from Louisiana and…"

"Did you say "Louisiana?""

"Yes, why? Do you know some Summerville people in Louisiana?" Babette inquired.

"No, not really, but I've heard of a couple from New Orleans who owns large plantations in southern Louisiana. Are they on board?"

"I don't know if these are the people you heard of, but there's a Summerville couple aboard. And these two are planning to get their hands on some of your money."

Betty sipped on her practically empty drink, and then she said, "Listen, Babette, in all the years I've been managing the enterprises I own or overseeing their operations, I've heard this sort of threat more than once. I know what it takes to avert such a problem or redress it in case it goes too far. Generally, though, the people who intend to fleece me"—*there's that word again*, Babette thought—"are experienced thieves, they have a record with either the SEC or IRS. So, a phone call to one of my friends will get rid of them in the blink of an eye."

"I'm glad to hear that, Betty," Babette said, a smile coming across her lips, "because I wouldn't want to be responsible for leaving you in the dark when you were caught unawares."

A few tables away from Betty's, Tiffany and Michele were in deep discussion with a large fellow, who seemed very intent in what he had to say.

"I am so happy you've invited us, Ms. Sylvan," the man said, "but I would like to make sure people on the ship understand that the performance is not generally done to entertain our public."

"Yes," Tiffany agreed, nodding. "I have prepared a little speech that I will be sure to make before you start tonight, Senor Salvatore. Here it is." She handed him a sheet of paper.

Ladies and Gentlemen, what you are about to see is exceptional. In fact, the people who have consented to perform for us tonight have done so, because we have promised them the respect the performance is meant to have. Let me explain: The Virgin of Candelaria is the patron of the Canary Islands. Every year, in February and August, the people of the island go on a pilgrimage designed to make offerings to their patron. In honor of the pilgrimage many of the men dress in their Guancho attire and dance in honor of their patron – which is the performance they have prepared for us.

"Thank you, Ms. Sylvan. That will do very well. It's actually not a dance per say, it's perhaps better compared to a happy walk," Mr. Salvatore said, with a chuckle. "But the dancers, the Spanish troop, should certainly entertain the passengers with their traditional steps and costumes."

"I'm sure they will," Tiffany replied. "We'll be happy to see all of you."

When Mr. Salvatore left the table, Michele turned to Tiffany. "Do you think we should have a back-up plan?"

Tiffany showed her surprise when she asked, "What for? Do you think these two groups will not be enough of an entertainment?"

"They might well be, but Mr. Salvatore mentioned his people were only going to do a "happy walk" as he called it; I wonder how long it will last."

Tiffany nodded. "You're right. It'll probably take them five minutes at the most. And the Spanish traditional dance will last about that long, too. So, yes, we need someone else on the board. What do you have in mind?"

"Well, Constantine arrived this afternoon. He's not due to perform until tomorrow night when we're at sea, but maybe I can charm him into doing a closing comedy number for us."

"If you think you can do that, it would be wonderful. At least this evening's entertainment might not be long but it will be high in laughter.

Tiffany was not done with her meetings for the day. She had yet to discuss Mr. Brogans' upcoming lecture. He was renowned throughout Europe for the wine tycoon and connoisseur he truly was. Laurent Brogans grew up in Cognac in the Charentes – South of France. He breathed wines and liquors since he was three feet high. His parents' winery made all the difference. He saw how hard it was to work in the vineyards – without a promise for a good crop or for an excellent cru. It all depended on the weather, the soil, the care one took of the vines, the crushing method, the fermentation and ultimately the aging of the vintage. Whether white or red, whether champagne or liquors, every bottle one consumed was the product of arduous efforts and years of patience. Laurent learned it all. He learned how to plant a vine properly, how to care for it, how to cut the grapes and everything else it took for him to make the best wine in the Lower Charentes' region. He then went to university and learned to handle the profits from the vineyards ... until he ultimately made his first million Euros. There was no stopping him then. He bought neighboring vineyards, trained his pickers, crushers, and his office employees to make money out of grapes.

Sitting in her office, Tiffany was reviewing Laurent's lecture proposal when the man came in. He was on time. An elegant fellow in his fifties now, Laurent breathed charm and money. He knew he had always made an impression on the ladies. Twice married and twice divorced, the man exuded old country charm. Tiffany had to admit later that she would have been smitten by him, if she hadn't been in love with Alan.

Once seated and the preambles over, Laurent asked, "So, did you have a chance to go over the lecture?"

"Oh yes, Mr. Brogans..."

"Please call me Laurent, it's easier that way."

"Alright then, Laurent. Yes, I have read your lecture and I think I will want to organize the entire session a little differently..."

"Oh? And how do you propose to do that, my dear?" Laurent sounded altogether cautious, curious and perhaps slightly offended.

"Nothing of your lecture would change, of course, Laurent. But I was thinking that an all-encompassing wine-tasting affair would be much more attractive for our passengers. We could organize it so that we offer one series of wines and liquors before the lecture and another assortment afterward. We could serve champagne as an introduction to the evening, and then finish the soiree with sweet wines or liquors, cognacs and ports perhaps."

"Grand idea! Very good initiative, Ms. Sylvan. I will have some of the wines you don't have on board flown in from my own cellars tonight. They should be here and loaded aboard *The Contessa* in the morning before the ship sails."

"Do you think what we have on board might not be sufficient?"

Laurent shook his head vigorously. "Absolutely not, Ms. Sylvan.

I've seen your wine lists, of course, and I can tell you, if I am to represent my house, I want the very best wines to be served."

"That's very generous of you, Laurent…"

"That's not generosity, Ms. Sylvan, that's simply good marketing. When you want to sell a cruise or even a choice of cabins, are you going to show your would-be traveler the average cabin only? No, n'est-ce-pas? You are going to show them the best accommodation possible, aren't you?"

"I guess you've got a point there," Tiffany had to agree. "And what do you say about the cheese I plan to serve?"

"That too is a point worth raising, yes. You need to think that Americans love these pasty, tasteless cheddars and have no idea that there are hundreds of cheeses much more palatable than cheddar when serving wine. I will give you a list, and I will ask William, my assistant at the vineyard to add a couple of boxes of cheese with the wine shipment. Would that be acceptable?"

Tiffany was all smiles. What appeared to be somewhat of a dull lecture at first perusal was now turning out to be the best entertaining event thus far.

"More than acceptable, Laurent. Thank you. And, by the way, I think it will be simpler if you called me Tiffany."

"I'll be honored to do so, Tiffany, thank you."

Wow! French chivalry is not dead after all.

Following another long day spent between the Santa Cruz beaches, lunches at the marina or nearby restaurants and on various tours of the island, the passengers were ready to "put their feet up" and relax. The evening promised to be enjoyable. Most everyone had heard of the Guancho tribes by now and was keen to see the men dressed in their sheep skins, shod in furry slippers and armed with their polished walking poles. They didn't have to move: they were an attraction all unto themselves.

Following their "happy walk" and waddling dance, the Spanish traditional dancers put the stage on fire with a couple of flamencos and tangos. Every guest was visibly delighted. Their performance was a crowd pleaser, no doubt about it.

But then, when Constantine stepped in the middle of the cabaret floor and took the microphone, the audience went wild. Many of the passengers had either heard of the comedian or had attended his performances in New York and LA.

"Ladies and Gentlemen," he began, when the applause had somewhat abated. "I'm really grateful for your welcome. It's great to hear that people of the oceans such as your good-selves appreciate bits of humor same as the aliens on land do."

Of course, renewed laughter accompanied the remark. Passengers appreciate being considered "different" from the people living on land. These are the aliens they meet along their journeys inhabiting strange lands.

"And since I've been told that you might need a few more stimulating words," Constantine went on, "before going to bed, I thought I would tell you about what happened to one of these aliens – my boss – the other day. Talk about a hair-raising experience. Poor guy, he couldn't sleep for three days afterward." He turned to Tiffany and winked. She smiled from her table in return. "So, here's my boss, Mark is his name. That morning he needed to call one of the key office employees with an urgent problem. He dialed the employee's cell phone number and was greeted with a child's whisper, "Hello?" Feeling put out at the inconvenience of having to talk to a youngster, Mark asked, "Is your Daddy home?" "Yes," whispered the small voice. "May I talk with him?" To Mark's surprise, the voice whispered, "No." Wanting to talk with an adult, Mark asked, "Is your Mommy there?" "Yes," came the answer. "May I talk with her?" Again the small voice whispered, "No." Knowing that it was not likely that a young child would be left home alone, Mark decided he would just leave a message with the person who should be there watching over the child. "Is there any one there besides you?" Mark asked the child. "Yes," whispered the child, "A policeman." Wondering what a cop would be doing at his employee's home, Mark asked, "May I speak with the policeman?" "No, he's busy," whispered the child. "Busy doing what?" asked Mark. "Talking to Daddy and Mommy and the Fireman," came the whispered answer. Growing concern and even worried as he heard what sounded like a helicopter through the earpiece on the phone, Mark asked, "What is that noise?" "A hello-copper," answered the whispering voice. "What is going on there?" asked Mark, now alarmed. In an awed whispering voice the child answered, "The search team just landed the hello-copper." Horrified, concerned and more than just a little frustrated, my boss then asked, "Why are they there?" Still whispering, the young voice replied, along with a muffled giggle: "They're looking for me"."

The entire cabaret-restaurant exploded in applause and laughter. Tiffany was relieved. The short evening of entertainment had been an extraordinary success.

Constantine then concluded, saying, "Ladies and Gentlemen, you've been a fantastic audience. But for now, I'll bid you good night. I'll be back, you can be sure."

CHAPTER TEN

You can expect a mutiny

THE LIGHT WIND FROM THE COAST was hot and dry. The sea was a sheet of glass; one would have believed *The Contessa* was gliding on the surface of a lake. The thermometer was playing games. It had been nearly a hundred degrees throughout the day, but as soon as the sun decided to hide, it simply plummeted to nearly fifty degrees Fahrenheit. Alan had heard of this climate oddity but had never experienced it first-hand. Although the African coast was not yet in sight, since they had left the Canaries the climate steadily became drier and either intolerably hot or decidedly cold. On the other hand, the clean air and seemingly unadulterated atmosphere allowed the passengers to have a clear view of the firmament. The myriad of stars enveloped the ship as if it was piercing the swell under a dome of small, but brilliant diamonds.

Tiffany and Alan were in awe before the greatness of God. One didn't have to be a religious person to be astounded by the beauty before their eyes. Silence was not a request but a must. You would not want to talk to intrude in the tranquility of this night. The two of them had finished work for the day – although Alan was still on call – and they were enjoying an evening stroll along the promenade before retiring for the night.

"Do you think we're lucky, or is this a common occurrence?" Tiffany asked as they stopped walking and leaned against the railing.

"Perhaps a bit of both," Alan answered. "It's very common, in my experience, to find yourself under a dome of stars at night in various seas."

"I wish it was a little warmer though."

"Well, Tiffany, you can't have everything at once. You know that."

"No harm in wishing, is there?"

Alan chuckled quietly. "Absolutely not. And I wish every night was as quiet as this one. Whether cold or hot, this tranquility, this absolute silence is to be savored."

"Except for the hum of life behind and below us," Tiffany remarked, "I would agree with you."

"Yes," Alan said, turning toward the elevator hallway a few paces from them, "but I think if we make it to the camel drive, we are promised the same type of silence."

"It's almost creepy though. It's as if everything or everyone had died and only sand had been left behind."

"That's a reasonable description of what might have happened when the Earth suffered its most recent upheaval. The fauna and flora that occupied this part of the continent disappeared and only sand remained."

"Quite incredible, isn't it?"

"On the contrary, Tiff. When you look at what is happening to unrestricted farming in East Africa, you can see the land slowly becoming devoid of vegetation until all life is irreversibly eradicated."

"Thanks to irresponsible humans, I suppose?"

Alan nodded. "Partly, yes, but we are the ones who should be able to inject some sense and education into the lives of those who need the crops to survive."

"But isn't that what all of these charitable organizations have been trying to do?"

"I would say so, but every time there is enough peace in one of these countries to start something worthwhile, someone is sure to come and disturb it."

"I guess, no one is at fault when it comes to Ebola. Who could have foreseen such a disaster?"

"No, Tiffany, we're not talking about an uncontrollable event such as a typhoon or a tsunami, we're talking about a disease that could have been quelled or prevented. Ebola is not a new disease. It has disseminated entire populations before now, but most scientists were busier finding cures for rare ailments or financially profitable ones than looking at what was staring them in the face. Which government was going to grant any funds for research into a disease that only erupts every hundred years and in insalubrious regions? Not one."

"I guess, charity begins at home as they say," Tiffany said reflectively.

"Yes, but if we wanted to prevent an outbreak of unprecedented proportion, there was a lot of work to be done. Unfortunately, not every nation in the West Coast of Africa will accept being told to "clean up their act", literally. Water has always been scarce everywhere on this continent, and keeping diseases away requires plenty of water and soap."

"Hygiene is not at the top of their list of requirements, I guess?"

"No, Tiffany. Although I've never been there, from what I learned in other countries plagued with lack of hygiene is that survival and food are on top of the list – not soap and water."

"I suppose we'll have to watch everything we do or touch if we go for a visit inland."

"Of that you can be sure, Tiff. And although we both have vaccinations, it doesn't mean that we don't need to be careful."

"Talking about being careful," Tiffany said, a smile drawing at the corner of her lips, "look who's coming…"

"Well, if it isn't our Sioux mate?" Alan said as Simon Albertson made his way to join the couple.

"Yeah, Doc. I've been looking all over for you…"

"Have you heard there's a "new invention" called a cell phone…?"

"Okay, Doc." Simon looked at Tiffany. "Sorry about the intrusion, Ms. Sylvan, but I've got to talk to the doc here for a minute. Do you mind?"

"Not at all," Tiffany said. "I'll be in the lounge," she added, talking to Alan.

Both men watched the young woman walk away.

As Tiffany reached the cabaret lounge on the upper deck, she remembered Constantine was performing tonight. She smiled to herself and took a seat at the back of the room.

Constantine was in the middle of recounting a series of events or conversations he had with people during his many travels.

"…Then she explained: My husband and I purchased an old home in Northern New York State from two elderly sisters. Winter was fast approaching and I was concerned about the house's lack of insulation. "If they could live here all those years, so can we," my husband confidently declared. One November night the temperature plunged to below zero, and we woke up to find the interior walls covered with frost. My husband called the sisters to ask how they had kept the house warm. After a rather brief conversation, he hung up. "For the past 30 years," he muttered, "they've gone to Florida for the winter." And I guess that's why I'm here, Ladies and Gentlemen; I can't watch my house melt down in the spring."

Truly, the man is quite amazing, Tiffany thought as she smiled at the approaching waiter. She had to wait for the applause to die down before she could give him her order.

In the meantime, on the promenade deck, Simon was saying, "It's about the vaccines, Doc…"

"What about them?"

"Well, I was in the mess when I heard the Frenchy talk about the canisters…"

"You mean Mr. Albert?"

"Yeah, that's the guy. I've heard him say something about the cases going ashore. He wondered why he couldn't be told which case contained the vaccines. He sounded pretty mad about it."

"Yeah, I got the same impression when I last talked to him about the operation. I told him that not even I or my nurse will know which case will contain the real vaccines and which case will contain vials of water."

"Why would he be so irritated about it though?"

"Because he's a hot head?" Alan offered with a smile.

"Always emotional these guys; yeah, I agree. But it bothers me anyway. I don't know what he's got in mind, but to my way of thinking it's a fuse you don't want to ignite."

"What do you mean?" Alan was truly curious.

"I mean if he starts rumors saying that we're intending to give these poor sods in these countries watered down vaccines, or some such rot, I can see us having a mutiny on our hands."

"Let's not over-dramatize the thing, Simon," Alan suggested calmly. "But I agree with you, though, we should stop the guy from spreading false rumors or any rumors concerning the vaccines."

Simon nodded. "I just wanted to let you know what's going on, Doc. And don't worry about my crew; they wouldn't believe a word of what the Frenchy says. They know better."

Although it was late in the evening, Alan decided to go down to the security office after he escorted Tiffany to her cabin. He might join her later. A matter of keeping her warm.

Gregoire Albert was on his satellite phone with someone in France when Alan came in. Gregoire stopped talking, and said, "Désolé mais je dois racrocher. Au revoir," and hung up. He definitely didn't want Alan to listen to his conversation, even if only one-sided.

"Doctor, what can I do for you?" Gregoire said, sitting down at his desk. "Please have a seat."

"No thanks. What I've got to say won't take long…"

"Oh? What is it?"

"It's about you being annoyed and spreading rumors about not knowing which case will contain the vaccines. I told you: only the WHO people will have that information. You, as the security chief on this vessel should appreciate their assistance in this regard."

"Is that it?" The arrogance in Gregoire's voice was all too audible.

"Yes, Mr. Albert, that is all I have to say for the time being. But, if I hear one more peep from the crew regarding what you have told them about these vaccines, I'll have you kicked off this ship at the next port, is that clear?"

"Couldn't be clearer, Doctor. Thanks for the warning," Gregoire said resentfully as he returned to his paperwork.

When Alan left the security office, he was certain this was not going to be his last encounter with Mr. Albert. Somehow, he couldn't bring himself to trust the man.

Relaxing in their cabin, Adele Muesli and Gregory Ashton were happy about the progress they made in searching for Betty's nephew. Père Gilbert had already contacted the monastery in Tambacounda and apparently there was an old monk who remembered "Lionel – the little white boy" very well.

"And I talked to Betty this evening after she was told that it wouldn't be that much of a problem for us to go to that town, Taba-something, when she intends to fly to Timbuktu while the ship is in port in Dakar."

"That's all fine and dandy, Addy, but do you think she'll let us come with her? You've seen how these WHO guys are; no one off ship unless they need to …"

"I know all that, Gregory, but we're not there yet. I've got to tell Betty why I really want to go to Taba…"

"Tambacounda," Gregory said.

"Yeah, that place. Because, up to now I've only told her about the possibility of her nephew being given to a white monk…"

"Why didn't you tell her the rest of it; about Père Gilbert and what our nice missionary found out?"

"All in good time, Greg. I'm not intending to rush anything, in case we're totally wrong and the *little white boy* turns out to be someone else's boy or nephew."

CHAPTER ELEVEN

Nothing but sand . . .

MAURITANIA WAS ONCE PART OF French West Africa, an enormous territory south of Morocco. There was nothing there but sand. The territory had no capital. It was administered – if administering nomadic tribes was ever possible – from Saint Louis in Senegal. In 1957 someone decided to name Saint Louis as the capital of the territory. By the end of 1958 Mauritania was born as an autonomous republic. The powers-that-be didn't like to be associated with the Senegalese tribal administrators. Senegalese tribes were trying to usurp power over the nomadic itinerants and no Touareg or Berber would have anything to do with those "who knew nothing of the desert." Thus, in 1960 Mauritania became an independent country with Nouakchott as its capital. Nouakchott comes from the Berber meaning "Place for the Winds" – and if anyone asks; it's a perfect name for it.

Mauritania is not a hospitable land. People are poor and in search of the elusive oasis every day of their lives. Although there is an enormous subterranean lake beneath their feet, called the Trarza Lake, it, too is threatening to run dry by the middle of the twenty-first century. The average temperature being 80 degrees Fahrenheit all year round, some Mauritanians choose to live underground. There are entire neighborhoods of "hole housing."

Perhaps the only saving grace to this unforgiving piece of land is the fact that someone found copper in them-there-hills. Chinese they were. And prosperity was finally knocking at the door of Mauritania in 2000.

Arriving at the Port de l'Amitié, the only deep water seaport along the coast, gives one the impression of an uninterrupted landscape meeting one's eyes. That was the impression Babette and Betty got when *The Contessa* approached its berth. Where the water ceased, the sand began. There was nothing but sand for miles and miles ahead of them.

"How terribly awesome," Babette remarked. "The blue of the ocean dying in white foam against the copper sand is almost as if the painter's palette had no other color with which to adorn the canvas."

"But where is Nouakchott, that's what I'd like to know," Betty queried.

"I suppose we'll see it soon enough. But if you recall what it said in the pamphlet; there are a lot of shanty neighborhoods and nothing resembling a thriving city of nearly two million people."

"I guess we'll have to wait and see," Betty added, looking disappointed.

"They said they were going to have several cars, or SUVs, I should say, waiting for us."

"I sure hope so, because from the looks of it, so far, we're a long way from any sort of civilized gatherings."

"That's where your adventurous mind should take over, Betty. Let's see what's behind the next sand dune sort of thing."

"Okay, okay. I hear you. But I don't even see any camels – where are they?"

"One thing at a time, alright?" Babette was starting to think that Betty had lived too long inside the four walls of her office; she seemed afraid to step out into the unknown.

"Okay, I'm sorry, Babette. I like things to be planned out ahead of time and even if the plan doesn't work, I know I have tried to organize the journey."

"Yes, I noticed that about you." Babette paused. "Okay, why don't we have a hearty breakfast and then get ourselves dressed for the occasion?"

Betty giggled. "Good idea; I can hardly wait to get myself all bundled up to go out in the burning hot sand!"

"Odd concept isn't it?"

"That it is, that it is, my friend," Betty concluded.

When the two ladies arrived at the café on the upper deck, it seemed as if the atmosphere had changed somehow. Every waiter and server was dressed in a light cream-colored uniform; the tables were bare of placemats and cutlery, and the counters were all devoid of the usual bowls of fruit, bread and cereals.

When Babette asked one of the waiters what was going on, he replied that when the sand starts blowing, all the food would be covered with it.

"And we're to expect these sand storms to reach the ship?" Babette asked, slightly taken aback.

"That's what we've been told, ma'am. We're going to keep all the terrace doors closed, of course, but apparently the sand gets through everything anyway."

"You know," Betty interposed, "that's true. I had a friend who lived somewhere in northern France and she told me that when you live near these beaches where there's nothing to stop the sand from blowing onto everything, it's a real nightmare."

"Okay then," Babette said to the waiter, taking a seat at one of the tables near the open windows, "why don't you bring us some tea, orange juice, a couple of yogurts and a choice of cereals?" She looked at Betty. "Would that be okay with you?"

"And I'll have a couple of those French croissants and a cup of mixed fruit, too."

"No problem, ladies," the young man replied, "I'll be right back with your order."

As soon as he was out of earshot, Babette said, "This is promising to be an interesting stop over."

"A surprising one, I should say," Betty countered.

A couple of hours later, Babette and Betty, along with a dozen passengers and several crewmembers descended the gangway toward the awaiting SUVs. They seemed to be on loan from the copper plant and port facilities, judging from the logos adorning the side doors.

Alan and Olga were on hand. They were going to accompany the passengers on their camel ride to an oasis about ten miles out of Nouakchott. Everyone had been told the camels were ready to travel and waiting at their stables.

People seemed generally anxious rather than curious. For Alan this little sortie was a first as well. Olga was the only one who had a little experience with West Africa, but not of the Sahara as yet. However, help was approaching in the form of a tall and handsome man. He was dressed in a black twab and abayah. His head was surrounded with a white keffiyeh or yashmagh, which went around his neck. He held a leather strap in his right hand.

"My name is Samir Alhassan, Ladies and Gentlemen; I will be your guide and caravan master for today." His English was perfect. No intonation of any sort. Babette was surprised and so were most of the passengers. Perhaps they had expected some old carpet seller to grovel and demand alms for his services – but no, this guy was the genuine article. One did what the man wanted you to do – no ifs, ands or buts about it!

"First of all, I would like to ensure that all of you realize that we will stop in a couple to three hours at our destination; before that, it will not be possible for any of us to stop anywhere for any reason what so ever."

Alan gathered, as did everyone else, that meant no pee stop anywhere.

"For those of you who have never been near a camel, I would like to remind you that it is a beast of burden, first and foremost. It is not a pet that you want to caress or cajole. It will bite you and I am certain the doctor here"—he threw a glance at Alan—"is not keen on treating that sort of wound. And mind the spitting; the camels have no manners what so ever," Samir added, which his remark ignited a round of laughter from the passengers.

"Next, clothing. I see that many of you are wearing loose garments and adequate attire for the desert. For those who have not heard of the dress requirements for this ride, I have some spare abayahs or twabs, and keffiyehs for all of you, in the back of each SUV." He paused and looked around. "Last, water. Each of you will be given a calabash of water, which will be attached to the pommel of the saddle. Don't try drinking while you ride; you will regret it! And throwing up on the saddles is not something the camel owners welcome."

Amid the titters and chuckles, the SUVs' drivers then took over while Samir shouted one more thing: "As-salamualaykum to all of you."

"Waalaykumu s-salam," Alan murmured in reply, which brought a gentle smile to Samir's face.

"How did you know what to say?" Olga asked, as the two of them were walking toward the last SUV.

"I've visited a few Muslim countries in my *troubled past*," he joked, "and I finally learned how to say 'you're welcome' in Arabic."

Driving through Nouakchott was an eye-opener for everyone. "A city by any other name would still be a city, I imagine," Betty remarked as they were slowly trying to fray themselves a passage through a population of all ages and descriptions. It was difficult to see if you were driving past a store, a hovel, a place of worship or a residence, for every habitation seemed to be everything in one or none of the above. Women carrying children on their backs or on their tummy as if they were sacks of rice; men trotting to some unknown destination through the sandy streets; donkeys pulling carts filled with bags and bags of fish or roots of some sort; wagons being pulled by a couple of men, all of it seemingly wanting to drag you down in time to some other era, two or three thousand years ago perhaps.

Alan could not take it all in at once. The people, the children, the houses, the shops, the hustle and bustle seemed to send his mind in a whirlwind of new and old adventures. As for the passengers, they were quiet. There was no need for explanation of any sort. It was laid before their eyes – nothing hidden. The wounds of civilization were bare. There were a few cars driving past or parked in front of what looked like government or administrative buildings, but not many to speak of. The other edifice that truly stood out from the rest, and perhaps slightly out of place, was the mosque. A gift from Saudi Arabia, this impressive structure, with its spire-like minarets, dominated the skyline, as if daring to challenge its nearest religious opponent to a battle for power. Unfortunately, the opponent was unmemorable. The only remnant of Catholicism in the city was the St. Joseph Church, which is still attended by a few devout and overseen by the archdiocese in Senegal.

As the cars reached the stable, the offensive odor of camel dung reached everyone's nostrils. Babette was not the only one who found it a little much for her. But she decidedly hadn't come thus far to experience a camel ride to turn back now.

As soon as he exited the vehicle, Alan went to her. "Okay, Babette," he said, holding her under her arm, "We're going to do this together. We'll soon be out of here and the odor will only be a bad memory."

Babette nodded but didn't say a word. She looked up at Betty who stood beside her with a handkerchief over her nose and mouth.

Samir had seen the doctor approach and hold Babette by the arm. He came to meet them.

"Ms. Babette; please come with me," he said, gently taking her arm from Alan. "She will be just fine, Doctor; she will be riding with me."

Alan immediately felt relieved. He knew Babette would be all right in Samir's arms. The man sounded and acted as responsible as one should be in these circumstances. As for Betty, she smiled at Alan. He took her arm and they followed the other passengers to the row of camels 'sitting' near the stable gate.

Samir showed each rider to his or her camel and then asked everyone to watch him mount his méhari.

"His name is Katoof," he said to Babette with a smile. "He is the best. I've raised him myself, but he still a little shy; so please don't touch him."

"Oh don't worry, Samir, I'm not going to; he's much too big for me." She giggled.

"Okay, Ladies and Gentlemen, here it goes," Samir said, laughing. And in one swift move he practically jumped over the saddle to land in it and to sit across his mount.

"Your driver will help you do the same," he added, nodding to his own servant. While the passengers tried their best to imitate Samir, with moderate success and humor, Samir came down, and lifted Babette into his arms to her great surprise.

"Oh my! Really?"

"Yes, really, my dear. I wouldn't want you to fall off before we leave."

Alan was amazed. Samir was a gentleman and he seemed to care as much as he himself would for his dear friend. He looked on for a few moments longer before he helped Betty onto her camel and finally climbed aboard his own.

When everyone was in the saddle, including Babette astride in front of Samir, the latter uttered a few orders in Arabic to the drivers. In one chorus of movement, the camels extended their hind legs and then their front ones.

Babette hadn't expected to be thrown forward with such a force but was grateful for Samir's arms wrapped around her waist.

"Good grief," she exclaimed, "Is Katoof always this surprising?"

Samir laughed heartily and grabbed the rein – a tress of camel hair adorned with a red tassel, indicative of his chieftain.

Before getting out of the city limit, Samir told everyone to cover their faces with their keffiyehs. "The sand will start flying in your faces as soon as we begin trotting; so leave only a slit through which you will see ahead of you."

And then the fun started. The drivers – those who had helped everyone onto their beasts – caught up with the passengers and their mounts and ordered the camels to begin trotting.

Alan had to admit; Samir had been right, eating or drinking anything at this time would have automatically been emptied from the intestinal tract. Your stomach, along with every other organ was dancing around your abdomen as if someone had installed a rhythmic drum inside of you – "Two to the right; two to the left; two ahead and two back; and there we go again…" he sang silently and laughed out loud. This was better than any ride at the fairground.

He wondered how Babette was coping.

She was doing much better than most. Samir was holding her close to him so that she moved in time with Katoof's rhythm rather than against it.

Once they were all well on their way, the wind began to whip at their faces. Once again Samir's advice had paid off. Alan could feel the millions of needles hitting the keffiyeh around his face with such force that he had to keep his eyes closed for a little while.

As soon as the caravan managed to reach the protection of an immense dune to their left, the wind died down. The beasts shook their heads and everyone breathed a sigh of relief.

An hour later, they were literally in the middle of the desert. There was nothing ahead of them, nothing behind and nothing on either side of them. Only a faint trail of hardened sandy rock was visible underneath the camels' feet.

"This is extraordinary," Babette blurted, turning her head up to Samir.

"What is, my dear lady?"

"This silence, the vastness, the heat, but the incredible freshness of it all."

Samir chuckled. "Yes. It surprises most people. It's very peaceful and relaxing, in fact. There's nothing to disturb you or your thoughts."

"No wonder the nomads can hardly wait to get out of the city," Babette remarked. "I would too if I were them."

"I gather you don't like the cities," Samir asked.

"Oh but I do. It's just that if I wanted to seek refuge somewhere, this is the place I would come. This is "immaculate tranquility." Thank you…"

"For what?"

"For your patience and taking the time to drive all of us to the oasis. I bet you could have left the job to any of the drivers behind us, couldn't you?"

"Yes, I could have, but then I would have missed a lovely ride with a famous playwright, wouldn't I?"

"Don't tell me you know about me."

Samir nodded and smiled. "Yes, my dear lady. You're the talk of the town in Paris…."

"You live in Paris?" Babette sounded incredulous.

"Why? Because I lead a camel ride from time to time, I have to be illiterate and ignorant?"

"You know I didn't mean it that way," Babette scolded. "You do not sound ignorant to me, and you're certainly not illiterate, judging from the way you speak three languages fluently. But I am surprised that you live in such a busy city as Paris. You could live anywhere – why Paris?"

"Because Paris is an enchantress, a lady to whom you can't say no, Ms. Babette. Besides, my wife is French and she is as enchanting as the city of her birth."

CHAPTER TWELVE

Water, at last . . .

A COUPLE OF HOURS LATER, as promised, an oasis was in sight. The green of the plants, palms and shrubs was a blot on the backdrop of an immense blue sky. The ocher sand only made the oasis look a lot more striking. It looked strangely out of place. Samir slowed the caravan down to a walking pace, to everyone's gratefulness. Alan felt as if he had been put through a cocktail shaker. He had a hard time describing the sensation. Betty, an experienced horseman, had adapted to the trotting rhythm fairly early in the ride and was quite satisfied with the sort of exercise she had just experienced. Olga was holding her tummy as she dismounted her camel.

"Remind me next time not to have breakfast before going on a camel ride," she said to Alan as she waddled toward him. "Do you think it's okay to drink some water now?"

"I would wait for a few more minutes before you try drinking anything," Alan answered. "Give your stomach some time to settle down."

Samir helped Babette down their mount and offered her a drink from the calabash of water he had grabbed from around the pommel of his méhari. *Water, at last...,* she thought.

Samir waited until everyone had dismounted and then asked the passengers to gather under the main tent at the back of the oasis.

Generally, the Touaregs' tents consist of long strips of cloths woven from black or brown wool and goats' hair. The strips are sewn together into a roof and separate sides. When erecting a tent, the men extent the wooden poles upward, which support the roof while the women pin the separate sides to the roofing. They then extend ropes from the poles to hold the structure in place. The open side faces away from the winds, and vertical curtains usually separate the interior of the tent into three sections: 1. the men's section, where the family gathers to eat and talk, 2. the sleeping section, and 3. the kitchen. Rugs, either woven by the women of the tribe or purchased in market towns, cover most of the ground. A brass mortar and stone pestle, and coffeepots stand at the ready at the tent's entrance. This is in front of the hearth, dug in the sand and covered with an iron grid. This marks the spot where guests are welcome to sit down with the man of the family. The tent, or home, belongs to his wife. If she sees a troublesome husband unfit to have about the place, she has the right to oust him without recourse.

Apart from raising children, fetching water and fuel, feeding and watering goats and camels, women also weave cloths, rugs and other pieces of clothing worn by everyone in the tribe. Bedouins, Berbers and Touaregs alike are entirely self-sufficient and they are regarded as the repositories of manly virtues. They are proud, fiercely independent, resourceful, courageous, loyal, hospitable and generous.

Babette, holding onto Samir's arm for balance in the uneven sand, walked toward the tent with a smile on her face. She was truly pleased with the whole scene. Alan, Olga and Betty joined her and Samir when they all stopped in front of the fire burning in front of the tent's entrance. An old man was sitting cross-legged behind the fire, pounding coffee beans with the traditional stone pestle into a brass mortar and keeping an eye on the steaming coffee pots resting on the grid that lay over the hearth. He smiled when he saw Samir approach him. The two men exchanged a few words in Arabic and then their host stood up. He stretched an arm toward the inside of the tent and said, "Come, come, we will have coffee."

Samir repeated the invitation and urged the guests to sit on the carpet. Betty inhaled a sigh of admiration when she looked down at the so-called carpet. That large Moroccan, hand-woven masterpiece would be worth an absolute fortune in any of the New York Interior Decor stores. Its intricate design and luxurious softness to the touch was truly a surprise for the passengers who slowly took their seats around a copper table.

Soon the women emerged from the kitchen part of the tent and brought a coffee cup to each of the guests, into which the host poured some coffee. It was dark and smooth to the taste. Many passengers had never drunk "real" coffee and were pleasantly surprised by the taste of it. When it came to the snacks, the biscuits were dry but very tasty. Afterward everyone was given a large glass of water – fresh from the well. The liquid was as transparent as the glass in which it was poured. It was refreshing and incredibly cold.

When Betty leaned over to whisper into Alan's ear that she might like to go to the ladies' room, he smiled. He then got up and went to chat with Samir who had been sitting with the host in front of the tent.

Samir listened to the request and got to his feet. He turned into the tent and told everyone that there were only "ladies' quarters" in the oasis. The women would show the guests where they could use the washroom. The men had to find a spot 'outside' for themselves.

When Betty returned from the ladies' quarters, she was grinning.

"I tell you, Babette," she said, as she returned to her seat beside her friend, "I never thought I would see the day when I would once again crouch to go…. You know what I mean."

Babette erupted in laughter. "A bit of a surprise, was it?"

"You can say that again. I mean one has to watch where one steps. There's only a very deep hole in the sand in which they put a pipe, and that's it."

"Okay," Babette said, getting to her feet, "I'll have to inspect this *ladies quarters* then, won't I? Sounds like a variation of the standard in India and many Arab countries."

An hour later, once everyone was refreshed and had had time to tour the oasis, which spread over a relatively large area, perhaps the size of a small park, the travelers rejoined their drivers who were ready and waiting for them at the back of the oasis. The ride back was uneventful and now that most passengers knew what to expect, the ten-mile trip seemed much easier and much shorter.

It had been an experience the passengers would never forget. They would have stories to tell for weeks to come.

As they climbed the gangway after thanking Samir profusely for being a "fantastic" and caring guide, Babette and Betty were tired; exhausted would be a better description of how every part of their bodies felt.

Alan didn't feel much better, neither did Olga. Truth be told, everyone who had participated in this little expedition needed a few hours' rest before they could function normally again.

That evening Babette decided to have dinner in her suite. She was no longer a young woman and although she did not regret the camel ride into the desert, she thought she better take it easy that night and get to bed soon after her meal.

Edmund had not said a word since Babette came in. He waited until she had taken a well-deserved bath and had joined him in the living room to finally appear in the seat across from her.

"I guess it was quite a harsh excursion," he commented.

Babette nodded, then shook her head and giggled. "But it was so much fun and so interesting, Edmund, I am very glad I mustered the courage to do it. I won't regret it."

"Did you go very far into the desert?"

"No, not really, only ten miles from the city's outskirts. But it seemed as if we were in the middle of nowhere. It was so peaceful, and so refreshing; I couldn't grasp the idea of going across one of the hottest pieces of land on Earth and finding it refreshing. It didn't make sense to me until our guide, Samir, explained that most of the desert is void of polluting substances in the air. They've either been burnt off or dissolved by the time they touched the ground." She paused musingly. "It truly felt as if I was 'drinking' a bowl of fresh air with every breath. Amazing really."

"I'm sure you'll find a way to include this experience in one of your plays, won't you?"

"I had already used a little bit of this sort of travel in one of my plays; if you recall, when Lord Bratton came back from the Middle East.... Of course, it was not first-hand experience. To portray such a ride and visit of the oasis would be truly difficult, I think." She paused again. "Anyway, we'll see." She looked at Edmund. "So, what happened around here while I was away? Anything interesting?"

"Well, nothing as interesting or exciting as to what you've just experienced, my dear, but I believe Adele Muesli and Gregory Ashton are making excellent progress in finding Betty's nephew. They've been busier than ever since reaching the port. They're in contact with a White Monk in Mali who has heard about a white boy being raised in Senegal at some monastery in a city called Tambacounda..."

"But that's marvelous, Edmund. Have they told Betty yet?" Babette shook her head. "Maybe I was wrong about these two..."

"Not so fast, milady. They have decided not to say anything until they're sure the boy in question was Leon Archer. By my way of thinking, it's very wise on their part. Let's say the boy wasn't Leon, but some other child. Betty would be even more disappointed when she would learn that all of their efforts had been for naught."

"I guess so. But if it were me, I would like to be informed every step of the way and if I found I was following the wrong trail, I would return to the starting point – no harm done."

Edmund chuckled. "Yes, but that's you, Babette. Betty is quite a different woman. She would sooner call the Tambacounda boy "Leon Archer" than admit defeat."

"I have to agree with you on that point, Edmund. Betty is a great friend and an admirable woman, but she won't admit losing the game or even a hand very easily." A knock at the cabin door interrupted them.

Edmund disappeared instantly from view. When Babette

answered the door, she was glad to see the steward standing in the doorway, holding a tray of goodies. She was terribly hungry. She told him to come in and to deposit the tray on the table. As soon as the young man left, she went to sit down.

She had ordered a large crustacean and fish salad with rice and nuts. A small bottle of Riesling was standing beside a wine glass; while a cup of fruit for dessert completed the repast.

"That must be as good as it looks," Edmund commented, returning to his seat.

"And it is," Babette answered, picking up a shrimp from the salad bowl. "I love anything fishy. I must have been a fish or maybe a hermit crab in another life."

Edmund had to laugh. He had a hard time imagining Babette seeking a home in an empty shell and hanging one claw out to grab her next meal in passing.

They both started laughing out loud when Edmund described what he had just envisioned.

CHAPTER THIRTEEN

Wedding vows

WHEN ALAN HAD RECUPERATED sufficiently, two hours of sleep later, he came back to the medical center to find one of the WHO personnel waiting for him.

"Oh, I'm terribly sorry," Alan said when he saw the man sitting in the waiting room, "have you been waiting long?"

The man waved a hand in front of his face. "No-no, Doctor, not at all. I had checked with your nurse earlier and she told me that you would be back at about this time. So, here I am." He paused and smiled. He was probably in his forties and sported a red beard. He looked like a man who had traveled the world over. "The name is Julian, Dr. Julian Hatfield." He extended a hand for the doc to shake and stood up. "I just came to give you the heads' up in regards to our next stop."

"Oh yeah?" Alan answered cordially. "Why don't we go to my office?"

As soon as the two men were sitting down, Julian began explaining the reasons for his visit. "You see, Doctor, Saint Louis is the first port where we will have to drop some vaccines at the clinic and perform some inoculations ourselves." Alan nodded. "Where it will become a little tricky is when we'll have to deliver the vaccine to a village near the border with Mauritania..."

"But isn't Saint Louis located near the Mauritania border anyway?"

Julian nodded. "Yes, but we're talking about a village located east of the city along the Senegal River. We were even thinking of taking a pirogue or two and go down the river to the village, instead of traveling by road. In my view, it would be less risky when it comes to the vaccines being exposed to theft."

"I'm sorry, Doctor," Alan said, "but you've lost me after the word 'pirogue'. From all accounts, I've been told that Saint Louis is one of the most civilized if not the cleanest cities along the coast. I know it's located at the mouth of the Senegal River, but why would you want to travel along the water ways?"

"Practicality, Doctor. You see, we could all pile up into a couple of SUVs and make our way out of town, but we could risk being attacked during the trip. These people have been waiting for relief for months now. And the body count is only climbing. So, Dr. Ashford and I thought we could travel along the river much faster, and we wouldn't attract that much attention. We haven't divulged this plan to anyone."

"And you would not say anything about it even after our arrival; is that the intent?"

"Exactly. Everyone would expect us to travel with the SUVs when in fact we would have taken a couple of fishermen into our confidence, and paid them of course, to take us to the village." Julian paused. "But we wanted to pass the idea by you and hear what you might have to suggest."

"Well, thank you for letting me in on the plot. I think it's a great idea. However, how do you know you could trust these fishermen not to blab to their families and have all of the population of Saint Louis up in arms because of the planned subterfuge?"

"It's a risk both ways, I know," Julian agreed. "Yet, one of our team members has a cousin in Saint Louis who's well acquainted with a fisherman's family. Dr. Ashford thought he might be trustworthy enough, since these people cannot (or will not) betray family confidence, especially in circumstances such as these."

"I don't know," Alan said reflectively. "At first thought, I'm not sure I would want to trust one of these boats. I know they're very sturdy, but…." Alan paused. "Why don't you let me think about this for a few hours? I'll get back to you before bedtime. How's that?"

"No problem, Doctor," Julian said, rising from the visitor's chair. "I'll give you a call before calling it a night, okay?"

"By all means, and please, tell Dr. Ashford for me that I'll be fine with any final decision you guys make."

That evening, Tiffany was looking forward to having Constantine perform again. He had been such a success thus far, that the passengers were looking forward to his return to the Cabaret.

Alan came into the restaurant after finishing his reports for the head office just as Constantine was about to start his routine. He took Tiffany's hand in his and whispered in her ear, "How would you like to go on a gondola through Saint Louis tomorrow?"

She turned her head to him and giggled quietly. "I'd love it," she said, squeezing his hand.

"Good evening, Ladies and Gentlemen," Constantine began as the applause died down. "Tonight, I thought we'd talk about marriage…" which announcement was met with a few chuckles. "Yes. I know this is not a familiar topic of conversation anymore. Divorce is at the top of the list of subjects preoccupying the minds of most young people these days. They're about to get married and they're already talking about who will get what when (not if) they part company." The audience had to interrupt him with a wave of cackled laughter. "Actually, one of my friends – hum, well yes, he's still a friend – when it was time to recite his marriage vows, he really got the surprise of his life." The laughter cut him off again. "Anyway, let me tell you what happened: during the wedding rehearsal, the groom (my friend) approached the priest with an unusual offer: Look, I'll give you $200 if you'll change the wedding vows. When you get to me, and the part where I'm to promise to 'love, honor and obey' and 'forsaking all others, be faithful to her forever,' I'd appreciate it if you'd just leave that part out." He passed the clergyman the cash and walked away satisfied. It is now the day of the wedding, and the bride and groom have moved to that part of the ceremony where the vows are exchanged. When it comes time for my friend's vows, the vicar looks him in the eye and says: "Will you promise to love her always monetarily and physically, obey her every command and wish, serve her breakfast in bed every morning of your life and swear eternally before God and your lovely wife that you will not ever even look at another woman, as long as you both shall live?" My friend gulped and looked around, and said in a tiny voice, "Yes." My friend then leaned toward the priest and said under his breath, "I thought we had a deal." The priest put the $200 back into his hand and whispered back, "She made me a much better offer"."

The laughter didn't die down for at least a half a minute. After which Constantine said, "And that, Ladies and Gentlemen, is the way it is with some of our most loved ladies. I'm sure my friend is well on his way to a divorce right now – poor guy!" He paused to let the applause travel around the room. He then resumed, "Talking about sweet nothings murmured in the ear of our beloved partners, I met someone the other day who had a terrible problem. This elderly gent was invited to his old friends' home for dinner one evening. He was impressed by the way his buddy addressed his wife with endearing terms, calling her Honey, My Love, Darling, Sweetheart, Pumpkin, etc. The couple had been married almost 70 years – 70 years, imagine that? – and they appeared to be still very much in love. While the wife was off in the kitchen, the man leaned over and said to his buddy, "I think it's wonderful that, after all the years you've been married, you still call your wife those loving pet names." The old man hung his head. "I have to tell you the truth," he said, "I forgot her name about ten years ago." The laughter, whistling and applause didn't let Constantine say another word for a few more seconds. Then he finally said, "Once again you've been a fantastic audience. I'll see you soon. Thank you!"

Captain Hildebrandt was on hand when the WHO team was ready to disembark from *The Contessa* in Saint Louis. This was one of the first of a long line of vaccination expeditions to West Africa. The captain was clearly honored that "his" vessel had been chosen to carry out this mission. He was also all choked up when he saw the WHO team emerge onto the platform near the gangway.

"Doctor Ashford," he said, "Please accept my sincere thanks on behalf of all those who are waiting for you and your team. It's been my privilege to take you thus far in the journey. And I wish you the best of luck." With these words, he shook the doctor's hand.

The latter smiled and said, "thank you, Captain. We'll do our best. And thank you for letting Doctor Mayhew lend a hand in this mission. I'm glad to have him on our team."

Alan lowered his gaze and bowed his head. He generally didn't know how to take compliments very well.

As for Gregoire Albert; he was on hand. He looked at the five cases that were latched to the doctors and nurses' wrists with handcuffs. He obviously hadn't expected that. Given that Alan had not trusted the young man since the beginning of the cruise, he had charged Simon with a little mission in Nouakchott: to buy some form of handcuffs at the market. Only too pleased to be of assistance, the Potty Man had brought back a half-a-dozen of these cuffs (with their keys) to Alan. In turn, last night, Alan had told Drs. Hatfield and Ashford why he suggested taking this precautionary measure while he also accepted taking the trip inland aboard the fisherman's pirogues.

Mr. Albert looked dumfounded. He approached Alan and whispered in his ear: "Whose cuffs are these? Do they always wear them?"

Alan shrugged. "I don't know, Mr. Albert. I suspect they've been told to expect thieves to try taking the cases away from them and that was the best solution. Don't you agree?"

Gregoire gulped and nodded. "Yes, I suppose you're right. And Dr. Ashford told me that after the clinic in Saint Louis, you're taking pirogues to a village inland, did you know about this?"

"Yes, but I was only told last night. And it's a good idea, I thought. But I wouldn't worry about it, since you're going to be in charge of traveling by road with the SUVs with some of the WHO assistants and supplies, aren't you?"

"That's what I've been told, yes. But it seems these guys are doing everything at the last minute, aren't they?"

Alan chortled. "Yes, Mr. Albert, that's the way dangerous missions have to be run. No one will know what to expect next – especially the thieves."

Saint Louis is probably the last resort-type city still thriving on the West Coast of Africa. It has a colorful past and is located at the mouth of the Senegal River. Saint Louis is endowed with a very refreshing and positively agreeable climate. The houses in the better neighborhoods of the city are reminiscent of New Orleans in the States. The French flavor is everywhere. From the cars, the restaurants, the hotels, the markets, the shops and even the couturiers, Saint Louis seemed to have preserved a piece of France in its midst even after being divested of its function as capital of the Senegal Territory in 1960.

The clinic staff and doctors were all on hand when the WHO team arrived at the local clinic. The director had ordered that a room be emptied and reserved for the team to change into their protective garments, since they were going to tour the small hospital before proceeding with the inoculations. During the visit, Alan had to admit he had never experienced such desolation and such powerlessness. There were entire families dying together. They were praying and not even looking up as the doctors and nurses came in. They knew the end was near for all of them. On the other hand, he was pleased to being able to administer some thirty vaccines to the people most at risk; those who had been exposed to the disease in the past few days. The gratefulness in the faces of those children was worth all he could ever have wished in an entire lifetime. Alan knew they would have a chance at life now.

Traveling along the Senegal River is a treat. One could think they were somewhere in Florida with all the palm trees swaying between the old houses. The walkways along the piers would make for pleasant evening strolls. The pirogues are all painted with many colors, which added to their appeal. They also bear the name of their owners on the sides. So, there couldn't be any mistaking which pirogue belongs to who.

The kids in charge of pushing the vessels into the water and the older fishermen were waiting for the team. Mandaye was the name of one of the doctors' cousins. He was not an old man but his face was definitely marked by the burden of weather. When he saw Tiffany who had just arrived at the beach by taxi, his smile broadened.

"She you wife?" Mandaye asked Alan, after observing the doc take Tiffany's hand to lead her to the pirogue.

"Not yet," Alan answered enigmatically.

Mandaye erupted in laughter before ordering the boys to push the boats into the river, once everyone was aboard.

CHAPTER FOURTEEN

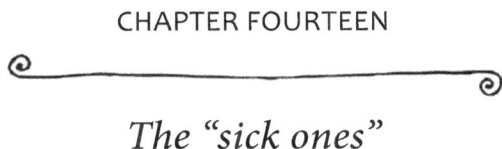

The "sick ones"

DEFEATED IN HIS INITIAL GOAL of stealing the vaccines' cases, Gregoire was wondering what he could do next to respond to his French accomplice's demands. The money was certainly too good to refuse. He couldn't simply turn down such an offer. He had to pay his gambling debts. Without the $50,000 in his back pocket, he wouldn't dare show his face in Monte Carlo again. Besides, the people in Senegal were going to be impatient to get the vaccines sooner rather than later, too.

While Gregoire, in one of the SUVs, was churning black thoughts and trying to find a solution to his problem, Drs. Ashford and Hatfield, Alan and Tiffany were sitting across the benches in the front pirogue, while two WHO nurses and other members of staff were aboard the second pirogue. The scenery was more peaceful than one somehow would expect in this part of the world. The recurring and all-enveloping silence returned to adorn the sights as they treaded the tranquil waters of the river. The old houses on the one side reminded one of the once opulent and thriving city, which was Saint Louis. Unfortunately the ramshackle huts, hovels and small corrugated iron shacks on the other side recalled you to the reality of the day. There was a disease that had a stranglehold on the city and was slowly but surely killing every one of its inhabitants. Alan was all too conscious of what Ebola can do and was currently doing to the men, women, and children of Africa. For Tiffany, it was the first time she had come face to face with such despair and misery. As they approached the village of Mokhana, Dr. Ashford was the first to break the silence.

"Ms. Sylvan, if you do not want to go through the village with us, you may stay here with Mandaye. But if you want to meet the people, I suggest you slip into one of our protective suits. Dr. Mayhew will show you what to do."

Tiffany nodded and turned to Alan. "Do you think it's okay for me to go with you?"

"Entirely up to you, Tiff. But this is no ordinary tourist visit of a village. People are liable to beg for your help. You just have to stay close to the team and if you wish to help, I'm sure the personnel or the nurses can use a hand."

"Okay then," Tiffany answered, slightly anxious, perhaps a little afraid as well. "I'll see the nurse in the next boat for the protective gear, shall I?"

"Yes, Ms. Sylvan," Tiffany and Alan heard from behind them. "I'm Annie. I've got just the thing you need," she added, handing a plastic bag to Tiffany as everyone disembarked from the pirogues.

"Nice meeting you, Annie. I'll be sure to stay close to all of you," Tiffany said, while pulling the protective garments out of the bag and slipping into them.

The children who had dragged the pirogues to shore were in awe of these men and women dressed in white and blue moonsuits. Everyone carried their cases or medical bags and the vaccine cases until they reached *la place* where the village chief had gathered his people. He was dressed in white garments and held a fly swatter in his left hand.

The villagers' chatter, from infants to old men and women, quieted down as soon as the WHO team emerged from behind the huts lining the river shore.

Doctor Hatfield thanked the chief for assembling his people in "la place" (the center of the village) and asked him to show him where the sick ones were.

The chief pointed to a hut at the end of the alley. "They are all very sick, Doctor," he said in French. "We give them water and rice to eat but we don't know what else to do for them."

Dr. Ashford nodded and asked Annie and Olga, who had just arrived in the SUV with Gregoire, to get the vaccines ready in the chief's hut while he and Alan would take some vaccines to the people at the end of the lane.

Two hours later, they had done all they could for the "sick ones" and vaccinated everyone who was probably more at risk of contracting the disease.

Tiffany was still silent when she returned to the pirogue with Alan. She had talked to some of the women in the village as they were inoculated and had held some of the little ones in her arms. Now she understood why Alan dedicated a lot of his free time to help the more disadvantaged communities around the world. The feeling was one of blessed privilege and grace. She felt gratitude that she was privileged to be young, healthy and able to give some of her time to those in need. Time is a gift that cannot be exchanged, replaced or denied.

Alan whole heartedly agreed with the sentiment. Taking her hand as they traveled back to Saint Louis aboard Mandaye's pirogue, he said, "I'm glad you came with me. I always feared you wouldn't understand. Especially when I want to sacrifice some of our time together in favor of going to some places like these and lend a hand to the ones who need me."

"To be sure, Alan, I'll never question you. You just have to say the word and I'll be right beside you. If I can help too, I will."

Meanwhile, Babette, Betty, Adele Muesli and Gregory Ashton were part of a tourist visit of Saint Louis with their guide, Abdulaye Salame. He was a young man who spoke English rather fluently and looked as if this was his first time taking a group of visitors through his city. Yet, once people began asking him questions about his life in such a beautiful and peaceful city, Abdulaye seemed to relax a little.

The dozen passengers toured the city, the shops on promenade along the pier and visited the mosque.

Babette was surprised to find the doors of the large edifice wide open. No one seemed to be around. There were immense carpets strewn about the marble floor and lanterns descending from the ceiling to illuminate the interior of this vast prayer hall. The passengers were asked to take their shoes off and leave them by the entrance. Babette could not believe, once again, how soft the woolen carpets were underfoot. Adele was in awe of the Arabic lettering carved in the stone adorning every wall around them. The four rows of colonnades, that were equally ornate, seemed to punctuate the respectful tranquility that enveloped the place, and which surprised the visitors somewhat.

"Where is everybody?" Gregory asked quietly.

"It's not prayer time yet," Abdulaye answered. "We have five prayer times every day. If you can come to the mosque, you come when the imam calls you from the minaret. But if you're at work or home; you pray where you are."

"And when are these prayer times?" Betty asked.

"At sunrise, mid-morning, early afternoon, late afternoon and at sunset."

"And everyone kneels down and faces east, is that right?" Gregory queried.

Abdulaye nodded. "It's best to face your God when you pray," he replied timidly.

When they exited the mosque, after walking inside it for a while, Babette still wondered why the doors were never closed. She asked Abdulaye why that was.

"All children of Allah, or your God, are welcome anytime day or night. No need to close the doors."

"What about thieves?" Babette asked. "There is literally a fortune in carpets and copper lamps in the edifice; aren't you afraid people will steal these things when they're hungry?"

Abdulaye bowed his head and smiled. "A thief would not come

close to stealing anything from the mosque, madam, he'd have his hand cut off as soon as he came out of the door."

"Oh, I read about that," Adele said, "about thieves having their hand cut off when they were caught, but I thought it was an old custom and no one would do such a thing these days."

"I know, mademoiselle, but I don't know anybody who would try stealing things from the place of Allah. He would be dead by morning, I'd say."

That was a sobering statement for everyone. There didn't seem to be any ifs, ands or buts about it. If you were caught with your hand in the till, so to speak, there would not be any technicalities or legal loopholes to save you from being sentenced most harshly and from having your hand amputated.

Babette thought of Matthew's words: "Wherefore if thy hand or thy foot offend thee, cut them off, and cast them from thee: it is better for thee to enter into life halt or maimed, rather than having two hands or two feet to be cast into everlasting fire."

Next, the group stopped by the artisans' market. It was the first time most of the visitors saw gold being melted in crucibles over an open fire. Babette was fascinated. The filigree process was another thing that was enticingly interesting. The jewelers were literally tatting gold threads in a lace pattern with imperturbable patience. "Simply amazing," Babette said as she came out of the jeweler's shop. But when everyone went next door to the gem keeper, Babette was even more surprised. There were gemstones of all kinds being cut, facetted and polished before being set into rings, necklaces and bracelets, all sitting before each of the artisans.

Here again, the security system appeared to be nil. All one saw was a couple of officers walking through the market and watching the jewelers at work with interest. Everybody seemed to be a friend with everybody else. It was a community rather than just a place to sell your crafts.

The one thing that Babette noticed was Mr. Atkinson's absence from the tour. One would have thought he would be most interested in the jewelers' work and in the setting of the gemstones. But no, he had not been seen for several days now, which worried Babette a little. She didn't want to say anything to anyone about it for the moment and decided to wait until they were back on the ship. *Maybe Edmund can have a quick look in his cabin,* she thought.

When the group left the jewelers, it was time to visit the leather shops. There again, the visitors were agape in front of the patience these artisans displayed when working the skins and pelts into items as small as wallets and coin purses or as large as vests, coats and jackets. Everything was soft to the touch and sewn by hand.

Many of the passengers could not resist buying a few things from the shops and all of them returned to *The Contessa* with at least one shopping bag – Babette included. A bracelet and a small leather bag had been her choices.

As soon as she entered her suite, she saw Edmund waiting for her. He smiled when he saw the small shopping bag.

"Ah-ha, milady has succumbed to the temptation, hasn't she?"

"Oh yes, Edmund, I have, and I am proud of myself for not buying anything more than I did. They have so many things a woman would love to buy. From jewelry, garments, leather jackets and shoes – quite incredible actually."

"Your description reminds me a little of the markets I visited in India or around the Far East. You don't know where to turn, really."

"Exactly. And that brings me to a thought I had while we were walking through the jewelers' market; I was wondering where Mr. Atkinson was. As a jeweler himself I thought he would have been most interested in visiting these markets."

"Maybe, he's seen many of these in his time and now he does not want to waste the time."

"And you don't believe that, do you?"

Edmund shook his head. "No, not really, milady. I would say, like you, that it's strange that we haven't seen anything of him for some time now."

"Perhaps you could have a quick look in his suite while I am taking a shower?"

"I can certainly do that, my dear. And if he's not in his suite, would you like me to locate him?"

"What do you think, Edmund?" Babette replied jocularly.

As Edmund left Babette's suite, he recited a couple of verses to himself:

"First god created earth, then He rested . . .

Then He created man, then He rested . . .

Then He created women and no one has rested since," and flew to the next deck, smiling to himself.

CHAPTER FIFTEEN

Depressing truths

AS ALAN OPENED HIS EMAILS the morning following the Saint Louis vaccination mission, he had to smile: his friend Mark had sent him what he called "Depressing Truths."

God grant me the senility to forget the people I never liked anyway, the good fortune to run into the ones that I do, and the eyesight to tell the difference. As I've grown older (but refused to grow up) I've discovered:

ONE - I started out with nothing, and I still have most of it.

TWO - My wild oats have turned into prunes and All Bran

THREE - I finally got my head together; now my body is falling apart.

FOUR - Funny, I don't remember being absent minded...

FIVE - All reports are in; life is now officially unfair.

SIX - If all is not lost, where is it?

SEVEN - It is easier to get older than it is to get wiser.

EIGHT - Some days you're the dog; some days you're the hydrant.

NINE - I wish the buck stopped here; I sure could use a few . . .

TEN - Kids in the back seat cause accidents.

ELEVEN - Accidents in the back seat cause kids.

TWELVE - It's hard to make a comeback when you haven't been anywhere.

THIRTEEN - The only time the world beats a path to your door is when you're in the bathroom.

FOURTEEN - If God wanted me to touch my toes, he would have put them on my knees.

FIFTEEN - When I'm finally holding all the cards, why does everyone decide to play chess?

SIXTEEN - It's not hard to meet expenses... they're everywhere.

SEVENTEEN - The only difference between a rut and a grave is the depth.

EIGHTEEN - These days, I spend a lot of time thinking about the hereafter ... I go somewhere to get something and then wonder what I'm here after.

Alan had to laugh. Truths they were, but depressing they were not. He closed the email folder just as Betty entered the medical center. She rushed into Alan's office, panting a little.

"It's Adele, Doctor Mayhew, my assistant; I think you should have a look at her."

Alan got up and rounded his desk. "Calm down, Mrs. Palmer," he said quietly. "Have a seat first and tell me what happened." He sat on the edge of his desk.

"I think she's sick -- maybe she's contracted the disease." Betty looked up at the doc pleadingly. "I don't know that she was vaccinated –" She shook her head in despair. "I don't know anything anymore, Doctor."

"And what makes you think that she may have Ebola? I am quite sure that everyone who registered for a visit of any of the ports along the coast has been vaccinated."

"Could you check, please, Doctor? Because her going ashore yesterday was a last minute thing."

Alan went to the door of his office and called Olga. She came in with her tablet. "Could you check if Ms. Adele Muesli had her Ebola vaccine, please?" he asked her.

Olga scrolled down the small screen and nodded. "Yes, Doctor, she was inoculated before we left Tenerife."

"Thanks, Olga," Alan replied. "Could you get me my medical bag and watch the fort for a while; I want to pay a visit to Ms. Muesli, okay?"

Olga nodded and walked out to fetch Alan's medical bag.

By the time she had it ready with fresh supplies and meds, Betty and Alan were waiting for her by the center's door.

When the two of them reached Adele Muesli's cabin, Gregory was waiting for them outside, by the door. "Thanks for coming, Doctor," he said, opening the cabin's door.

Alan turned to her. "Sorry, Betty, I think it's best if you stay outside until I determine what's wrong with Adele."

Betty nodded and watched Alan go inside the suite with Gregory.

Inside, Alan immediately noticed the aroma of marijuana. He shook his head. *The idiot; she may have overdosed on drugs...* He stepped into the bedroom and checked the unconscious woman's pulse. It was tachycardic. She was sweating profusely. He took her temperature. It was elevated, and so was her blood pressure. Next, he checked for any needle marks anywhere on her body. Smart users no longer shoot themselves in the arms, but often they can find a vein in the foot or ankle. He saw no obvious needle marks on her exposed body.

Much to his dismay, he had to wonder what was wrong with Adele. She must have smoked a joint or two with Gregory, but did she smoke enough to pass out? In any case, he wanted to transport her to the center to run some tests on her.

"How's she?" Gregory asked when Alan took off the stethoscope and exited the cabin with him.

"Just answer me one question, Mr. Ashton: did you smoke a joint with Adele before she passed out?"

Betty's facial expression passed from one of worry to one of outrage in a fraction of a second. "How could you? You idiot!" she yelled at Gregory.

"I am sorry, Mrs. Palmer," Alan interposed, "but I will have to take Adele to the medical center for further examination." He turned to look at Gregory. "As for you, Mr. Ashton, one; I need to know exactly any other drugs you might be using in addition to marijuana. Two; I think you would do well to get rid of any and all types of drugs you may have in your cabin. If security finds anything, you'll end up in the brig or disembarked – is that clear? There is a strict no drug policy on all ships."

"And if you think that you'll stay in my employ when you're a druggie, you're sadly mistaken, young man," Betty uttered, practically spitting the words in Gregory's face.

"Mrs. Palmer, I'm sorry; I know how it looks," Gregory blurted, "but Adele was already feeling bad before I shared a joint with her…"

Alan frowned. "I'm sorry, Mr. Ashton, did you say Ms. Muesli was feeling unwell *before* she smoked a joint or had a drink with you?"

Gregory nodded. "We just had a couple of shots of vodka like normal and she felt dizzy and she said she wanted to throw up. So, I thought maybe a puff or two would settle her stomach down." He threw a pleading glance in Betty's direction. "I only wanted to help. And when she fell asleep and I couldn't wake her up, that's when I called you, Mrs. Palmer. I'm sorry, believe me."

"Okay," Betty said, somewhat appeased, "but, as Doctor Mayhew said, just throw away any of the stuff"—she waved a dismissive hand in front of her—"or whatever you call it, in the toilet and spray the room before anyone else finds out that you've been smoking and report you to the captain. Okay?"

"Yes, ma'am. I'll do that as soon as Dr. Mayhew has taken Adele out of here."

Alan then called Olga to have one of the stewards come up to the suite with a gurney. He also told his nurse that he wanted Adele isolated until they had determined what was wrong with her and to get the lab equipment and an IV ready.

On her way back to her cabin, Betty stopped by Babette's suite. She wanted to have a chat with the playwright regarding what just happened. Then, on second thought, she decided not to say anything to anyone. *One never knows who's listening,* she told herself as she returned to her cabin. As she turned the corner along the corridor leading to her suite, she bumped into a handsome, middle-aged fellow. He was accompanied by a very pretty woman.

"Oh gosh, my dear woman," Leon Summerville said, "I am so very sorry about this..."

"As usual, you're not looking where you're going, dear," Linda added, turning to Betty. "So sorry, ma'am, but my husband here does not know what he's doing sometimes."

All the while Betty didn't listen to the apologies; she stared at the man before her. *I must be dreaming,* she thought before saying, "I'm the one who's sorry, sir, I wasn't looking where I was going. I'm Betty Palmer," she added, extending a hand for Leon to shake.

He did with a broad smile adorning his tanned face. "I'm Leon Summerville, and this is my wife Linda."

"Very nice meeting you, Mrs. Palmer," Linda rejoined. "Could we treat you to some refreshment upstairs... to make up for our bumping into you?"

"Perhaps later," Betty answered, "my assistant is a little under the weather, and I think she left me with a few things to do before this evening's dinner." For some reason, Betty wanted to distance herself from the man. There was something strange about him. Almost eerie.

"Maybe we can meet up later?" Leon ventured.

Walking away, Betty said, "Yes, yes, of course. We'll meet later."

When she entered her suite and closed the door, Betty leaned her back against it. Leon Summerville's face wasn't leaving her mind. It was as if it had been imprinted in her memory. Once her respiration returned to normal, she went to the desk and picked up the framed photograph of her sister and her son. She stared down at the little boy. *Could it be that Leon Archer is in fact Leon Summerville? No, that would be too extraordinary. Way too much of a coincidence.*

In the meantime, Edmund had been searching for Isaac Atkinson throughout the ship with no result. The man's suite was bare. It almost felt as if no one was occupying it, although there were several bathroom articles still standing on the vanity near the sink. There were clothes in the closet and a robe thrown over a chair in the bedroom. Edmund gathered that the man had perhaps been visiting Saint Louis and wasn't back yet. So, he decided to wait for the gentleman to return to his cabin. When ten chimed on the clock on the night table, Edmund began to worry and made his way to Babette's suite. He hated to report that he couldn't find the gentleman. Edmund was by no means an alarmist, but this very much resembled an unwarranted disappearance on the part of the jeweler.

When Edmund came down to sit in front of his dearest friend, she was reading the latest "On Board Bulletin" sipping on a small cognac. She lifted her gaze to him and asked, "So, where is the dear man? Snug as a bug in a rug, I suppose?"

"I am afraid not, milady." Babette stared. "I cannot locate him."

Babette's brow furrowed. "Have you searched the theater and all the empty rooms or cabins?"

"Yes, Babette, I have. And it's only when I heard the ten o'clock bell that I decided to come back and tell you."

"Where could he have gone, do you think?" Babette asked as if posing the question to herself.

"The only reason I could think of for his disappearance is somewhat alarming, I'm afraid."

"You mean he could have been kidnapped by someone who had heard about the diamond and wanted to hold him for ransom. Is that what you're thinking?"

Edmund nodded. "You see, Babette, the man did not hide the fact that he travels with something that would attract any respectable thief instantly."

"I just don't think it's the answer in this case, Edmund. I would rather think the fellow will re-appear in the middle of the night after remembering that we're leaving at dawn."

"I hope you're right, dear lady. I would hate for anything to happen to the old gentleman. I think his mind has been disturbed and even invaded by evil thoughts for far too long. The poor man does not deserve to be bothered by superstitious ideas."

"I agree. What's more, I still can't understand why he would want to return the diamond to its place of origin, thinking that the curse will be lifted if he does so."

"Oh but, milady, greed itself is a curse. Evil uses it every day in every way possible. So, if Mr. Atkinson has decided to return the diamond to its country, perhaps he will be free of greed then."

CHAPTER SIXTEEN

It's my job, if not prison . . .

IN THE MEDICAL CENTER, a quick look at Adele's pre-boarding medical form showed that she had no major medical conditions, that she was taking a non-steroidal anti-inflammatory and an anti-malarial medication.

Alan started testing her electrolytes, blood sugar, and ran a CBC while Olga started an IV and attached the leads for an EKG. Although the differential diagnosis for a suddenly unconscious patient is many, Alan had to remember that they were in Africa. Many of the tropical diseases like Malaria can cause coma. The nausea Gregory mentioned could be from the alcohol, something she ate, hypoglycemic coma, some other drug laced into her marijuana, or even Dengue or Chikungunya fevers if she had been bitten by an infected mosquito.

She was still in a coma and sweating profusely. The finger stick blood sugar was extremely low, confirmed with the lab testing so Alan said, "Olga, please reconstitute one milligram of glucagon and give it in her IV and change her IV to D5W. Looks like this lady is in hypoglycemic shock. Just to be sure, let's get the results of the other lab tests. In particular let's do an HbgA1C, titers for Dengue and Chikungunya fevers, a thick blood smear for malaria, and an alcohol and drug screen. I know the rapid test was only positive for marijuana, but let's do the more complete test too."

Olga asked, "Should we continue to keep her under isolation, now that we are pretty sure that her coma was induced by the hypoglycemia?"

"Yes, until we are sure of some of the other tests," said Alan, as Adele started regaining consciousness.

"Hello, Adele, how are you feeling?" Adele looked up from her pillow, visibly dazed. "You are in the medical center. You passed out in your cabin."

"Did I?" Adele sounded hesitant. "What's happening to me?"

"You just passed out. Has that ever happened to you before?" Alan asked.

"Not that I remember, no." Adele raised herself on her elbows.

"I think it would be better if you lay down for a while longer..."

"I just felt dazed and then the room disappeared..."

"Tell me; do you know if there's a history of diabetes or hypoglycemia in your family?"

Adele shook her head. "No, nothing like that. And what's that hypoglycemia anyway?"

"You suffer from low blood sugar. Some doctors call it diabetes' first cousin."

Adele looked nonplussed. "Do you mean I could be a diabetic someday?"

"There's nothing for sure in that regard, but it's something you need to be aware of, Ms. Muesli. For now, we'll run several more tests and raise your blood sugar count."

"Does that mean I'll have to eat sugar?"

Alan laughed. "Not really, Ms. Muesli, but you should not avoid it either. Besides, protein and glucose go hand-in-hand when it comes to treating hypoglycemia."

"And how long do I have to stay here, do you think?" She sounded frustrated now.

"Maybe a couple of days will see you right as rain."

Adele nodded again and switched her gaze to Olga. "Will I be allowed visitors?" she asked with a broad smile on her lips.

Olga returned the smile. "By all means, Ms. Muesli, once we've run the rest of the tests, and as long as we've got enough chairs for every one of your admirers, I'm sure it will be fine."

Alan let the two girls giggle happily and returned to his office to write his reports.

Meanwhile, and after talking for a while longer, Edmund left Babette to go to bed. He, for his part, returned to wait for Isaac in his suite.

Babette had been right. Isaac had spent two days with some friends in Saint Louis and, now, at three a.m., was rushing up the gangway to return to his suite where Edmund saw him instantly. He observed him for a while and once the man was *snug as a bug* (as Babette described it) in his bed, Edmund left Isaac's cabin. He was on his way to Babette's suite when he saw something that aroused his curiosity. Two crewmen, who were assisting some of the men on the pier before raising the gangway, rushed up to the platform with metal cases that looked exactly like those that the WHO team used to transport the vaccines. Before *The Contessa* could leave the port of Saint Louis, there were a lot of matters to attend to. The supplies had to be loaded, the ballast water had to be checked, the pumps and other apparatuses had to be checked, and so on and so forth. This all meant that there was a hype of activity mostly on the lower decks and port side of the vessel. However, it was rather easy for Edmund to keep an eye on the two men who had brought the cases aboard. He followed one of them going down to his cabin, and saw that he left the cases under his bunk before returning to his assigned duties. Edmund used his kinetic powers to move the cases from under the bunk and slide them near the door. He then flew to Alan's cabin. He had seen him go in with Tiffany earlier that night when he was still searching for Isaac. He hated to wake him, but this was too important a matter to let his great-grandson sleep away the night.

When Alan heard it at first; he groaned. But when the train whistle blew for the third time, he sat up and swore under his breath. Tiffany turned around and opened her haggard eyes, looking at Edmund floating over their bed. "Good Lord, Granddad, what on earth are you doing here at this hour?" she blurted, her gaze not leaving the hovering ghostly figure.

"Nothing that should concern you, my child. It's my great-grandson that I want out of bed."

"I gathered that!" Alan grumbled, still obviously annoyed. "What is it that you want?"

"I want you to get dressed and get down to the crew's cabins. Two of the crew have brought vaccine cases aboard this ship."

"What are you talking about?" Alan demanded, getting out of bed now. "Those might be cases they bought for their own..."

"Tsk, tsk, son. Let's get on with it. The sooner we get this straightened out, the sooner you can get back to bed, alright?"

"Okay, Granddad, but I hope we're not going on a wild goose chase."

"You know, son, even wild geese are worth chasing – they're very beautiful to watch flying in formation."

"Good God," Alan said, following his great-grandfather out of the cabin.

When they reached the two crewmen's cabin, Alan knocked before he used a master keycard to open the door. As soon as he set eyes on the cases, he knew his great-grandfather had been right. These definitely looked like the WHO cases. He crouched down to open them. When he did, once again he could not come to any other conclusion. Those two cases were meant to be substituted for the WHO cases; and the vaccines stolen.

Alan then asked Edmund where the cases had been when the men brought them down to the cabin. When his great-grandfather told him, Alan replaced the cases under the bunk bed and walked out of the cabin under his great-grandparent's displeased gaze.

"Don't say anything, Granddad," Alan told him. "I know what you're thinking. But I would prefer catching these two red-handed rather than pointing an accusatory finger when I could never prove that they brought the cases aboard if I have them in my possession."

"Alright, I see your point, son. But how do you intend to catch them red-handed, as you said?"

"I think you can help in that regard, Granddad, but let's get back to my cabin before I attract attention. Babbling to myself or to an invisible entity in the corridor of the ship in the middle of the night is not something I would want to be caught doing."

Edmund nodded and Alan made his way back to his cabin in silence. He had to think how he was going to entrap these two men, but most importantly, how was he going to catch the organizer of the proposed vaccine heist?

In the morning everyone seemed to be out of bed rather early. The heat was becoming intense. The heavy humidity and unrelenting sunshine seemed to weigh on every bone and muscle of one's body. The cabins and suites were air-conditioned, of course, but most passengers preferred to be outside before the heat became literally unbearable. The scenery was again of only two-tone blues with a dash of white as the wavelets lapped the sides of the ship. The sky and ocean seemed to meet happily on the horizon undisturbed by any cloud.

As for Alan, he had not been able to go back to sleep when he returned to his cabin. Tiffany was asleep when he slipped underneath the blanket and since he didn't want to wake her, he lay there until he couldn't take it anymore. He had to get up, take a shower and get some breakfast before getting to the medical center. The second nurse had arrived the night before. She was a top-notch lady with a background in the military. Alan had known her for years. Alice Muller was just the woman he needed to mind his medical center right now.

As soon as he was ready, he kissed Tiffany on the forehead while murmuring sweet words in her ear. She turned, yawned and opened her eyes just in time to see Alan close the door behind him.

When he reached the café, every table was occupied already. He looked around for Alice. And yes, there she was, sipping on her coffee. When she lifted her gaze to him, a broad smile adorned her lips.

"My God, Doc, why are you up so early? Don't tell me we've got an emergency already. Do we?"

"Good morning to you, too, Alice. How are you?"

"Just fine, Doctor, thanks. And top of the morning to you. But why so early to rise?"

"A problem, Alice. Not an emergency, but a problem. We've got a rogue chief of security and I would bet my bottom dollar, he's planning a heist of the Ebola vaccines in the near future."

"You don't say! Who's the guy? That chief of security, I mean. Anyone we know?"

"Not really. I've never worked with him. And like many of the crew on this particular cruise, he's French. Mind you, I don't have anything against the French personally, seeing that I am French descent myself, but this guy is a little too irritating for my liking. He's got something up his sleeve; I'm sure of it."

"Okay, I'll have a chat with him as the new nurse and see what "he does not say". That usually helps define what he would love to say but can't."

"You sound like you've interrogated people before. Have you?"

"Not really, Doc. But, you know, being an army nurse you see and hear all kinds of things. And best of all, you learn to take note of what people can't hide."

Alan nodded vigorously before getting to his feet. "Do you want a refill or something else to eat?" he offered.

"Not now, thanks, Doc, I'm fine."

"Okay, I'll be back in two ticks then."

Once they had finished breakfast, it was high time to relieve Olga and for Alice to start her shift. When Alan and Alice arrived at the center, they found Olga playing cards with Adele Muesli. Alan had to smile. Adele looked definitely better. Her cheeks had regained their rose hue while her eyes were bright and clear.

Alan made the introduction and told Olga to gather her winnings – three candy bars – and be prepared for a long, well-deserved rest. He didn't want to see her back until ten o'clock that night. Alice and Olga then had a short chat about the routine the doc had adopted on this cruise, particularly in regard to the vaccines, and the crew's check-ups and physicals.

As soon as Olga left, Alice and Alan sat down to discuss the discovery of the two cases in the crew's quarters.

"How did you know they had come aboard with the cases?" Alice asked.

"I was observing some of the loading of supplies," Alan lied, "when I noticed the two guys being handed metal cases from someone on shore. I could not really see who the person was, but I distinctly saw the two men returning aboard with the cases just as the gangway was about to be lifted."

"And you followed them to their cabins?"

"Only one of them – the one who took both cases down to his cabin and slipped it under his bunk."

"Do you think maybe the guy and his friend are trying to steal the vaccine to help some family members ashore?"

"I don't know, Alice. But my instincts tell me that Gregoire is mixed up in this somehow. I am quite sure he is trying to steal the vaccines. The fact that I sent Simon, in Nouakchott, to buy some handcuffs to tie the cases to their carriers, really threw a wrench in the works for him. I am sure he's answering to some higher authority in France. I've surprised him on a couple of occasions talking to a French party, using a satellite phone. I do understand some French, after all."

"What about the vaccines in here? Are they all real or are some of them bogus vials?"

"They're all real, unfortunately. We've got two fridges. One belongs to our company, the other to the WHO team. These vaccine vials are all digitally recorded on the pharmaceutical tablets. Every morning, you'll need to scan the vials and verify the count..."

"What if we put some bogus vials among our own? So that if anyone tries taking them, all they'll get are vials filled with water."

"I thought of that too, Alice. And the WHO nurses fill some vials with water, which they put in the dummy cases when we go ashore. But doing it with our own vaccines, I don't think I want to take the risk. If one of these vials disappears for any reason, it's my job on the line – if not imprisonment for felony-theft."

"Okay, Doc, why don't we leave it for a bit? I need to think about this while I get used to this new routine. Let's talk about it later, okay?"

"Sure. I'll do the same while I write the reports and get the supplies counted with you."

The day had been a busy one for all crew, especially since most passengers had stayed indoors due to the unrelenting heat pounding the ship hour after hour. That night everybody was ready to stay outdoors and enjoy an outside cabaret that Tiffany had organized for the "over-heated" passengers.

When Constantine grabbed the microphone from one of the men in the band, people took no time to return to their seats. They were ready to have a laugh.

Constantine was his jovial self again. He started by looking around the audience and soon spotted Drs. Hatfield and Ashford eating some of the roasted vegetables the chef had served with crab on the grill.

He began by saying: "Ladies and Gentlemen, good evening. Thank you for your patience and tolerance. I know sometimes I can be long winded. I mean when I tell stories, not the way our good doctors speak of our 'winds'…" That remark ignited laughter. "Did you know," Constantine went on, "that we've got no less than twelve qualified medical practitioners aboard *The Contessa?* Oh yes, our lady of the seas is well endowed with medical assistance. You and I can be sick anytime – just say: "Is there a doctor in the house? And twelve of them will come running. Can you imagine that? Having twelve opinions about the "winds" you've just passed?" There was no stopping the laughter now. Constantine had everyone's attention.

"Anyway, I have to tell you about Brian. He's a friend of mine. He's always in need of a doctor, the poor guy. So, due to a job transfer, Brian moved from his hometown to New York City. Being that he had a very comprehensive health history, he brought along all of his medical paperwork, when it came time for his first check up with his new doctor. After browsing through the extensive medical history, the doctor stared at Brian for a few moments and said, "Well there's one thing I can say for certain, you sure look better in person than you do on paper!"

Dr. Ashford said to Hatfield, "I had a Brian in my clinic…" as he chuckled at Constantine's story.

Constantine continued, "Anyway, Brian, as you have gathered by now, Ladies and Gentlemen, is one of the world's greatest hypochondriacs. One day at the supermarket, he bumped into his doctor. "Doc!" Brian exclaimed, "I've been meaning to tell you, remember those voices I kept on hearing in my head? I haven't heard them in over a week!" "Wow! What wonderful news, Brian! I'm so happy for you!" his doctor said, truly happy for my friend.

"Wonderful?" asked a dismal-looking Brian. "There's nothing wonderful about it. I'm afraid my hearing is starting to go now!"

The laughter didn't die down for a couple of minutes, until Constantine resumed, saying, "And you know, doctors hate to be wrong. Yes. You can't tell your doctor he's wrong, otherwise you might have to cope with some terrible side effects from his latest prescription…" the laughter interrupted him again. "I knew this old man; he went to the doctor complaining of a terrible pain in his leg. "I am afraid it's just old age", replied the doctor, "there is nothing we can do about it." "That can't be," fumed the old man, "you don't know what you're talking about." "How can you possibly know I am wrong?" countered the doctor. "Well it's quite obvious," the old man replied, "my other leg is fine, and it's the exact same age!"

"Enjoy the fantastic barbecue, Ladies and Gentlemen. You've been great," Constantine concluded as he slipped through the side entrance of the café under a roar of applause and laughter.

CHAPTER SEVENTEEN

Gorée Island

THE JOURNEY DOWN TO Gorée Island was not a long one by any means. *The Contessa* dropped anchor near the small island and the tenders were ready by midday. Gorée Island is a piece of paradise with a troubled past. The modern, colorful beach homes neighbor the 'slaves' house', as if taunting history to retreat behind the veil of horrors Gore represents. The 'slaves' house' is a construction sealed on practically all sides, designed to conceal and detain the prisoners for any length of time. The opening onto the ocean is a mere square carved out of the outer wall through which slaves were thrown onto the boats destined for the New World. Napoleon is largely to blame for the continued slave trade that existed between the French colony and the plantation owners of Louisiana. Napoleon's wife, Josephine, maintained some friendships with people in the New World, particularly those located in the South. She encouraged Napoleon to restore slavery in 1802 after France had abolished the trade in 1794 during the French Revolution. Then, in 1815 Napoleon definitively abolished slave trade during the "Hundred Days" of his political comeback.

Gorée Island was the last stop before the slaves would embark on the ships to cross the Atlantic. Gorée Island is a beautiful and horrible place all in one. The passengers could sense the ambivalence and ambiguity between the gorgeous setting and the evil reminders of days gone by as soon as they disembarked onto the pier.

Babette was taken aback by the contrasting effect the island seemed to have on everyone. The solitary beach on the west side of the island was bordered by beautiful houses, small villas and a couple of open bar-terraces. She walked with Betty toward the bar-terrace rather quickly. The sand, even with their sandals, was blazing hot. They sat down and ordered a tall orangeade from the waiter. He was as black as a black man can be. Babette noted that the white of his eyes and that of his teeth was probably the only thing that would be noticed in the darkness of night. He was very cordial and it seemed as if he was strangely unconcerned when Babette asked him, if there had been many people sick on the island. He chuckled a little, and replied, "The devil had enough to do with us in the past; he can't be bothered anymore."

Babette didn't know what to say. Betty looked up at him before she said, "Do you mean Ebola has not affected anyone over here?"

"No, ma'am, it has not. You see, as soon as the mayor heard of the disease spreading over Dakar, he stopped the ferries from coming in. We get our supplies from the international volunteer doctors who live with us on the island."

"How extraordinary!" Betty said, truly amazed at the mayor's presence of mind. "And that's the reason we were allowed to come ashore unhindered, isn't it?" She looked at Babette.

"I suppose so," she replied.

Seeing Babette's hesitation, the waiter said, "The name is Moise, ma'am. If you wish to have something to eat later, I'll bring the menu."

"Yes, thanks, Moise," Babette was quick to answer. "But we're fine for now. Thank you."

As Moise walked away from the table, Babette said, "Don't turn around now, Betty, but here come the Summervilles…"

"Oh God, no. Don't tell me they're coming to this terrace."

Babette smiled in reply and looked up at Linda and Leon Summerville as they approached the bistro's terrace hastily.

"Mrs. Palmer, how are you?" Leon exclaimed genially when he

and his wife reached Babette and Betty's table.

"Just fine, Mr. Summerville, and you?"

"Oh, we're just peachy, my dear," Leon said, looking around him briefly. "Don't you find it a bit hot around here?"

Since he ignored Babette totally, she returned the favor and watched the children running over the hot sand and plunging into the waves.

Linda noticed Babette's obvious disinterest and turned to her. "I'm sorry, I am Mrs. Linda Summerville. Haven't we met earlier on the cruise?"

"I don't recall," Babette said indifferently, "but I'm Ms. Babette. Pleased to meet you. Is this your first time on the island?"

Betty was surprised. She didn't expect Babette to be so abrupt with her query.   Betty had related her encounter with the Summervilles the day before to Babette. She had also mentioned Leon's uncanny resemblance with her nephew; she wanted to find out a lot more about the man and his wife – but not right away. For some reason, it seemed as if Betty was afraid to find out the truth.

"Not for me, it isn't," Leon replied. "I was here on holidays a few years back. But it's Linda's first visit, yes."

"Leon told me so much about Africa," Linda said, "and all the places he visited before we met, I was very excited when he booked this cruise for us."

"And what other places have you visited? Were they on the west coast?"

"No, not all of them, but since we're plantation owners from way back when, there's history for us around here."

"You mean your family owned slaves from this island...?"

"I don't rightly know," Leon said hesitantly, "but I suppose at one point there were slaves held on our properties, yes."

Betty was agape by now. She could not reconcile the idea of being the aunt of this man. He seemed totally unashamed of his ancestors' malevolence. On the other hand, if he indeed was her nephew, he wouldn't have known anything about his ancestors' misdeeds. Being an orphan, he could not offer an apology or any form of regret for something in which he didn't participate.

The four of them continued talking about this and that after the Summervilles sat themselves down at the ladies' table. When it was time to take a tour of the island and enjoy the shady streets leading to the Gorée Castle, Babette was glad to get away from the Summervilles. She felt uncomfortable in their company. As sensitive about people as Babette was, she felt as if Leon Summerville was not at all what he purported to be – far from it.

Yet, Babette wanted to help Betty, and to do so; she wanted to find out a lot more about the man and his wife.

As beautiful and enticing as the island was; the group of passengers that had taken the tour were now ready to return to the ship. Babette wanted to have a discreet chat with Adele Muesli. She had learned from Edmund that Adele and Gregory had possibly located the monastery where Leon Archer had been brought up. She wondered if it would be possible for her (Babette) to talk to the monk who had unearthed the information in the first place.

When she phoned Adele and Gregory's cabin to find out when they could meet for coffee, Gregory told Babette about Adele's condition and being confined to the medical center until they reached Dakar. Babette said that she wouldn't want to disturb Adele while she was getting over her illness and would catch up with both of them later.

In the meantime, there was someone whose presence had been literally ignored by everyone. Gaston Giroux, the Summerville's secretary. He had followed his employers during many of their excursions and shopping sprees in Tenerife and Saint-Louis. He had also remained in contact with someone else on the ship: Gregoire Albert, the chief of security. He was of particular interest to Gaston. The latter had a lot more experience with certain types than one surmised when meeting him. He had dealt with quite a few supply thieves during his tour of duty in Afghanistan. Their only purpose or goal was to amass enough money to enable them to disappear for a long time – or until their ill-gotten gains had been consumed. As far as Gaston was concerned, this guy Gregoire, was one of *them*, a "piece of shit" that he would dispose of at the first opportunity, if he were still in the Middle East. But this situation was quite different and far removed from the troubled fields of battle in Afghanistan. They were aboard one of the most luxurious vessels roaming the seven seas, and they were skirting the West Coast of Africa on what could only be described as a rescue mission. Gregoire Albert was obviously intending to steal the vaccines – Gaston was sure of it. The only way to do it, now that the cases were carried ashore by people who had their wrists fastened to the case handles, was to steal the cases or even the vials from the point of origin, which, in this instance, was the medical center. Gaston had no choice; he had to alert Dr. Mayhew of what he had observed thus far and what he thought would be Gregoire's next step.

Since Linda and Leon had not returned from Gorée yet, Gaston took the opportunity to have a chat with the doc. As soon as he entered the medical center, he was met by Alice's cordial welcome. Gaston told her that he wasn't sick but needed to talk to Doctor Mayhew rather urgently. Alice sensed this was important, but she sensed something else.

"Where were you stationed, Mr. Giroux?" she asked him.

"Third battalion, near Kandahar, ma'am," Gaston replied without batting an eyelid. He had recognized a fellow soldier in Alice.

"Well, Mr. Giroux, let's see if our commanding officer can see you now."

Gaston's face snapped into a broad grin as a reply.

As soon as he went into Alan's office, the doc got up and shook Gaston's extended hand. The doc was slightly surprised with Gaston's unexpected visit, but would soon find out the reason for it.

"And to what do I owe this surprise visit, Mr. Giroux?" Alan asked as he sat down again.

"Please, Doctor, call me Gaston. Maybe this is a "fool's errand" (me being the fool) but I have to relate something to you that might help the WHO people in their mission and, in turn, might help you as well."

"Now you intrigue me, Gaston. What is this all about?"

"It's about the vaccines, Doctor. They are going to be stolen. I'm sure you are aware that a lot of people, including honest people, on the West Coast of the continent would pay a king's ransom for them."

Alan nodded. "Yes, I am well aware of the temptation these vaccines represent. But can you perhaps get to the point?"

"Well, hum, yes. You see, I've spent many months in Afghanistan and I have had the opportunity to observe thieves in action, and even nabbed a couple before they could deprive entire villages of their much needed supplies."

"And you believe we have a thief aboard *The Contessa*..."

"I don't 'believe' it, Doctor, I am absolutely certain, Gregoire Albert is getting ready to steal some vaccines from your medical center."

Silence fell between the two men.

"May I ask how you know this?" Alan asked, having brought his forearm to the top of the desk. "Are you acquainted with Gregoire?"

"As a matter of fact I am, Doctor. When I came aboard with my employers, Mr. and Mrs. Summerville, I wondered about applying to work in the security department of a vessel such as this one. From the outset, I was surprised by the lack of organization and effective security in Mr. Albert's department."

"And from there you deduced that the man was probably after something else than keeping his job on the ship?" Alan was sure the young Gaston was on the right track, but he wanted to get the whole story before divulging what he himself had deduced thus far, regarding a possible theft.

Gaston cracked a smile. "No, Doctor. As I said I met a few of these eels in the Middle East, and I wanted to befriend him before I took another step in any direction." Gaston paused. "As soon as we left Tenerife, I began asking Gregoire a lot of questions about the vaccination mission, feigning interest as a possible candidate for a security job with the cruise line company."

"And did Mr. Albert answer all of your questions?"

"No, not all of them, but he certainly alluded to the fact that he himself was looking at leaving the company for a more lucrative job in France. Being of French descent myself, I had no problem getting interesting answers to my questions. For example, when the cases didn't leave this center without being handcuffed to their carriers, Mr. Albert was dreadfully concerned. Under normal circumstances, he should have been the one suggesting that the cases be transported in that manner." He coughed to clear his throat. Alan remained silent. "In any event, when you came back from Saint-Louis, he was truly annoyed. He told me to mind my own business, which didn't bother me, since I knew he was most probably in trouble with his masters in France. You had relegated him to driving an SUV with dummy vaccine to the village along the Senegal River and Gregoire was really offended. But then he came round to my cabin this morning and asked me if I would do him a favor. He wanted to know if I could have a look at the security system installed on the fridges." Alan nodded and smiled. "An honest man should have come and asked you himself. He is the Chief of Security after all, isn't he?"

"Exactly, Gaston. And I am very glad you came to tell me all this. It will make my job a lot easier. In fact, I am going to do something very irregular, if you don't mind…"

"No, not at all, Doctor; the more irregular it is, the more I like it," Gaston replied, cracking a laugh.

"Good. Let me discuss my plan with my nurse first and I'll get back to you before we sail for Dakar tonight. But, in the meantime, should you change your mind, let me know, okay?"

"Will do, Doctor. And thank you for hearing me out."

As Gaston was leaving the center, Alan leaned back in his chair and played with his pencil pensively. He smiled.

An hour later, Alan went to fetch Gregoire out of his office to bring him up to the medical center. He sat him down and said, "It's about time I get some real help from you, Mr. Albert. You see, tomorrow we'll be going to the hospital in Dakar. This is going to be the largest drop of vaccines we will do during the cruise. So, before we do, I thought I would show you where the vaccines are kept. That way, you could come up in the morning and help me and the WHO team fill the cases."

Gregoire smiled from ear to ear. Finally, he was going to get closer to these blasted vaccines.

When Gregoire left the medical center, Alan phoned Gaston, saying: "We're all set, Mr. Giroux. Alice and I will meet you later this evening."

The evening, once again was better spent outdoors. The day had been a scorcher. The trip to Dakar had just taken under an hour. As soon as *The Contessa* found her berth, the passengers began taking pictures of Dakar's skyline before going to dinner on the upper deck where the evening air was quite pleasant. Mack and Joe had found their stools at the bar. They had spent the better part of the day – after coming back from the Gorée Island tour with their wives – in their cabins, relaxing and watching a few movies while their wives were at the spa.

As they were watching the cello player setting her instrument down and the other strings getting themselves ready for the short recital, Mack turned to Joe and said, "You know my wife plays the violin…"

"Does she now?"

"Oh yeah she does. She was supposed to play for my niece's wedding just before we left to come on this cruise."

"That's nice," Joe said, taking another sip of his scotch.

"Yeah, except that my mother-in-law was there too…"

"Oh! What did she do?"

"Well thank God she didn't do anything much, but it's what she said that really stuck in my mind."

Joe was getting a little impatient. "Okay, let's have it: what happened."

"Well, as my wife was about to start, one of the strings snapped on her violin. My mother-in-law didn't wait for it to be repaired. She got up, took the microphone and said something like: "I'm sorry, but Jill cannot play the violin as in the program, her G-string has just snapped!"

People behind the two friends wondered what their laughter was about but just smiled and prepared themselves to listen to the string quartet playing a piece in *G-minor!*

CHAPTER EIGHTEEN

Caught red-handed

AS THE EVENING DREW TO A CLOSE, Alan and Alice prepared themselves for what promised to be an interesting night. He had told Gregoire Albert that since it would be a long day tomorrow, he was closing the medical center early that evening. Alan had sent Olga back to her cabin to have a good night's rest. He told her he would be busy filling out the reports since he would probably have to spend the whole of the next day at the hospital in Dakar. As for Alice, after helping Adele Muesli back to her cabin and grabbing a couple of hours' rest, she came back to the medical center around eleven o'clock that night. A few minutes later, Gaston Giroux came in. He and Alice had devised a plan by which they would grab the thief, whoever he was, 'red-handed'. Alice would leave the medical center's fridge unlocked while doing something else in the storeroom. They didn't have to wait too long. The chief of security used his master keycard to come in. In the dim light, using only a small flashlight, he made a beeline for the fridge. He smiled when he found it unlocked. He opened it. He placed six vials into the slots of each of the cases he had brought with him. These were the cases that Edmund observed being brought aboard by the two crewmen. Alan switched the lights on as soon as the cases were filled while Alice and Gaston jumped the surprised Gregoire. He offered very little resistance since Alice and Gaston knew exactly how to subdue a man in less than a few seconds. Alan emptied the cases, replaced the vaccine vials in the fridge and locked it. He was seething with rage by this time. He had always hoped to be wrong about Gregoire. He was still a young man and now he would spend the better part of his life behind bars.

Alan shook his head before he called the staff captain. The latter was well liked among the crew. He had just embarked in Saint-Louis to replace Gregoire's "Good Friend." The "Good Friend" in question had made one-too-many mistakes and the Captain had seen to it that the man was ousted at the next port. When Alan confirmed the capture of the thief, Robert Ekelton, the new staff cap, told him that he would take charge of the prisoner immediately and contact the company tonight.

"I have been told the company has been able to locate Chief Gilbert Evans already. They cut his vacation short," Ekelton added. "He'll be flying into Dakar ASAP and will be replacing Mr. Albert in a day or two."

Gregoire was taken away by two of Simon Albertson's *larger men* – two moving mountains. Gaston and Alice high-fived each other. It seemed as if Gaston had come alive again. *Yes, he definitely would be an asset to any security department,* Alan thought. He would certainly write a reference for him, should Gaston decide to apply.

Now that the vaccines were safe, that the thief was under lock-and-key, Alan was ready to retire for the night. He invited Alice to do the same. However, his nurse told him that she was far too wound up to go to bed now. She would read for a while and then sleep for a bit until Olga was due to arrive at six the next morning.

This was going to be a big day for Betty Palmer. She and her two assistants were going to visit the Dakar General hospital. There, they were to review the plans for the construction of the new wing. This wing was destined to host a research center for infectious diseases and an in-patient center for disease management and prevention. Upon signature of the agreements with government officials and the release of funds to the various authorized contractors, the work would begin, most probably in the next three months. In the meantime, and today in particular, the focus would be on the inoculations of the people who were exposed to the Ebola virus on a day-to-day basis. The WHO team would also visit many of the clinic and medical facilities in and around the city to administer as many vaccinations as they could in the one day.

In order for Betty, Adele and Gregory to visit the hospital, they had to be fitted with protective garments. They ultimately would wear a hood when entering the facilities they would visit.

Watching Olga as she gathered the garments and necessary accessories, Alan thought of a little prank a nurse played on a friend of his a long time ago.

When Olga was ready and now waiting for Betty and her two assistants to arrive Alan went to sit with her in the examination room.

"You know, when I was watching you gather the garments for Mrs. Palmer, I thought of something that happened to a proctologist friend of mine."

"Oh, and what's that?" Olga asked a bit distractedly.

"Well, he told me the story about a man who came to his office for his first proctology exam. His nurse told him to have a seat in the examination room and that the doctor would be with him in just a few minutes. When the man sat down and began observing the doctor's tools, he noticed that there were 3 items on a stand next to the doctor's desk. 1. A tube of K-Y jelly; 2. A rubber glove; and 3. A beer." Olga smiled. "When my friend finally came in, the man said, "Look, Doc, I'm a little confused. This is my first exam. I know what the K-Y is for, and I know what the glove is for, but can you tell me what the BEER is for?" At that, my friend became noticeably outraged. He flung the door open and yelled, "Damn it, Rachel, I said A BUTT LIGHT, not a Bud Light!"

Olga stared for a fraction of a second and then erupted in tittering laughter.

A few minutes later, Mrs. Palmer rushed through the door of the medical center, Adele and Gregory in tow, all excited.

"Doctor Mayhew, you don't know what this means to me. I'm so looking forward to this. Finally, I am going to be able to see for myself where the funds are going to go."

"Yes, Mrs. Palmer," Alan said, "but first, I think you should prepare yourself to see what Ebola does to human beings, and it's not pretty or exciting, I can assure you."

"I realize that, Doctor, of course I do. But to be able to do something about a dreadful disease, that's what I've been waiting for practically all my life."

Adele and Gregory didn't say anything and remained quiet while Olga helped them into their suits. Once the three of them had gone through their practice demonstration and had been given their suits in a plastic bag, they went down to the foyer to wait for Alan, Olga and the WHO team to join them.

A few minutes later the WHO guys arrived and it was time to fill the vaccine cases. There would be at least twelve cases going today and twelve more tomorrow. Olga, Alice and Annie, the WHO's head nurse, took almost fifteen minutes to load the cases and record the vial numbers on their tablets. Drs. Hatfield and Ashford were on hand, of course, and visibly impatient to get to work.

In the meantime, at the Dakar airport, Gilbert Evans was as impatient as ever to get to the ship. He was keen on getting back to work. *Holidays and vacations are fun but then they get boring,* he had told the Human Resources person. She had contacted him with his latest assignment just two days earlier. He could not get to the ship fast enough. But he had to make a stop in New York City to be vaccinated. The Ebola vaccines had only reached a few hospitals in North America and the closest to his home was in New York. The good thing about this was that there was a direct flight from New York to Dakar twice a week and he was lucky enough to get a seat on the Friday flight. This was unusual to get the company to pay for the direct flight. Generally, the arrangements were to use the most inexpensive ticket to get the crew there. Flights like leaving at 5:00 am and waiting in four airports before finally getting to the cruise port two days later were normal occurrences. This is why those in the know asked what their budgeted expenditure for the 'cheapo flight' was and had them apply that to your pay. Then one made their own plane and hotel reservations and just absorbed the added cost, for sanity sake.

His arrival at the Dakar Airport was an eye opener. If one does not like crowds, one should stay away from this airport's arrival concourse. Let's say it's "semi-modern" but quite inadequate for the number of passengers landing in that city every day. On the plane, the pretty stewardess walked through the cabin holding two industrial-size cans. She sprayed everyone (literally) with some sort of bug repellent (or killer – who knows) before the doors were opened. After gagging from the spray, one has to make one's way into the intense heat to the concourse. You hope that the customs' forms one filled in beforehand are in order. Once Gilbert had gone through immigration without any more trouble than being looked at curiously when he said that he was staying aboard "*The Contessa*," he made his way to the luggage carousel. He hoped that his bag had made it. He doubted very much that, if it hadn't, anyone would ever find it. When it came out of the tunnel, it was amazingly still unopened and bearing all of the right tags. It was then that a horde of porters, literally *leashed* to their trolleys, rushed him. They pushed their carts against his legs and demanded that he let one of them take his bag through to customs. One of them even yelled in Gilbert's face when he was having none of it. This assault only stopped when a customs' official came to Gilbert's rescue. He grabbed him by the arm and led him unceremoniously to an office, away from the crowd, where he asked him what he was "really" doing in Dakar.

"This is not a place for a white man right now, sir," the officer said. "So, what is the deal?"

Gilbert handed him his passport, his vaccination booklet and his engagement papers. He didn't say a word.

The officer went through the engagement papers, which stated that he was a security officer aboard *The Contessa* accompanying the

WHO team on their mission along the West African coast. The custom man looked somewhat appeased. He then asked Gilbert to open his bag. The chief did so and let the officer rummage through his belongings before he finally let him go.

Once Gilbert was able to get out of the airport, he came face to face with another sort of trouble. In most every city of the world, it's generally not a problem to hail a cab at the airport. But in Dakar, there is absolutely no discipline when it comes to the taxis lining up in front of the arrivals' doors. The cabbies are out of their cars, yelling at one another or screaming the latest, outrageous fare at the arriving tourists. In Gilbert's case, he wasn't surprised. He had seen this sort of thing in some of the Middle East and Asian cities, but he was nonetheless annoyed with the whole thing. His gaze traveled around the assortment of vehicles parked haphazardly in front of the doors and chose one that looked as if it would get him to his destination without falling apart.

After the necessary bartering session with the driver, Gilbert was finally on his way to the port. Going through Dakar was an experience in itself.

This city is a relic of an Old French settlement with busy streets and narrow sidewalks. People fray themselves a passage amid the dense horde of cars, buses, donkeys, horse-drawn carts and hobbling beggars. Even the many Parisian-style large tree-lined thoroughfares, bearing such names as 'Avenue George Pompidou' or 'Boulevard Charles de Gaulle', ail from the seldom-interrupted traffic jams.

Throughout the years of abundance, this old city kept its charm. But because of years of hardship, in Dakar you can find the most luxurious mansions abutting the poorest shacks and the cleanest beaches not far from the filthiest fishing coves. It is not unlike a small version of Marseille, with its very busy port, markets everywhere, selling everything. If you need *it*, you'll find *it* in Dakar.

CHAPTER NINETEEN

To express their gratefulness

READY TO MEET WHOEVER and whatever was expecting them when Alan and the nurses, with Gilbert Evans and the WHO team arrived at the hospital, they climbed down from the government SUV to be immediately surrounded by armed guards. The men from "the presidency" were on hand to escort the group and their precious cargo inside the hospital. Although the hallways leading to the rooms that would be used for the inoculations were bare, Alan sensed that beyond these doors and walls there were people receiving or in need of medical assistance.

The Chief of Medicine, an aging black fellow, judging from his graying hair and sagging eyes, met Drs. Ashford and Hatfield as soon as they went through the last door at the end of the hallway. Alan let the "Docteur en Chef" make the introduction. As soon as Dr. Beaudieu set eyes on Betty Palmer, his smile broadened.

"My dear lady," he said in perfect English, "you have no idea how long I have been waiting for this day. Now the suffering will be over soon, and the healing can begin."

"So happy to be here, Dr. Beaudieu," Betty replied, holding the old doctor's hand in hers. "After so many conversations on Skype, I feel as I am meeting an old friend."

"Thank you, dear Madame. You have been our savior and now these doctors that you brought with you"—he looked at Drs. Ashford and Hatfield—"can begin to end our suffering. Thank you for being here."

A half-hour later, the nurses and physicians started their inoculations. There was a line-up down the hall and through the treating rooms. It seemed as if half of Dakar's population had been selected to receive the Ebola vaccine. Outside, the guards ordered the crowd to sit on the ground and not to try approaching the hospital doors. These soldiers, armed to the teeth as the saying goes, meant every word of their menaces. They had an animalistic instinct for survival. One wrong move and they wouldn't hesitate to kill the one stepping out of line. The vaccines being administered inside the hospital were the first signs that relief was in sight and that the disease was soon to be beaten. However, and in the meantime, no one should rush the process. No one was to step out and take matters in their own hands. The soldiers knew it and so did the people on the ground.

When eleven o'clock sounded in the hospital chapel, oddly enough so did the chant from the imam began from the minaret at the nearby mosque. Except for the soldiers standing around the people in front of the hospital, everyone in sight – those who were not working – began praying, rolling their chaplets between their fingers.

In West Africa most religious denominations rub elbow with one another. Entire families will have different beliefs. They're "observant" devotees. Most people abhor radical behavior of any kind. If you are Muslim in your heart, so be it. If you are Christian in your heart, so be it. Even if you are Jewish in your heart, no one has the right to take away your faith. Perhaps, one of the most intriguing persons in this society is the shaman. He is the one you pay to hear truths about yourself and the probabilities surrounding your future. He is perhaps a cross between a psychologist, a spiritual healer, and a fortune-teller.

Alan had heard of a ritual that called for the groom and his bride to bathe or shower in chamomile tea to calm the sexual urges that the young couple would face before the marriage ceremony. Perhaps laughable for a westerner, but it was a practice still respected throughout a few parts of West Africa.

It was not uncommon to find a shaman attending a marriage ceremony. Nor was it unusual to have a bride alone attending the wedding. Her husband was not making any promise to her, she was to him!

After prayer, all that were still sitting on the ground, stood up slowly and returned to whatever task they had started before the WHO team arrived at the hospital. For some reason, the prayer or the imam's words had calmed them down. They were no longer so intent in entering the hospital.

Meanwhile, inside the premises, Betty and Dr. Beaudieu had joined a number of government representatives in the boardroom of the hospital. They all had been inoculated prior to coming up to the meeting. These twelve men and five women represented the powers-that-be in Senegal. They were the prime movers in a society where a mistake is not easily forgotten or forgiven. If Betty Palmer was not to make good on her promises, she would never be forgiven and never forgotten either. These seventeen people had to affix their signatures on the dotted line today. The palavers were over. The bartering was done. A common-accord had been reached. But with all that came responsibilities. Each of the people in the room, including Betty herself and Dr. Beaudieu would have to ensure that every single thing that had been promised in the accord was indeed made a reality.

Senegalese are particularly belligerent people. They are hunters. They will survive against all odds. They rarely cry or express an emotion that would 'diminish' their stature or standing in the community. They're fiercely loyal but will lie if it means the untruth can avoid someone being hurt. They rarely complain since complaining is a sign of weakness. However, they will not shy from showing you how much you owe them. If you have a big house, you will have to employ as many servants as it takes to maintain the house, to do the cooking, the laundry and the shopping for you. You have the money – they don't. So, if you want to stay in their country unharmed, you spend that money on them.

At the exit of the meeting, Betty felt exhausted. She had attended many meetings of this kind in her working life, but she did not recall one being as intense as this one had been. She looked at Adele and Gregory, as the three of them were on their way to the elevators, and shook her head. "I'm sorry," she said, as they entered the lift, "but I've never experienced something like this before. Being escorted by armed soldiers everywhere and signing the most important document in my life is a little more than I expected." She paused. "Although I had been told what would happen today, I am truly amazed."

"Are you relieved?" Adele asked. "I mean are you relieved to have finalized the agreement?"

"Oh yes, my dear, I am. And now you and Gregory will have a lot of work to do. You see"—she raised her gaze to the young man—"they are expecting us to deliver, but I will be expecting them to follow every clause of that agreement to the letter. If they want to see the hospital wing erected, opened, and maintained properly for years to come, I am not going to be flexible with working deadlines or reports. The doctors and medical staff that will be working here, as well as the researchers, will count on us to ensure that the government stays out of their hair. This hospital will no longer be a place to entertain an idea, but a place where that idea becomes a reality."

"Wow, that's the speech these guys should have heard after you signed the agreement," Gregory remarked. "And you still think your nephew is the answer to holding the reins on this project?"

They exited the elevator and came face to face with another three soldiers.

"Well, Gregory, at this point, I don't know," Betty replied. "I don't know my nephew. If I judge him capable of handling my affairs around here and elsewhere, I'll hand him the reins, of course. If not, I will cross that bridge when we come to it."

The WHO team and Alan, Olga, Alice and Annie finished this round of inoculations in the early part of the afternoon. It was time for them to leave. After the meeting upstairs, Dr. Beaudieu had joined them to participate in the inoculations. It seemed as if the old doctor was most happy when he could talk to "his people." For him to being able to assure these men, women and children that Ebola was now a thing of the past, seemed to be a crowning event in his life. The glistening eyes, the firm, yet striated hands appeared to express his inner sentiments. The doctor was thoroughly happy.

When everyone returned to the ship, they were tired, yes, but excited. Olga could not stop talking about the children she saw come through the treatment rooms. They were all shy, but wanted to have "le vaccin." Generally, children are frightened of needles. These ones *wanted* to receive their inoculations. Alan, for his part, was looking forward to going back to the hospital the next day and visiting the facilities with Dr. Beaudieu. He had heard that, for many years, this hospital had treated people coming from all parts of West Africa. It had been a center for the practice of medicine since the 1930s. Many young doctors had done their internships in that hospital along with many teams assigned to the treatment of tropical diseases. This was by no means your regular developing world hospital. It had been severely damaged since Senegal's independence, but once the government realized how important a center the Dakar hospital was for many of their neighbors, the successive presidents had seen to its maintenance if not its modernization.

While discussing what they had seen and experienced that morning, Alan, Olga and Alice were ready to attend to the tasks left undone while they were ashore.

In the meantime, the now minister of cultural affairs, the famous singer Youssou N'Dour had been invited to attend the captain's dinner and the cabaret performance. Youssou N'Dour is perhaps one of the better known singers in the western world. His presence aboard and his contribution to the understanding of West African culture was appreciated by everyone. Surprisingly, the minister had offered to bring the national company of dancers and drummers with him to entertain the passengers that evening. Tiffany could not have hoped for a better gift. This was going to be the climax of a cruise already vibrant with memories.

Before the dancers were to start their performance, Tiffany had asked Constantine to break the ice.

As he came on the floor, the applause accompanied his taking of the microphone.

"Ladies and Gentleman, I have to tell you a story," he began. "This afternoon after coming back from a few hours of shopping in Dakar's most intriguing markets, our entertainment director was pacing the floor, waiting for me in the foyer. She was so nervous; I thought there had been a death in her family. But no, nothing like that had occurred. She was shaking from head to toe when she finally told me what was the matter with her: Youssou N'Dour was coming aboard!" The wave of laughter that accompanied the remark was hard to contain. Even Youssou N'Dour himself couldn't help but laugh and applaud the irregular introduction. "And then Ms. Sylvan went on to tell me, with a straight face, that sixteen dancers were going to accompany Mr. N'Dour." He paused. "That; I had not expected! I dropped my shopping bags and asked her: "What can I do to help, Ms. Sylvan?" The passengers were laughing uncontrollably by now. "Would you like me to try imitating them? She looked at me as if I came down from another planet. "No-no," she said, I just want you to tell everyone who they are." Constantine had to break into a grin while people chuckled and applauded. "Don't you think they will know who they are? It's not like they're wearing tuxedoes, now are they?" That was it. That's all Constantine had to say. The drums cut him short as the performers came onto the floor. In one chorus of movement, the passengers stood up and applauded until their hands hurt. These people had just gone through hell and back and they managed to come on board to dance to express their gratefulness.

Truly amazing!

CHAPTER TWENTY

Tambacounda

PERHAPS THE MAIN REASON FOR Senegal being one of the countries least affected by Ebola is its prosperity. Since the early 1990s following the discovery of a large gold deposit, named Sabodala, located south-east of Tambacounda, the country has reaped the benefits of mineral ore mining on a grand-scale. The story of Sabodala began with the determination of a highway robber by the name of Ousmane Ahne to make good on his promise to "bring fame and fortune to his people." He literally set up camp where he had found gold dust practically covering the ground as far as the eye could see. His earlier thieving; mostly bringing stolen gems from South Africa into Senegal, and selling them profitably, brought him to the door of a fantastic venture. He bought crusher equipment in the States, had a Canadian company design a processing plant and erect it where he thought there was enough gold to crush the rocks into an early fortune. However, his initial thieving activities and the jealousy on the part of government parties saw him imprisoned for his misdeeds.

As soon as the gold prices began climbing on the stock exchange's trading board, a Canadian company, with some vision, decided to have another look at the Sabodala claim. Today, it's one of the largest (if not the largest) open-pit gold mine in West Africa.

Alan had once met the woman who recalled participating in the early negotiations to acquire the Sabodala mining rights. She had talked and worked with Ousmane Ahne for a while. She admired his enthusiasm and his stubbornness to reach his goal. Today Alan was looking forward to flying over the site and see what that woman's idea had become some twenty years later.

Betty, for her part, was on tender hooks. Adele and Gregory had arranged to charter an aircraft to take the three of them together with Drs. Hatfield, Ashford and Alan to Tambacounda. The plane belonged to the mining company, which made regular trips to eastern Senegal.

The other two parties interested in visiting the back country were Leon and Linda Summerville. Yet, before Betty accepted having them join the flight, she had a long chat with Gaston, as per Alan's recommendation.

"It's not that they're really thieves per se, Doctor Mayhew," Gaston explained when he and Alan had their little debriefing chat after Gregoire's arrest. "It's just that Leon is too smart for his own good. For as long as I've known him, he's never taken anything that didn't belong to him; neither did Linda for that matter. That said, he does know how to persuade people to put their signature on the dotted line of one shady scheme or another. It's all virtual investments. Most of the companies he's dealing with only exist on a piece of paper. The SEC and IRS are the ones that I'm watching closely. Leon and Linda are making money mostly on getting a cut on what they sell on line. They both have investors' licenses and use those licenses when an *idiot* falls into their trap."

"But what do they want with Betty Palmer, is my question. If they intend to pull a fast one on her, they won't hear the end of it. She is no "idiot" and won't fall into the first snare they put in front of her feet."

"I admit," Gaston went on, "it surprised me also. She is a bigger shark than they are and swimming in the same waters would be dangerous for Leon, I agree. Yet, I think there's something else behind Leon's uncaring façade." He paused. "I know"—he chuckled—"I sound like the advocate of a man condemned to be executed in the morning, but I believe Leon deserves the benefit of a background investigation."

"That's an interesting suggestion. What gave you the idea?" Alan asked.

"It's Mrs. Palmer's attitude toward Leon. Every time they are face to face, Mrs. Palmer is staring at him. It is as if she is recognizing him, but who is she seeing in him, I really don't know."

"Yes, and I think you're right, we should ask Gilbert Evans to run a background check on Leon Summerville. That's a good idea actually."

"What about Linda; do you think it's worth doing the same with her?"

"I'll ask Gilbert about that when I've explained the situation to him."

A day later and a few hours before everyone was due to board the aircraft, Gilbert reported on Leon Summerville. He apparently moved to the States after being taken from an orphanage in *The Gambia* and brought to Louisiana. He inherited a cotton plantation when the owner died. He married his benefactor's niece soon after the man's death. He's been officially living in Louisiana since then, but traveled extensively for his many business interests worldwide.

Alan summarized the report for Betty and advised her that it might be prudent to take the Summerville's with her. "If someone recognizes him at the Tambacounda monastery, then it would be time to move forward, but not before."

The flight was a pleasant one. The aircraft was well appointed and seated at least fifteen people comfortably. When Alan asked the pilot and co-pilot how long they had been working in Africa, they both replied that they were on a rotation schedule. They would switch with another team every six weeks.

"And don't worry, Doc," the co-pilot said, "We've all been vaccinated as soon as the vaccines came out of the lab."

"Well, glad to hear it. What about the people at the mine, have they been vaccinated?"

"I have no idea, but I think the doctors from the World Health Organization will be able to tell you that better than we can."

"Yes, I'm sure they will, actually. Anyway, thanks for the info," Alan said before returning to his seat across from Betty and Babette.

"I don't really know what I should expect, Alan," she said, while the plane was taxiing toward the runway.

"What do you mean, Betty? You're going to visit an interesting part of this country, and tomorrow, you're going to have accomplished a stated dream of yours."

"What if the monastery has no record of my nephew? What if everything was destroyed somehow?"

"Come, come now, Betty, let's stay positive about this," Babette put in.

"I know, I know, Babette, but I can't help wondering where all this will lead me." Then with a very pensive look on her face, she added, "Just grant me the senility to forget the people I never liked, the good fortune to remember the ones I do, and the eyesight to tell the difference, especially with this Summerville issue."

Alan crossed his arms over his chest. "Babette is right, Betty. You need to stay positive. Even if no one recognizes Leon Summerville in Tambacounda, it's just one more thread to pull out from the skein. Since we've just learned that he came from an orphanage in The Gambia that means that the monks in Senegal had him moved. Alternatively, maybe the social services did, since he was a white boy with a better chance of being adopted in a country still under British rule."

"So, if we don't find evidence around here, we can continue searching when we get to The Gambia, right?"

"Yes," Babette said, patting Betty's hand gently. She then looked at Alan in the seat facing hers. "Did you or Gilbert have a chance to chat with the Summerville's about all this?"

"No, Babette. Neither of us did. We really don't know what the Summervilles are up to on this cruise, based on their track record." Alan fixed his gaze on Betty. "If Gaston is right, Leon Summerville is going to make a move pretty soon. Maybe he'll try selling you some mining shares in Sabodala…"

"You mean the open-pit mine; the one south of Tambacounda?"

"Yes, the very same."

"But those shares are not his to sell, as far as I can tell. Unless he's a shareholder himself, then, of course, he could offer the shares." Betty seemed pensive for a moment. "But do we know much about this mine?"

"You'll have to ask Gregory to do a search on Google. But I can already tell you it's a very profitable venture. Actually, I've asked the pilot to fly over it because you need to see where 'an idea can lead you'. Twenty years ago a man had an idea; he believed there was gold in *them there hills* and although he never reaped the rewards of his labor, the seed was planted and it blossomed into a fantastic project which is now feeding a nation. What you have done for the hospital and for the health of West Africa easily equates to the Sabodala Project. That mine feeds a country, your idea will ensure that the health of its inhabitants are preserved."

"Have you ever thought of entering politics?" Betty asked Alan, a broad smile affixed on her lips now.

Alan had to laugh. "No way, not really my scene. Politics is the art of looking for trouble, finding it whether it exists or not, diagnosing it incorrectly, and applying the wrong remedy, and as Will Rogers said, 'The trouble with practical jokers is that very often they get elected.' But as long as my patients understand what I'm saying that's all the politics I would want to manage."

Less than an hour later, the aircraft was circling over the mine. It was an impressive enterprise to say the least.

Leon and Linda were seated at the back of the plane. Leon turned to his wife to say, "Can you imagine owning a piece of that mine?"

"Oh I can imagine it, yes, Leon, but do you think Mrs. Palmer would agree to buying a piece of it?"

"I have no idea, Linda. Unless I can talk to the woman, alone, I won't be able to answer your question. And you know, there's something about her that's been nagging at my mind. She reminds me of someone. For the life of me I don't know who."

"Could it be that you've met her when you came over here a couple of years back?"

"No, I don't think so. I've been wracking my brain since I first met her. But I truly can't place her. Besides, when I asked Gaston about her, he said that it was her first trip to West Africa. So, it's not like we might have met in passing around here."

"And when do you think you'll throw the bait in the water?" Linda asked.

"When I know a little more about Mrs. Palmer and her business, there will be plenty of time then to make a move.

When they finally landed in Tambacounda, Alan was agreeably surprised to see how clean and well-kept everything was. He thought it was probably because of the mine's proximity. There was added infrastructure, such as paved roads, proper airport runway and tarmac in addition to other well maintained city amenities.

"That was quite impressive, I mean seeing that mine from the air," Babette said, as she was walking out of the airport with Betty and Alan. Adele and Gregory stayed back to collect the small cases and process the luggage through customs. Security was as tight as in any city in the States. Coming out of the airport, everyone was clearly impressed.

"This is quite amazing," Dr. Ashford said to the chauffeur who was going to take him and Dr. Hatfield, Alan and the nurses to the hospital. "Everything is very nice."

"Yes, Doctor," said the driver, "we have strict rules since the epidemic started. The doctors at the hospital have really worked hard to make sure we don't get sick."

"We can see that," Alan said, snapping his safety belt on. "Do you know how many people have been infected?"

"I really can't tell, Doctor," the driver replied. "But I have seen a couple of people coming from Guinea by the south road and going to the hospital. They were sick."

"What about the people at the mine; have they been vaccinated?" Dr. Hatfield asked.

"I don't really know. But I think the chief of medicine at the hospital will be able to tell you."

Relaxing now in the back seat, Alan wondered how many people would have crossed the border unnoticed and unchecked. Even if the city was as clean as it looked, who could stop the nomadic tribes from traveling cross-country? He would soon find out he supposed.

CHAPTER TWENTY-ONE

The monastery

THE MONASTERY OF KEUR-MOUSSA has been modernized over the years, yet it still remains an "old" religious community and edifice. The church itself is beautiful in its simplicity. There is no organ; there is no organized choir, but there are dozens of voices singing the "cantiques" at the sound of balafons and drums. It's an odd combination of soft tunes and imposing but discreet rhythm.

When Betty, Babette and Alan were admitted into the "parloir," the abbot came in. The older gentleman radiated with peacefulness. It was even strange.

The abbot spoke in undertones, addressing Betty first.

"I received your letter, Mrs. Palmer, and I welcome your visit. Please sit down," he added, indicating the seats behind them. "I am afraid you will be disappointed to hear that I have not met Leon Archer while he was working here as a young boy." Betty lowered her head. "Yet, the fact that I was not looking after this monastery at the time is not a problem. If nothing else, the Church keeps excellent records of everything that happens within its walls." He paused; fixing his gaze on Betty's querying face. "Therefore, I have contacted the abbot who served the Lord in those days. He has sent me a photograph of the only white boy who resided here at the time." He pulled an envelope out of his cassock's pocket. "Perhaps you could take a look at this picture, and tell me if you recognize your nephew in it."

The abbot handed the envelope to Betty with a gentle smile. She opened it, took the old black and white picture out of it and gasped. The boy in the picture looked exactly the same as the one in the framed photograph Betty kept on her desk. "Yes, Father, this is my nephew. I would recognize him anywhere. Thank you." She replaced the picture in the envelope and wanted to hand it back to the abbot.

The latter waved a hand in front of it and said, "Keep it, my dear. I have no use for it."

Alan looked at Betty before he asked, "I'm sorry, Father, but where could we find the other monk who looked after Keur-Moussa in those days?"

"He is living in France now, Doctor Mayhew. You see, living in Africa is not easy for anyone. Although, the Lord provides for us in most everything we need, it is still difficult for some of us older men. Father Joshua retired about ten years ago and I will probably do the same in another ten years." He smiled.

"Do you hold mass in the church for the Christian population sometimes?" Babette asked, opening her mouth for the first time.

"Yes, we do. There are quite a few Catholics among the people living in this area. Besides, from time to time, we hold a special service for the expat men and women working at the mine. We hold midnight mass at Christmas and perform Easter services for the community as well."

"That's so good to hear, Father. And do you think we could attend a service while we are here? I know the few people who are working at the hospital right now and those who have accompanied us on this tour would appreciate it."

"I thought one of you would ask me," the abbot replied. "I have already organized a service to be held tomorrow morning, before you leave for Timbuktu."

"But... but how...? How did you know?" Betty asked, taken aback.

"Well," the abbot said with a tentative smile cracking his lips, "as it happens, Mrs. Palmer, someone else in your group was interested in our monastery. The man and his wife came in an hour ago. They asked to tour the premises. Mr. Summerville – that is the man's name – was quite impressed with the cloister. He seemed to recall some other monastery with similar features."

"Did he really?" Betty sounded amazed.

"Yes, he did. I truly had to wonder, for a fleeting moment, if Mr. Summerville was perhaps your nephew. But I will not advance such a proposition at this time, since, as I've said, I was not the one who looked after the boy."

"And he mentioned our upcoming trip to Timbuktu?" Betty asked, still visibly puzzled.

"Yes. You see, Mrs. Palmer, Westerners have the habit of segregating people into religious or societal boxes, whereas we shouldn't, of course. All places of worship are just that – places of worship. A place where the Lord – whatever name you wish to call him – is ready to hear your prayers, contemplative thoughts or devotions. When Mr. Summerville asked me what he could expect to see in Timbuktu, I had to describe it as I would any other sanctuary. It was a place of pilgrimage for the believers for centuries before the concept of religious segregation came about. And that's what it still is. It is a place of peace. I am sure you and your group will find it amazingly retiring. I myself liked to go to the Sahel and rest my head in Timbuktu or even in Djene – another Malian place of pilgrimage and worship."

"I wish you could come with us, Father," Babette put in, obviously impressed by the abbot's description.

When they came out of the monastery, Babette was still pensive.

"What are you thinking?" Alan asked her.

"Well, Alan, I am thinking that one day, in the near future actually, I will come back here. Perhaps for a week's 'retreat'. The atmosphere in this monastery is imposingly tranquil. You cannot but feel calmness invade every part of your mind. I am just very impressed with it."

"Same here," Betty chimed in.

The three of them stopped at the back of the monastery and looked up. The modesty of the edifice was once again reflecting the peacefulness that one could find inside its walls.

Still impressed by their visit, they went into town to have some lunch at the hotel where they would stay for the night. Alan was tired from the heat and so were the ladies with him. They were glad for the air-conditioned restaurant and the superbly clean amenities. Alan still could not believe he was in the middle of Africa. Although, this was a tourist hotel, and not necessarily reflecting what was happening in the villages surrounding the town center.

They were eating some rice with vegetable sauce – quite a spicy dish – when Drs. Hatfield and Ashford came in with the nurses. They looked satisfied with their morning.

"Hello-hello, everyone," Dr. Ashford said cheerfully as they approached the table.

"Why don't you pull up a table and some chairs and have some of this," Alan offered, pointing at the large tin tray in the middle of the table. "It just tastes great."

The doctors didn't have to move. A couple of waiters and the hotel manager eased another two tables in near Alan's. The doctors, with the nurses' help, gathered enough chairs around them for everyone to sit down.

As soon as they were settled, Dr. Hatfield ordered the same tin tray of rice and vegetables for everybody.

"It does look very good," Annie remarked her eyes riveted on the rice dish.

"Here, take my spoon, dear," Babette said, wiping it with some sanitizing tissue, "and dig in. It's absolutely delicious."

A few seconds later, as Annie was to grab the spoon from Babette, one of the waiters appeared out of nowhere and handed her a clean one. "The other tray will be here soon," he added, before retreating quietly.

"So, how was the day at the hospital?" Alan asked.

"Just as expected," Dr. Ashford replied. "About the same as what happened in Dakar, except this time we had a whole contingent of European nurses and doctors to lend a hand."

"Really?" Alan sounded as surprised as he was.

"Oh yes," Hatfield rejoined. "It's because of the mine. There are apparently hundreds of workers in the pit and working the machinery. We mostly looked after the women and children that live in and around town today. The workers will be vaccinated on site, at the mine. While we were at the hospital today, we sent an order to Toronto to have vaccines flown in. Hopefully by tomorrow or the next day."

"What about the border problem we discussed last night," Alan inquired.

"They have security patrols all along the borders between Guinea and Senegal apparently. But if someone slips through the barriers, there's nothing we can do. In any case, the hospital staff is well aware of the danger. Since most of them have been vaccinated now, the risk of infection is minimal."

As the waiter deposited another larger tray in the middle of the combination table, the door of the restaurant opened. Leon and Linda Summerville came in. They stopped when they saw everyone sitting around the adjoining tables.

"There you are," Betty exclaimed, oddly cheerful toward the couple suddenly. "We were wondering if you had gotten lost in the mine or something."

"Well... no... not really," Leon blurted, obviously taken aback. "We've been visiting the monastery..."

"Let's get you another table," Alan offered, getting up and beckoning for the waiter to come over.

"Yes, we know," Betty went on. "We've been there ourselves. Wonderful place, isn't it?"

"Oh yes. Absolutely," Linda piped in as she took a seat beside Babette and across from Betty and Alan.

"It's a gorgeous place," Babette said. "I'm even thinking of coming back for a week's retreat. The monks' cantiques are just unbelievable."

"Oh, did you stay for one of their devotions then?" Leon asked.

"Just to listen to them sing. No, not really a devotion. The abbot will perform a mass service for all of us early tomorrow morning."

"That's wonderful," Linda said. "I can hardly wait to hear them sing."

The remark sounded as if Linda was preparing herself to go to the opera, Babette mused ruefully.

Once everyone had eaten and the trays were nearly empty, Alan decided to retire to his room. The hotel had the luxury of a broadband connection in the room, not Wi-Fi mind you. Since they were ashore and he didn't have to search out an Internet cafe, he wanted to read some of his emails and contact Gilbert with the latest about their trip inland.

His friend Marc had done it again. There were a couple of jokes waiting for him. Alan always enjoyed reading them. They inevitably put him in a good mood for the rest of the day.

His message read:

Hey There,

After reading about your exploits with the thief and the med center's fridge, I thought this was an appropriate lesson to be learned.

A student named Jacob was sitting in class one day and the teacher walked by and Jacob asked her, "How do you put an elephant in the fridge?" The teacher said, "I don't know, how?" Jacob then said, "You open the door and put it in there!" Then Jacob asked the teacher another question "How do you put an ape in the fridge?" The teacher then replied, "Oh, I know this one, you open the door and put it in there?" Jacob said, "No, you open the door, take the elephant out, and then you put it in there." Then he asked another question: "All the animals went to the lion's birthday party, except one animal, which one was it?" The teacher a bit confused and said, "The lion?" Then the student said, "No, the ape because he's still in the fridge." Then he asked her just one more question; "If there is a river full of crocodiles and you wanted to get across it, how would you?" The teacher then says, "You would walk over the bridge." Then Jacob says, "No, you would swim across because all the crocodiles are at the lion's birthday party!"

And this one is for later....

Dr. Parker, the biology instructor at a posh suburban girl's junior college, said during class, "Miss Smith, would you please name the organ of the human body, which under the appropriate conditions, expands to six times its normal size, and define the conditions." Miss Smith gasped, blushed deeply, then said freezingly, Dr. Parker, I do not think that is a proper question to ask me, you should be asking a boy. And I assure you my parents will hear of this." With that, she sat down, very red-faced. Unperturbed, Dr. Parker called on Miss Johnson and asked the same question. Miss Johnson, with composure, replied, "The pupil of the eye, in dim light." "Correct," said Dr. Parker. "And now, Miss Smith, I have three things to say to you. One, you have not studied your lesson. Two, you have a dirty mind. And three, you will someday be faced with a dreadful disappointment."

Have a grand day, my friend.
Marc

Apart from the jokes, Marc had picked up a link about the Keur-Moussa Monastery on the Internet. The link led Alan to a site where they had a fantastic series of cantiques sung on videos. He promised himself to send the link to Babette. Those were to be kept somewhere safe – they were the perfect souvenirs from their trip to Tambacounda. What a wonderful town it was.

CHAPTER TWENTY-TWO

Timbuktu

THE NEXT DAY, THE GROUP arrived at the Keur-Moussa monastery bright and early. The cantiques were already invading the church as everyone filed in to attend the morning mass.

The abbot had many words! Those that left the greatest imprint on the visitors' memories were his prayers.

He first asked everyone to close their eyes. "Feel the holy silence all about you. Know that God is with you. He will hear your prayers. Speak to him quietly and reverently. This is the most sacred time of your day."

After communion, he recited a prayer for the ill. "Please close your eyes. Feel silence and stillness all about you. There are those in hospitals here in Africa, at home, on the road, and even in the fields who carry the burden of infection, pain, fear, or guilt. For them and for ourselves, we pray together each in our own words or by repeating this prayer, "Heavenly father may thy blessings descend as a healing balm on all who need thy help."

And when it was time to leave, the abbot closed the service with, "I will lift my eyes unto the hills, from whence cometh my help. My help cometh from the Lord. These words are born for the purpose of the universe. As we lift our eyes unto the hills, let us see beyond. Let us lift our deeds to set them on the highest purposes. Let God touch our every day with magic and understanding and give our lives the full meaning that may shine in the radiance of thy love.

"Almighty God, we entrust all who are dear to us to your never ending care and love, knowing that you are doing better things than we could ever imagine. Open our hearts and enter in, abide with us and bless each of us this day and every day."

Babette was crying silent tears at the end of the service. She had made up her mind. She was definitely coming back to this place.

If one ever wants to take a trip back in time, Timbuktu is the place to do so. Since the sixth century, this small city of pilgrimage has been dedicated to those crossing the Sahel and the Sahara en route to North Africa.

Abutting the southern rim of the Sahara, the Sahel stretches its immensity to the northern banks of the Niger River. Much like the devil's playpen, Mali is endowed with everything beautiful the Sahel has to offer and everything treacherous it could bestow on its inhabitants. Its nomadic routes are traced and retraced at the whim of devastating sandstorms. When the fury of the monsoons descends upon the Sahel, the Niger bulges out of its banks to inundate towns, villages and fields for weeks without respite. This, of course, brings fertility to the flooded earth like a mother nurturing her children. The spirit of the Sahel shapes the lives of everyone living there or attempting to travel its paths. It becomes the master of one's mind and existence. Once trapped in the Sahel's enveloping magnitude there is no escape from the thralls of its sensuous desires and passion for adventure.

Northern Mali, as viewed from the air, looks like a postcard painted in orange and green. In places, the sandy terrain was as red as blood, while in others the golden ocher and orange hues seemed to tease the green of the trees and bushes, which sparsely furnished the landscape. The Niger is still a handsome river flowing across the continent. It forms a natural divide between the Sahel and Sahara. Timbuktu is now located about five miles from its northern shore. Originally, the city and its mosque were constructed within a stone-throw of it. Today, however, the women of the town have to travel the five miles to the river several times a week to fill their troughs with their daily water needs.

One of the interesting things about Timbuktu is that the mosque resembles a sandcastle. As one can remember from beach time as a kid, this is not a type of construction, which would stand the test of time. In fact, this edifice would never have withstood the fierce sandstorms whipping the region every year if it hadn't been for Timbuktu's residents. Every year, they rebuild the corner, the façade, the broken wall or the fissure near the door of the mosque. They will not let time erase what their faith and ardor had constructed generations ago.

When Babette and Betty, along with everyone in the group alighted from the aircraft, they were surprised to see a modern airport at the end of the runway. However, beyond the airport lay an ancient world where camels, donkeys and dray carts seemed to have stepped out of one's story book.

Almost instinctively, the women in the group pulled their scarves over their heads before walking the distance separating them from the couple of government SUVs waiting for them.

The doctors and their vaccine cases were soon to find themselves surrounded by several soldiers holding machine guns. Since Al-Qaeda's invasion of the city three years previously, the government had sent reinforcement troops to guard the city from these unwelcomed visitors. This was to be the first and only delivery of vaccines in this remote part of the Sahel. Because of its remoteness from populated and infected areas along the west coast, there had not been any Ebola cases reported thus far in the city. However, due to the influx of travelers and pilgrims crossing the Sahel during the approaching Ramadan, the government had decided that precautionary measures were indeed needed.

As they came to the door of the city, Babette remembered what the Keur-Moussa abbot had said, *"You will find the place very retiring."* He was right. She felt that strange sense of detachment and peace she had felt when she traveled with Samir on the camel's back. Although, and once again, the heat was incredibly intense, the freshness of the air was unmistakable. Babette felt that if she could store all that clean air in her lungs, she would live to be a hundred.

The group was to gather in a "hotel" after the WHO team dropped off the vaccines at the local clinic. As rudimentary as the medical building was, the equipment was rather modern and more than adequate. The people living in secluded Timbuktu were generally unaffected by the diseases found in the larger centers.

"Do you realize how long it has been since I wanted to see this?" Betty asked Babette.

"Probably since the first time you learned of the city's existence."

"Exactly. At first, I didn't think this place really existed, but when I began researching my nephew's antecedents, I realized that my "dream place" was actually real."

"Do you think Leon Summerville ever knew you existed," Babette said. "I know, it's not really my place to ask, but I was wondering if his adoptive parents, the ones who took him out of Africa, ever talked to him about his mother or his biological family."

"I truly don't know, Babette. But you said something that's quite interesting to me. You talked about Leon Summerville as if he was, in fact, my nephew. We don't know that yet, do we?"

"No, you're right, we don't know. Yet, judging from your reaction, starting with the very first day you two set eyes on each other, there must be a filial connection between the two of you. You two are definitely in the same vortex."

"You really think so?"

"Yes I do, Betty, and you do too. But I think you're afraid to admit it even to yourself. He's not a boy; he is a middle-aged man with a past, which has never included you, or his mother. He will have a hard time reconciling the fact that someone in his family has looked for him for all these years and that his mother abandoned him when he was just an infant."

"I know what you're saying, Babette. And you're probably right.

That's another reason why I would like to get a DNA screen to make a comparison between our two blood samples." Betty shook her head. "But how do you tell a man that his aunt has never had the guts to try finding him until her own husband was dead and buried. How do you explain my cowardice?"

"Perhaps you're punishing yourself for nothing. You're definitely not looking at this problem in the right light, Betty…"

"I am sorry to interrupt, ladies, but we have arrived," the chauffeur said, parking the SUV in front of the gigantic mosque's feudal walls surrounding it. As they stepped out, Betty and Babette wondered how many travelers had stood in awe before this strange "sandcastle." It was enormous.

"Somehow, I had imagined it to be much smaller than this," Betty remarked. "This is indeed an imposing building. And I can see why people would call it a sandcastle. It looks exactly like the ones I built when I was a kid."

When all the SUVs arrived on site, Leon and Linda walked toward Betty.

"Isn't this something else?" Leon said. "Quite an incredible mosque, don't you think?"

"Oh yes, that it is, Mr. Summerville," Betty answered. "It's too bad we can't visit it."

"From what I've heard, when Al-Qaeda was here, they did a lot of damage inside of it and even disturbed or vandalized some of the mausoleums and Mufti tombs."

"Why would Al-Qaeda destroy a mosque?" Linda asked. "Aren't they Muslims?"

"Oh yes they are, ma'am," an old man replied in very good English as he walked toward the little group, "but you see, all Muslims are not the same. Al-Qaeda and its followers are Islamic radicals. They are sectarians. When they were here, our women could not even carry out their duties as usual or be dressed as they did traditionally. They had to wear a hijab and hide from the public view of males."

"I guess order has been restored, has it?" Babette asked.

"Yes, ma'am, in a way it has." He smiled. "My name is Ishmael Mamadou. I will be your guide while the doctors do their duty at the clinic." He paused and returned his gaze to Babette. "Actually, it is more a question of freedom than it is of order. You see, in Timbuktu, you are welcome to go on bended knee or prostrate yourself in front of your God the way you were raised.　Islam, at its origin, was welcoming of all men. Since its inception, however, there has been a lot of dissention among its believers – some more strict than others, and some very violent."

"That is not a trait singular to Islam," Leon said. "There are many sects born from and within Christianity, some of which are 180 degrees from the general population in their strict practices."

"That's right," Babette agreed. "Many of the original Christians were of the same heart until the crusades, I believe."

Ishmael smiled benignly. "Yes, yes. But you are not here for a religious discourse I think." He began walking in the direction of the outdoor market that seemed to have popped up out of nowhere on the side of the mosque. "Let's have a look at what the artisans have made for your group."

Ah-ah, Babette thought, *our Ishmael is probably getting a commission on the sales of Timbuktu souvenirs.*

Perhaps this was true; nevertheless, the visitors were agreeably surprised by the wood carvings and the exquisite replicas of some of the mosque's doors. The doors in question are centuries' old. They are apparently the only "solid" part of the whole edifice. Although, there was no water to be seen for miles around, most of the market stalls surrounded a lonely tree at the corner of the mosque. It was a testament that its roots had found water below the surface.

For some reason, Babette seemed reluctant to buy anything. She felt as if taking anything from this place was not appropriate. She wanted everything to remain the way it was. Even the leather pouches and sacs the artisans were selling were tempting, but she resisted buying anything.

CHAPTER TWENTY-THREE

The sorcerer

AS SOON AS THE GROUP RETURNED to Dakar and to *The Contessa*, they were greeted by Gilbert Evans, the newly appointed chief of security, a couple pursers and a tall fellow dressed with what looked like white pajamas. Tiffany was standing beside the imposing black man. He was wearing some kind of bandana around his head and was swatting the absent flies and mosquitoes from his shoulders with what resembled a feather duster. Alan had to use all of his power of restraint not to explode in rude laughter. This was too much of a sight! Imagine you're coming home and your wife (girlfriend) is standing beside a tall, handsome, but curiously dressed fellow.

"This is Abdulaye Charrod," Tiffany said by way of introduction, as soon as the WHO team had vacated the foyer.

Alan dropped his bag by his side and extended a hand for the man to shake, which he did. The smile that came with the handshake framed a beautiful set of white teeth. "Very nice meeting you, Mr. Charrod," Alan said. "Why don't we have a seat in the salon," he added, pointing to a sofa and chairs against the far wall and grabbing his medical bag.

"I'm sorry, Dr. Mayhew," Gilbert interrupted, appearing suddenly from behind the giant man, "May I have a word, please."

"Sure, Gilbert, what is it," Alan answered, leaving Tiffany to guide their strange guest to the seats.

"This Charrod fellow says he is a sorcerer…"

"Really? How interesting. Did he say why he's here?"

Gilbert shook his head. "Didn't say really, except that he wanted to talk to you about the disease."

"Okay then, I guess that's what I'll do."

When Alan rejoined Tiffany and Mr. Charrod, it seemed the two of them hadn't spoken a word since he went to talk to Gilbert. "Now, Mr. Charrod, what brings you to our ship?"

"No-no, Doctor. I did not want to come to the ship; I only wanted to leave a message with your officer for you and Miss Sylvan here to come to me."

"Is that so?" Alan sounded incredulous. "And why would you want me to visit you? Is a member of your family sick perhaps?"

"No, Doctor, you are!"

"Truly, Mr. Charrod, I do not understand...."

"There is nothing I can tell you now. Come to my place, where the spirit inhabiting my house can talk to you and Miss Sylvan in peace."

"And where is your place?" Tiffany asked.

"In town, Sister." Although Tiffany was slightly surprised by the man calling her "sister," she didn't correct him.

The latter smiled and returned to beating his shoulder with his fly-swatter, which gesture brought another grin to Alan's lips.

"I will only talk when I am in my house," the man said suddenly, getting to his feet. "As I said, I will need to consult the spirits while we talk." He then took a business card from his trousers' pocket and handed it to Alan. "Both of you can come after eight o'clock tonight and I will talk to you then."

As he got to his feet Alan thanked the man for the visit and accompanied him to the gangway.

When he returned to the foyer, he sat down by Tiffany again. "When did he come in?" he asked.

"This afternoon; about a half-an-hour before you came back. It was strange actually. He knew you were on your way back from the airport. Did you see anyone at the airport – I mean anyone looking like him?"

"No, I didn't. But to tell you the truth, Tiff, this airport is quite busy. It's like people are waiting for a plane to land even when none are scheduled to do so." He paused to look at Mr. Charrod's card. "Do you want to come with me tonight?"

"What a silly question? Of course I'll go with you. But I think we should take Simon and a couple of his guys with us. You never know; it may be an ambush of some sort…"

"That's exactly why I don't think it's a good idea for you to come with me."

"On the one hand, I think it will be prudent for me to stay here, but on the other, I don't want to offend a sorcerer," Tiffany said, a broad grin appearing on her lips, "You never know what spell he could cast on me, now do we?"

"I rather think the man is hiding something and he wants to unburden his secret to us while we're at his place."

"What about the virus? Do you think someone in his family is sick and he's come to ask for help?"

"Maybe. He certainly looks like a man too proud to admit he does not have the power to cure a patient suffering from Ebola."

"Okay then," Tiffany said, rising from her seat. "I'll ask Constantine to open the cabaret–casino night with a few intros and I'll get ready to accompany you."

"Yes, and while you do that, I'll call Simon and ask Gilbert to come with us."

For her part, while all this was going on in the foyer, Babette and Betty had returned to their suites. Babette was truly tired. This cruise had been very taxing somehow. During previous voyages, there was ample time to rest between ports and ample time to visit a place of interest without having to rush between airports, airplanes, SUVs, monastery, mosques and markets.

As she plopped down on the sofa, Edmund made his appearance in the seat across from her. "Glad to see you've made it back to the ship in one piece, milady."

"Just about, just about, Edmund. One more SUV ride, one more mosque, one more camel ride and one more market might have been the death of me. I am ready for bed. I don't even care to eat right now."

"Gracious Lord," Edmund exclaimed, "you must really be tired then. Refusing a few oysters and a glass of champagne for dinner is certainly not like you."

"Did I hear you say champagne and oysters?"

"Yes, dear lady, champagne and oysters was what I had in mind for you tonight – to welcome you home sort of thing."

Babette had to smile. "That sounds absolutely divine, Edmund. I guess I don't have to eat right away; I can have a little nap and then order that delightful dinner." She paused and sat up. "But before I do all that, tell me how is our jeweler, Mr. Atkinson?"

"Oh, he's a busy little fellow. Every day since we're been in port, he's taken a taxi outside of the port facility and gone to visit people he seemed to know in town."

Babette opened her eyes wide. "Do you mean you've been able to follow him?"

"Of course I did. As you will surely remember, I have been able to follow you on several of your town visits in other ports."

"Yes, yes. That's right. Anyway, were you able to listen to his conversations?"

"Yes. Actually, most of the visits he made were to European people who worked at the mine back east, or jewelers who were buying stones from South African countries. He sounded interested on reopening talks – his words, not mine – with stone exporters. There was no mention of diamonds, though. I think he's got all the connections he wants or needs in that regard."

"Well, that sounds like he was working rather than enjoying the sights, doesn't it?" Babette remarked.

"Yes. I would believe he's been here before and even lived here, judging from the way he talked about the place."

"That's good to know." Babette got up. "As long as he's in good health and staying active, it won't hurt him to keep busy." Walking to her bedroom, she added, "I'll see you in an hour or so. But for now, it's cat-nap time for this lady."

As they crossed the treed boulevard, Alan, Tiffany, Gilbert and Simon wondered what the next hour had in store for them. Alan checked the address on the business card once again and looked up at the building. The front entrance was barred by a large porte-cochere. Gilbert looked on the side of it. There was a single doorbell affixed to the wall. He pressed it.

A moment later, a small man rushed to open the door for the guests. He didn't say anything but stretched an arm toward the inside courtyard.

If Alan and his companions were expecting to be taken upstairs to an apartment, they were mistaken. A white tent stood in the middle of the courtyard, large enough to host ten people easily. Their shoes resounding on the cobble stones, Charrod must have heard their approach for he came out of the tent to meet them.

"Come in, come in," he said to the four companions. "I am sorry for the modest accommodation, but my habitation would be really too small to host all of you."

As they entered the tent, they saw that the floor was covered with several mattresses and cushions. There was a lantern hanging on the side of the center post. The notable thing about the décor was that all the linen was white. Charrod, dressed in his white pajamas, practically melted in the décor when he sat down. He then invited everyone to gather around him. They did as bidden.

"Thank you for coming, Doctor. I did not expect you to bring friends with you, but I understand caution. I have to adopt prudence as a companion often myself."

"I'm sorry, Mr. Charrod," Alan said, "but could you satisfy my curiosity. Why have you asked us to visit you here, in town?"

"Because, Doctor, you have been endowed with power to

accomplish a great healing mission..."

"But I'm not alone..."

Charrod lifted a hand. "Please, Doctor, let me give you the explanation you seek." He paused for a few seconds. "As I was saying you have a healing mission on this continent. Everyone in Africa knows that you and your companions are here to help. But I am here to help you!"

"And how do you propose to do that?" Alan asked.

"I think chastity is the best course of action." Alan was about to smile, but refrained from doing so.

"Who's to be chaste?" Tiffany ventured to ask. Beside her, Simon and Gilbert were about to erupt in laughter, but knew it would be unwise to do so.

"You are, my dear," came the reply.

"But how or why will chastity help me or Ms. Sylvan?"

"Your mind is occupied by her beauty; therefore it impairs your work, Doctor. If you were to stay out of her reach, you would accomplish your task much better." He stopped talking and fetched something that resembled a heavy, black chaplet out of his pajama's pocket. He handed it to Alan. "Since it may be difficult to stay away from your lady friend, let me give you this gri-gri. If you wear it around your neck, you will be protected in your work and life while you travel through Africa."

Alan didn't want to refuse the gift. He put the gri-gri around his neck and smiled to Tiffany. After giving a white gri-gri to Tiffany with the same recommendation, the four guests left the tent. To say they were all puzzled would have been an understatement. The four of them had no words. They were baffled. The little man accompanied them back to the porte-cochere. But before opening it he extended an open palm to Alan. "Baksheesh," he said, meaning "tip." Of course he wanted some money for his master and himself probably. Alan handed him a five dollar bill. His eyes lit up and his smile told it all.

A little after ten o'clock, Constantine opened the cabaret-casino night with a welcome round of applause. As he grabbed the microphone, he looked around the room. "Is anyone here personally acquainted with Hillary Clinton?" A wave of titters, giggles and chuckles was the only response he obtained. "Alright. But if I hear from *my people* that *her people* are displeased I'll know where to look for the guilty party." He let the chuckles die down. "So, as you gathered we're going to talk about Hillary's departure. She passed away last week from an overdose of diet pills..." The laughter stopped him. He smiled and then resumed, "Hillary Clinton died and went to heaven. As she stood in front of Saint Peter at the Pearly Gates, she saw a huge wall of clocks behind him. She asked, "What are all those clocks?" Saint Peter answered, "Those are Lie-Clocks. Everyone on Earth has a Lie-Clock. Every time you lie, the hands on your clock will move. "Oh," said Hillary, "whose clock is that?" "That's Mother Teresa's. The hands have never moved, indicating that she never told a lie." "Whose clock is that?" "That's Abraham Lincoln's clock. The hands have only moved twice, telling us that Abe only told two lies in his entire life." "Where's Bill's clock?" Hillary asked. "Bill's clock is in Jesus' office. He's using it as a ceiling fan."

When the laughter finally died down, Constantine said, "Thank you so much, Ladies and Gentlemen. And to show you my gratitude I think it's a good time as any to talk about cold places – to cool us off a little." He paused to look around the tables. "Anybody here has gone ice-fishing up north?" No one put their hand up. "Well let me tell you what happened to my friend then. He was a little bit over the limit, if you know what I mean. And since we live in Boston, you can go ice-fishing in a few places outside the city. So, my buddy did on that particular night. He packs up all his tackle and sets out in search of a suitable spot. Eventually, he stumbles across a huge area of ice and decides that he'll give it a go. Taking out a saw from his tackle box, he starts to saw a hole in the ice. Suddenly, a loud voice booms out at him, "There's no fish in here." My buddy looks all around him but can't see anyone. He decides to ignore the voice and carries on sawing. Again, the voice booms out, "I've told you once, there's no fish in here!" He looks up again but there's still no sign of anyone, so he returns to his task. "Stop it!" shouts the now very angry sounding voice, "You'd better pack up your stuff and get out of here or there'll be trouble." "Who are you?" shouts my buddy, "you don't scare me!" "Look," replies the voice, "I'm the manager of this Ice Rink!" When Constantine bowed to leave, the laughter and applause accompanied him all the way to the back of the cabaret-casino.

CHAPTER TWENTY-FOUR

Conakry

WHEN TIFFANY AND ALAN RETURNED to the ship, their two companions could not stop laughing, chuckling while trying to keep a straight face.

"Really, Alan? Are you two going to use the chaplets?" Simon asked, disbelief written all over his face.

"What do you think?" Tiffany answered for Alan. "It's our duty, isn't it?"

"What do you mean *it's our duty*?" Gilbert queried. "Simon and I haven't been asked to wear a chastity chaplet around our necks, have we?"

"I think I'll save it and wear it when we get to our next port of call," Alan told them."

"And the rest is history for us to record," Tiffany quipped. "We're not going to kiss and tell."

"And you two are not to say a word about this to anyone, understood?" Alan ordered.

"Aye, aye, sir," Simon replied in jest.

"I'm mute as a tomb," Gilbert rejoined before the two men exploded in renewed laughter.

As soon as the gangway was lowered in the port of Conakry and the customs' officers were ready to meet the passengers in the port facility, Mr. Atkinson made his way down the stairs. One person was certainly surprised at his hurry to disembark from the ship. The man didn't want to follow the jeweler immediately and make his presence obvious. He wanted to remain as inconspicuous as possible until it was time to strike. So, he waited for a few minutes and made his way down the gangway with Adele Muesli and Gregory Ashton. The man had noted that Mrs. Palmer's companions were often visiting the ports-of-call in the absence of their employer. He also noticed that Adele was in the habit of carrying a voluminous bag wherever she went. Both notations were well anchored in the man's memory and would remain there until they would come to be useful in carrying out his ultimate plan.

If riches could be had from the gold dust covering the hills of Sabodala, in Guinea the "dunes" of bauxite near the port of Conakry resealed its prosperity for years before the republic's declaration of independence. The red *terrils* of bauxite, as they are called in French, were a reminder of what the people of Guinea had fought for in years past.

A man by the name of Sékou Touré had ruled Guinea for the best part of twenty-five years. He had sold his country and his soul to the USSR. The many children who attended school in the nineteen-sixties and seventies were taught by Russian or Eastern European teachers. The official language was French, as it had been since the days of colonization. Sékou Touré was known for two things: his tyranny and his philandering. The man loved women. He thought that his position allowed him to call upon any woman he desired to spend the night with him. His mistresses were of many colors and shapes. He chose them at random until he fell ill and died in the mid-eighties.

In regards to the man's tyranny, perhaps visitors couldn't readily recognize it. The gold jewelry that adorned the ladies' bosoms, wrists, ankles and the rings on their fingers or earlobes somehow attested to the capitalistic traits Sékou Touré wanted to display to anyone visiting his country. He was called a tyrant by his enemies and a benefactor by his supporters. The USSR tried to convert the man to communism – he refused. He didn't like the equality it implied. He hated to be considered second fiddle to a powerful nation. He wanted Guinea to become a power to be reckoned with. Of course he couldn't do it alone. And his so-called supporters were thieves waiting for his demise or his faltering in the meantime.

For all the bad things that Guinea displayed during Sékou Touré's reign, there was one thing that always amazed not only the neighboring countries but also his Islamic brothers – the power he bestowed upon the women of his country. There were guilds, committees, unions comprised solely of women. They were revered and had a place in society much to dismay of the Islamist radicals that were roaming the country during an era when terrorism wasn't yet part of the Westerners vocabulary.

However, there were distinctions made between men and women in many instances. Boys were educated in lyceums, which offered a range of disciplines from literature to sciences and engineering, whereas women had to go to secretarial or commercial colleges. There, they learned to commercialize the goods they would make at home or in artisans' classes. Some, of course, would excel in their chosen trade and would end up owning a fair share of the goods markets throughout the country. As for the secretaries, they learned to infiltrate the men's domains and become a forceful voice behind those in power.

But, this was the past. Today the country suffered from chronic poverty. The schools, which were once the pride of the city and the country were closed decades ago and also the hostelries shut their doors long ago. Only a few clusters of French communities have re-installed themselves in the once "elegant" parts of the city. These beautiful old mansions and commercial establishments were ex-pat establishments, which catered mainly to Europeans or to the richer commercial travelers who navigated their way along the West African Coasts.

The Hotel de France was one such establishment. Mr. Atkinson was due to meet someone in the lobby as soon as he disembarked. He carried a briefcase and was probably looking forward to making arrangements with this person to buy some of the more valuable stones dredged out of the Baoule River in the southeastern hills of the country.

Entire communities of "private prospectors" living in the Upper Region of Guinea had dredged diamonds. There, they had found some of the most precious stones on earth. These were generally not large or brilliant diamonds, such as the ones you find in Botswana or in South Africa but they were rare because of their colorings. A five-carat tiger diamond could be worth nearly five million dollars to the collector. And Mr. Atkinson was such a collector.

He wanted to buy a treasure to replace the one he was about to give back to Sierra Leone. The Star of Sierra Leone had been his doom since the day he bought it. But now that his outlook on life had changed for the better, he wanted to get a 'rose diamond' or another of the more expensive stones found along the Baoule River.

Yet, "found" is the wrong word to describe how these stones had originally been dredged. The young boys, sons of prospectors, would dig a "rabbit warren" of tunnels along the river and bring up handfuls of stones. Not all the stones were precious diamonds, but could feed their families for months. Unfortunately, the Baoule property had been developed at the cost of many lives – ex-pats had died in a community uprising in the mid-1980s. AREDOR was today the owner of the dredging facility. The peculiarity about this company was that they didn't have to pass through De Beers' sanctioning approval of sales in Switzerland to distribute their diamonds. They were 'freelancers' as it were. This was another attractive aspect about Atkinson's prospective purchase. He could do it directly with the AREDOR owners without going through De Beers' taxing vultures.

When he arrived at the Hotel de France, Atkinson made his way to the reception desk and asked for Mr. Huffner. Mr. Huffner's father had paved the way for AREDOR's initial success in Guinea. An Australian by birth, Huffner had been instrumental in the original deal that had been struck between his company and President Sékou

Touré.

When the two men shook hands, Atkinson immediately recognized a fellow merchant in his interlocutor.

They went to the restaurant to have some refreshments and began their trade discussions under the watchful gaze of Atkinson's fellow passenger.

When the WHO team, accompanied by Alan and Olga, disembarked that morning, they were met by a team of doctors at the door of the port facility. The team was surprised at the number of "physicians" waiting for them.

"They're not all MDs," Ashford murmured in Alan's ear. "They wear a lab coat and gloves so that the customs' officers will let them stay by the door."

"Do we know who we're supposed to meet over here though?" Alan asked.

"Oh yes-yes. Hatfield will soon sort that out."

"And we've got another trip up-country to make, I gather?"

"Hum yes," Ashford replied. "Well, we'll see what's really needed when we talk to the health authorities in town."

"You mean there might be a safety concern involved?"

"Exactly. This is a very volatile region. With the diamond dredging compound on the one side of the border and the gold production smelter on the other side – in Sabodala – you've got the perfect pot-of-gold target for ISIS radicals to come and steal whatever they find to pay for their crimes."

A sobering thought indeed.

Alan and Ashford remained silent for the rest of the trip to the general hospital.

There, they found misery and dilapidation. People were dying in the corridors; screaming patients were on their last breaths; doctors and nurses were trying to ease the pain of those who were ready to pass: all of which were memories to be anchored in Alan and Olga's minds forever.

As soon as the team had donned their protective suits, they began to work. Hour after hour, they inoculated numbers of patients, isolated some others, and began cleaning the wards of any remnants of the infection. It was a labor of love for Alan. He now truly understood the extent of the epidemic. What he and the team had witnessed to date was nothing in comparison to what they had seen that morning. The helplessness he felt was incomparable. Yes, he had vials upon vials of vaccines in the cases, all of them capable of saving numerous lives, but what about those he could not save because they were too far along in their disease?

The Western Governments were not here to see what their research grants had *not* done. They had been dedicated to popular diseases and popular gimmicks, while the rest of the world was dying.

Harping on such a subject was not useful. What was useful, however, was the matter of being able to ensure that such a catastrophe didn't happen again.

In the old days, leprosy and tuberculosis as well as small pox and cholera had devastated entire city populations, and today Ebola had done the same in Africa. Yet, there was hope today. A vaccine was now available and distributed as fast as possible.

Meanwhile, Mr. Atkinson was very much engaged in his conversation with Mr. Huffner.

"Would you like to see for yourself where the stones you will buy come from?" Huffner invited.

"Of course, of course, but, you see, Mr. Huffner, it's not as simple as that. I believe we're only in Conakry for a couple of days and I don't have transportation to the dredging site."

"Don't you worry about that, Mr. Atkinson, I'll have our field chopper pick you up in the morning and bring you back before nightfall."

"But I thought AREDOR's facility was some six hundred miles inland – isn't it?"

"Oh, yes, yes, of course, but we're working downstream now. We should be able to get there in two hours at most."

"Well, yes." Atkinson was nothing if not cautious. "Let me call you from the ship," he told Huffner, "to confirm the time and place where you will pick me up."

"Alright then, mate," Huffner replied jovially, getting to his feet. "I'll wait for your call."

The man, who had followed Mr. Atkinson from the ship to the hotel, retraced his steps to *The Contessa* an hour later. He had heard every word of the two men's conversation thanks to a small listening device he had planted in Atkinson's coat pocket while they went through customs. As soon as the two men climbed the gangway, the man hurried past Mr. Atkinson, bumped into him and recovered his device.

That poor devil doesn't know what he's getting into with Huffner, he mumbled to himself as he went up to his cabin.

CHAPTER TWENTY-FIVE

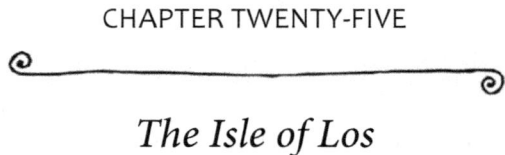

The Isle of Los

THERE ARE PROBABLY VERY FEW THINGS more appealing in life than watching ocean waves roll slowly onto a white sandy beach. Yet, and in this instance, there was nothing appealing or calming about the rolling wave of the Isle of Los. This enormous wave does not respond to a tidal schedule. It does not abate. It does not stop rolling. It is enormous. Measuring over twenty feet at its peak, it slams tons of water onto the small beach facing it. Nobody has yet been able to explain the phenomenon of the Isle of Los to its visitors. The roar of the furious wave can be heard all the way to the other side of the island. The passengers disembarked from the ferry, looking forward to seeing and even filming "the wrath of God" in action. There was nothing to say or describe along the way to the Atlantic coastal beach facing the wave. The rocky terrain was not easy to manage, but everyone felt as if they "needed" to see "the unexplained". Curiosity kills the cat they say; in this instance, it would certainly kill you to try surfing that wave. The only redeeming factor was that if you were to plunge into the mouth of the wave, it would automatically throw you back onto the beach. Even if you didn't know how to swim, it wouldn't matter; you would find yourself back on land, sand-scraped, but quite okay as you opened your eyes to the blasting sun overhead.

As the passengers arrived on the ledge overlooking the wave, they stopped looking at their feet and raised their gazes to the wonder of God. It was the perfect spot for what Babette wanted to do that morning. The day before, she had approached a few of the people she knew were Christians or in need of a prayer perhaps. On larger ships there are services held in the chapel every week, or there is a Chaplin aboard, who will perform a service from time to time. In the case of *The Contessa,* although there was a small chapel at the stern of the vessel, a Chaplin was only due to join the cruise in Sierra Leone, the worst affected part of Africa. In the other parts of the West Coast, many clerics accompanied the WHO team and doctors as soon as they disembarked.

Out of her capacious bag, Babette took out a dozen candles and handed one to each of the participants to this impromptu devotional. Although the din emanating from the rolling wave seemed to eclipse her words, all attending heard her clearly. As she lit a candle, so did the others in the group. She then said, "This candle is for the people who obviously have passed on the Isle of Los. As a match touches a wick, a light is born, and in the same manner, may we renew the light of God which is within each of us. As this candle glows, may our words of reverence and love arise and glow with warmth and love forevermore."

There were no residents on the island. Although there was a ferry that traveled regularly between all of the islands bordering the coast of Guinea and that of Guinea Bissau, the Isle of Los was not hospitable. There was no fresh water stream traversing the island and no well had ever been dug to find the water at depth. The rocky terrain made it quite difficult to cultivate the soil or even to walk. However, when Alan and Gilbert arrived on the island, they were interested to see that a few children were playing near an old ship wreck beached on the southern side of the island. Where there are children, there are generally parents. Sure enough, as the two men approached the rusted vessel, they saw a couple of women hanging clothes on the ship's railing. Where there is washing, there must be a family nearby.

"Hello there," Alan said when he saw a young fellow come out of the water and walk toward him. "Are you living on the ship?" he asked him in French.

The young fellow nodded as his siblings came to join him. They looked as if they had not eaten in days (or weeks even).

"Yes, Officer," he replied now. "My family cannot go back to Conakry. Everybody is dead."

"Have you got some food on the island?" Alan asked.

"We get food from the cooks on the ferries," he said. "I am called Mamoud, and you?" he looked at Gilbert.

"I am Gilbert, Mamoud, and this is Doctor Mayhew," the chief of security said in broken French.

As soon as he heard the word "doctor", Mamoud's eyes lit up. "You come to cure us?" he asked Alan.

"Is someone sick here?" Alan was quick to ask, fearing the worst.

"No-no, Doctor. Everybody is fine here. We came here soon after my aunt and grandfather died. Dad said we have to leave before the Evil Hand catches us. *La Main du Diable– so, that's what they called Ebola,* Alan thought.

"Well, if you are here tomorrow, I will come back with a vaccine to inoculate your family, so that you can go home afterward."

Until then Mamoud's siblings hadn't pronounced a word, but when they heard Alan say that they might be able to go home, they went to grab him and Gilbert and dragged them to the steps leading to the deck of the old vessel. Their joyous screams alerted their parents. A man appeared on the top step. He asked his children who the two men were.

Once they were introduced, Alan and Gilbert made their way up to the deck. The ship seemed to have been a pre-world-war vessel, probably a cargo ship by the looks of things.

The man, Hassan Tamara asked if what Mamoud was saying was true. "You are coming back tomorrow with vaccine?"

"Yes, sir. I will come back to vaccinate your family so that you can go home. But I don't know what we can do about food. There's really nothing left in town."

"I know, I know," said Hassan, "but we have friends in the country. They have a farm and if they are okay, maybe they have rice and eggs. Maybe vegetables too. We should be okay."

"Are they close to a village?" Gilbert asked.

"Yes. They live in Forecariah. It's not too far. We can walk there. Or go by taxi…"

"Maybe we can do better than that," Alan said. "I will not make any promises at this point, but I will tell you tomorrow when I come back, okay?"

A broad smile illuminated the man's face now. "Yes, yes. That is nice, Doctor," he said. "We will wait for you."

When the passengers returned to the ship, Edmund was anxious to see Babette come back. He had news for her.

"Alright, alright, Edmund, what is it? Did you find out something about our friend, Mr. Atkinson?"

"Yes, milady," the ghostly figure replied as Babette plopped down on the sofa of her suite. "He left the ship early and went to meet a man at the Hotel de France…"

"Did he now?" Babette cut in, massaging her sore feet.

"Yes, but that's not the interesting part…"

"What is then?" Babette interrupted him again.

Edmund stayed mute. Babette looked up at him. "Well?"

"Milady, if I may be permitted to finish my story before you start asking questions, I think that would be much better."

"Alright then, Doctor, go ahead," Babette said, crossing her arms over her chest now.

"As I was saying, the interesting detail is that a man followed Mr. Atkinson from the ship to the hotel. And the same man followed him back to the ship. His name is Agent Daniel Crosby of Interpol."

Babette raised both eyebrows and mumbled almost inaudibly, "And what would an Interpol agent be doing with our New York jeweler, I wonder."

"Exactly, milady. I wondered the same when he showed his badge to the customs' officer at the port facility. So, I followed him to his cabin, number 304 by the way, and watched him send a report to his office. Apparently, Interpol is not watching our Mr. Atkinson per se, but they're more interested in the latest goings on at the dredging facility in southeastern Guinea. The Mr. Huffner who met with Mr. Atkinson at the hotel is a "person of interest" it seems. I gather that Interpol or another agency is suspecting the man of selling diamonds from the dredge and pocketing the money. Perhaps the property owners have found out something about the man and have alerted Interpol."

"And how is Mr. Atkinson involved do you think?" Babette asked since it seemed that Edmund had come to the end of his recital.

"I believe our New York jeweler is intending to buy some rare diamonds from Mr. Huffner. But I don't think he knows that Huffner is suspected of fraud at this point."

"And our Mr. Atkinson is not seeing what's in front of his nose; is that what you're saying?"

"Exactly, milady. Let's say Huffner is not interested in Atkinson's money, but in his diamond – the Star of Sierra Leone – he could kidnap the man and demand to get the Star in ransom for the jeweler's life. What do you think?"

"Yes, Edmund, I think you're right. I think we need to protect the little man against the very devil that occupies his mind constantly."

"What do you mean?" Edmund asked, somewhat curious.

"I mean that, when it comes to diamonds, our Mr. Atkinson is totally blind to the snares that may be laid before him. He loves these little stones. He couldn't care less about anything else. Every minute of his life is devoted to the acquisition and sale of the most precious stones on earth. He is not here to appreciate the beauty of the continent, or even the devastation a disease has had on its population; no, he's only here to buy more precious stones. He wants to replace the one he will give back."

"And he doesn't realize that all of his woes and troubles have not been caused by his ownership of the Star, but by putting all of his enjoyment in life in the possession of diamonds. Is that what you think?"

"Yes, Edmund. I can't help but think that our Mr. Atkinson is heading for trouble. He's the type of man who will cross the street thinking that every car will stop for him, or not even thinking at all."

Since the afternoon was coming to an end, the two gentlemen decided to have a game of golf on the upper deck. Of course, the links were only a holographic representation of some fabulous golf course or other. They hadn't wanted to visit Conakry since they had been told the devastation throughout the old city was far from worth a visit. They were in the middle of their game when Steve, one of the two guys, erupted in laughter when he saw his friend Bert doing a small shuffle in front of the golf ball perched on its tee.

"What's the matter?" Bert asked, "Did I do something funny?"

"No, not you," Steve said, "but you doing the shuffle in front of your tee reminded me of something that happened to a friend of mind."

"What's that?" Bert asked, straightening up to listen to Steve's story.

"Well, picture this: Gaston, a married man and his secretary were having a torrid affair. One afternoon they couldn't contain their passion, so they rushed over to her place where they spent the afternoon making passionate love. When they were finished, they fell asleep, not waking until eight o'clock. They got dressed quickly. Then the man told his secretary to take his shoes outside and rub them on the lawn. Bewildered, she did as he asked thinking him pretty weird. The man finally got home and his wife met him at the door. Upset, she asked where he'd been. The man replied, "I cannot tell a lie. My secretary and I are having an affair. Today we left work early, went to her place, spent the afternoon making love, and then fell asleep. That's why I'm late."

The wife looked at him, took notice of his shoes and yelled, "I can see those are grass stains on your shoes. YOU DAMN LIAR! You've been playing golf again, haven't you?"

CHAPTER TWENTY-SIX

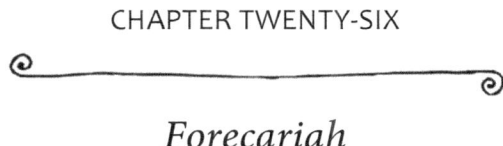

Forecariah

AS SOON AS ALAN AND GILBERT came back to the ship, they went to find Drs. Ashford and Hatfield. They invited them to have a drink at the bar upstairs and soon began relating Hassan Tamara's story to the doctors.

"We know Forecariah, Doctor Mayhew," Ashford was quick to say. He looked at Hatfield. The latter nodded. "I don't think there's any need for us to visit the Isle of Los, but when you're ready to come back, I think we should wait for you at the ferry terminal to take the Tamara family with us to Forecariah."

"Yes," Hatfield rejoined. "We have to travel through the city anyway when we go up country."

"Are you going to fly to the mountains?" Gilbert asked.

"I think we'll go as far as Kissidougou by road and then we'll take one of the dredging plant's choppers to go and visit the adjacent villages and dredging teams."

"You're sure to be back before we sail, though?" Gilbert asked.

"Oh absolutely, Mr. Evans. We don't intend to do any sightseeing," Hatfield added, chuckling lightly.

As they were about to change the topic of conversation, Gilbert noticed that someone was listening to them. He wondered who the guy might be.

He didn't have to wait very long, for the fellow got up from his table and came to join the four men. He stood beside the table and introduced himself.

"I'm sorry to interrupt, gentlemen," he said, "My name is Andrew Crosby from Interpol." He opened his wallet containing his identification and insignia, before replacing it quickly in his jacket pocket. "I was eavesdropping and heard you mention that you were planning to use the AREDOR chopper tomorrow; is that right?"

"Yes, Agent Crosby, that's the doctors' plan," Gilbert answered, getting to his feet and pulling a chair for the man to sit beside him. "Is there something wrong with that?"

"No, there's nothing wrong with the planning, but the execution of that plan might be a problem."

"Can you explain what you've just said," Alan asked as Andrew sat down.

"Yes, of course, Doctor. You see, we are suspecting some of AREDOR's men of defrauding the company by bribing the dredgers and then selling rare stones to the highest bidder. One of the buyers would be none other than Mr. Atkinson."

"When you say, "would be"," Gilbert asked, "is he buying or is he only window shopping?"

"Oh I think he intends to purchase a couple of very rare stones alright, but our seller and fraudster – a guy by the name of Huffner – has something else in mind for our New York jeweler."

"What would that be?" Ashford asked, a frown appearing across his brow.

"Kidnapping, Dr. Ashford."

"Did you say "kidnapping"?" Hatfield asked, obviously surprised.

"Oh yes, Doctor. You see, Mr. Atkinson has a stone worth millions in his possession. The price on his head – the ransom – will be for someone to bring the Star of Sierra Leone to Kissidougou where you're intending to board the chopper to the BaouleRiver.

"If everything goes according to plan, Mr. Atkinson should be released while the Star would disappear, never to be seen again."

"Have you alerted Atkinson of the danger?" Gilbert asked Andrew.

"Not as yet. I wanted to make sure first, that you, Doctors, were still planning to go up country tomorrow," Andrew said.

"But shouldn't we stop Mr. Atkinson before he agrees to go with this Huffner character?"

"Absolutely, Dr. Mayhew," Andrew replied. "And I can assure you, Mr. Atkinson is no fool. He's already told Huffner that he will "think about his offer" and contact him later."

"What if he's contacted him already?" Ashford asked Andrew, obviously getting worried.

"It doesn't matter whether he does or not; we will stop Mr. Atkinson from leaving the ship in the morning, if he does not agree with our plan," Andrew said.

"Won't Huffner smell a rat when Atkinson doesn't show?" Alan asked.

"That's exactly where I would like to ask for your help, Doctors."

Alan, Ashford and Hatfield exchanged a glance. "What could we possibly do?"

"Offer Atkinson a ride in your SUVs instead of him accepting a chopper ride with Huffner from Conakry to Kissidougou. This way we will be in control of the situation. Once we get to the village, we can catch Huffner red-handed, hopefully with stones in his pocket, and save Mr. Atkinson the ordeal of being kidnapped."

"But wouldn't Huffner find it suspicious, if Atkinson tells him that he's going with us rather than with him?"

"Whether he does or not, I don't think it will prevent him from trying to abduct Atkinson in Kissidougou. The stakes are too high, gentlemen. He needs to trap the jeweler whether here or up-country."

"Have you asked for the chopper to be available in Kissidougou already?" Alan asked Hatfield.

"Yes. Actually I sent a message to AREDOR this morning. I'm still waiting for an answer, though."

"And I believe," Andrew put in, "our Mr. Huffner is waiting for Atkinson's reply before he sends you an answer, Doctor."

"From everything that you've just explained, Agent Crosby, I think you're right," Gilbert agreed.

"Why don't we invite Mr. Atkinson to join us and explain the situation to him?" Alan suggested.

"That would be a way of settling the matter," Ashford said, looking around the table for his companions' approval.

"Maybe I should go and get him," Andrew said, getting up.

Gilbert pulled down on the sleeve of his jacket. "Let me go, Agent Crosby. He doesn't know you and you're not wearing a uniform. He might not want to go anywhere with you."

"Alright, Mr. Evans, I'll just come with you, if you don't mind."

"Suit yourself, Agent Crosby. Let's go then."

In the meantime, Constantine was rehearsing a few lines for this evening's performance. A real performance it was to be this time. Tiffany had organized a "Vaudeville Production" to be presented on stage with Babette's help. Tiffany had engaged a few of the kitchen hands – good singers they were – and a couple of guys from the spa and gymnasium to do some dances with the girls. It didn't have to be perfect, just a lot of fun, like "in the old days".

"Ready for the rehearsal, Ms. Babette?" Constantine shouted from the stage to the playwright who was sitting a few rows up from the orchestra section of the theater.

"Whenever you are, Mr. Constantine. Go ahead."

"I was in the bar after work when I heard a rather confident young man address a stunning woman sitting at the next table. He gave her a quick glance, and then casually looked at his watch for a moment. The woman noticed him and asked, "Is your date running late?"

"No," he replied, "I just bought this state-of-the-art watch and I was testing it."

"Intrigued, the woman said, "A state-of-the-art watch? What's so special about it?"

"It uses alpha waves to telepathically talk to me," he explained.

"What's it telling you now?" she asked. "Well, it says that you're not wearing any panties." The woman giggled and replied, "Well it must be broken then, because I am wearing panties!"

The man exclaimed, "Damn! This thing must be an hour fast"!"

Still laughing, Babette nodded to Constantine. "Okay; very good, Mr. Constantine. But now could you mix this with something lighter perhaps?"

"I've got just the thing, Ms. Babette…," Constantine said, stepping back from the edge of the stage. "But I think it would be good if I had a little boy to do this skit with me. Do you think that's possible?" he asked Babette.

"Sure, I don't see that as being a problem, but why don't I listen to the joke first?"

"Okay, Ms. Babette, no problem. Here it goes." Constantine then began: "I believe who's ever dressed a child will appreciate this. My boy's teacher was helping one of her pupils put on his boots. He had asked for help, and she could see why. Even with her pulling, and him pushing, the little boot still didn't want to go on his foot. By the time they got the second boot on, the teacher had worked up a sweat. She almost cried when the little boy said, "Sorry, Miss, they're on the wrong feet…" Babette, imagining the scene, broke into laughter right then. "Sure enough," Constantine went on, "they were! Unfortunately, it wasn't any easier pulling the boots off, than it was putting them on. She managed to keep her cool as, together they worked to get the boots back on, this time on the correct feet. He then announced, "These aren't my boots." She bit her tongue, rather than get right in his face and scream, "Why didn't you say so?" like she wanted to. Once again, she struggled to help him pull the ill-fitting boots off his little feet. No sooner had they got the boots off when he said, "They're my brother's boots but my Mom made me wear 'em today." Now she didn't know if she should laugh or cry. But she mustered up what grace and courage she had left to wrestle the boots BACK onto his feet again. Helping him into his coat, she asked, "Now, where are your mittens?" He said, "I stuffed 'em in the toes of my boots." She'll be eligible for parole in three years."

Babette had tears in her eyes from laughing when Constantine bowed to his imaginary audience.

"This is excellent, Mr. Constantine, excellent indeed. Given that many of our passengers have children and live above the forty-ninth parallel, I'm sure they'll appreciate this. And I don't think you need a child to act this skit with you. I would even prefer you to lead your audience the way you usually do. You do it so well, no need to change anything."

Several decks above the theater, Mr. Atkinson had come with Gilbert and Agent Crosby to join the doctors at their table.

As always, a bit leery of strangers, the jeweler sat beside Alan and smiled at everyone in turn as they were introduced.

"Mr. Evans tells me that you fellows have some qualms, shall we say," Atkinson began, "about my going with Mr. Huffner to the dredging site; is that correct?"

"Not quite, Mr. Atkinson," Crosby said. "We have no problem you going up country to visit the dredging site, but we have a problem with the person who's proposing to take you there."

"Oh? You mean Mr. Huffner is "the problem"?" Atkinson asked as if stating a fact rather than asking a question. "Well, I had a chat with Mr. Huffner this morning and I have formed a first impression about the man. I do not trust him, Agent Crosby."

"And why would that be?" Alan asked.

"Well, Doctor Mayhew, Jewish people have an innate distrust of their fellow man. And in the case of Mr. Huffner, his comportment and his words led me to believe the man is a fraud."

"Could you explain what you just described, sir?"

Atkinson nodded and went on, "Yes, yes, absolutely, Mr. Evans. You see, Mr. Huffner told me that it would only take a couple of hours to reach the dredging site by chopper since the dredging team is now working downstream." He paused. "I did not believe a word of it."

"Why would that be?" Crosby queried.

"Well, Agent Crosby, most jewelers, like myself, are geologists in their spare time. And when I looked at a map of the Baoule stream bed, there is no "downstream" to speak of. The stones are found at the source of the river not downstream. Besides, I don't see why Mr. Huffner proposed having me go all the way up-country, when all I was asking him to do is to bring me samples of the stones his company – not himself – would be able to offer me."

"You mean you didn't see the need to go up-country with anyone if Mr. Huffner could not show you stones worth purchasing, is that what you're saying?" Hatfield asked, quite interested in this little sleuthing episode. It was a welcome break from their dreary, not to say dreadful daily task and operation.

"Better than that, Doctor. If I were interested in any of the sample stones, I would not buy them here or at the dredging site – De Beers would close my New York operation down the next day if I did so." The people around the table looked at each other. This was slightly out of their field of purview. "You see, diamond sales and purchases are highly regulated. If I want to buy a diamond from the AREDOR site, I most likely will find a case for sale either at a broker in London or in Antwerp. And I would have to buy a whole case of maybe six diamonds (if I'm lucky) sight unseen. So, this is why my visit here is so important. I simply wanted to see what kind of stones I could expect to buy in London."

Silence fell around the table. It appeared that Agent Crosby had been right; Mr. Huffner was indeed after the little jeweler.

CHAPTER TWENTY-SEVEN

A harrowing experience

THE MORNING CAME FAR TOO SOON for Alan and Tiffany. The Vaudeville performance had been a huge success and had drawn practically every passenger to the theater and cocktail party in the foyer. Yet, it was 5:00 a.m. and time to get to the Isle of Los to get the Tamara family back to the mainland. The WHO vehicles would be waiting for Alan, Gilbert and the family in front of the port facility, near the ferry terminal.

When Alan and Gilbert made it to the old ship, they were both surprised to see the family waiting for them, sitting on sacs and sacs of clothes, linen and what seemed to be rice or grain of some sort. Alan and Gilbert exchanged a glance. They were immediately wondering what they were going to do with all the "baggage" once they got back to Conakry. They sure couldn't take any of that stuff with them. *But let's take it one step at a time,* Alan thought.

"Okay, let's get out of here," he said cheerfully, once he had administered the vaccine to the seven members of the family. Then the parents and their five kids and their "baggage" were ready to leave.

Hassan Tamara was all smiles. "You know, Doctor Alan, I didn't believe you would come back," he said as they were walking to the ferry pier.

"And why would that be, Mr. Tamara?"

"We hear a lot of promises in these parts and many of them are really empty. People want a lot out of us, but they're not prepared to give back."

"You mean white people don't keep their promises," Gilbert inquired as he and Mamoud shared the carrying of the load of a large bag of linen and clothing.

"Not all white people, Mr. Gilbert. Blacks too. When people have money, they promise things to get more money or services for free, and then they don't pay or don't give what should be a share of the goods."

"I know it's sad, Mr. Tamara," Alan said, "but as you can see, we're not like the people you describe."

"I can see that, Doctor Alan," Hassan said, chuckling.

While Mrs. Tamara was busy rounding up the children as soon as they reached the port of Conakry, her husband went with Alan and Gilbert to meet Drs. Ashford and Hatfield.

The two explained that they would be able to fit the family in the SUVs but their "baggage" would be a problem.

"No problem, Doctor Ashford," Hassan said, "Let me show you."

Under the amazed gazes of the three doctors, Hassan directed the chauffeurs to get all of the "baggage" on the SUVs roof-tops. Since they always carried ropes in the back of the vehicles, it was easy to tie up the lot in a matter of minutes.

As Alan took some pictures, he had to grin and shake his head. He was reminded of some of his trips up country in Asia where packing everything (including the kitchen sink) everywhere you go is of prime importance.

Ashford and Hatfield didn't say anything – what could they say? They had offered to transport the family, so if loading the SUVs like mules crossing the desert was what was required, that's what they would do.

A half hour later, everyone was aboard the three SUVs. The passengers included Mr. Atkinson and Agent Crosby. These two had become inseparable. The little jeweler knew his life was now in danger. Huffner wanted the Star, and short of swiping it from its hiding place on *The Contessa*, he was not going to put his paws on it if Crosby and Atkinson had anything to say about it.

Yet, Huffner was not to be defeated. He had fought tooth and nail to get AREDOR's dredging permits and much of his efforts cost him a fortune, a fortune he was not likely to recover any time soon. In his position as a major partner in the enterprise, he was at liberty to take stones out of the compound but not without leaving his ID card and passport with the office beforehand. Without these two items, he would be unlikely to leave the country easily. However, where there's a will there's a way, as they say. And Huffner had found a way years ago. He had bribed customs' officials along the way and was still doing it to date. If he wanted to leave the country without his "real" passport it would cost him dearly. The forgery he carried would do him for another two years, after which he would retire with the proceeds from the sale of the Star of Sierra Leone. He had a buyer lined-up and waiting in Fiji. The man would be waiting for him for as long as it took for Huffner to get the Star out of Guinea, down to South America and to Fiji.

It was an elaborate plan, and one that he would start executing this very morning. Huffner had received a call from Atkinson telling him that he was going to travel with the doctors to Kissidougou where he would be pleased to accompany Huffner to the dredging site.

It had put a kink in his initial plan, but Huffner wasn't too worried. He knew he would be getting his hands on Atkinson in the next few hours anyway. What's more, he liked the idea of having two famous World Health Organization doctors available – these two could certainly be taken hostage, too. As for manpower, he had plenty. He had greased so many palms over the years; he was the "Bwana" of Guinea. *What I say goes;* he sniggered as he sat in the company chopper, preparing to take off for Kissidougou.

Since they were expecting some trouble, Alan asked Alice Muller to accompany them this time. Olga would stay aboard and mind the medical center for the day. Alice was pleased to get out and was actually looking forward to some action. She would have taken Huffner across her knee and given him a good-old-fashioned spanking if she could, although what she had in mind for the man was quite different. If he were to make a move toward the little jeweler, she and Agent Crosby were ready to make mincemeat of the guy. Huffner would probably not have his day in court.

When the team reached Forecariah, it was as if the whole village had assembled along the roadside to welcome the vehicles. They applauded their passage and ran after the cars until they all stopped in front of an old house in dire need of a coat of paint.

An elderly woman stepped out first and put a hand across her brow to shade her eyes from the sun.

As soon as Hassan Tamara rushed out of the vehicle, she smiled.

"Grand-mama, I am home!" he shouted, taking her in his arms and lifting her off the ground.

"You big fool," she replied, brandishing her cane, "put me down this minute!"

"Meme, Meme, Meme," the kids screamed in turn, as they surrounded the old woman.

Alan was choking. He could not believe how this simple scene touched him. He would have cried, but smiled instead while he helped the chauffeurs and Mamoud unload the baggage from the top of the cars.

Once the family had been re-united with their ancestor (by the looks of the old lady) and their friends, the team went to the hospital to carry on with their duties for the day. Although there were quite a few patients that had not escaped the virulent disease, it seemed that the epidemic had found its nemesis in the region. They carried on with the vaccinations and helped with some of the isolation measures, but other than that, Forecariah wasn't in great danger at the moment.

As they were about to return to the vehicles, Mamoud came running to the hospital to grab Alan by the hand.

"Doctor Alan, Meme has prepared a meal for all of you. You need to come and eat," he said, practically out of breath.

Alan looked up at his companions. They were smiling and shaking their heads.

"Well, what do you think?" Alan asked Dr. Ashford.

"Why not?" was his reply.

"Okay, Mamoud, lead the way," Alan told him, pushing him into the SUV.

Even Mr. Atkinson seemed happy to follow Mamoud to the old house. When everyone exited the SUV they were surprised to find a long table, set up with all sorts of dishes and trays populating its entire surface, under the baobab. It was as though the entire town had contributed to the pot-luck lunch.

Alan went directly to Meme and thanked her profusely. His French grammar was not the best, but there wasn't any need for words, the old woman understood.

Once they finished their meal, they returned to the SUVs and prepared themselves for the rather long journey to Kissidougou. It would have been much shorter to cut through Sierra Leone rather than following the border all the way to their destination, about 250 miles from Forecariah. Yet, crossing the border into Sierra Leone at this point would have been unwise.

In the end the journey wasn't too bad. They arrived in mid-afternoon and were pleased to see that the town was quite clean and even inviting.

Someone was waiting for them at the hospital. Huffner was there with two gendarmes armed to the teeth – he didn't look too happy.

They're obviously in his back pocket, Alan mused and wondered what two officers were doing in the hospital.

"Gentlemen, and ladies," Huffner began, "I know this must be a surprise to you, but you see, we've got our own rules up here. And if you wish to remain in this town for another minute, you better do as you're told!"

"Are you crazy, Huffner?" Agent Crosby snapped. "These are the World Health Organization doctors and nurses – they have free passages wherever they please…"

"Oh hush your face, Agent Crosby," Huffner hissed. The Interpol agent frowned. "And don't look so surprised – I know who everyone is before they enter my city."

Except for Alice, whose jaws were clenched in seething rage, everyone was wondering what was happening right now.

"And what do you want from us?" Doctor Ashford asked, somewhat firmly. "We're only here to vaccinate the children and aging folks first and then see if any of the men need our attention."

"I understand that, Doctor, and I don't have any problems with it. However, I do have a problem with the ones that are not really here to perform any vaccination."

"You mean me?" Atkinson said, stepping in front of the astounded team.

"Yes, you, Mr. Atkinson. We had an appointment to visit the dredging site, remember?"

"Yes, I remember, Mr. Huffner, but I also remember telling you that I wanted to see some of the stones I could buy…"

"And so you shall, Mr. Atkinson, so you shall," Huffner sniggered and then turned to his gendarmes. "Get him to the chopper," he ordered while pulling a handgun out of the back of his belt. "As for the rest of you, you can go back to Conakry with a message for your captain. If you don't come back here with the Star at the same time tomorrow, Mr. Atkinson will die – is that understood?"

As he asked the question, and as his gendarmes marched away with Atkinson, he approached the people facing him menacingly. He seemed to enjoy seeing frightened faces staring at him.

But that was all Alice needed – a fraction of a second of distraction on the part of Huffner – she pounced on him like an enraged panther.

It was so quick that no one in the group even had time to realize what was happening. Agent Crosby didn't leave all the action up to

Alice though, he grabbed Huffner's gun before he could fire it and tackled the man to the ground.

The two gendarmes were now staring at the scene with fear in their eyes. They knew they were in trouble. Huffner had been their guardian angel for far too long. The only thing they could do was to run for their lives, literally.

As soon as they had done what they came to Kissidougou to do – vaccinate the part of the population in need of their assistance – the team members climbed back into their SUVs and were happy to drive back to Conakry. Huffner – in handcuffs – was riding in the AREDOR's security Landrover under Agent Crosby's able guard. He would be deported back to the states after facing the Guinean courts and possibly a lengthy jail sentence.

It had been a harrowing experience for Mr. Atkinson. And it increased his resolve to return the Star to its country of origin as soon as he could. He never wanted to see the stone again.

CHAPTER TWENTY-EIGHT

A cassette worth the trouble

WHILE ALAN AND THE WHO TEAM were on their way back to the ship, Babette and Tiffany were having a late afternoon tea at the terrace café. The day had been hot and unpleasant. The humidity was overwhelming. None of the passengers were keen to visit Conakry and some of them even returned to the Isle of Los. The wind from the Atlantic Ocean kept the temperature down on the island. However, Babette didn't want to tire herself again today. She had spent most of the day writing the rest of her play, which she intended to stage as soon as their mission in Sierra Leone was completed.

"And you know, Tiffany," Babette went on saying, "sometimes it is difficult to lighten the scene or ease people into laughter after they've just experienced some difficult incidents."

"I imagine it's not as easy as flipping a switch, is it?" Tiffany remarked.

"Exactly. Let me give you an example." Tiffany was all ears now. Babette's stories were always – without fail – enjoyable. "A woman had just returned to her home from an evening of church services, when she was startled by an intruder. She caught the man in the act of robbing her home of its valuables and yelled: "Stop! Acts 2:38!" (Which reads: Repent and be baptized in the name of Jesus Christ, so that your sins may be forgiven.) The burglar stopped dead in his tracks. The woman then calmly called the police and explained what she had done. As the officer cuffed the man to take him in, he asked the burglar: "Why did you just stand there? All the old lady did was to yell a scripture to you." "A scripture?" replied the burglar. "She said she had an axe and two 38s! That was enough for me."

Tiffany erupted in laughter and nodded. "I see what you mean. That's very clever."

"It's just difficult to do. It's like your brain cannot change gears. Like you're wiping the floor with a heavy mop and then you switch to wiping fragile porcelain – nine times out of ten, you're going to break the porcelain."

"But, tell me," Tiffany inquired, "what is the play about this time?" She knew Babette wouldn't divulge the content of the play to anyone, yet, she also knew that Babette would need to stage the performance with her assistance.

"It's called "The Black Hand of Death"," Babette replied.

Tiffany's eyebrows shot up. "Isn't that what they call Ebola around these parts?" She poured herself another cup of tea. "That sounds somber…"

"Of course it does," Babette said, "but that doesn't mean the play is going to depict the ravages the disease has done in West Africa. On the contrary, I aimed to engage the audience in understanding what this plague is all about. It's the story of one man…" The playwright stopped abruptly. "Anyway, it's not finished. I may change my mind yet."

"When were you thinking you could give me a list of the actors and the props required, so I can begin working on it?"

"Don't you be so anxious, Tiffany. You know you'll have plenty of time to arrange all of that once we've passed the gap…"

"What gap is that?"

"As I told you; once we're out of the woods, so to speak, and sailing away from Sierra Leone, I think there will be plenty of time to get ready to make the appropriate preparations."

"What about the actors?" Tiffany insisted, knowing that Babette might just get up at that point and leave her to her queries.

"They'll be joining us in Freetown. Since the quarantine has been lifted – or so they told me – they'll be able to land and join the ship." Babette smiled. "Don't worry about all this, Tiffany. Truly, I will give you ample time to stage the play."

As soon as they returned to the ship, Alan and Alice went back to the medical center, while Agent Crosby made arrangements to have Huffner detained until the Guinean authorities decided what they wanted to do with the man.

Meanwhile, in order to appease the diggers' community, AREDOR's management decided to wash their hands of the whole affair. They invoked an injunction against Huffner so that he would never be able to return to the dredging site.

As for Mr. Atkinson, he practically ran to his cabin when he reached the top of the gangway. He had enough. He wanted nothing anymore to do with West Africa. He knew he would probably regret the decision someday, but for now, saving his life was more important than obtaining a few diamonds from that awful place.

However, he was surprised when he heard a knock at his cabin's door and found a man standing in the embrasure when he opened it.

"Yes, what is it?" Atkinson asked politely.

"I'm very sorry to disturb you, sir," the tall and handsome black man said, "but I would like to speak to you for a moment if I may."

The man was impeccably dressed. His linen suit, shirt and tie had probably been purchased from an expensive Parisian tailor.

"May I ask who you are?" Atkinson asked, obviously unimpressed by the man's attire.

"I'm Maitre Alhassan Sangare, sir. I'm an attorney at law. AREDOR is my client. And I am here to make amends, if I may."

"Well, Maitre Sangare, why don't you come in then," Atkinson replied, extending an arm toward the small lounge room of his suite. "Please have a seat."

Once seated, Sangare went on: "I have flown from Kissidougou this afternoon after I heard what happened to you and after I had a chat with my client."

"I must apologize to Mr. Strauss," Atkinson said, "It was rude of me not to meet with him after he extended such a kind invitation to visit the dredging facility."

"Sir, please don't worry, Mr. Strauss is the one who wants to apologize for the way Mr. Huffner has treated you. Most of the company directors knew or were somehow aware of Mr. Huffner's activities, but we could not move without fear of repercussions. He paid the local gendarmes well to keep the company directors and me at bay."

"I see," Atkinson said concertedly. "But I'm afraid it is now too late for either of us to do anything about the current situation. This ship is sailing tomorrow morning and I am much too tired to contemplate another trip up country."

"The directors expected that to be so, Mr. Atkinson, therefore, they've asked me to give you a cassette from the dredging plant. It was sealed this morning." Sangare pulled a small wooden case from his breast pocket. "I don't know what the cassette contains. As you are probably aware, no one can open it until the recipient breaks the seal, which I suggest you do once you're home. To avoid the customs' queries, you understand."

"My, thank you so much, Maitre Sangare," Atkinson said, taking the cassette from the attorney's hand with renewed eagerness. He looked up at the man sitting across from him. "Do you have any idea of the total worth contained in the cassette?"

"No, sir, I don't. Yet, I know Mr. Strauss wouldn't want you to be disappointed with its content. It seemed to us that you have faced enough frustration for the time being."

The two men continued talking for a while until Maitre Sangare took his leave. Atkinson had to smile as soon as he closed the door on the attorney. He went back to sit down and took the little cassette in his hands. He turned it over a couple of times and promised himself to resist the temptation of breaking the seal before getting home. He was happy enough to have renewed ties with Albert Strauss. However, he knew Strauss was a scoundrel. He couldn't readily trust him, yet there was some dignity and a smidgen of integrity left in the man's character, Atkinson was sure. After all, he had resurrected a dying enterprise and made it the pride of the diamond trading community.

While all of this had taken place, Betty Palmer was making some progress in identifying her nephew. With her assistants' help – Adele Muesli and Gregory Ashton had done more than their homework. With their information, she was practically certain that Leon Summerville was her relative. There was only one thing left to do which could confirm the fact – a DNA test. Betty was more than willing to have Alan draw some blood and to have it sent to Marseille for analysis; but how was she to get some blood from Leon, was the question.

"You could get DNA from practically anything these days," Alan suggested after he had placed Betty's vials of blood in the fridge. "If you have any items that he has licked, such as an envelope or a stamp, it would do the trick."

Betty shook her head. "Come on, Doctor, who's licking envelopes or stamps these days?" she asked mockingly.

"You're right. Maybe you could find a hairbrush or even a razor…"

She shook her head again. "I think it's time I'll come forward. There's been enough covert actions regarding this matter. If Leon Summerville is my nephew and he is as good as he appears to be, then I will do the right thing by him. If not, he will not get his hands on a fortune he does not know exists."

"I have to disagree with you, Mrs. Palmer," Alan countered. "If Leon suspects that there is a pot of gold at the end of the rainbow, he will do everything he can to get it."

"Perhaps he knows already about the pot of gold, as you call it, Doctor, but it's not for him to access without my naming him as my heir."

"He will contest your will, Mrs. Palmer. I can be almost sure; the man will do everything possible to get your money upon your death."

"Well, Doctor," Betty concluded, getting up from the chair in the examination room, "let me think about it. But if Leon comes to you for a blood test, please do me the favor of not speaking of my intentions to him."

"Of course, Mrs. Palmer, all of our conversations are privileged. You know that."

"Yes, yes, Doctor…," she added before exiting the room, "nevertheless, I would prefer that none of this become public before we know for sure who we're dealing with here."

"Totally, Mrs. Palmer. Mum's the word."

Returning to her suite, Betty decided to stop by the terrace café. She dearly wanted some sort of refreshment. "That heat is getting to me," she grumbled to herself. As soon as she neared the café she saw Babette and Tiffany in the middle of what seemed a rather intense discussion.

"Sorry, ladies," Betty said, taking a seat at the ladies' table, "Am I am interrupting?"

Babette smiled before she said, "Not at all, glad you did actually, Betty. This young woman here"—she nodded in Tiffany's direction—"is insisting on driving me up the wall with questions about my upcoming play."

Tiffany erupted in laughter. "No, I'm not, Mrs. Palmer. I can assure you…"

"I am curious too," Betty said, turning to Babette, "what is the play about? Please do tell?"

Babette shook her head emphatically. "Not a word from me," she declared.

Laughing their consensus, the three women decided to order a couple of *blueberry teas* to give their little gathering a bit of a kick.

As soon as they were served, Betty explained that she wanted their advice and why she did.

Babette was the first to suggest, "Why don't you enlist Gaston's help?"

"Who?" Betty asked, wide-eyed.

"Gaston, Leon and Linda's secretary. Apparently he's a straight arrow, according to Doctor Mayhew. He could certainly get you something with Leon's DNA on it. Why don't you ask him?"

"Won't he go straight to his employer and tell him what I'm intending to do?"

"Perhaps you should enlist Doctor Mayhew's help on this one," Tiffany suggested. "I'm under the impression that the two of them have talked already."

"Maybe you're right, Tiffany. I think I'll go back to the medical center tomorrow and ask him. But for now, let's enjoy our very *special tea*, shall we?"

The ladies tittered – quite amused at their own daring.

CHAPTER TWENTY-NINE

Gaston?

"LISTEN TO THIS . . ." Simon said as he sat at his crew's table.

"If that's another set of your re-runs, I swear..."

"Shush, Ivan, these are brand new – I've just got them off my laptop, okay?"

"Who are they from?" Ivan demanded, still worried that they heard it all before.

"They're from a mate on *The Baroness*. They've got this doctor who collects jokes every single time he's on line. It's like his hobby or something." Simon looked around him. "Anyway, do you want to hear them or not?"

"Yeah-yeah why don't you go ahead," Ivan said, crossing his arms over his chest.

"Okay, here goes nothing: The teacher asked, "How can you prevent diseases caused by biting insects?" The kid replied: "Don't bite the insects!"

"Very good," Ivan said between chuckles.

"Okay, here's the next one: Doctor: We need to get these people to a hospital! Nurse: What is it? Doctor: It's a big building with a lot of doctors and equipment.

"Doctor: You're in good health. You'll live to be 80. Patient: But, doctor, I am 80 right now. "Doctor: See, what did I tell you?

"A man speaks frantically into the phone, "My wife is pregnant, and her contractions are only two minutes apart!"

"Is this her first child?" the doctor queries.

"No, you idiot!" the man shouts. "This is her husband"!"

After the laughter died down, Simon said, "Have you guys heard what happened to our doc this morning?"

"What else...?" Ivan asked. "He's had more strife than any man I know. Wasn't he up country with the jeweler and the WHO guys?"

"Exactly," Simon said, nodding, "and the only reason he went with them was to make sure the jeweler didn't get kidnapped..."

"Are you serious?" Ivan asked, goggle-eyed now.

"Oh yeah. We heard all about it from the chauffeurs when the guys came back and we had to dispose of the empty vaccine vials safely."

"So what happened?" another crew member asked, quite curious now.

"Apparently, the super from the dredge site planned on taking the little jeweler hostage until the doc got back to that village with the Star."

"You mean the super was planning to kidnap the little guy?"

"Yeah, that's what I'm saying, but thanks to that Interpol guy who was with them, they captured the super and brought him back – he's in the brig right now."

"I wish we'd get rid of that darn stone," Ivan said, shaking his head, "it's spelling trouble wherever people keep it."

"It's a tempting rock though, you've got to admit," Les said. "I wish I could see it."

"I don't," Ivan countered hotly. "Keep the darn thing away from me!" he added, getting to his feet. "I'll be down where I can be as far away as I can from that thing, Simon. I'll see you guys later."

As he walked out of the crew's mess, Simon said to his other two companions, "you know, Ivan might be right; that stone is really attracting the worst kind of people to it."

Several decks above, Betty was having a late night liquor with Gaston Giroux. She didn't want to wait until the morning to talk to him.

When things need to be said or done, might as well say and do all of them now, had been Betty's motto on quite a few occasions. She liked to *beat the iron while it's hot* sort of thing.

"Do you miss the action?" Betty asked the young man while they sipped on their pousse-cafés.

"Not the action, ma'am, but the camaraderie and the purpose," Gaston replied.

"What do you mean by purpose?"

"We knew why we were there; what we were doing and we knew that we served a purpose."

"And you don't find that at home?"

"No, ma'am, I don't. I have a job, which is great, but if I were to go elsewhere tomorrow, no one would miss me. There's no greater purpose; there's no camaraderie and nothing else than money in your bank account."

"That's quite a defeatist attitude isn't it?"

"Not really, ma'am. I have to look at the life I had in the military and the life I have today. The one was filled with goals to reach, with purposes to fulfill while the other is rather empty. I keep the Summerville's accounts in order, I keep them happy and I try to stay away from thinking about the past."

"I see," Betty said musingly and then paused for a few moments. "I have something to confess, Mr. Giroux..."

"Please call me Gaston," he interrupted, with a broad and inviting grin drawing on his lips.

"Thank you Gaston, and as I was saying, I've got a confession to make. You see, I've been looking for my nephew for some years now – actually since my husband died. He wanted nothing to do with "the bastard child", as he used to say. My nephew was born many years ago out of wedlock and given to a monastery in Senegal for adoption. The rest of the story is blurry. Not for the lack of trying, mind you. I found the monastery, thanks to Adele and Gregory, my assistants. In turn, I learned that the boy had been adopted and moved to The Gambia. After that, I have no idea what happened to the child."

"And what has that got to do with me, Mrs. Palmer?" Gaston queried, rather curious now.

"I don't know at this point that it will have anything to do with you, Gaston, but it may have a lot to do with Mr. Summerville."

"You mean Leon could be your nephew?"

Betty nodded, and sipped on her crème de menthe.

"Wow! That would be a stroke of luck!"

"How would it be a stroke of luck, Gaston?"

"I mean, the man is certainly a mystery but I believe his instability – if I may call it that – stems from his having no family to support him. It's like he's climbing a glass wall all the time. He gets himself stretched to the limit and then he can't go any further because no one has told him how."

"That's an interesting metaphor, Gaston, but what are you really saying?" Betty asked, not quite understanding what Gaston was trying to explain.

"I'm sorry, Mrs. Palmer, I'm not making this very clear, am I?" Betty shook her head. "Well, Leon has had his fingers in many pies; he is very successful in most of his enterprises, but then he can't help but con a few people here and there. It's like he enjoys the challenge and then lets the reins go while the horse gallops to their death."

"You mean he doesn't know how to stop a runaway train, is that it?"

"Exactly. Whether it's a good investment or a bad business decision, he doesn't know how to reverse the throttle. And when it all crashes, he calls it fate. It's a very childish attitude, I know, but that's where I try to intervene. I show him how to stop the train or how to make a U-turn before the car crashes into the next wall."

"And whose money does he use to do all this?"

"Whoever signs up for his investment advice. And before you ask, he's a licensed investment advisor, but every case is different..."

"Of course it is. Has he ever swindled anyone?"

"Yes, he has, but he's never forced anyone to sign on the dotted line. He's not always given the right advice to people, and he tries not to scheme, but I have to admit, he's a con. Yet, I believe Leon Summerville is rather honest at heart."

"What about his wife..., Linda is it?"

"Yes. Well, Linda is a lovely woman, but that's about it. She loves to spend her husband's money and travel the world. She hates cooking, staying home or having to take any responsibility. She is the ideal spoiled brat!"

"I see," Betty said again. "But would you be able to find out where he was born or who his parents were?"

"Oh absolutely," Gaston said, putting down his snifter of Cognac. "I have a birth certificate somewhere in their passport files I think. I could check on my laptop if I've got their files with me." He paused. "But it won't tell you much about his background, I'm afraid. Even if Leon was adopted, these records were sealed long ago and probably inaccessible right now."

"Yes, I know," Betty admitted, "but it's a place to start. And with the monastery records, we might be able to piece this puzzle together."

"May I ask why you are so interested in finding out if Leon is really your nephew?"

"Apart from the fact that I'd like to meet the man who's probably the last surviving member of my family – aside from me of course – I rather not say at this point, Gaston."

"I understand. I'll check my laptop in the morning and let you know," Gaston concluded with a conspiratorial smile.

Alan was in the middle of a dream when a train whistle pulled him out of his slumber rather abruptly. He truly didn't know where he was when he opened his eyes. Apparently, he had been the only one hearing such noise, as Tiffany was sleeping quietly beside him. He sat up and pulled himself out of bed. He was about to sit at his desk when his great-grandfather appeared to him.

"Granddad, what's going on? Why the early call?" Alan asked, whispering the words so as not to wake Tiffany.

"It's Gaston," Edmund replied. "I think he'll need medical attention rather quickly."

"What's happened? Where is he?" Alan asked, already slipping into his trousers. "Olga is on call at the med center; I better give her a call…"

"Before you wake everyone, maybe you should see the patient for yourself."

"Okay, okay, but are you going to tell me what happened?" Alan demanded as he opened the cabin door quietly.

"Gaston and Betty Palmer had a drink tonight, and when they left the bar, I saw Gaston go to his cabin – he was alive and well then…"

"Are you telling me he's dead?"

"Listen, son, if you didn't interrupt me all the time, I'd be able to answer your questions." He stared at his great-grandson for a few seconds before he resumed his account of the events that occurred in the last few hours.

"And where is he now?"

"He's in the theater – in the front row."

"What on earth…?"

"That's exactly what I said to myself when I found him. The last time I saw him, as I said, he was alive and well and entering his cabin."

"What about Betty, did you follow her?"

"Yes. She was as well as can be and seemed happy when she left the bar."

As they reached the theater, Alan noticed that Gilbert was already looking around the foyer.

"Hey, Doc, nice of you to come down. I didn't mean to wake you…" He looked at Alan questioningly. "But how did you make it down so fast. I just called Olga a minute ago."

"I couldn't sleep and thought I'd take a stroll when I decided to come down to have a look at the program for the week."

As the two men were talking, the elevator doors opened at one end of the foyer while the doors of the theater opened at the other end.

Olga came out of the elevator, gasped and let out a shriek before she pointed to the opposite end of the foyer. Gaston was standing with a knife in his hand, his chest covered in blood and looking haggard.

Alan rushed to Gaston while Gilbert ran to Olga as she was about to faint.

"Gaston?" Alan called out to the young man. "What's happened?"

"Drugs, Doctor, drugs, that's what it is…" That's all he had time to say before he passed out in Alan's arms.

CHAPTER THIRTY

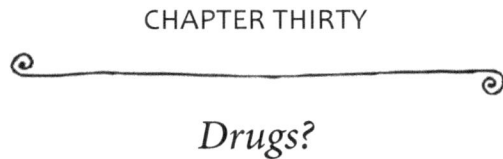

Drugs?

"REMEMBER WHAT I TOLD YOU, Doc?" Gaston asked Alan when he tried explaining what happened after he left Betty Palmer. Alan frowned. "I told you that I had seen a few things in Afghanistan in my time, and this little knifing venture only served to remind me that I learned a few good lessons while I was out there."

"That certainly seems to be the case, Gaston," Alan replied as he dropped the last of the suture threads in the tray. "And this particular "knifing venture", as you call it, was very well learned I suspect. You're alive to tell the story." He paused. "Why don't you tell me about it now? How did you get the tip of that knife in your chest? Who attacked you?"

Gaston smiled. "Can we make it one question at a time, Doc? I'm rather confused right now."

He suddenly closed his eyes… Alan looked at the monitor behind the patient for a fraction of a second, afraid that Gaston would either go into shock or flat line. He checked his pulse and waited. When the moment of crisis passed and his vitals returned to normal, Gaston opened his eyes while Alan exhaled a sigh of relief together with Olga, who was standing across the bed, assisting him.

"Yes…, where was I?" Gaston asked, looking at Alan inquiringly.

"You were about to tell me what happened in the theater."

"Well…, hum, yes…" He hesitated. Alan wasn't sure he could pressure him any further at this point. Some of the men who returned from the Middle East or other regions where warfare was a daily occurrence associated current events with those they experienced in the battlefield. In this instance Alan had no doubt that Gaston had faced an enemy brandishing a knife and the theater event only served as a trigger to unwanted recollections.

"Okay, no need to talk about it right away, Gaston," Alan said, nodding to Olga. "We're going to leave you alone for a bit, so you can get some sleep, okay?"

Gaston nodded and closed his eyes again, obviously grateful to be left alone. PTSD is not a forgiving mental disease. Although Alan did not think Gaston was one of the worst cases; he displayed some signs of suffering from it. Actually this last event might have unbridled suppressed memories, especially those related to knifing someone to death; an event perhaps associated with some drug running operation. Alan wasn't sure of anything at this point, but he didn't want to put any undue stress on his patient either.

He returned to his office then, sat down and was about to write an email to one of his colleagues in the medical corps when Gilbert came in.

"Do you mind if I sit down for a minute?" he said, plopping his butt in one of the visitors' chairs across from Alan's desk.

"Why don't you?" Alan replied with a smirk on his lips.

"Okay, thanks. How's our patient? Did he tell you anything when he woke up?"

"Not in so many words, no…"

"What does that mean?"

"It means that he remembered having a similar experience during his last tour of duty, but then he clammed up on me. I think he's suffering from a slight case of PTSD and has difficulty speaking about this particular event."

"You mean it reminds him of something he lived through in Afghanistan and doesn't want to talk about it?"

"Precisely. And before you ask, no, I did not ask what he meant about "drugs". Perhaps that too is related to something that happened to him out there."

"And when do you think we'll be able to get some answers from him?"

"I frankly don't know, Gilbert. As soon as he's fit to return to his cabin, it'll be time enough to interview him."

"That's all fine, Doc, but if we've got a killer aboard, I'd rather know about it now, if at all possible. We've got quite a few people whose lives we wouldn't want to lose, don't we?"

"I know, I know, Gilbert, but I don't want to be responsible for Gaston's case worsening either. I can assure you he's no killer. He's probably an excellent soldier who could execute any man when in the field of battle, but when he's home, I don't think he would hurt anyone willfully."

"I have to agree with you there, Doc. From what I've learned, Gaston is everything a good guy should be. If I read his CV correctly, he got an honorable discharge and hasn't even gotten a parking ticket since he came home."

"What about drugs?" Alan asked. "Does his military record say anything about him using drugs for any purpose?"

"No, not a peep. He's been sick a couple of times apparently but nothing that a couple of aspirin wouldn't cure. Do you think he was referring to drugs on this ship?"

Alan got up. "Why don't we pay a visit to his employers?"

"You mean the Summervilles?"

"Who else?"

"And what would you want to ask them?"

"Perhaps it's time we knew a little more about Mr. Leon Summerville. Nothing of what I've heard thus far about him is very re-assuring." Alan rounded his desk while Gilbert got to his feet. "Have you told them what happened yet?"

"Not yet. I don't think they're awake at this hour though."

"Maybe you're right. I think I might as well get in the shower myself before I go anywhere."

Gilbert had to smile. Alan was still in his t-shirt and blue scrubs.

The early morning freshness being the only time when the passengers could enjoy the outdoors without being fried alive on their lounge chairs or boiled like poached eggs in the pool, most passengers would make their way to the upper decks before the sun was up above the horizon. Most were either going for a swim in the pool or having a game of golf on the imaginary course.

Mack and Jeff were on their way to the holographic links when Mack started laughing. Jeff turned to him as he planted his tee in the artificial turf.

"What's the matter; did I do something wrong already?"

"No-no, mate, not you. I was thinking of my wife..." Mack said, shaking his head.

"What has the poor lady done now?" Jeff asked, before driving his ball to the first hole with a near-perfect swing.

"Well, she's done nothing today, but she won't have a game of golf with me anymore."

"Oh? And why would that be," Jeff queried somewhat mockingly.

"Just imagine this: A man (me) staggers into the emergency room with a concussion, multiple bruises, and a five iron wrapped around my neck. Naturally the doctor asked me what happened. "Well, it was like this," I said. "I was having a quiet round of golf with my wife, when at a difficult hole we both accidentally sliced our balls into a pasture of cows. We went to look for them, and while I was rooting around, I noticed that one of the cows had something white in its rear end. I walked over and lifted up the tail, and sure enough, there was a golf ball with my wife's monogram on it stuck right in the middle of the cow's butt. That's when I made my mistake."

"What did you do?" asked the doc. "Well, I lifted the tail, pointed, and yelled to my wife, "Hey! This looks like yours!"

"Ha-ha-ha-ha!" Jeff was doubled-up in laughter. "I'm sure you're exaggerating, aren't you?"

"Well, maybe a little, but I tell you, don't ever play with Irene – she's got a temper and a half when it comes to losing a ball."

As soon as Alan had taken a shower, and had explained what happened to a bewildered Tiffany, he got dressed and went out to leave his lovely lady in peace.

When he got to the upper café restaurant, he spotted Gilbert immediately.

"Okay, here I am," Alan said, sounding eager to get on with their interview with the Summervilles. "Did you have breakfast yet?"

"No, not quite," Gilbert said, pocketing his cell phone. "I was just talking to our Potty Man, to see if he – or some of his guys – could conduct a search for drugs in the less accessible parts of the ship. I just want to have all of our bases covered before we go any further."

"Okay then, let's have breakfast, shall we?" Alan said, getting to his feet again. Gilbert followed him to the counter.

They both helped themselves to some cereal, fruit, yogurt and coffee.

They ate in silence, probably thinking of what they would be discussing with the Summervilles.

Alan was sipping on his coffee when he noticed Leon and Linda Summerville going to the breakfast counter.

"It looks like Mohamed has come to the mountain," Alan said almost inaudibly, his eyes following the couple in their progress up the queue.

Since Gilbert had his back to the line, he bent over the table to say, "You mean they're here?"

Alan nodded. "Yeah. And I think we shouldn't have our conversation in the café. I suggest we leave as soon as you're done and wait for them after they leave; what do you think?"

"Good plan. And it will give Simon and his guys a bit more time for their search. I just hope he doesn't find anything. These drug cases truly irritate me. Going back up the chain to get the mastermind or "drug lord" is a real hassle."

"Have you thought of enrolling the services of our eminent Interpol agent? The only job he has right now is to watch over our jeweler."

"That's an idea. I don't think he'd mind a bit of diversity in his assignment, now that Huffner is locked up."

"Okay," Alan said, standing up. "I'll go back to the med center to get Alice up to date. Olga has had enough for today, I think."

"Right. Why don't I phone you when I get some answer from Simon and see the Summervilles leave?"

"Good plan," Alan agreed. "See you then." He waved and disappeared along the deck a moment later.

Not waiting a minute longer, Gilbert punched Agent Daniel Crosby's cell phone number.

The man answered with a yawn. Admittedly it was only 7:00 a.m.

"Hello, Agent Crosby, sorry to wake you. This is Gilbert Evans…"

"Ah, yes, Mr. Evans. What can I do for you?"

"First of all, you can call me Gilbert – everyone does – and then maybe you can join me for breakfast at the upper deck café; what do you say?"

"I say, I'll be right there, Gilbert. And please call me Daniel. I'm on holiday right now, understood?"

"Perfectly, Agent… I mean, Daniel. I'm waiting."

"Give me ten."

Ten minutes later – on the dot – Daniel Crosby was pulling up a chair to sit across from Gilbert. His breakfast tray couldn't have been fuller. He had picked up enough fruit to make a salad for four, to be sure, three little yogurt tubs and four slices of toast to enjoy with his coffee. Gilbert looked at all this in amazement.

"Are you sure you're not expecting company?"

Daniel erupted in laughter. "No company, no, just enough to keep me going for a few hours, that's all." He took a bite of the banana he had just peeled. "Okay, tell me; what's going on?"

Gilbert put down his second cup of coffee and advanced his body closer to the table again. "Something happened last night – rather early this morning – and I'd like your help in the investigation, if you don't mind. Or at least your input."

"No problem," Daniel replied. "But first tell me what happened."

"Okay – here it goes…" Gilbert then told Daniel about Gaston's knifing; his agitated comments regarding the incident being "all about drugs" and his relationship with the Summervilles. He then summarized the Summervilles possible relationship with Betty Palmer (for the little he knew of it) and Alan's qualms about Leon's honesty.

"Right," Daniel said while stirring some berries into his second tub of yoghurt. "Has Gaston said anything about his remarks or about the person who attacked him?"

"Not yet, no. The doc is afraid that he might have a PTSD episode if we push him."

"You mean Gaston is a vet?"

Gilbert nodded. "Model soldier with honorable discharge and a Purple Heart to boot."

"Okay, I think your idea of interviewing the Summervilles is a good one. But like you, I'd like to see if your Simon guy found anything like drugs hidden aboard."

Gilbert nodded. "He should be calling me before you're done scoffing that breakfast."

Daniel chuckled again. He was lucky. He was one of these fellows who could eat anything as much as he wanted without gaining an ounce.

CHAPTER THIRTY-ONE

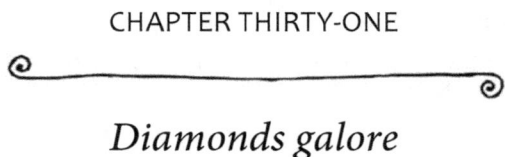

Diamonds galore

THE SUMMERVILLES WERE finishing their breakfast when Gilbert felt his phone vibrate in his shirt pocket. Simon was calling.

"Hey you?" he started, which instantly put an instant smile on Gilbert's lips. "I think you better come down to the head."

Gilbert chuckled. "You mean the sanitation room?"

"No, you knuckle head, I mean the mess *lavatory* if you want to be formal about it."

"You found something?" Gilbert was all ears now.

"Yes, and this ain't no drug that I recognize. It's more like ice, if you know my meaning."

"You mean…?"

"Yes, exactly. You got me. So, can I expect you down here soon before people begin to wonder what I am doing locked up in this stinking stall?"

"Be right down!"

With a significant nod to Daniel – who guzzled down the last of his coffee – both men got up and raced down to the crew mess. As soon as they entered the washroom, Gilbert hollered: "Come out, come out, wherever you are!"

"Okay, I'm coming," Simon answered, flushing the toilet.

Gilbert and Daniel exchanged a puzzled glance.

"Did you really call for us to come down here to attend your morning release?"

Simon came out of the stall and stopped. He looked Daniel up and down, noting the absence of uniform. "Who's he?" he asked Gilbert, pointing a thumb to the smiling agent.

"That's Daniel Crosby. Interpol," Gilbert answered, throwing a glance at Daniel.

"Seriously?" Simon said, walking to the basin to wash his hands. Without turning around, he added, "And you've come on this cruise, why?"

"Because there's a stone and a jeweler on board that deserve some protection; that's why."

"Oh, I see, you're that guy! I thought I recognized you from when you came back from the dredging site." Simon dried his hands and extended the right one to the agent. "Welcome to our precious diamond-holding vessel, Agent Crosby."

"Call me Daniel. Simpler and less conspicuous."

"Sure, but you'll need more than addressing you by your first name to get anyone to say boo to you around here, I can assure you."

"Why's that?" Daniel asked.

Oops, Gilbert thought, *wrong question to ask Simon.*

The latter opened his shirt to air the scars on his chest. "That's why, mate. Interpol and some forensic outfit got me bombed and almost killed. So, no, your first name alone ain't gonna cut it around here."

Daniel shook his head. "Yeah, I can see where you're coming from, man. We've had our share of mistakes, and this is one of them obviously, which I sure won't try to repeat, believe me."

"Okay, let's leave the past where it is, and concentrate on the present," Simon said, returning to the toilet stall he had just left. He lifted the metal panel covering the flushing mechanism and pulled out a small plastic bag from its hiding place. "Here you go, gentlemen. If I am not mistaken, these are not sugar crystals but genuine stones from somewhere around these parts."

Gilbert and Daniel were looking at the diamonds through the clear plastic bag in awe. There must have been at least fifty stones in the bag.

An hour later the trio was seated in Gilbert's office. The chief of security had called on Mr. Atkinson to assist them in evaluating their find.

"There you are!" Gilbert exclaimed when Mr. Atkinson came in. "Thank you so much for accepting to come and help us, sir."

"Yes, yes, of course. I could not resist the temptation, you see. As soon as you mentioned that you found some stones hidden aboard our vessel, I had to come down to see for myself what you had discovered."

"Please sit down, sir," Daniel said, getting up from his seat to leave it vacant for the jeweler to sit down.

"Thank you, Agent Crosby," Atkinson replied, lowering himself into it. "And I must thank you again for saving my life yesterday. It was just what I had expected of our Mr. Huffner. As soon as he mentioned going to the site, I knew I would be in trouble..." He looked at Simon. "I'm sorry, officer, I don't believe we have been introduced."

"No, we have not, Mr. Atkinson. I am Simon – the Potty Man on this vessel!"

Obviously, the jeweler had not expected such an introduction. A fraction of a second later, he chuckled. "I see, officer, a grand job you hold; without your service, we all would be 'congested'."

"It is Simon who found the stones, Mr. Atkinson," Daniel said, after he came back from the operations' room with another chair.

"And where would that have been?" Atkinson asked, looking from Simon to Gilbert.

"In the toilet, where else?" Simon replied jokingly.

This time Atkinson erupted in loud laughter. "You don't say? Quite a find, I should think."

"That is if they are diamonds and not some synthetic imitation," Gilbert remarked.

"Of course, of course," Atkinson said. "May I see the 'toilet loot' then?"

Upon hearing these words, Simon decided he liked the man. There was something good about the little guy.

"There they are," Gilbert said, putting the little plastic bag in front of the jeweler.

"That is really no way to treat diamonds," he remarked. "Such wonder of nature deserves to be laid on a bed of velour or silk – not inserted in a plastic bag as if they were items of groceries."

"Sorry," Simon said, "I didn't have any velour or silk on me when I went to the toilet this morning. Didn't think of taking any with me. I generally wipe with the cheap stuff the ship provides."

Once the chuckles had died down, Mr. Atkinson pulled the bag toward him, opened it and took one of the stones out. He then took a jewelers' loupe out of his vest pocket and adjusted it in front of his right eye. He examined the stone carefully before taking off the loupe from in front of his eye, and drawing a broad smile on his lips. "Totally genuine, gentlemen," he declared. "Of course, I will have to analyze every one of them and give you an estimated value for each stone, but as of now, I believe you should keep this treasure locked away properly."

"Of course, Mr. Atkinson. But would you be able to tell us where these stones were mined?"

"Not mined, my dear Mr. Evans. No, these stones have been dredged out of some river. Although they have no sign of wear, they have been slightly eroded over millions of years, which gives them this smooth and rounded allure. The same as the Star of Sierra Leone, I would assuredly believe they came from West Africa."

"Do you think they were dredged in upper Guinea then?"

Atkinson shook his head. "No, Mr. Evans. The stones in Guinea are very particular and exceptional. They vary in color and in flaw content, which makes them extremely rare. These ones, unless I am mistaken, are white diamonds – probably flawless. Of course, they're of great value, but they are not exceptional."

When Alan learned of what the Potty Man had discovered in the mess' washroom, he and Gilbert decided to defer their meeting with the Summervilles until Gaston was fully recovered. He still hadn't been able to come to terms with the knifing incident and didn't want to talk about it – for the moment. Alan then thought that Alice could have a chat with Gaston. After all, they both had gone to the Middle East and had faced similar incidents perhaps.

This said, he told Alice that he would prefer her to have this conversation with Gaston the next day, when the patient had time to recover from the shock.

That night, Tiffany had organized another cabaret for the passengers. They seemed to enjoy these most of all. Until they were out of the danger zone and had gone past the epidemic area, most passengers preferred spending time on board.

Of course, Constantine was at his rendezvous with center stage. He grabbed the microphone and began by saying, "Good evening, folks. Glad to be alive. Truly, these past few days were absolutely disastrous for me..." At this point everyone thought he was going to talk about Ebola and its nefarious effects on one's body. But no. All hopes of hearing anything about the disease were soon dashed, for he went on with, "my wife contacted me and we had this weird conversation which turned my world upside down. Here is what she told me: I phoned the local gym and I asked if they could teach me how to do the splits. At that point, I truly wondered why would my wife want to learn how to do the splits? Never mind; here is what the instructor told her: he said, "How flexible are you?" My wife said, "I can't make Tuesdays..." The audience broke in chuckles and snickers. Then Constantine went on: "I think at that point we lost the connection because all I heard her say was: "I'm going to chop off the bottom of one of your trousers' legs and put it in a library". I thought: That's a turn-up for the books." He paused. "Truly folks, phone connections at sea are terrible. The next item my wife had to report concerned her latest shopping trip I believe. She told me, and I quote: "So I was getting into my car, and this bloke says to me, "Can you give me a lift?" She said, "Sure, you look great, the world's your oyster, go for it." Really? I had to wonder who she was talking to at that point. And then she added: "You know somebody actually complimented me on my driving today. They left a little note on the windshield. It said "Parking Fine."! That was nice, wasn't it, dear?" I didn't have the courage to ask her "how much?" Now the laughter interrupted Constantine for several minutes.

When cackles and titters had subsided, Constantine resumed the description of his conversation with his wife.

"So Helen – that's my wife – said, "So, I went to buy a new watch and the man asked me if I wanted an Analogue. I said, "No, I just wanted a watch. After that, I stopped at the houseware department and asked the man if someone could find me a good mixer. He told me to go for *Kenwood*. And I really looked, you know, dear, but I couldn't find the man anywhere! The strange thing is, folks, is that we have Kenwood appliances at home already – I had to wonder what was happening to my dear wife while I was away." The applause then drowned his last comments. He then concluded saying, "Thank you! You've been excellent company once again."

Alan bent down to whisper in Tiffany's ear, "He's better every time I listen to him."

She turned to him while they were still applauding the man. "This is only tidbits of what he can really do apparently. And he writes most of his material. I have no idea where he finds all the jokes…"

"I'd say in everyday life," Alan said. He then looked around to see if the Summervilles were in attendance. They had been told about Gaston's "accidental knifing" and had paid a visit to their secretary at the med center.

According to Alice, Gaston had first told them that he was trying to help the stage manager to set some lights – just to pass the time – when the knife slipped and slashed his chest. It seemed highly unlikely that the stage manager would allow a passenger to help him.

They didn't question him or ask him who the stage manager was apparently. Alan had made himself scarce during the interview. He felt that if they were involved somehow with the young man's knifing, he wanted more than hearsay or suppositions before he talked to them.

Mr. Atkinson, for his part, had been very busy with the evaluation of the stones. He was now sure these diamonds came from Sierra Leone. He wondered who had brought them on board. They were beautiful stones – every one of them. He estimated the total value to be around four million dollars if cut properly. Waste was always a concern, of course, but these days most jewelers would put to good use almost every diamond chip or even dust. If the quality was there, the size didn't particularly matter. Once he finished the work and listed all of the stones for Gilbert, he dug a small cassette out of his briefcase – the one he was going to use if he had had the chance to collect some stones in Guinea – and laid all of the diamonds on a bed of blue silk. They were indeed magnificent. He shook his head, closed and sealed the cassette, readying it to take to Gilbert's office. One of the security officers had stayed with the jeweler all day. The two of them were now waiting for the elevator to take them down to the security office's deck.

The elevator was full. Most people came out on that floor and someone bumped into Mr. Atkinson. The gentleman excused himself profusely and went on his way. By the time the little jeweler and the security guard made it to Gilbert's office, the cassette had disappeared.

CHAPTER THIRTY-TWO

Who wants ice?

THE CONTESSA WAS DUE TO DOCK the next morning in Freetown. The journey from Conakry had been a short one. The landscape had changed somewhat. With mountains as the backdrop, Freetown is located in the foothills which descend gently in rolling hills and valleys to the ocean shore. This rather large city is endowed with green expanses extending as far as the eye can see. Some parts of the city have been abandoned for years. These are the neighborhoods where poverty has taken hold and does not seem desirous of releasing its clutches on the families inhabiting its slums. On the other hand, there are parts of the city which are a reflection of its wealth. If corruption would let go of its vice-hold on the government, perhaps Sierra Leone could become one of the most prosperous countries in West Africa. The discovery of diamonds in the upper forest put the country on the map, so to speak. Sierra Leoneans are either business people or men of the forest.

Practically the entire country is covered in lush jungle or natural gardens. Quite a fascinating place if it were not for the fact that it has been ravaged by Ebola in the last year or so.

Because of its large population, the disease spread like a proverbial wild fire. There wasn't any way to stop its advance or encroachment into the mountains. The *Hillside Station*, which, originally, was one of the favorite spots for tourists visiting Freetown, had been vacated months ago. The hotel and resort had been left empty soon after the epidemic had been declared. This is where Alan and the WHO team were going to be staying for the next few days. Located some ten to fifteen miles out of the city, it would prevent the physicians and nurses from being in direct contact with the population near the shore.

However, before berthing the vessel in port, Captain Hildebrandt insisted that none of the passengers disembark from his vessel until the WHO physicians had completed their visits of the hospitals and had established their operation headquarters at the Hillside Station. Making sure that the situation was at least manageable for the passengers was paramount.

Meanwhile, Babette and Betty Palmer were standing by the upper deck's railing, taking photographs of the bay incurving Freetown and the nearby hills. The contrasting colors of the city sprawls with the green of the foothills were amazingly attractive. The whole picturesque landscape held a certain charm.

Babette said to Betty, "You know, this is one city I would love to visit. It looks so inviting. A little like New Orleans. Viewed from here, I would say it's a very well appointed city."

"Speaking of New Orleans," Betty said, "Have you heard what happened to Gaston, the Summerville's secretary?"

Babette turned to her friend and frowned. It was obvious she hadn't heard the latest. "No. Pray tell, what's happened?"

"Well, I haven't heard all of the details except that Mr. Evans came to see me the morning after the incident..., yesterday morning that is."

"Why on earth would he come to talk to you?" Babette asked, even more puzzled now.

"Because, you see, I wanted some inside information, as it were, on the Summervilles and who would be better placed to answer my questions than their secretary."

"But why...?"

"Hold on, let me tell you. We just had a late drink at the night-bar and after that, I just went to bed. But from what Mr. Evans told me in the morning, Gaston didn't go to bed. He apparently went to the theater…"

"The theater you say? But why…?"

"Dear Babette, if I knew that, I believe there wouldn't be any mystery behind the fact that he's been knifed."

"Are you saying the poor man was attacked?" Betty nodded. "But why?"

"As I said, there wouldn't be any mystery if…"

"Yes, yes, of course," Babette said. "I'm sorry if I sound so baffled, it's simply because I am. Why would anyone want to kill Gaston?" She paused. "Did Mr. Evans tell you if he survived?"

"Oh yes; I mean he did say that Gaston will be fine according to Doctor Mayhew. But apparently he doesn't – I mean Gaston doesn't want to talk about what happened because of his PTSD."

"You don't say!" Babette looked at her friend as if a little green man had just landed on the deck from outer space. "This is too incredible for words."

"Well, I would perhaps say the same thing if it weren't for the fact that we had a drink together…"

"Are you saying that the attacker may have thought Gaston would have talked a little too much or revealed things about the Summervilles that should have remained unsaid?"

"Something like that. Although I truly cannot think of one single item he said that could have been damaging to the Summerville's."

"Did you tell Gaston that you thought Leon was your nephew?" Babette inquired.

"Yes, I did, I'm afraid. But I had the impression it wasn't news to him. He didn't tell me as much, but he certainly sounded less surprised than I would have thought he would be." Betty turned toward the hallway at their backs. "Why don't we go for a nice ice-coffee? It's getting hot out here again." She tittered. "Where are the days when someone hurried indoors because the weather was foul outside?"

"Just across an ocean, my dear," Babette replied, following her friend to the nearest elevator.

When the theft of the diamond cassette was discovered, Gilbert was literally up in arms. He was terribly upset. Alan didn't want to let him interview Gaston yet about his knife wound. And now, Gilbert was even more upset since the diamond cassette had been swiped from the jeweler's pocket. Someone was playing games, and Gilbert did not like it. Four million dollars is worth getting into a lot of trouble – and somebody was looking down the barrel of all the trouble Gilbert wanted to inflict on the perpetrator – once he could lay hands on him, of course.

He phoned Alan. He wanted to try one more time to let him, Gilbert, interview Gaston. It had been more than 24 hours since the incident and he should have recovered well enough to face the music as it were.

"Hi, Doc..."

Alan frowned. "The answer is still no, Gilbert."

"But why? I need to know why he was attacked. I want to know if he knew anything about the diamonds that we found downstairs."

"All in good time, Gilbert. You'll get all of your answers, I promise, once Alice is finished talking to him."

"Is that because Alice was a vet – I mean is a vet like Gaston?"

"Exactly. These two have many things in common. And one of these things is the fact that they will talk about their memories of the battle field freely..."

"And you think he's going to open up for her."

"Yes, Gilbert. That's exactly what I'm hoping will happen."

In fact, Alan had been right. Gaston was talking to Alice as if the two of them had served under the same command. At one point Alan heard them laughing. He would have liked to interrupt but thought the better of it.

"...and we had this Aussie guy in our platoon who was mad – I mean he had the worst jokes," Gaston recalled, "Like this one:

Imagine the blokes in the Melbourne International Airport control tower…" He told us. "You gotta love this one even if you've never lived in Melbourne…

Melbourne Tower: "Pakistani Air 511 – you are cleared to land on runway9R."

Pakistani Air: "Thank you, Melbourne – acknowledge cleared to land on infidels runway 9R.Allah be praised.

Melbourne Tower: "Iran Air 721 – you are cleared to land on runway 9L."

Iran Air: "Thank you, Melbourne. We are cleared to land on infidel's runway 9L. – Allah is great."

"There was a pause in the transmission for a bit and then the Pakistani Air pilot came back with: "MELBOURNE TOWER– MELBOURNE TOWER!"

"Melbourne Tower: "Go ahead Pakistani Air 511…"

Pakistani Air: "YOU HAVE CLEARED BOTH OUR AIRCRAFT FOR THE SAME RUNWAY GOING IN OPPOSITE DIRECTIONS. WE ARE ON A COLLISION COURSE … INSTRUCTIONS, PLEASE!"

Melbourne Tower: "Proceed to your destination and tell Allah we said "Hi!"

"You see what I mean?" Gaston asked Alice, after their laughter had subsided. "Totally crazy, right?"

They continued talking for a while longer, but when it came to the knifing incident a day and a half ago, Gaston's recollection of it was prompt and accurate.

"You see, Alice, I had been talking to Mrs. Palmer. She's got it into her head that maybe Leon Summerville is her nephew. I don't know if that's correct, but it certainly makes sense. There are a lot of pieces of that puzzle that seem to fit." He paused for a minute, took a drink of water and resumed. "Anyway, after we talked, she said she was tired and we decided to call it a night. Well, I'm sure she went to her cabin, but me, I wasn't sleepy yet. Since I came back, see, I've had lots of trouble going to sleep…"

"I know what you mean," Alice interrupted. "It's the same for me. That's why I like to work at night – no need to go to sleep." She smiled. "But anyway, I cut you off. Go on. What happened after that?"

"Well, I thought I would get a magazine in the foyer and have a read of it in the theater." He shook his head. "And don't tell me I could have done that in my cabin. Frankly, I can't. It's too small. It's good when I can sleep or take a shower, but for anything else, it's really like a cell. So, anyway, I took my magazine and went in."

"It wasn't locked?" Alice sounded surprised.

"Yeah – I mean no, it wasn't. And, you're right, that's something that I found kind of strange. But who am I to know what should be left open or locked on a ship. So, I went in, there were a few lights on and although it was a bit dark to read, it was quiet and peaceful like." He paused to drink another gulp of water. "I was about halfway through the article I was reading when I felt a belt going around my neck." Gaston placed his hand at the base of his neck and swallowed as if he could still feel the belt. "I grabbed it and pulled it hard and fast. The man holding it came with it. He must not have expected my reaction because he swore and landed on his feet so fast, I thought I was facing a gorilla of some kind. He had that belt in the one hand and the knife in the other. He swung it a few times; I dodged it and was about to grab his arm – to crash him – when he swung the knife at me. I backed out just in time, but not soon enough. He had managed to plant the tip of it in my chest."

"And why didn't you tell this story right away to the Doc?" Alice asked.

Gaston shook his head. "It's because I thought I saw that guy in Afghanistan. He looked familiar anyway."

"And you say he's a big guy?"

"Oh yeah. At least six-two. And muscles like you wouldn't believe."

"What did he wear, do you remember?"

"No, not really. It was too dark to see anything, but I remember his hands. He's probably dark skinned."

"You mean he's black?"

"No, not black, but really dark. Oh, and he's got some kind of short haircut. Not bald but very close to it."

"Okay, that's great that you remember," Alice said, taking the empty jug of water. "And I think I'll let you sleep for a bit now. You need it." She smiled and turned on her heels to leave the room.

"Oh, and thanks, Alice. I think I will sleep now," Gaston said, turning on his side and grimacing a little – his wound, obviously, wasn't healed yet.

When Alice came back to bring him a fresh pitcher of water, Gaston was fast asleep. She smiled and went out of the room silently.

She went to Alan's office and sat across from him.

After she related what Gaston had described of the incident, she said, "You know, Doc, I think his story is very close to reality."

"You think he's left something out?"

"No, I don't think that's it. I think it all happened the way he said, but the man who attacked him is not the person he described. I believe that he's transposed the story from Afghanistan onto this one. I also believe that he is absolutely convinced that the man who attacked him while he was out there is the same man who tried killing him the other night."

"How do you think we can convince him to dig deeper into his recollection?"

"Sorry, Doc, I don't think you can, because the two men in his mind are one and the same person. The only way he might change his story is if he's confronted with the real perpetrator, assuming we can catch him before he leaves the ship."

"Okay, Alice. Let's revisit the problem tomorrow when he goes back to his cabin."

"Oh, sorry, Doc, I forgot to mention, but that's another thing. He feels confined inside his cabin and can't seem to be able to rest in there. It reminds him of a cell."

"Alright then, let's see what we can do about that."

While Alice had been talking to Gaston, Gilbert was still pacing the length of his office. He had no clue of what might have happened to the young man. When Alan called him and told him that Gaston had described what happened, Gilbert's first question was, "What about the drugs? Did he say anything about that?"

"No, I don't think he did. And for now I believe that he recalled being attacked when he was in Kabul – maybe something to do with drugs then, but not here, not now."

"Okay, Doc, I'll take the bread crumbs until we find the loaf. But what do you suggest I do about the diamonds? The thief is obviously an excellent pickpocket, but what bothers me the most is the fact that he was aware of the diamonds being in Mr. Atkinson's possession. How could he have known, do you think?"

"Maybe someone other than Agent Crosby is very interested in our jeweler and is observing his every move."

"That's a given, Doc! But what I'd like to know is who the interested party is."

CHAPTER THIRTY-THREE

How did he know?

ALAN HAD TO WONDER indeed. There were very few passengers interested or even aware of what was happening during this journey apart from what they saw, heard or watched during the entertainment soirees. Perhaps Betty Palmer's assistants were a pair worth watching. They had been very circumspect lately, losing themselves in the crowd, so to speak. While everyone had their eyes on Mr. Atkinson and his comings and goings, perhaps one should keep an eye on those whose eyes were more focused on the little jeweler than others.

Nothing much was known of Miss Adele Muesli and Mr. Gregory Ashton. Along the way, and because of Betty Palmer searching for her nephew, a lot of Leon and Linda Summerville's past and background had emerged. However, when it came to Adele and Gregory, the information was rather meager.

Alan had been right.

In their cabin, Adele and Gregory were in the middle of a rather heated discussion.

"Now what? What do you expect me to do with this?" Adele asked, pointing at the little box on the table of the small sitting room of their suite.

"I don't know… Maybe we should get the real thief…"

"Hold on a sec, Greg. What do you mean, the "real thief"? You're the one who stole it from the jeweler. Who else is involved in this?"

"Well, they're not Atkinson's diamonds…"

"How do you know that?"

"Well…"

"Never mind," Adele bellowed. "Do you know who the "real thief" is by any chance?"

Gregory shook his head. "I haven't a clue. I just know Atkinson was asked to value the stones. Apparently they were found in the crew mess – or at least that's what I heard. I just took the opportunity to pick Atkinson's pocket when he came out of the elevator. It was like he was begging to be robbed."

"You're a child, you know that?"

"These are worth a real fortune…"

"They probably are, but if we keep them, the only fortune we'll get is to play Bingo in prison."

"And you are such a party pooper," Greg retorted, walking toward the door.

"Where are you going?" Adele demanded.

"To get some air. It's much too stifling around here."

"Oh no you don't!" Adele yelled, practically jumping from the sofa to the door – barring Greg's exit. "You better take these with you"—she handed him the cassette—"and lose them somewhere." She glared at him. "I mean it, Greg. Don't come back with them, you hear me!"

Shrugging, Gregory took the cassette from Adele's hand, pushed past her, opened the door and walked out. Adele slammed the door shut and went back to the sofa. She plopped down on it and pouted, much like a little girl who had her first fight with a school friend.

Edmund, who had the same inkling about the cassette's whereabouts as his great-grandson did, was smiling to himself when he watched "little" Adele sulking on the sofa. But there wasn't any time to lose. Edmund had to follow Gregory. The disgruntled young man might do anything imaginable with the diamonds. Edmund wouldn't even be surprised if he threw the cassette overboard.

But, no, Gregory was not to be swayed in his purpose. He was going to keep the diamonds. Where would he hide them, was the question that encumbered his mind as he walked along the promenade deck. The afternoon was hot. It seemed that everyone had taken shelter in their cabin or the upper deck restaurants. Gregory did not want to be distracted if he was to find a place for the cassette. *But where?*

While Edmund was on Gregory's tail intent on not losing sight of the young man, Gilbert decided he needed to have that talk with Gaston. The latter would be moved to a larger cabin later that day, since his claustrophobia seemed to prevent him from sleeping in his current quarters. Gilbert wanted to interview the young man before he was moved. Besides, he wanted Alice to be in attendance. His reasoning being that maybe he would open up to him, if she was around.

As Gilbert entered the medical center, he noticed someone he didn't expect to see sitting in the waiting room – Gregory Ashton. Gilbert first wondered where his other half was – Adele Muesli usually never left the young man's side. Yet, Gilbert wasn't there to chat with Gregory but with Gaston.

He knocked on Alan's door. He was on the phone. He waved at Gilbert to come in. He sat down and waited for the doc's conversation to come to an end. It sounded as if he was organizing his "sortie" to the *Hillside Station* with one of the WHO physicians.

"Okay, Gilbert, what can I do for you," Alan asked as he hung up the phone.

"I wanted to have a chat with Gaston, if that's okay with you?"

"Sure; not a problem. He's going to his new cabin later today and he should be as fine as rain in a day or two – as long as he doesn't exercise or pull on his sutures."

"Okay, I won't be long," Gilbert replied, getting up from the visitors' chair. I've got diamonds to find."

Alan smiled. Gilbert stared.

"Why the grin, Doc. What's the matter?"

Alan crossed his arms over his chest after he stood up. "I am not going to tell you how I know this – it's just a hunch on my part – but I believe the person who took the cassette is sitting in our waiting room."

Gilbert was about to turn around. "Don't you dare look!" Alan said, "I don't want you to spook him."

"But, Doc, how do you know this? How did you find out?"

"It's just what he said when he came in that made me think he was probably the one who took the cassette."

"What did he say?" Gilbert was more than puzzled now – let's make that truly baffled.

"He had something he wanted to put in the fridge…."

"How very clever of him. I would never have thought about that. *Ice in the fridge!*"

"Exactly. But I haven't seen the cassette or the diamonds yet. So, I suggest you keep this under wrap and have your interview with Gaston while I get the story from Gregory."

With a smile on his face, Gilbert turned around, strode out of Alan's office and walked past Gregory without as much as a greeting.

When Gilbert took a seat beside Gaston's bed, the young man was all smiles. *It looks as if it's my lucky day,* Gilbert thought. Things were finally moving in the right direction.

"Mr. Evans," Gaston said, "Sorry I wasn't able to talk to you sooner. Memories of other battles were preventing me from seeing things clearly."

"Don't mention it, Mr. Giroux…"

"Please call me Gaston; Mr. Giroux makes me sound so old." He chuckled.

"No problem, Gaston," Gilbert replied. "I just have a couple of questions regarding what happened the other night." Gaston nodded. "The first relates to what you told Alice when you were first moved here to the med center: Why did you say that you were helping the stage manager with the electrical wiring?"

"Sorry, Mr. Evans, but I don't remember saying that, although I do remember seeing a man come out of the side stage at one point when I was reading my magazine."

"Okay, you saw a man come out of the side stage; did you talk to him?"

"No. I wasn't paying much attention. He wasn't paying attention to me either, it seems."

"What made you think that you were helping the man with the electrical wiring?"

Gaston shook his head and looked up as Alice entered the room.

"Well, Mr. Evans is keeping you company for a bit I see," she said, sitting on the other side of the bed.

"Yeah. You know it's strange, but Mr. Evans was just asking me about what I said when I first got here after the accident; something about my helping the stage manager with the electrical wiring… I can't recall ever doing anything like that."

"That is certainly okay, that often happens, Gaston," Gilbert said. "Why don't you tell me what you remember happening? And if you recall the face of the man who attacked you."

"I don't think I can give you a description of the guy," Gaston said, turning to Alice. "As I said to Miss Muller, I know he was as big as a gorilla; he was dark skinned and he smelled…"

"That's good recall, Gaston, what did he smell like?"

"I hate to say this, but he smelled like shit!"

"You mean like someone who's just pooped in his pants?"

Count on Alice to be direct.

"No, not really. More like sewage refuse. It's like the guy came out of the sewer."

"That's great, Gaston," Gilbert said, truly excited with the description Gaston just gave him. Not many people on a ship could smell like sewage.

"And, perchance, did you see him leave?"

"Just the same way he must have come in – the stage door."

Alice and Gilbert exchanged a glance.

"You saw him come in then?" Alice asked. She hadn't heard this version of the story yet.

"Well, yes. I mean at first I thought he was the stage manager – I don't know why – but then I didn't think about it until he tried strangling me with that belt... I mean a wire-like belt. That's probably why I thought he was doing the electrical wiring."

"Can you describe the belt-like wire?" Gilbert asked.

"Yeah. It was like one of those heavy-duty extension cords. It looks like several wires spliced together."

"Was it a long cord or just a small piece, do you remember?" Gilbert asked.

"I'd say it was about three feet long – no more than that," Gaston replied.

"Okay, that's great, Gaston," Gilbert added, while taking notes. "One last question; could you describe the face to a sketch artist you think?"

"I don't know, Mr. Evans. Like I said to Miss Muller, the guy reminded me of a man I encountered in Kabul. He was big too. But this one was more agile. When I flipped him over, he seemed surprised. He didn't expect my reaction, whereas the guy in Kabul knew all the moves."

While Gaston was relating his story to Gilbert and Alice, Gregory was telling his own story to Alan.

"And you say you found the cassette in the foyer?" Alan asked the young man.

"Well..., yes."

"What if I told you I don't believe you?"

"Okay, okay, Doc. If I were you, I wouldn't believe me either. I just took the opportunity when it presented itself, that's all."

"And what opportunity was that, Mr. Ashton?"

"Well, I had seen Mr. Atkinson go into his cabin, accompanied by one of the security guys. At the time I thought the jeweler was probably examining the Star before giving it back to the authority here in Freetown. But then, a while later, I saw him again, as I came out of the elevator. I thought he must have "it" on him as there was a big bulge in his jacket pocket – and I just picked it."

"What did you think when you got it back to your cabin?"

"I don't know – I talked to Adele. She was furious. She wanted me out of the cabin and to take the Star with me…"

"And you still believe it's the Star you've got in that cassette?"

"What else could it be?"

Alan knew instinctively that Gregory was lying. "Come on, Mr. Ashton, what are you not telling me?"

"Okay, okay, Doc. I saw Mr. Atkinson going to the security office yesterday and come out in the company of a security officer. So I followed them. I don't really know anything else other than I thought why all the fuss about the Star if Atkinson is not going ashore yet…"

"You've been busy, haven't you, Mr. Ashton?"

"You could say that. I just want you to keep the cassette in the fridge. Maybe there's going to be a reward for the one who found it… What do you think?"

"Listen, Mr. Ashton, you've admitted taking the cassette from Mr. Atkinson's pocket, do you think for one moment anyone is going to reward you for stealing the diamond or diamonds – whatever the case may be?"

"Just as long as I don't get arrested – Adele would be furious."

"Alright, since you've come clean about your actions, I don't think anyone is going to press charges. But don't you go picking anyone else's pocket from now on; otherwise I'll be forced to tell Mr. Evans all about your sticky fingers?"

Gregory nodded, obviously relieved.

CHAPTER THIRTY-FOUR

A consultancy gone wrong

DRS. ASHFORD AND HATFIELD were riding in the first van with Alan, as usual. During their two-days in Freetown, the WHO team would visit three hospitals. Before they started their assignment, however, they established a camp, so to speak, at the Hillside Station. It had been deserted since the beginning of the epidemic. Since they didn't know the conditions in which the resort and hotel had been abandoned, Gilbert decided to get a couple of stewards to accompany the group, together with a cook. They also brought all the provisions they needed to spend the two days in relative comfort. The last thing they wanted to do was to go to town to fetch food or missing items.

The winding ride up to the resort reminded Alan of one of his assignments in Europe. Physicians routinely consult for organizations in setting up programs, or ensuring that programs are appropriately performed, and produce various protocols for the clients. The clients are often governments, NATO, European Commission, etc. One always tries to work for reputable employers, given that doctors are hired on a hand-shake and a promise. And sometimes the promise is broken – no pay is forthcoming at the end of the consultancy assignment.

As Alan was recounting his misadventure to Dr. Ashford, the latter nodded emphatically.

"And you're not the only one to have been taken for a ride, Dr.

Mayhew. I, for one, recall what happened to me in Eastern Europe. I was party to doing a long consult for a country brokered by a consulting firm (originally based out of Canada but then which strategically moved to Austria where laws protect these guys). I ended up being $8,000 out of pocket for expenses and did not get paid for the consulting or lost time when I could have been doing other work. Some of the people I worked with, including industrial hygienists, psychologists, administrators, and other doctors ended up losing much, much more than I did." He paused. "As I recall, this guy Norman got the contract with the EC country and then got us to do the work, which benefited people in that EC country, of course. For all that, we got naught, while he got paid big bucks. He never paid any of us our consulting fees or expenses. Norman took his ill-gotten gain and relocated to Vienna where he could not be touched because of Austrian laws."

"I can only sympathize with you, Dr. Ashford. I have been faced with similar scams myself as I said, and truly, I wish we could stop these agents from abusing our goodwill."

"But it's up to each of us to distrust these agents when we do not get to see the contract signed and sealed in advance from the government agency."

"Do you have contracts with the World Health Organization?" Alan asked.

"Oh yes. None of us would lift a finger or think of going anywhere without a contract, an advance payment for travel expenses, and a deposit in our bank account before we leave."

"I suppose that organization wouldn't stand for their reputation being smeared if they dared cheat their physicians and nursing staff out of their salaries."

"Exactly. We are engaged to save lives, and they are not paying us for their conspiracy."

"I've never thought about it that way, I must admit," Alan said, glancing out of the van's side window now.

The doctors all sat back and tried ignoring what was glaring at them in the streets along which they drove. There was nothing they could possibly do for the poor people who were still suffering from the disease or died hours before. It was a nightmarish scene. It was much like one probably would have seen in the scourges of ancient Rome and major cities of Europe during the Black Plague and other epidemics that have affected humanity. They didn't want to take home this memory, but probably would carry it with them for the rest of their lives.

Dr. Hatfield had been quiet thus far. Suddenly, he turned to his companions and said, "I heard you talk about losing money, but did you realize most of us are losing money every day because we don't drink enough beer?"

Alan and Dr. Ashford exchanged a glance.

"Could you explain that?" Alan asked.

"Well, if you had bought $1000.00 worth of Nortel stock one year ago, it would now be worth $16.00. With Enron, you would have $12.50 of the original $1,000.00 invested a year before bankruptcy. With WorldCom, you would have less than $4.00 left. If you invested $1000.00 with Bernie Madoff you would have $0. But…, if you had bought $1,000.00 worth of Budweiser (the beer, not the stock) one year ago, drank all the beer, then turned in the cans for the 10 cent deposit, you would have $215.00. Based on the above, my current investment advice is to drink heavily and recycle."

Both Alan and Dr. Ashford laughed loudly over the road noise.

"Trust my friend to come up with the right joke, Dr. Mayhew. Hatfield's not a bad guy when it comes down to it…"

"What do you mean; "not a bad guy"? I think I'm pretty darn patient when it comes to traveling with you, Ashford," Hatfield replied jocularly.

"Yeah, you're *pretty* alright but I don't know about *patient* though. I've seen you in action, remember?"

Alan was happy to be working with these two. He considered himself quite lucky in fact. There's nothing worse than having to work for days on end with someone you can't stand.

A half hour later they came up to the entrance to Hillside Station. As expected there wasn't anyone to meet them, although a man and a woman came out of the nearby woods when they saw all of the people alighting from the vans.

Alan went to them. "Do you live near here?" he asked.

They looked at one another and nodded.

"Have you been sick?"

"No-no, sir," the man answered. "We live in the mountains and come down with vegetables for the market every week. But the market woman told us not to come down – they were all sick she said."

"My name is Dr. Mayhew," Alan told them. "I have come with other doctors to give vaccines to people in Freetown so you won't get sick. Do you think I could vaccinate you?"

They exchanged a glance and nodded in unison before the man said, "I am Mamadou Simon and this is my wife Annie." He looked at the woman briefly. "We have children – five of them – and we would prefer you give them the vaccines, Doctor. We want them to be safe."

"I understand," Alan said, "But I will have to inoculate everyone for them to be safe. So, as soon as we're settled, if you bring your family over, we can give an injection to all seven of you. Would that be okay with you?"

"Sure, Doctor," Mamadou said before turning to Annie again and nodding. "Do you have vegetables?" he asked.

Alan had no idea if they had brought anything else than canned food. He turned to the stewards. "No we haven't got any fresh vegetables, Doc. Only cans of peas, carrots, beans and corn – that's it."

Alan returned his gaze to Mamadou. "I don't know how much we could buy since we're only here for a couple of days, but anything you can bring us would be welcome, I'm sure."

"Do you like strawberries?" Annie asked.

Alan smiled. "Oh yes – love them. Why? Do you have strawberries?"

Annie nodded. "Yes, Doctor. We grow them at this time,

especially for visitors. We have many baskets. Do you want some?"

By this time Henry, the cook, had made his way to the little gathering. "Yes, ma'am. And if you like them yourself, I'll cook you the best strawberry cake for tonight's dinner – how's that?"

If she wasn't as black as coal, Alan would have sworn that Annie was blushing from ear to ear. "Yes, thank you, sir. But the cake will be for the children. For us, we will eat whatever is left…"

The humbleness in the woman's words touched Alan's heart. "Okay then, that settles it," he said cheerfully, "let's get us all settled and then if you, Annie, will bring the kids down the hill for everyone to get a vaccine we can start our tour of the hospitals."

Mamadou hesitated before he asked, "Are you going back to town?"

"Yes, Mamadou, we will. We have to visit all of the hospitals," Dr. Hatfield said.

"Because, sir, I mean…, Doctor, I have my brother… I mean he works at the Central Hospital. I don't know if he… I mean if he is sick. Can you look for him? He is a nurse. His name is Christian Simon. Maybe you can ask around?"

"Of course, we'll do that, Mamadou. And if he's there; do you want me to give him a message?"

"Just let him know that we're okay, Doctor. We'll be going back to town when we know the disease is gone."

It took Alan and the team about two hours to get everyone settled in their various duties and to have the rooms ready for the people who were going to stay overnight. After that, they went back to town and left the hotel "management" in Alice's hands. When she saw all the vegetables being brought into the large kitchen, she beat a quick retreat – cooking wasn't her forte.

Back on board of *The Contessa*, Mr. Atkinson was getting nervous. He knew that he would have to meet with the prime-minister the next day, and return the Star of Sierra Leone to its rightful owner. On the one hand, he was glad the whole ordeal was soon to be over. On the other, he felt as if he was going to part with a child, something that had grown to play an integral role in his life. The Star had been his pride and joy for nearly forty years now. He would be sad to see it go back to the hills where it was found – unless the country president had other ideas for its destiny. Mr. Atkinson only hoped he wouldn't have it cut, because, the jeweler was sure, he would not succeed. No one had managed to split it thus far, and Mr. Atkinson did not think – in fact he was almost sure – it would ever happen.

The curse which accompanied the Star was real as far as he was concerned. He had been fighting one disease after another since he had bought the stone and now he didn't want to risk his life by keeping it.

Another person who was rather nervous was Daniel Crosby. Tomorrow he would accompany Mr. Atkinson to the presidential palace where he would attend the ceremony of the return of the Star of Sierra Leone to the prime minister. He was glad to see the end of that assignment. There had been very little to worry about, apart from that little incident in Guinea, of course. But after the ceremony was over, he would have his hands full with finding the owner of the stones that had been stolen, hidden in the crew mess lavatory and then stolen again, only to be turned over to the doc to be stored in his fridge – under lock and key. Someone, somewhere aboard *The Contessa* was probably very unhappy right now. He or she was out four million dollars, not a little sum to lose at the hands of the Potty Man.

Thinking of the Potty Man, Daniel needed to attend to the man's safety. It would be the worst kind of luck if something were to happen to him; he, Daniel, would probably be facing suspension if not dismissal. Yet, from what he had seen on board, there weren't many people apt to protect the Potty Man from harm. None that he knew had military experience and from what he heard, Gaston Giroux and Nurse Muller were the only two who had been in "the field", as it were. Perhaps, Gaston would be the guy to enroll for the rest of the cruise, *unless I can get headquarters to get someone else involved,* he thought. Getting someone else involved would mean opening another case file. Daniel didn't know if he wanted to do that. The thief was aboard this ship. He was sure of it. He would not leave without his stones. Where did the stones come from in the first place; Daniel would have to find out. Yet, when you can't even walk through the city, or question anyone without being exposed to a deadly disease, things can become very difficult indeed.

CHAPTER THIRTY-FIVE

The scourge of progress

WHEN COLONIZATION PREVAILED, Africa was suffering from the wounds of tyranny and progress. None of the people who had been colonized for centuries knew the bane of progress. Modernization has its price when not consumed properly. For the people of Freetown, many living in Sierra Leone, and other countries of West Africa, progress had been intolerable. Much like toddlers in a toy shop, the African men and women were given new toys, new means of easing their toils, new means of transporting goods and people, and new products that supposedly would make their lives easier. Did they need or want an "easier" life? Most did not want anything else but freedom. Freedom from tyranny, freedom to choose the life they wanted to lead. They didn't want new cars, new stoves, new washing machines– they wanted to be left alone to make the choice as to how they wanted to live.

Freetown is perhaps one of the best examples of ambivalence in the mind of those who populate it. The choice of life, the choice of existence and taking what was on offer was the freedom the inhabitants of the city endeavored to keep. Some lived in what appeared to be poverty; others lived in the abundance left behind by the colonial masters, but most lived the life they chose to live. None had been forced to abide the invasion of progress.

Alan seemed well aware of the choices these people made when he looked at the various faces that came through the doors of the hospital. Those who were sick – mostly with Ebola – seemed to be resigned to their fate. They hobbled in, sat down in what used to be a fairly decent waiting area, and waited either for a doctor to take a look at them or waited until death came to fetch them.

The sight of these people left to their own devices was disheartening, to say the least. The people of Sierra Leone had chosen to live where and how they did; but now the choice was costing them their lives.

The sanitary conditions in the shanty towns near the center of Freetown had been their downfall. These people would have been better off returning to the forest and hills when the colonialists left the country. They would have benefited from Nature's own healing process. Like Annie and Mamadou, they would not have been affected. Yet, the affected had chosen to stay close to the *toy shop*, to benefit from progress while ignoring the frequent menaces of diseases.

For those who came into the hospital to accompany the sick ones, they only realized too late that they too would soon be victims of Ebola and die much as their family or friends would beside them.

Alan and the WHO team set out to work as soon as they came out of the vans, already wearing their protective gear. A hospital administrator, the one who had survived thus far, had organized for the people most in need to be vaccinated. They were to line-up along the hallway on the ground floor.

When Alan and the WHO team came down the corridor, applause and cheers accompanied them to the first ward where they inoculated over three hundred people in the next few hours.

It had been exhausting work which demanded constant attention. A mistake could cost a life. Alan wished he could have worked without his protective suit. It made every move more laborious. But, in the end, he was happy to have been able to assist so many in regaining their health.

As for the nurses and assistants, they gave a leaflet to everyone who could read and explained how to prevent another epidemic where they lived. They basically taught them (as much as they could through a translator) how hygiene worked when faced with progress.

Henry, the cook had come down with them in one of the vans with coolers filled with sandwiches, fruit juice and oranges. Water was what most of the team wanted when they were finally able to take off their hoods and masks.

"I wish they would invent something to refrigerate these suits," Dr. Ashford noted, sweat soaking his shirt, as he sat on the bench outside of the hospital. It used to be an English Garden for the long-term patients. It had been neglected for years and resembled an abandoned, weedy backyard.

"You and I both," Alan agreed, taking a bite of his sandwich. "Perhaps, Mylar suits would be better. They keep the heat out and conserve your body temperature while you wear it."

"You mean like those Mylar suits the first astronauts wore in the sixties?"

"The very same. It even became a fashion among young adults at the time."

"That must have been funny – everybody dressed in foil, looking like the left over roast beef," Hatfield remarked, chuckling.

"I guess, but it made for great raincoats."

The conversation died for a moment and then Alan said, "Have you seen any male nurse in the group that worked with us this morning?"

"No, why?" Ashford asked.

"I just wondered if we could find Christian Simon – the veggie-man's brother."

"Oh yeah, I heard him mention something like that," Hatfield agreed. "When we're done with lunch, maybe we could ask the administrator to locate him."

"Grand idea," Ashford said.

"Yeah, I really would like to bring our veggie-man a bit of good news."

It was almost nightfall when the vans pulled up to the Hillside Station. Mamadou and Annie were waiting for them by the side of the driveway to the resort.

The smile of Alan's face couldn't have been mistaken for anything else than good news.

"You found him?" Mamadou asked eagerly.

Alan nodded. "Yes, we found him, Mamadou. And he will be well now."

Tears pearled at the rim of the veggie-man's eyes. "Thank you, Doctor, thank you," he said, shaking his hand. "When can we go back?"

"Not yet, Mamadou, not yet. In a couple of weeks, maybe. It is still too early for your family to visit the market. It will be a while before you'll be able to sell your veggies again." He paused and watched Annie stringing her chaplet. He turned to her. "You are Christian people aren't you?"

Mamadou nodded. "We go and see the monks up mountain since we don't have a priest anymore. He died the first week people were sick."

Alan nodded. "This has been an ordeal for you, hasn't it?"

"Yes, Doctor, it has been terrible. But we are the lucky ones."

"Why do you choose to live in the hills?" Alan asked.

"It is just better for the children. The air is good up here. And we love to grow the vegetables. It's like we give life to the ground."

"You are very wise, Mamadou." Alan then turned his gaze to the Hillside Station and the hotel behind him. "Have you eaten today?"

"Oh not yet, Doctor," Mamadou answered, turning to Annie. She lowered her gaze timidly. "Annie is a very good cook. She prepares the best meals. But we eat very late in the night, when the heat is gone."

"Again very wise," Alan concluded. "But why don't you two and the children come to the hotel and spend a bit of time with us?"

"That would be very nice, Doctor, thank you," Mamadou said, nodding.

The evening was a relaxing one for those staying at the Hillside Station. Aboard *The Contessa*, Simon Albertson, the Potty Man, was busy entertaining the troops, as it were. Obviously, none of the crew had been allowed ashore which Alan was very grateful for. So, tonight some of the men had pulled a few tables together to have a bit of a rest.

"Okay, Simon, let's have it," Ivan coaxed him. "You said you'd reserve the best one for such a gathering..."

"Oh don't you be so pompous, Ivan," Gilbert said, "Let the man compose himself before his performance, why don't you?"

"Okay, okay, Mr. Diamond Security..." another man said, amid the chuckles. He then turned to Simon. "We're all waiting, Mr. Potty Man – let's have it!"

"Alright, alright. Here it goes: Once upon a time there lived a beautiful Queen with queenly large breasts. Nick the Dragon Slayer was obsessed over the Queen for this reason. He knew that the penalty for his desire would be death should he try to touch them, but he had to try.

"One day Nick revealed his secret desire to his colleague, Horatio the Physician, the King's chief doctor. Horatio thought about this and said that he could arrange for Nick to more than satisfy his desire, but it would cost him 1000 gold coins to arrange it. Without pause, Nick readily agreed to the scheme.

"The next day, Horatio made a batch of itching powder and poured a little bit into the Queen's bra while she bathed. Soon after she dressed, the itching commenced and grew intense. Upon being summoned to the Royal Chambers to address this incident, Horatio informed the King and Queen that only a special saliva, if applied for four hours, would cure this type of itch, and that tests had shown that, among all of the citizens of the kingdom, only the saliva of Nick, the Dragon Slayer would work as the antidote to cure the itch.

"The King, eager to help his Queen, quickly summoned Nick to their chambers. Horatio then slipped Nick the antidote for the itching powder, which he put into his mouth, and for the next four hours, Nick worked passionately licking the Queen's large and magnificent breasts. The Queen's itching was eventually relieved, and Nick left satisfied and was hailed by both the King and Queen as a hero.

"Upon returning to his chamber, Nick found Horatio demanding his payment of 1000 gold coins. With his obsession now satisfied, Nick couldn't have cared less, knowing that Horatio could never report this matter to the King and with a laugh told him to get lost.

"The next day, Horatio slipped a massive dose of the same itching powder into the King's underwear. The King immediately summoned Nick.

"The moral of this story is: Pay your damn bills!"

Roaring laughter accompanied Simon's punch line.

Gilbert was pleased to be where he was right now. He liked Simon and his crew. These men had seen practically everything there was to see at sea, except perhaps for piracy – something Gilbert always feared, especially aboard a ship like *The Contessa*. No one was safe these days from the idiots who believe they have the right to steal and murder to satisfy their hunger for misery and pain.

CHAPTER THIRTY-SIX

His name was Samuel

THE NEXT MORNING, everyone who would participate in the diamond ceremony, such as it had been dubbed, was in the foyer of the ship, waiting to disembark as soon as the president's town car pulled alongside *The Contessa*. Daniel Crosby was in attendance when Armand Guillaume, the Chief Purser put the case containing the Star of Sierra Leone in Mr. Atkinson's hands. The little jeweler was trembling when he took the large cassette and put it in his briefcase. Once locked, Daniel slipped one handcuff around the briefcase's handle and the other around his wrist. He gave the key to Mr. Atkinson and smiled. Both men nodded and followed Armand Guillaume to the platform where Captain Hildebrandt was waiting for them.

"Mr. Atkinson," the latter said, "While I secretly hoped that the Star would never leave my ship or would never leave the United States, I understand your decision. I'm sure you will not regret it in the end."

"Thank you, Captain. I will not forget the particular care and attention you paid to me during the first part of this voyage. I will however, be relieved when the Star is returned to its rightful owners. I had no right to take it. Such as any country's relics, the Star belongs to Sierra Leone."

And with these words, the captain shook Mr. Atkinson's hand. "Be safe, sir," he told him.

The car was a large Mercedes town car. The chauffeur opened the doors while an officer in uniform watched Daniel and Atkinson climb aboard.

Many of the passengers had watched the jeweler's departure and had observed the man accompanying them from the upper deck promenade.

Babette said to Betty, "Can you imagine, loving a gem such as the Star so much that you would risk life and limb for it?"

Betty smiled. "I know you are not a materialistic person, Babette, but when you have worked hard to satisfy one of your desires, whatever it may be, you don't want anyone to steal the item or even the moment when you feel the most happy. Do you?"

"You're right, I suppose. If someone were to steal one of my plays or even copy it somehow, I would be devastated. These plays, the stories I have written are truly part of me. I know they may not be compared in value to the Star of Sierra Leone, nevertheless, they are very dear to my heart."

"There you are then. Mr. Atkinson is a jeweler – has probably been one since he was a youngster – and his pleasure resided in owning the largest dredged diamond on earth and having it on display in his home…"

"Do you think he displayed it?" Babette asked.

"Perhaps not for everyone to see, but certainly somewhere he probably showed it to visitors or friends. For him it was like an objet d'art I suppose."

"I guess you're right. I just couldn't spend that much money on something like that. I wouldn't be able to sleep at night."

When the car pulled inside the gate of the presidential palace, another officer opened the back doors of the town car to let the passengers out.

The Vice-President, Mr. Samuel Sam Sumana was in attendance.

He came down the few steps and bowed to Mr. Atkinson.

"Welcome to our country, sir," he said. "Please come in. We have prepared a little reception for you."

"Too kind, I'm sure," Atkinson replied. "I'm just glad that I could return the Star to its country of origin."

They walked with Mr. Sumana through the magnificent foyer of the old mansion and entered the ballroom, as soon as the doors were opened. People in attendance stood up and applauded Mr. Atkinson's arrival.

He walked with Daniel Crosby all the way to the table that had been set up at the far end of the room. The people sitting on one side were all older men, dressed in their traditional grand bou-bou. They seemed somewhat ill-at-ease with this whole ceremony thing. Mr. Atkinson presumed they probably were local miners or geologists ready to examine the Star.

He didn't know how he was going to handle it. He had never allowed anyone to touch the stone. But now he had to remind himself, the Star was no longer his to do with as he pleased; it belonged to the people of Sierra Leone.

Surprisingly enough, no one shook hands with Atkinson. He lifted his gaze to Daniel, who bent down and whispered, "They don't want to contaminate you, sir."

Atkinson nodded imperceptibly, smiled and went round the table to take his seat. Before he did, however, the Vice President made his little spiel and welcomed Atkinson, once again, to Sierra Leone.

And then the moment of truth came.

Daniel got the key from Atkinson, unlocked the handcuffs and gave the briefcase back to the jeweler. He laid it on the table and opened it. He took the case out and placed it in front of the Vice President and invited him to break the seal, which he did as he opened it. The Star seemed to be brighter than ever....

The next thing anyone knew, a shot rang out, Mr. Atkinson fell beside Daniel, bleeding profusely from the left shoulder.

Ever vigilant, Daniel had seen where the shot had come from. He ran down the aisle while people screaming, tried to flee from the room through the French doors or out into the foyer.

Mr. Samuel Sam Sumana surreptitiously took the Star and put it in his jacket's inside-pocket before he went down to place a table napkin over the jeweler's shoulder. Mr. Atkinson stared at the man looming large above him.

"Don't worry; it's safe with me, sir. I've called the ambulance. It will be here in a moment."

He then straightened up and disappeared through the French door nearest to him.

As soon as he was able to regroup, so to speak, Daniel called the ship on his cell.

"Gilbert, get down to the pier," he ordered. "Atkinson's been shot. I'll get the ambulance to drive up to meet you. Maybe you could call Dr. Mayhew and have him get back to attend to our jeweler. Okay?"

"No problem, mate. I'll get down there with a couple of my men. I'll wait for you." He hesitated. "What about the Star?"

"I'm not sure, but I think the Vice-Pres took it as soon as the shot rang out."

"Are you going to try to get it back?"

"Nope. It's their business now. We've done what Atkinson asked. Now these guys can work it out amongst themselves."

"Okay, I'll call the doc now. See you soon," Gilbert said, hanging up.

"Yeah, Gilbert. What can I do for you?" Alan said as he was finishing his breakfast.

"Can you come back to the ship on the double? Atkinson has been shot. Daniel is getting him back to the ship by ambulance. I don't know what happened, but apparently the Star was stolen during the ceremony."

"Say What?"

"You heard me. We need you, doc. So, please, leave the vaccinations to the others and come back. Okay?"

"Sure will, Gilbert. I'll make it as quick as I can."

When Alan hung up, he looked at his expectant companions.

"Mr. Atkinson has been shot. I need to get back, fellows. Do you mind if I borrow one of the vans and a chauffeur?"

"I'll come with you," Ashford said firmly. "I'm a surgeon. So, if there's a bullet to get out of this man's chest I'll be the best one to get it out."

"You sure?" Alan asked, throwing a glance at Hatfield.

"No problem, Dr. Mayhew, I'll be here when you two come back. We've got almost all the inoculations on the schedule done anyway, so you go ahead."

"Thanks, Hatfield," Ashford said, patting his friend on the back.

As they were driving down toward town, Ashford asked Alan, "Do you have the equipment needed to perform an operation in the med center? Or do you want to commandeer an operating theater at the Central Hospital?"

"Yes, we've got everything we need aboard the ship, no worries. And..., we have sanitary conditions. I don't think I would risk operating on anyone in any of these hospitals. It would take us more time to get the theater sanitized than what I gather we have."

Ashford nodded. "Especially if our patient has lost a lot of blood. No time to waste."

"Exactly. Besides he's not a young man and not in the best of health either."

When the ambulance came through the gates of the palace, President Ernest Bai Koroma had been alerted and was talking to Daniel.

"I am so very sorry at what happened, Agent Crosby. I was not able to attend the ceremony, as it were. We had a meeting scheduled with some delegates from China regarding some port reconstruction..."

Daniel nodded. "I understand, Mr. President. And believe me when I say Mr. Atkinson won't blame any of you for what happened. There are criminals everywhere. I'm just sorry that the Star has been stolen."

At that moment the paramedics came out with Atkinson on a

gurney which they placed inside the ambulance.

Daniel said, "I'm sorry, Mr. President, but we'll have to go now. I'll be in touch with your office with a report later today."

President Koroma nodded and waved discreetly when the ambulance pulled away down the drive.

Inside, Daniel was not going to take any chance. He didn't want to be faced with a kidnapping on top of it all. He took his gun out of his holster and aimed it discreetly at the driver's head. "Okay, you're going to drive this thing to the pier and stop in front of the ship, right?"

The driver looked in his rearview mirror and saw the barrel of the gun. "Yes, sir. That's where we're going." He turned to his companion, sitting in the passenger seat. "You better call Ahmed and tell him we'll be delayed."

"NO CALLS!" Daniel erupted from behind the two men. "You're not calling anyone. You just drive. Okay?" *That diamond is enough to pay for another ISIS' strike,* he thought. I don't want to be beheaded at dawn just because I helped our little jeweler do the right thing.

Ten minutes later the ambulance pulled up in front of the ship's gangway. Gilbert and two of his men were in attendance. They aimed their side arms at the driver and paramedic while Daniel helped Olga and Alice unload their patient. Gilbert had also called Simon to come down. His men looked more menacing than any guns. Ivan and Serge came down the gangway, grabbed the gurney as if it were a yoga mat and made their way up.

Daniel, meanwhile, returned the ambulance keys to the driver, pointed the gun at his head and ordered him to leave "NOW!"

Knowing full well, they couldn't get away from this ambush, the two men turned the ambulance around and left the pier under the astonished gazes of the customs officers and local police.

As soon as Alan and Ashford reached the ship, a few minutes later, they ran up the gangway and rushed to the med center where Alice was waiting for them. She directed them to the prep-room where they went through the usual pre-surgery scrub and slipped into their blue gowns.

"Greetings Olga," Alan said, as he and Ashford entered the operating room, "You remember Dr. Ashford, don't you?"

"Yes, of course," Olga said, nodding to the surgeon. "Welcome to the med center team, Doctor."

"Thanks," Ashford replied from behind his mask. "Let's see what we've got…" he said before starting the surgery.

Alice took on the role of anesthesiologist, while Olga assisted in the surgery.

The bullet was lodged between the clavicle and the humerus. Not a very accessible spot. Whoever shot Mr. Atkinson was a poor shot, or didn't want to kill him.

Two hours later, the patient was resting comfortably in the recovery room under Olga's vigilant eye. Meanwhile, Alan and Ashford had no time to spare, they had to return to the Hillside Station and resume their interrupted inoculation schedule. They were on their way down the gangway, when Gilbert called them back.

"Doc, Doc, please stop!" he yelled. "Come back aboard, Dr. Hatfield is being held hostage…"

Alan and Ashford exchanged a quick glance and returned to the deck.

CHAPTER THIRTY-SEVEN

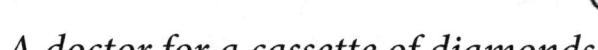

A doctor for a cassette of diamonds

NEEDLESS TO SAY Captain Hildebrandt was up in arms as soon as he heard what had been happening. Not only had one of his most respected passengers been shot while ashore, a World Health Organization physician had been kidnapped now.

"Mr. Ekelton, what do you know about this?" Hildebrandt demanded of his staff captain.

"At the moment, nothing more than you do, sir," Ekelton replied, obviously dumbfounded. "I cannot believe what is happening either."

"Well, you better start believing that we're in trouble, Mr. Ekelton. The company will not stand for The Contessa being detained in port for an hour more than required. Besides, no one wants to hear any more about such things as shootings and kidnapping on my watch; do you understand?"

"Yes, I understand, sir."

"Well then, you had better get your arse in gear and solve this problem before 0500 hrs. tomorrow. And have Dr. Mayhew report to me as soon as he is available. I want a written report on Mr. Atkinson's condition a-sap. As for Mr. Evans, I want to hear – no, make that a written report as well – of the incident in town."

To say the captain was in a foul mood would have been the understatement of the year.

"Any word from the kidnappers yet?" Hildebrandt asked before Ekelton had a chance to step out.

"No, sir, nothing as yet."

"Keep me informed, darn it!"

"Yes, sir, of course, sir," Ekelton said, closing the door of the captain's office. As soon as he was able to do so, he took his cell phone out of his pocket and clicked on Alan's number.

"Doctor Mayhew," he said the moment Alan was on the line, "Mr. Ekelton here, I'm sorry to disturb you, but the captain needs a written report on Mr. Atkinson's condition. As soon as you can have it on his desk, would be much appreciated."

"I thought he would," Alan replied. "I'm just finishing it. I'll bring it up to him in a few minutes." He paused to switch the phone from one shoulder-hold to the other. "But tell me, have you or Mr. Evans received any word from the abductors?"

"Not as yet, Doctor. I'm on my way down to Mr. Evans now. I'll catch up with you if I have anything more."

"One more thing, Mr. Ekelton... I'm sorry, but could we keep Dr. Ashford in the loop. The man is going to have a heart attack if we don't watch it."

"Is he sick?" Ekelton asked: his voice sounding quite concerned indeed.

"Not yet, but he is not a young man, and I would prefer if we kept him informed."

"Okay; why don't you do that then? And where is he right now?"

"I've sent him to his cabin, in case Dr. Hatfield gave his kidnappers the cabin number."

"Good idea. I'll be in touch. And maybe you should come down as soon as you've had a chat with our captain, okay?"

"I'll do that," Alan replied before hanging up.

It took him a couple more minutes to complete his report – a short one at that – and to leave everything else at the med center in the hands of his two rather unnerved nurses.

As soon as he walked in the captain's office, Hildebrandt said, "Ah, Alan, there you are. Come, come in, have a seat." He pointed to the visitors' chairs opposite his desk.

Alan did as bidden but not before handing his report to the captain. The latter sat down and reclined to the back of his seat while he read the condensed account of what happened since Alan left The Contessa the previous day.

"Very well then," Hildebrandt said, advancing his body to the desk. "I am glad to see that Mr. Atkinson will recover from the ordeal. Nice man that little jeweler." He paused reflectively. "And who do you think abducted Dr. Hatfield?"

"I can't be sure, of course, Captain, but I would suggest the two incidents are not related."

"You mean the shooting and the kidnapping are not connected?"

"Yes, that's my contention, Captain. According to Agent Crosby, the Vice-President is supposedly the one who took the Star "for safe-keeping". So, why kidnap anyone else, now that the man has gotten what he wanted?"

"I see what you're getting at. You think that our diamond thief – the one who's after the four-million dollar cassette – has made his way to the Hillside Station and is now holding Dr. Hatfield as hostage. The ransom being the cassette of diamonds. Am I correct?"

"Yes, sir, you are – at least that's my conjecture."

"Very well then. And are the diamonds still in the fridge in the med center?"

"Yes, they are."

"One last question, Alan, do you have any idea who could have done this?"

"I wouldn't like to say at the moment, sir. But there are only a handful of people who have any knowledge of the diamonds' existence and their current location."

"I see your point," the captain said, nodding and getting to his feet.

Alan followed suit. "I'll be in touch as soon as any of us hear from the kidnappers, sir," he said, turning toward the door.

"And do tell Mr. Evans that I don't want him to spare man-hours or expense to bring our Dr. Hatfield back to the ship alive and well – do you hear?"

"Yes, sir, I'll pass on the message."

When Alan was on his way down to the security office, he thought about the cassette's location. It was still in the vaccine fridge. Perhaps he should take it down to the engineers' vault in the bowels of the ship. Not everyone knew there was such a vault and where it was. At the moment, quite a few people knew where the diamonds were. Olga, Alice and Gregory Ashton – not to mention Mr. Atkinson – were all in danger. If the thief had an accomplice on board, most likely, this is the person who would be given the cassette when the exchange would be made.

Making a decision, Alan rushed back to the center, entered the storage room, took the cassette out of the fridge, and slipped it inside his shirt, making sure it wasn't readily visible, locked the refrigerator again, and walked out.

"Forgot something?" Alice asked from her desk, where she was having what looked like a salad and fish wrap for dinner.

"You could say that," Alan answered, rushing out the door.

Alice smiled and looked towards him as he closed the door.

Instead of going to the security office, Alan went down to the engineers' quarters. With the chief engineer's help, he placed the cassette in the vault, watched him close it and swing the lock in place.

"Okay, Doc. No one else but me knows the combination, so if you want the numbers I'll give them to you now…"

Alan shook his head. "Absolutely not, Jim. I don't want to know anything about any numbers. But…, I don't want you to open the vault for anyone else but me. Okay?"

"Understood, Doc. I don't even know why you're here." He chuckled. "We've all got our injections and we're not due for a physical for another month. So...?"

Alan laughed with him and made his way up to the outside deck. He took the long way round to get to the security office where he found Gilbert and Mr. Ekelton in the midst of a rather heated discussion. They stopped talking as soon as Alan came in.

"Don't mind me, fellows, I can make myself scarce if you want?" Alan said jokingly.

Ekelton and Gilbert shook their heads and smiled. "We were just arguing or rather betting on what the ransom would be," the staff captain said, watching Alan take a seat beside him and across from Gilbert.

"Yeah; I'm thinking someone is after the vaccines – that's what they'll want," Gilbert said. "I'd bet on it."

"Maybe," Ekelton said, "But I'm inclined to think that it's got something to do with the cassette of diamonds." He turned his face to Alan. "What do you think, Doc?"

"I think you might both be correct. You see, since the beginning of the cruise, there have been people wanting to get our vaccines to sell them on the black market throughout West Africa. No one has succeeded in putting their hands on any yet. But that's not to say the criminals are giving up on the idea. Maybe they want to exchange Dr. Hatfield for another shipment of vaccines – much larger and more lucrative than just the few cases they could swipe from any of the visiting doctors."

"See," Gilbert said, "What did I tell you?" pointing his pencil to Ekelton.

The latter smiled and returned his gaze to the doc. "But why did you say that we might be both on the right track?" he asked.

"Because, another of my suppositions is this: What if the diamonds we found were to buy the vaccines from someone on board? You know how tempting diamonds are. Maybe the thief is no thief at all, but some medical person or a tribal chief that gathered every diamond he, or his people collected from the dredging site in Koidu to exchange them for a supply of vaccines."

Gilbert looked from Alan to Ekelton. "What do you think, Mr. Ekelton? Could that be a possible explanation?"

"Yes, that makes sense, of course," Ekelton replied, but what were the diamonds doing in the crew lavatory, here aboard this ship? Why hide them? Unless, of course, they were trying to hide them from one of my regular crew inspections."

"We'll only know the answers to any of these questions when we hear from the kidnappers," Alan suggested.

He was about to leave when Daniel Crosby poked his head through the door. "May I have a word?" he asked, directing his gaze at Gilbert.

"Yes, yes, Daniel, come on in," Gilbert answered, "We were just having a chat about why Dr. Hatfield was kidnapped and who could have done the deed."

"And I gathered you haven't come up with an answer yet," Daniel said, nodding to Alan as he took the seat the doctor had just vacated.

"No, we haven't, Agent Crosby," Ekelton said, turning to the Interpol man.

"May I suggest that the diamonds you found in the crew area have something to do with it?"

"Dr. Mayhew had the same idea, yes," Gilbert said, looking up at Alan.

"Well," Alan said, "I just thought that the diamonds were to pay the WHO doctors or someone else, to bring a larger shipment to the West African coast. Some sort of bribe perhaps?"

"Yes, that's something worth considering, of course." Daniel nodded in agreement. "On the other hand, my boss at Interpol believes that a lot of this could have some link with ISIS. They've been trying to put their paws on the dredging operation in Koidu."

The four men fell silent. ISIS these days was casting long shadows everywhere one went.

This affair was getting more complex than anyone wanted to

contemplate. Until they heard from the person who held Dr. Hatfield captive they would not be able to move. However, Alan felt he needed to do something. He couldn't just sit and wait for things to happen. There was too much at stake. Thousands of lives could be lost if the vaccines were not distributed properly and rather quickly.

He decided to make his way to Dr. Ashford's cabin as soon as he left Gilbert's office. When (or if) Gilbert would hear from the kidnappers, he would most likely take the WHO van and travel to the Hillside Station to make the exchange.

Somehow, Alan didn't think anything like this was going to happen. He wasn't sure. He wanted to talk to Dr. Ashford first.

"How's the patient?" the doctor asked as soon as he opened the door of his cabin for Alan. "Please come in, come in and have a seat." He indicated the sofa in the small sitting room. "Would you like a drink?"

"No-no, Doctor. But thanks all the same. I won't stay long. I've just come from talking to our captain and to Mr. Evans. We're all very concerned about Dr. Hatfield, and that's the reason I'm here."

"You want to do something, don't you?"

"Yes. I don't know if you would be game to come with me, back to the Hillside Station, and have a look at the lay of the land. What do you say?"

"I'd say: what are we waiting for?" Ashford replied. He then looked at the cabinet along the far wall. "I have just the items we will need," he said, getting to his feet. He walked to the cabinet in question, opened one of the drawers, and extracted a satellite phone, high caliber gun, camera, and pepper spray from it.

"Oh, I didn't know you had a satellite phone," Alan said, smiling. "I was going to ask Gilbert Evans for his."

"No need. And this phone has a direct line to our head office in Washington. If we need something to be flown in or assistance of any kind, we will use it. Deal?"

"You've got a deal, Doctor."

With these words, both Alan and the surgeon left the cabin to make their way down to the engineer's room.

CHAPTER THIRTY-EIGHT

A thief among them

AFTER COLLECTING THE CASSETTE of diamonds from the chief engineer, Alan and Dr. Ashford made their way down to the WHO van, which was still parked on the pier. They climbed aboard after Alan called the chauffeur out of a little gathering sitting on the ground, where he was probably playing some game or other with his friends.

Alan had given a quick call to Gilbert, telling him of his intention and the reason why he had to get to the Hillside Station before nightfall. Gilbert had listened to Alan's proposed sortie and said, "It's your ass on the line, mate. If anything happens to either of the old goats, you'll be the one looking at early retirement – without pension." Alan had smiled inwardly, but knew Gilbert was right.

Once they were comfortably ensconced in the back seat, a knapsack filled with bottled water, medical implements and supplies at Ashford's feet, the WHO doctor smiled.

Alan was taken aback. He didn't think there was anything to smile about. They were on their way to meet men with deadly intentions...

"You know, Doctor," Ashford said, "in our job, Hatfield and I have seen the worst of human depravation and conditions; but one thing that always kept us going has been keeping a joke or two in reserve for such moments when we were faced with the horrors of life and death."

Alan understood now. Ashford wanted to ease the tension.

The old surgeon went on, "And we also had to suffer the silliness of some of the more fortunate western governments when it came to dealing with insurance companies."

Alan nodded. "Insurance and government regulation seemed to be attached at the hips when it comes to decide who receives medical treatment and who doesn't."

"Something like that, yes," Ashford replied. And it makes me think of this little story...." He paused. "Three nurses died at the same time & went to heaven where they were met at the Pearly Gates by St. Peter. To the first, he asked, "What did you do on Earth and why should you go to heaven?" "I was a nurse in an inner city hospital," she replied. "I worked to bring healing and peace to the poor suffering city children." "Very noble," said St. Peter. "You may enter." And in through the gates she went. To the next, he asked the same question, "So what did you do on Earth?" "I was a nurse at a missionary hospital in Africa," she replied. "For many years, I worked with a skeleton crew of doctors and nurses who tried to reach out to as many people and tribes with a hand of healing and with a message of God's love." "How touching," said St. Peter. "You too may enter." And in she went. To the last nurse, he asked, "So, what did you do back on Earth?" After some hesitation, she explained, "I was a nurse at an H.M.O." St. Peter pondered this for a moment, and then said, "Okay, you may enter also." "Whew!" said the nurse. "For a moment there, I thought you weren't going to let me in." "Oh, you can come in," said St. Peter, "but you can only stay for three days..."

As Alan was listening to Dr. Ashford, he turned his head to the back of the vehicle from time to time. There was a Landrover following them, he was sure. Moments later the driver of the vehicle on their tail started honking the horn. Alan and Ashford looked through the rear window and saw a man's hand wave at them out of the passenger window. Alan recognized the hand – Daniel was following them.

He asked their chauffeur to stop on the side of the road as soon as he could. When the van came to a halt, the Landrover did the same behind them.

Daniel climbed out before the doctors had time to alight from their vehicle.

"Sorry, guys. I just thought you driving a WHO van would be a little too obvious. If someone is watching the road from the Hillside Station – and I'm sure someone is – your van would make an easy target for anyone wanting to eliminate the invasive party before it got there."

"You really think someone is watching our arrival from the Hillside lookout?" Ashford asked, frowning.

"Wouldn't you?" Daniel said.

Alan nodded. "So what do you propose we do?" he asked.

"I think it'd be much better if you two came with me in the Landrover and let the van go back to the ship."

Alan and Ashford exchanged a glance.

"And I suppose you're carrying a gun of some sort," Ashford queried.

"What do you think, Doctor?"

"Yes, yes, I would say "you wouldn't leave home without it," now would you, Agent Crosby?"

"You got it, Doc." Daniel grinned. Ashford shrugged.

"I think it's a good idea, Dr. Ashford," Alan said, "I mean switching vehicles would certainly help us to move unnoticed. What do you think?"

"I think we should get going," Ashford replied, getting his bag out of the van. "You take the van back to the ship, Alfonse," he told the chauffeur, "and tell the guard that everything is fine. We are driving with Mr. Crosby now."

Alfonse only nodded, turned on the ignition and was gone down the road in a moment.

Daniel, Alan and Ashford climbed aboard the Landrover and resumed their trip to the Hillside Station a few minutes later.

Meanwhile, at the Station, Dr. Hatfield was cooling his heels, as the saying goes, in one of the hotel rooms. If it weren't for the unpleasant heat, he wouldn't have minded being detained at all. As for Henry, the cook, and the stewards, they had been gathered in one of the storage rooms in the basement of the hotel. None had been harmed, but the air-conditioning unit was hardly keeping the temperature bearable.

The man who had organized this kidnapping was a tall one. He had the allure and stature of a tribal chief. He was dressed in some sort of pantaloons with a black vest barely covering his chest, attesting to his ancestral background. He was a "coursier" – a messenger. He could run for miles up and down the mountains without breaking a sweat. The "coursiers" were men who would win the Olympic races, or the world marathons without effort and in record time.

When Alan, Daniel and Ashford arrived on site, the man approached the Landrover alone. He held a long stick in the one hand and stood erect in the courtyard of the hotel. His stature and demeanor reminded Alan of the pictorial displays found in the old geography books – he was the portrait of the "African Man".

"Good of you to come," he said to the three companions. "My name is Azar Abdouley." His English was flawless. "As you know, I have taken the liberty of detaining Dr. Hatfield for a while. It was the only way for me to recover my property." He looked at each of the doctors in turn. "And who might you be, sir?" he asked, fixing his gaze on Daniel.

"I am Daniel Crosby, sir. I am here to escort the doctors."

"Ah yes. You probably expected me to be armed, be totally out of my mind, or making unreasonable demands of the doctors, didn't you?"

"Maybe, yes. Frankly, though, we didn't know what to expect," Daniel answered. "But perhaps you could tell us."

"Before I do, Mr. Crosby, I will invite you to have a drink at the bar, as is customary when hosting such a party as ours," Azar said, turning toward the open lounge and bar to his left.

"I am very sorry, Mr. Abdouley," Dr. Ashford said, "but could we conclude our business first before we have a celebratory drink?"

Azar turned around to face the old surgeon. "No, Dr. Ashford, we are not going to conclude anything until you have taken the time to hear my plea and then return what has been taken from me." And with these words, the man marched in the direction of the lounge.

Alan and his companions followed. He was curious, as the others were, to hear what Azar had to say.

He, Daniel and Ashford went to sit at the bar, while Azar rounded the counter to get the glasses from the trays and serve each of his "guests" a glass of rather fresh water. He smiled as he handed a glass to Alan.

"I would believe that you are the one who organized this trip, are you not, Dr. Mayhew?" Azar asked.

Taking a sip of the well water, Alan nodded. "I thought we needed to settle this matter sooner rather than later, Mr. Abdouley. I presumed you had no means of communicating with the ship, and unless someone came up here, we wouldn't know what made you detain Dr. Hatfield here, at the station."

"Precisely, Doctor. When Mamadou and Annie came to tell me that you had arrived, I was happy to hear the news. You see, I had entrusted all the diamonds my family had gathered over the years to a friend of mine across the mountains. He worked at the Guinean dredging site. I was hoping that he would give them to one of you Doctors, to pay for extra vaccines. There are many men and women dying in the valleys far away and even in Mali. I wanted to buy some vaccines for them too."

"Very noble of you, sir," Daniel said, "but why do you think we found the diamonds aboard the ship and not in the hands of a doctor?"

"Perhaps the man, whom I thought I should trust, was the thief among us. Perhaps he took the diamonds for himself and was hoping to scamper with the loot once the ship dropped anchor at the next port of call."

Alan nodded. "Yes, I would tend to agree with your conjecture, Mr. Abdouley, except for the fact that we know of no one working aboard our vessel that has worked at the AREDOR site in Guinea. Perhaps you could describe your friend for us?"

"A better question might be where did you find the diamonds, Dr. Mayhew?" Azar asked, riveting his gaze on Alan.

"I did not find them, Mr. Abdouley. They were brought to me by one of our crew members – the man who found them in the mess toilet."

"I see. And you don't know how they ended up in that location, do you, Doctor?"

"No idea, no," Alan answered.

"Perhaps, I will be able to shed some light on this dilemma later. But first, let me see the stones and then we can all breathe easier."

"Dr. Ashford has the cassette in his knapsack," Alan said, looking down at the bag at the surgeon's feet.

"Yes, yes, of course," the latter said, bending down to retrieve his bag.

As he was doing so, Daniel took his gun out of his side holster and pointed it at Azar. Everyone froze.

Alan shook his head. "What do you think you're doing, Daniel?" he demanded, putting himself between Azar and Daniel.

"Get out of the way, Doc. I just want to make sure, Mr. Abdouley here is not about to make fools of all of us." Alan stepped aside. "Let's see Dr. Hatfield first, shall we?"

"Alright, Mr. Crosby, if that's the way you want to play it, we shall." Azar then turned to the side of the lounge, toward the patio leading to the pool. "Ahmed!" he yelled. "Get Dr. Hatfield to join us. Now!"

The four men saw nothing and heard no more than a rustle of leaves before a shadow disappeared in the bushes, presumably in the direction of the rooms. They all stayed silent and waited. A few minutes later, Dr. Hatfield trotted in front of the man Azar called

Ahmed.

"Hey, everyone?" Hatfield said, grinning, "I just spent the hottest day indoors, don't you know? Atrocious, truly atrocious…"

"Are you alright?" Ashford was quick to ask, stepping closer to his friend and colleague.

"Not so fast, Dr. Ashford. Let's not get ahead of ourselves here." Ashford turned to glare at Azar. "As you can see your friend has not come to any harm. But there is time yet for that to happen." He nodded to Ahmed. The machete he held then came down within an inch of Dr. Hatfield's ear. "You see, Mr. Crosby, by the time you pull the trigger, Dr. Hatfield would have lost his right ear. Don't you agree?"

Daniel didn't move. He stood stock still while he remained with his gun pointed at Azar's head. "Okay, let's call it a Mexican stand-off, Mr. Abdouley. I've no problem with that."

"Let's not go any further with this nonsense," Ashford said, grabbing the cassette out of his knapsack. "Here are your damned diamonds!" He threw it on the bar counter. "I have no idea how many there were at the outset, and don't expect me to tell you anything about them, because I don't know anything."

"Let's see," Azar said, breaking the seal and opening the cassette.

"Wow!" Alan exclaimed. He had never seen so many diamonds at once. Even uncut, these stones seemed to reflect the light rays exceptionally well. "They're beautiful!"

"Yes, Dr. Mayhew, they are," Azar agreed. "And I don't have to examine them. I know they're mine." He peered down at the stones with a tear at the rim of his eye. "I am not a violent man, Doctors. But these stones represent the salvation of many, and I cannot see any reason to keep them if they could buy health for my people."

Daniel had lowered his gun by now and Ahmed had slipped his machete to the back of his waist belt.

"Listen to me, Mr. Abdouley," Alan said, "I don't want to sell the vaccines I have on the ship. They are to be given free of charge. If you come back with me, I will give you a few vials and show you how to give a vaccine to some people you know, and to those who live too far for us to reach them." He peered in the coursier's eyes. "Would you like to do that?"

Azar nodded gratefully. "Yes, I would, Doctor, thank you."

Ashford smiled and added, "And I can call our lab in Washington and have them organize another vaccination mission for the people who live in the neighboring inland countries."

"You can do that?" Azar sounded incredulous.

"Believe me, Mr. Abdouley," Hatfield said, "if this old guy says he can do it, he can do it." He smiled. "But now, if you have something like a cold beer behind that bar of yours, I'd love to quench that thirst of mine."

Azar closed the cassette, placed it in a pocket amid the folds of his pantaloons and, after washing his hands, served everyone a tall glass of beer or water.

He also asked Ahmed to release the stewards and the cook so that they could have a meal.

Alan wasn't sure Henry would cook for his abductor, yet he had to ask him.

CHAPTER THIRTY-NINE

Drinking less

"SO ARE YOU DONE CHASING chasing diamonds and thieves?" Gilbert asked Alan when the two men were sitting down having a drink at the *Promenade Deck Bar* that night.

"I don't know that I am, Gilbert," Alan said, "but I do hope we can resume our vaccination program pretty soon without having to worry about our doctors being kidnapped or any of our passengers being shot, clobbered or knifed."

"You said it. I was getting a little antsy when I saw the WHO van come back this afternoon – without you or doctor Ashford – I thought for sure something else had happened to you two." He sipped on his beer.

"But I was glad Daniel came to the rescue," Alan admitted. "It was not so much the Abdouley fellow that concerned me, but his acolyte. The guy handled his machete as if it were a butter knife."

"Are you guys talking about me again," the two companions heard Daniel say behind them.

Gilbert and Alan turned to him in unison.

"Speak of the devil incarnate!" Gilbert said, guffawing. "Where have you been? I tried to get you on your cell to get my report – but it went through to voice mail." He stared at the agent.

"Sorry, you take second place, Gilbert, when it comes to reporting, don't you know?"

"Who's on first?" Alan quipped.

Daniel had to laugh. "I love that. You always make me smile."

"So, who's on first?" Gilbert repeated.

"My boss in Washington, of course. Who else do you think would be demanding an explanation of my time and expenses?"

"Your wife maybe?" Alan suggested.

"Good one, Doc. As if this man could ever get married? I am married to my work and to a very bossy lady at the main office by the name of Aileen McCarthy."

"Is she a redhead too?" Gilbert burst out, almost spitting the words in his beer. "With a name like that, what else could she be but a Scottish lass?"

"Aye, not all Scottish lasses are redheads … but this one is," Daniel admitted.

"So she's on first and I'm on second, is that the pecking order?"

"Yes, Chief. Except in this particular case I had to confirm the reason for our little sortie with my handler, who is not the Scottish lass."

"And I'm complaining about the reports I have to write to the company," Alan said. "At least I don't have a "handler"."

"But we do, Alan – right here – in the person of Mr. Ekelton. Let's not forget about the dear man, shall we?"

Daniel went to sit beside Alan and called for the bartender to serve him a *"lite"* beer. Gilbert looked at him and began chuckling.

Both Alan and Daniel stared at the chief of security.

He waved a hand in front of him and said, "Sorry, guys, it's just that when you asked for a "lite", it reminded me of a joke…"

"Which one?" Daniel asked.

"Never mind, Agent Crosby, you can catalogue it later, after you've heard it."

Gilbert nodded. "Well, there was this drunk guy who walked into a bar and approached the bartender, "Can I have a pint of *Less*, please?" he asked. "I'm sorry sir," the barman replied, looking slightly puzzled, "I've not come across that one before. Is it a spirit?" "I've no idea," replied the guy, "The thing is, I went to see my doctor last week and he told me that I should drink *Less*."

The three men chuckled with the bartender. He had overheard the joke and returned to his wiping the counter afterward, still smiling.

"This hot weather never lets up around here," Daniel said. "I could never understand why people – those who have a choice – would choose to live here."

"Oh, I've known people to live here for their entire lives," Alan said. "It's not so bad. Certainly better than having to shovel snow out of your driveway six months of the year, though."

"There's that, of course," Daniel agreed. "But I don't think I would like to have an air-conditioned office, car and apartment all year round."

"You know, what the best thing about working aboard a cruise ship is?" Gilbert queried.

Both Alan and Daniel shook their heads.

"Well, you can pick a place where you'd like to live for a while, then when you have enough of the scenery, you hop on the next ship and go somewhere else for another contract."

"Sure, if you don't get fired in between," Alan said, grinning at the thought. He knew having an "at will" contract as a doctor would never be a possibility.

"And if you don't have a lady waiting for you at the other end of the trip," Daniel added.

"Is someone mentioning a lady in my absence?" Tiffany said as she sat down on the stool Gilbert just vacated, beside Alan.

"Hi Sweetie," Alan whispered in her ear, "How are you?"

"Running my feet off and downright tired."

"Why, what's happening?" Gilbert asked after he went to sit on Daniel's other side.

"While you guys went gallivanting up country..."

"Wait a minute; did you say "gallivanting", Ms. Sylvan?" Daniel cut in, all smiles.

"Yes, that's what I said, Agent Crosby. Why, wasn't that what you were doing?"

"Let's not talk about our *gallivanting*," Alan suggested, "I'd rather hear what's going on around here. I've seen people rushing up and down the stairs and coming up here with some sort of backdrop for a play – is that what's happening? You're putting on one of Babette's plays up here?"

"Yes. Actually, as I said, while you guys were out *gallivanting* through the countryside..." The three men burst out in muffled chuckles. They knew they wouldn't hear the end of it if they didn't shut up at this point. "With the help of one of the hospitals' nursing staff we organized an open-air play for the children – the ones who lost their parents during the epidemic."

"You mean you've invited the little blighters aboard this ship?" Gilbert was shocked. "Has Mr. Ekelton approved this? And why haven't I been informed?"

Tiffany laughed at seeing Gilbert's amazed face. She nodded emphatically. "Of course Mr. Ekelton approved the open-air production – what else could he have done when Babette asked him? He couldn't have said "no", now could he?"

"I guess not," Gilbert answered, chugging his glass of beer.

"And when is all this going to happen?" Daniel asked.

"In about a half-an-hour. Everything is ready at the aft of the ship and the kids should be coming up in fifteen minutes."

"Will they come up alone?"

"Oh no; the nurses are with them and there's only about forty of them."

"I better go and see what's been done," Gilbert said, getting off his stool. "Thanks for ruining a perfectly relaxing evening, Ms. Sylvan;" he added jocularly, "I owe you one."

"Why don't we do the same," Alan said, getting up together with Tiffany and Daniel. "I wouldn't want to miss the play." He looked at Tiffany. "What is it about?"

"Why don't you wait and see," she replied, walking out of the bar inbetween Daniel and Alan.

CHAPTER FORTY

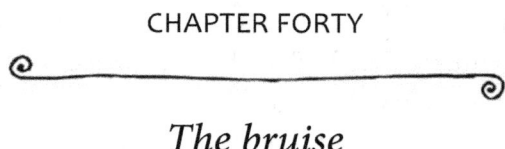

The bruise

BABETTE WAS ALREADY STANDING in front of her small audience. The children varied in age – from little ones of about four or five years old to teenagers who had their eyes on the smaller kids to see that they behaved.

Some of the passengers had also chosen to attend the little production and were seated or standing at the back of the gathering. Captain Hildebrandt, as well as members of the bridge staff, were in attendance too.

"Ladies and Gentlemen, and Children," Babette began when the deck lights dimmed and the spotlight fell on the playwright. "The play you are about to see is a reminder of what many have been through in the recent past. However, it is also a lesson for all of us to learn. Ebola is not just a disease but a warning. It warns us that evil is lurking and we need to be vigilant. We need to take precautions against such terrible afflictions. Ebola, like many other diseases, does not forgive our trespasses. We need to be very clean at all times. We need to have our little ones vaccinated. And remember, Children, needles do not hurt, they cure you."

The applause died down and silence returned. With curiosity on their faces, everyone's eyes focused on the swaddling blanket in which a baby seemed to be lying on the floor. It was surrounded by many colored scarves, a box, a gorgeous African drum with its playing stick, some banana peels, some palm leaves filled with handfuls of rice and three long sticks. The African red skies served as a marvelous backdrop to this strange assemblage of items. Everyone, including the children, wondered what the actors were going to do with these things. The acting cast was composed solely of African children with scripts in hand. He immediately wondered how Tiffany and Babette had accomplished such a tour-de-force in the time given to them. But, trust those women, they had done it.

The Bruise

AHMED: They just don't understand.

HASSAN: What, who doesn't understand?

AHMED: Everybody, about Ebola.

HASSAN: You have Ebola, get away from me.

AHMED: I won't hurt you.

HASSAN: I'm warning you.

SHARIA: Me too, I'm warning you.

HASSAN: No, don't sit or stand there, that is too close, go away, over there.

SHARIA: You shouldn't be allowed around people.

AHMED: You don't understand, by touching you, I can't give you Ebola.

HASSAN: I'm not tough for taking any chances. You go, you better go over there and stay away from him, he has Ebola.

SHARIA: I have Ebola too, but nobody else in my family has Ebola. Not even my baby brother, Laman, and I touch feed him all the time. Want to look at him? He's so cute.

HASSAN: You're all crazy.

(SHARIA takes out banana leaves and a small amount of rice.)

DEROOBA: Go away.

SHARIA: Is there somewhere where I can wash my hands?

AHMED: I'll show you. (They exit.)

DEROOBA: I'm hungry.

HASSAN: So am I. We could take their rice, it smells good and I'm so hungry.

DEROOBA: You are the one who said that they have Ebola and not to touch them. Do you want to catch the disease?

HASSAN: My hunger got the best of me for a minute.

(AHMED and SHARIA return.) Don't you understand their hands had to touch the food? Besides, I heard that they bleed over everything.

DEROOBA: Look at the sick one's hand and see if he has blood on it.

HASSAN: He has bandages on his knee.

DEROOBA: You are sure there's no blood?

HASSAN: Looks like it to me. You know what that means; they're just trying to hide the blood and the bruises from us. I saw a sick one once who just bled from his eyes.

AHMED: That's only because he waited too long before going to the Ebola clinic.

SHARIA: Want some rice, it's very good, I made it myself.

HASSAN: I would never eat with anyone who had Ebola.

DEROOBA: I never have and I never will.

(SHARIA turns away and cries - hands Ahmed a leaf with rice and takes a leaf for herself)

HASSAN: You eat with women?

AHMED: Oh her, Sharia, she's my cousin. It gets very lonesome for me, there are all women in my family and that is why I sit here day after day hoping that I will meet someone that I can call a friend.

HASSAN: What could you do for a friend?

DEROOBA: Do you have money?

AHMED: No, I don't have any money but I know some magic tricks that my father taught me before they took him to prison.

HASSAN: Why don't you do one great magic trick and make yourself disappear? (Laughs.)

SHARIA: Would you please do a magic trick for me?

DEROOBA: How can you do magic when your eyes are all blurry?

AHMED: (Waves hands, wiggles his fingers.) They're not blurry, the doctors in the clinic are taking care of me, in a year's time, I should be alright. (Stars are disappearing through the finger pointing) She went to the clinic sooner than I did all she has to do is take her medicine all the time. Did you take your medicine today?

SHARIA: Yes, I took it.

AHMED: You can touch the star.

DEROOBA: Will you show me how to do it? I think we could pick up some money.

HASSAN: Don't bother me with that.

(Drummer enters - beating his drum)

DRUMMER: The greatest dancers in all of West Africa will be here immediately following. (Sees children with Ebola, leaves mouth open, stops beating his drum). Are you a sick one?

AHMED: Yes, I have Ebola.

DRUMMER: I want you to get out of here.

AHMED: Why?

DRUMMER: You know why, because you are untouchable. If you stay here, you will be stopping everybody from wanting to come to the show.

AHMED: I'd just like to see the dancers. How could I hurt anyone?

DRUMMER: By just being around. Does she have Ebola?

(Pointing the drummer's stick at SHARIA)

AHMED: She's never seen any dancers.

DRUMMER: Well, get rid of her now and when I come back with the dancers, I don't want to see either one around here.

(Starts hitting on his drum) The famous, the greatest dancers in all West Africa (Exits)

BOY (named ISHMAEL): (Runs on stage) They are coming, hide, before it is too late.

DEROOBA: Who is coming?

ISHMAEL: The bad spirits. (Starts to go, HASSAN grabs him.)

HASSAN: Bad spirits, what do you mean?

ISHMAEL: You know, let go of me. (Tries to pull away)

DEROOBA: What do they do to you?

ISHMAEL: First, they cast a spell on you then, when they have you in their power, they can do anything they want with you, kill you or eat you alive. (Crosses near to AHMED) Or they prick you all over the place with these long needles.

DEROOBA: Where shall we go?

AHMED: Come, SHARIA, let's go back into the clinic.

(AHMED stands, holds the baby and they exit into the clinic, which is just behind the sign that says clinic but they squat and peek out)

ISHMAEL: Maybe we'd better go inside the clinic.

HASSAN: And get Ebola, you're crazy!

DEROOBA: Ahmed says you can't get Ebola by just being with people who have Ebola.

HASSAN: What does he know?

ISHMAEL: Well he has Ebola and the doctors have told him all about everything.

(Enters dancers followed by the drummer - drummer then runs ahead of them).

DRUMMER: Make way; make way, for the greatest dancers in all West Africa.

(The girls start dancing - ISHMAEL runs across the stage at the finish of the dance and crosses to exit left).

ISHMAEL: What did I tell you? You wouldn't listen, now you will be under their spell.

DRUMMER: You are making too much noise. (Takes his drummer stick and puts it into the back of Ishmael's shirt and pushes him toward Ahmed and Sharia – Ishmael, who is shaking allover trips over Ahmed, falls, knocking himself out – the dancers turn and whirl and exit right, Ishmael and Hassan following clapping and laughing).

SHARIA: What's the matter with him?

AHMED: When he fell, he must have lost consciousness.

SHARIA: Will you be alright?

ISHMAEL: (Moans) Mother... (Ahmed pats him on the face – Ishmael sits up) You...you touched me.

AHMED: I was just trying to help you.

ISHMAEL: (Stands). Help me get Ebola, thank you very much.

AHMED: You just can't possibly get Ebola by my touching you or you touching me.

ISHMAEL: Paces back and forth) Why would you do this to me, give me Ebola? My face... Sharia, what do you see?

SHARIA: A boy who is frightened and has no reason to be afraid.

ISHMAEL: (To Sharia) My nose, is it bleeding? (To Ahmed) My ears, do I have two ears, my two ears, are they bleeding?

AHMED:	Do you have any kind of bruises, Ishmael, on your body, yes bruises on your body?
ISHMAEL:	Am I all bruised up?
AHMED:	No, of course not. I meant if there is a bruise ready to burst open, say like on your arm.
ISHMAEL:	Let me look and see. (Examines his arms, muttering...) A bruise? What am I looking for?
AHMED:	If you touch it, it will start to bleed.
ISHMAEL:	Let me try that. (Runs his fingernail allover his arms). Woooo, that hurts.
SHARIA:	There's no bruise.
ISHMAEL:	(To Ahmed) You're sure?
AHMED:	Do you see any bruise on your arms, or legs, or stomach, how about your chest?
ISHMAEL:	Do I really have to go through that again?
SHARIA:	It's up to you, if you want to know.
ISHMAEL:	It's those demons, those dancers, they did it. I warned you, didn't I? (Paces back and forth.)
SHARIA:	They can't give you Ebola.
ISHMAEL:	(Sits down on the ground) Alright, I'll check. No bruises on this leg, no bruises on that leg.(stands) Do I have to test my legs with my fingernails?
AHMED:	Well, that's up to you.
ISHMAEL:	(Sits) Look what you put me through. (Starts to run his nails over his leg, sighing, moaning and so forth).
AHMED:	Are you satisfied? What about your face?

ISHMAEL: Not that same thing all over again.

AHMED: I could help you.

ISHMAEL: No, thank you, I'd rather do it myself. Do I have to stick my fingers in my eye?

AHMED: Of course not, try your nose.

ISHMAEL: (Screams) That hurt! Couldn't you do some magic and make sure I'd be alright?

HASSAN: Even if I were the greatest magician in the whole world, if you have Ebola, my magic wouldn't help. There is one magic though...

ISHMAEL: What's that?

HASSAN: Only if you promise to do it.

ISHMAEL: Yes, yes, I promise you anything. (Pause.) I said I'd promise. Well, I'm waiting.

HASSAN: The magic is in there. (Pointing at the sign) In there, the doctors can tell you if you have Ebola and they can give you a vaccine.

ISHMAEL: You said magic.

SHARIA: If you find out about Ebola in time, the vaccine the doctors can give you will be like magic.

ISHMAEL: (To HASSAN) That's a trick to get me in there.

HASSAN: What do I gain by getting you inside?

ISHMAEL: Another member for your untouchables, you, you sick-one. (Turns to walk away)

HASSAN:	Now that you've touched me, where can I go to see a doctor?
ISHMAEL:	There is nothing, absolutely nothing that will make me step one foot in that evil place.
HASSAN:	You have Ebola.
ISHMAEL:	I'm not listening to you. You liar. Walks two steps away from Hassan).
HASSAN:	It's true.
ISHMAEL:	How do you know that?
HASSAN:	Because I saw the sign. (Ishmael turns toward him).
ISHMAEL:	What sign, some of your crazy magic?
HASSAN:	No, the bruise on your back.
ISHMAEL:	I don't believe you. Just think what you're saying, what you'd go through to get me into that awful place. (Pointing) You are a liar as well as a sick-one. You think you're pretty smart, don't you? You had me check every place.
HASSAN:	You didn't check your back. You have to check all over.
ISHMAEL:	How would you expect me to see my back?
HASSAN:	(Shrugs his shoulders and turns away).
ISHMAEL:	How can I see way back there? (He tries to turn around and look at his back).
HASSAN:	The doctors could tell you.
ISHMAEL	(Screaming.) I told you that I am not going in there. (To Sharia) Do you have anything shiny, like a mirror

that would help me?

SHARIA: Why don't you take that stick and touch the bruise and see if it hurts or if it bleeds?

ISHMAEL: (To Hassan) Now, you have her telling me to make a fool of myself. What would people say if they saw me playing with my stick on my back?

SHARIA: They'd think you were scratching yourself.

ISHMAEL: My father might not like me to test my back, if fact, my entire family, that is my uncles, they are seven of them. The skinny one, well he is so mean. Then there's one with the mustache, he thinks himself so good and he wouldn't like unless it was his idea.

SHARIA: So they had to know about it.

ISHMAEL: I tell them everything. Yes, I would have to tell them and if the one with the mustache heard about it, he might make me leave the family. (Picks up the stick and runs it up his back.) If I do have Ebola, I'll give that uncle Ebola too. I... I'd like to do that. That's an idea. (He laughs.)

SHARIA: Ebola doesn't give you the right to...

ISHMAEL: I know; I was...

HASSAN: You're on the bruise now, press on it.

ISHMAEL: It hurts, but it's not bleeding is it?

SHARIA: Try it again.

HASSAN: Give it another try.

ISHMAEL: (Puts his stick down). Why did you do this to me?

You and your magic...

HASSAN: I may be a magician but I can't get you bruises. Think about that.

ISHMAEL: (He sits and cries)

SHARIA: Let the doctors give you the answer. Let them at least look at you.

ISHMAEL: Because I'm crying, I'm so beautiful to look at?

            (HASSAN, SHARIA and ISHMAEL all laugh).

SHARIA: What are you waiting for?

ISHMAEL: I want magic. (HASSAN points towards the sign)

HASSAN: In there!

ISHMAEL: Who's begging who now?

HASSAN: (To SHARIA) I'll be back. (Puts an arm around the Ishmael's shoulder and the boy puts an arm on him). Come along, I'll personally introduce you as my best friend.

(Exits, Sharia picks up the baby and runs after them).

CURTAIN

As soon as the lights came back on, and the applause abated, the children of the cast rushed to surround Babette. She was delighted. One of the nurses with a little boy came to the front of the stage to hand the playwright a huge bouquet of tropical flowers.

Alan had a tear in his eye. This lady, as far as he was concerned, deserved a hundred bouquets like this one.

CHAPTER FORTY-ONE

Our "little jeweler" is at it again!

MARK IS AT IT AGAIN, Alan thought when he opened his email. Apparently he had collected a couple of comments he had heard around the hospital where he was working.

Hey you!

Here is a joke or two to put a smile on your face. Have a great day, my friend.

Mark.

One patient in a big city medical center was to have abdominal surgery. She wasn't taking any chances, so she taped notes to her body, stating things like wash your hands; take your time; don't cut yourself. All the notes were of course removed before surgery, but after the surgery, the nurses found a new note: "anyone seen my watch and pen?"

Visiting a psychiatric hospital, an inspector asked one of the intake officers how they decided what ward to put the patient in lock down or open ward?

"We fill a bathtub with water and give the patient a teaspoon, a cup and a bucket."

"Oh I see, if they don't use the bucket, you know that they are not normal," asked the inspector.

"No, the more normal ones pull the plug."

Still laughing quietly, he heard the door of the center open. At this hour, he surely didn't expect to see anyone, except perhaps for a patient who had suddenly felt ill.

He got up from his seat to see if the visitor needed immediate assistance.

"I'm so glad to find you here, Doctor Mayhew," Betty Palmer said, stepping into Alan's office and plopping down in one of the visitors' chairs. "I've been mulling over all kinds of scenarios regarding the Summerville's and I can't find the right answer, I'm afraid."

"The right answer to what, Mrs. Palmer?" Alan queried, regaining his seat.

"Whether I should tell Leon that he's most certainly my nephew."

"But isn't that what you wanted to do? Didn't you want to find who he was and once you did, you would interview him?"

"Well, thanks to you, I did find out and DNA tests don't lie. The man is my nephew. However, I have a problem. Should I let him have the reins of my husband's company and have me oversee his work while I'm still able to do so, or should I simply surrender the lot to him, take the cash and run?"

Alan chuckled lightly. "I'm sorry, Mrs. Palmer, I know this is a troublesome matter for you, but I cannot personally see you 'taking the cash and run' as you say. You would soon try to return and take the helm again."

"Maybe you're right. In everything, there should be a trial period, shouldn't there?"

Alan nodded. "Yes. Even if you trust the person implicitly – and I am not saying that you don't in the case of Leon Summerville – but, you need to ease the person into their new position or in assuming their responsibility."

"So you recommend that I 'ease him into the job', do you?"

"Yes, I do. I think Leon is a sensible man, although you would need to be assured that he doesn't make the mistake of embezzling the funds he's managing. I think he would make a wonderful CEO in due course."

"But how do I tell him that I want to oversee everything. I mean he is no longer a child, is he? It's not like he is in his twenties and I can teach him the ropes. He probably has more experience in handling a profit center than I would ever have."

"Mrs. Palmer, please listen to me," Alan said, putting his forearms onto the top of his desk. "You have been in this business for a long time. Even though you might not have your husband's acumen, you are a leader and you made a success of what has been handed down to you. So, I wouldn't sell myself short if I were you. I would, however, sit down with Leon and put the cards on the table. Be honest and open with him. Tell him that you have reservations. Tell him you know that not everything he's done thus far has been totally legal. Tell him that you won't stand for any more of these shenanigans. Just be perfectly candid with him."

"I suppose you're right. It's just that I didn't think this thing through when I first started on this veritable quest. I never truly thought about the fact that I would find a grown man at the end of the trail. Somehow, I had this poor little boy image in the back of my mind, which was wrong, of course," she said, shaking her head in dismay. "You see, Doctor, I am very glad to have found Leon. I'm even happy that he made it as far as he did, even if some of his dealings were not totally kosher as they say, but I am not sure that he has what it takes to lead people."

"Many people are said to be born-leaders, yet I don't think it means much in this case. You had to learn how to handle the ropes when your husband died, and you did it without anyone's help. Surely, there was personnel who handled the day to day business, but there wasn't anyone to show you how to lead, was there?"

"No, you're right. I was alone and extremely frightened, I'll admit."

"Well, think of it as you giving lessons to your successor. Tell him where you succeeded, where you failed and what to do, so he doesn't fall into the same traps. Be the mother and father he didn't have."

"I knew I would find some of the answers I was looking for when I came to you, Doctor. I'm sure your friends are often lucky and grateful to get your advice." Mrs. Palmer then rose to her feet.

"Thank you for your comments, Mrs. Palmer. But it's only logical that you were seeking advice on such matters and I am glad to be able to provide some assistance."

"More than you realize, I'm sure, Doctor."

Alan accompanied her to the door of the medical center.

"If there's anything else I can do for you – apart from commenting on your business decisions – don't hesitate to let me know."

"Thanks again, Doctor," Mrs. Palmer said before Alan closed the door.

As he returned to his desk, he saw his great-grandfather sitting in the chair Mrs. Palmer had just vacated. He smiled.

"Alright, what are you doing here?" Alan asked his gentle ghost.

"I'm here to tell you that I cannot find our jeweler, anywhere."

"How could he have disappeared, Granddad?" Alan demanded, visibly astonished. "I sent him back to his suite yesterday to rest. He sure wasn't well enough to go dancing. So, unless he's been abducted, where is he?"

"I suppose there's always a chance that someone from Freetown – some of the ministers or government people – want to exchange his life for taking possession of the Star."

"You mean some thief from Freetown is aboard this ship?"

"I know, I know it sounds far-fetched, son, but why else is the man away from his cabin and nowhere on board?"

"Let me call Gilbert," Alan said, lifting the receiver from the phone on his desk.

"Doctor!" Gilbert answered. "What can I do for you? And please don't tell me you've got a diamond problem – I want to go to bed early tonight."

"Well, I'm afraid we're possibly faced with another kidnapping…"

"You're joking, right?" Gilbert sounded as stunned as he probably was.

"I'm afraid not. I just need you to check that my patient, Mr. Atkinson, is in his suite and has not absconded on his own. He still has a damaged shoulder and is not supposed to go gallivanting anywhere for a few days yet."

"Why don't you meet me up there?" Gilbert said, "I would prefer to have our Doc with me when I go and search the ship for a 'physically damaged jeweler'."

"Okay, okay, I'll be there in a few minutes."

When Alan hung up, he looked at his great-grandfather with a mixture of gladness and anxiety in his eyes. "Why don't you ever come to me with happy news, Granddad?" he asked, as he got up and made his way to the door.

When Alan reached the upper deck suites where Mr. Atkinson's cabin was located, he saw Gilbert talking to one of the stewards.

"No, no, Chief, I've not seen Mr. Atkinson or anyone else come out of his cabin, sir," the young man said. "He was there this morning when I brought him his breakfast. I asked if he wanted me to help him have a wash, but he said that he would manage just fine. So, I left him."

"Did you see him after that?" Gilbert asked, nodding to Alan.

"No, Chief. I mean, I came in to drop off his lunch and I heard the water running in the bathroom, so I didn't say anything. I left him."

"And when you collected the tray, was he in his room?"

"No, Doc. I mean I don't know. The tray was outside beside the door, which was sort of funny because he couldn't have handled the tray with the one hand. It's too heavy. I thought maybe some of the cleaning staff had been in and taken it out."

"Okay, Laurent. Thanks for that," Gilbert said, "But if you remember anything else, you call me, okay?"

"Sure will, Chief. He's such a nice man; I just hope he is okay, sir."

"So do we," Alan agreed, watching Laurent walk away in the direction of the service elevators.

"Well, what do you think happened?" Gilbert asked Alan.

"I don't know, but why don't we have a look inside, since Laurent didn't."

"Sure, but I don't think there's anything to see…"

"Okay, if you say so," Alan replied, opening the door anyway.

As the two men walked in, the odor of ether overwhelmed them.

"Good gracious," Alan exclaimed. "Someone's has tried – if not succeeded – in anesthetizing him."

"You mean like chloroform?"

"Just about like that. Unless the man used it for shining his glasses."

They walked into the bathroom to find dirty towels on the floor – some of them soaked in blood.

"This is definitely not a good sign," Gilbert said. "I better seal this room."

As Gilbert rushed out of the suite, Alan shook his head. He certainly hoped their "little jeweler" was all right. He also wondered who could have transported a bleeding man somewhere else on this ship without being seen. Unless, of course, the perpetrator killed the man, stuffed him in a piece of luggage and walked out of the suite. No one would question a passenger moving out of their cabin or disembarking the evening before *The Contessa* was due to sail.

Keeping that thought in mind, Alan made his way out of the suite and closed the door before Gilbert put a tape across the lock. It was a discreet way to tell the staff not to enter the suite until further notice.

Daniel Crosby was the first person Gilbert called when he returned to his office. Alan sat across from the chief of security.

Neither man held much hope of seeing Mr. Atkinson alive again.

As soon as Daniel appeared in the doorway, he asked, "Any idea who could have harmed an injured man? Whoever did is a real sadist in my view."

Both Gilbert and Alan agreed.

"What's more he's not worth anything to anyone, dead," Daniel added. "Who'd want to exchange a body for the Star – if that's the theory we're going with at the moment?"

"That may be jumping the gun a little," Alan said. We don't know that the man is dead. Maybe someone mishandled him and since his sutures have not had time to heal, he would have bled before passing out."

"So you think he's still alive, do you?" Gilbert asked.

"I honestly don't know what to think," Alan replied, shaking his head. "I only know that we have to inform Ekelton of what's going on and have the ship searched."

"That's the next move, of course," Gilbert agreed. He then turned to Daniel. "Any other suggestions, Mr. Interpol?"

"No suggestions, no, but getting ready to have my ass dragged over the hot coals, yes. This is a bugger of a situation. And I can already hear Mrs. Aileen McCarthy's words: "And what were you doing while someone was having a go at Mr. Atkinson, Mr. Crosby?" What do I tell her, that's what I'm wondering."

"Maybe we could search the ship before you send her your report?" Alan said.

"Okay, I'll go searching now," the Interpol agent said, getting up. "Can I borrow a couple of your guys…?" He looked at Gilbert.

"By all means, Agent Crosby. But I think we'll call Mr. Ekelton first and give him the 'Good News', shall we?"

Gilbert will not give up until he finds our "little jeweler", Alan thought.

CHAPTER FORTY-TWO

In the trash!

IF ANYONE COULD FIND a needle in the proverbial haystack, it was Simon Albertson. The Potty Man knew the ship inside and out. He could have found a rat or even a mouse if there was one hiding anywhere on *The Contessa*. Alan went down to see the man in the sanitation department. Meanwhile, Daniel, Gilbert and a number of security officers had been assigned to search the ship under Mr. Ekelton's supervision.

"Good Lord!" the Potty Man exclaimed when he saw Alan come down the steps leading to the platform overlooking the septic tanks. "Have you any idea what time it is, Doc?" He stared at the smiling Alan. "What have you been up to now? Don't tell me; someone has disappeared and you're looking for a body in my tanks?"

Alan had to laugh. "That's exactly why I'm here, although I dearly hope the person I'm looking for is not in one of your tanks."

"And who is it this time?" Simon asked.

"Mr. Atkinson."

Simon opened his eyes wide. "You mean our little diamond man – the owner of the *Star* himself?"

"Yes, that's the one," Alan replied, putting his forearms down on the railing.

"And you think somebody might have taken him and stuffed him in one of the tanks? But why?"

"I don't think we'll find him around here, Simon. As to why, I do believe he's been held for ransom. Someone is not happy with the fact that the Star of Sierra Leone has been stolen and now the prime minister, or some other higher-ups in this government wants the diamond back."

"And you think no one is worthy enough to be held for ransom in this frigging country?"

"I guess that pretty well sums it up, yes."

"And what can I do about it? You realize of course that we've got only eight hours before *The Contessa* leaves this port, don't you?"

Alan nodded. "And that's why I'm here. You're the one who knows *her*. You know where to hide someone or a body – God forbid – in her belly. So, any idea?"

"The only idea that comes to mind is the freight hull. This is the time when the boys will be loading the supplies and unloading the last of the rubbish. So, if our little jeweler is anywhere, it will be in the freight hull. I just hope he's not in any of the trash bins."

"Why is that?" Alan asked.

"Because, these things are compactors. Some of my guys go down at night to compact the rubbish if needed."

"And have they done so tonight?" Alan was truly getting worried. If Mr. Atkinson had been thrown in one of the trash bins, he would most certainly contract an infection and might die of septicemia in the next twenty-four hours – not to mention the risk of being compacted.

"Not yet. The trash is the last thing to go off the ship before sailing. So we've got another two hours to find him," Simon replied.

"Okay, let's go then…"

"Wait a little minute, Doc." Simon looked at the doc's immaculate white uniform. "You're not going anywhere dressed like that!"

Alan had to smile as he looked down at his impeccably ironed trousers. "What do you have in my size then?" he quipped.

"Come with me. The guys will get you dressed for the *debutante's ball* in no time."

Alan always appreciated Simon's sense of humor.

As soon as he was dressed with overalls, heavy rubber waders and gloves, he, Simon and another two men made their way to the bowels of the ship.

The doors to the loading docs were wide open, which surprised Alan until he saw two armed guards watching the stevedores and ship personnel loading the supplies.

Before reaching the enormous trash bins, Alan called Gilbert and told him to come down with two of his men.

"And where did you say you are?" Gilbert asked, sounding more baffled than ever.

"In...I mean near the trash bins near the loading bay and doors."

"And you think they dumped our little jeweler in the garbage?"

"I am not the one who came up with the idea, Simon did. He thinks it's the only place where no one would think of looking."

"Okay, okay, I'll be down with Daniel in a minute."

Simon grabbed the doc's phone out of his hand and practically shouted into it: "Listen, Gilbert, before you come down here, get yourself some overalls and waders from the sanitation department. Your uniform won't survive the brush with trash."

"Appreciate the heads up, Simon, thanks," Gilbert replied before hanging up.

Ten minutes later the group of men literally weaved their way through the freight hull and arrived in sight of the bins. They would be rolled out of the ship and loaded onto trucks to go to the dump site or incinerator, which ever the case may be. The recycling of garbage had not reached the shores of West Africa yet.

Simon's men were the first two to climb up the ladders to reach the top of the first bin. They looked down and shook their heads. Simon ordered one of them to climb down and see if there was a body hidden among the trash. The second man, who had remained perched on the rim of the bin, yelled that 'no' his companion had found no one remotely resembling a human being – some things came close, but not really!

As soon as the two men reached the top of the second bin, they raised their hands in surrender. For a moment Alan and his companions wondered what they were doing. Then they heard a voice say: "Get out of here or I'll kill him!"

"That's my cue, guys," Daniel said, taking his gun out of its shoulder holster. He waited until Simon's men were down the ladders and climbed up to the rim of the trash bin.

Gilbert followed him, climbing up the next ladder.

Everyone waited with baited breath; none more so than Alan. He wanted to get to Mr. Atkinson *now*. His patient was probably dying and he felt totally helpless standing down there and looking up.

When Mr. Ekelton arrived, he immediately asked Alan what was going on.

"Mr. Atkinson is being held hostage in the bin, sir," he replied, pointing to the huge garbage holder.

"And what is Agent Crosby hoping to accomplish?" Ekelton questioned, looking up at the Interpol agent.

"I don't really know, sir. I just hope he can get the man to cooperate so that I could get to Mr. Atkinson before he dies from unsanitary exposure."

They then heard Daniel shout: "Okay, man, I can understand where you're coming from. I'm just worried that you push this thing too far and you end up in front of the firing squad because you let your hostage die."

"This man has *my* diamond!" everyone heard the abductor say. "He tells me where it is and I will let him go!"

"Wrong!" Daniel yelled. "I was there when Mr. Atkinson gave the stone back to your government. If you want to take anybody hostage, get your prime minister…"

"What is happening in here?" they heard one of the Sierra Leonean guards' demand of the group. The two guards had come up the platform.

They all turned to look at the two men.

Daniel didn't budge. He still had his gun pointed downward at the man in the trash bin.

Once Ekelton had explained to the guards what was going on, the older of the officers yelled up to Daniel, "Sir, please come down. We will look after the situation."

Reluctantly Daniel ceded the ladder to the guard. The latter climbed up to the rim of the bin, pointed his rifle down, and fired.

Alan was stunned. He could not believe what just happened. The officer had shot a man without even asking any explanation for his conduct. He was appalled. Yet, he had to rescue Mr. Atkinson before he would succumb from this ill treatment.

Once Alan had climbed down into the trash bin and had examined his patient – as briefly as possible – Simon's crew lifted the poor little jeweler out of the bin and transported him back to the medical center.

Before returning to the med center himself, Alan waited for Simon's men to retrieve the body of the abductor, which they dropped onto a gurney. Alan examined him. He had been shot through the head. He wouldn't have suffered. He was just a young fellow. He had probably been coaxed into capturing Mr. Atkinson and in demanding that he return the diamond to him. How the young man had reached Mr. Atkinson's cabin or even knew where to look for him was another matter that would need investigating.

In the next hour Captain Hildebrandt was to receive the most sincere apologies from the Sierra Leone government. The messenger added that they were glad to have taken the criminal in 'flagrant delicti' and to have exacted punishment swiftly. The captain had no answer. According to Ekelton and the report he had received from Agent Crosby, the perpetrator was not aware that the Star had been returned to the government and had lost his life in a futile attempt at recovering what was supposedly his.

When Alan reached the med center, Alice had already undressed the jeweler and had fitted him with a clean gown before lying him down on one of the beds in the examination room. He was still unconscious – probably from being ill-treated or from the shock of being dumped into a garbage bin.

A few minutes after Alan had cleaned his wound and had replaced the dressing, Mr. Atkinson woke up. He looked around him and grabbed Alan's hand.

"They want the Star... I don't have it! Don't they know?"

"No one is here, Mr. Atkinson. Just Alice and me. We found you. Do you know who took you?"

"Some hooligans, Dr. Mayhew. They came in with the maid to make my bed..."

"Did you say the maid on your deck let them in?" Alice was astounded.

"Yes, my dear. There were three of them. Two guards and a younger man who kept saying that the Star was his. His father had found it. He wanted it back."

A picture began to take shape in Alan's mind. The two guards on the dock were probably the ones who transported the jeweler after drugging him. They let the young fellow do whatever he wanted to extract the information out of Mr. Atkinson until Daniel intervened. One of the guards had no choice; he had to kill the witness. Under the guise of getting rid of an abductor, he killed the only witness who could have plausibly identified him and his companion. As for Mr. Atkinson recognizing him, he was sure the jeweler couldn't put a name to the face he only saw briefly before falling unconscious.

"I'll get Gilbert to find the maid," Alan told Alice. "You look after Mr. Atkinson." He returned his attention to his patient. "I'll give you a mild sedative so that you can rest comfortably tonight, sir. We'll see if we can move you to another cabin in the morning, if that's alright with you."

"Just fine, Doctor, just fine. But before you go, this whole affair reminded me of what one of my friends told me when I told him that I was going on a cruise..."

"What did he say?" Alan asked.

Mr. Atkinson smiled and winked at Alice. "He said: "Don't forget to smile at the maid, Isaac, she is the only one you'll let into your cabin"…" He chuckled lightly.

Alan smiled. There must have been a private joke somewhere in there, but he couldn't quite grasp the meaning of it.

When Alan reached Gilbert's office, it was past midnight. He plopped down on the visitors' chair and crossed his legs. He let Gilbert finish his phone conversation and then said, "The maid did it!"

"What are you saying now, Alan?" Gilbert stared at his friend, goggle-eyed.

"I'm saying that Mr. Atkinson is awake; that he saw his assailants and that the maid let the two guards and the young man into the cabin."

"You mean the guard who shot the guy was in on it?"

Alan nodded. "Absolutely. The young guy probably knew the maid and promised her a cut of the profits after they had sold the Star. She agreed to let them in, and the rest is history."

"Let me see," Gilbert said, already consulting the list of housekeeping personnel assigned to Mr. Atkinson's deck. "There are a couple of girls looking after the six suites of the east deck. I gather the one from Guinea would be our first choice." He raised his gaze to Alan. "What do you suggest we do?"

"Ask Ekelton for an order of immediate dismissal – if she's still aboard. I actually think she's already gone. These guards, as you saw, don't play games. She probably knows what happened to her accomplice in the trash bin and has gone to the mountains, never to be seen again."

At 5:00 a.m. the next morning, Edmund was observing his great-grandson as he watched the sunrise with Tiffany from the upper deck.

"You two need some sleep time," Edmund said to them.

"You're right about that, Granddad," Tiffany replied.

Alan looked up at his ancestor. "I wish I could have spoken to our victim before he died."

"No matter what you would have said, son, his fate was sealed the minute he sought the diamond from our little jeweler. Death came too soon for him though, I agree."

CHAPTER FORTY-THREE

A surprise in a billion

WHEN BETTY PALMER DECIDED TO MEET with Leon Summerville and his wife Linda, she invited the couple to have dinner with her at the upper deck restaurant. She chose a table near the panoramic window but away from the dining crowd. She had told Gregory and Adele, her assistants of her decisions and had rewarded them for their efforts in tracing her nephew by depositing a serious reward in their respective bank accounts. But for tonight she didn't want to see them anywhere near the restaurant. Adele and Gregory were happy enough to leave the woman alone; they had plans to make and a future to envisage now that they were significantly richer than when they first stepped aboard *The Contessa*.

Leon had received the message from Betty Palmer with a mixture of excitement and relish. At first he wondered why the woman wanted to talk to him. He and Linda had their eyes on Betty's fortune for some time. With Gaston's assistance they would be ready to pounce and divert some of her personal funds into their pockets. What the couple didn't know, however, was that Gaston wasn't prepared to move in that direction. He was actually disgusted with the whole idea of stealing the lady's money. Playing with investments, tempting one's luck or playing the odds on the stock market with someone else's money was one thing. Diverting funds and stealing money, is quite another. The punishment for doing so would be imprisonment. Although Gaston had seen the inside of the worst of jails in this cruel human world, he was not prepared to step into an American prison gladly or waste the rest of his life ruing the day he would have accepted Leon's directives.

Linda and Leon didn't know what to make of Mrs. Palmer's invitation. Was she aware of their intentions?

"What do you think she wants?" Leon asked his wife, while he was slipping his tie under his shirt collar and looking at his reflection in the mirror.

"I have no idea, sweetheart," Linda replied evasively. She really didn't care to know what the woman wanted. "Having dinner with her could prove informative, don't you think?"

"Maybe so, but the woman does not spare a minute on empty chatter, from what I gathered from Gaston," Leon said, lifting the knot of his tie to the collar of his shirt. He then passed the brush through his hair and looked at his reflection with satisfaction. He turned to Linda. "So, what do you think?" He swiveled on his heels.

"This suit looks very good on you; glad we have the opportunity to get dressed properly for once." She returned to finishing her make-up. "This heat and vacation-like atmosphere is getting a little boring, don't you think?"

"Exactly. It's about time we get our hands on Mrs. Palmer's money, and get out of this hell-hole. I've spent enough of my youth around the black man to know that I have had enough of "his" company for a long while. Not that I don't appreciate what they've done for me, but I am as anxious as you are, honey, to return to the States."

"You know, with everything that's happened to that New York jeweler, I am very glad we didn't choose to fleece him. We would be suspected of all sorts of crimes by now if we had moved on him."

"You're absolutely right, sweetie," Leon replied, bending down to kiss his wife in the nape of her neck. "And you look absolutely ravishing tonight – or did I say that already?"

She lifted her gaze and smiled at her husband in the mirror.

A half hour later the couple showed up at the door of the

restaurant.

"Mr. and Mrs. Summerville, how nice to see you tonight," the maître d' said with a broad grin adorning his lips. "Mrs. Palmer is already seated. Let me show you to her table."

He walked ahead of the couple in the direction of Betty's table.

She had an aperitif in front of her. She smiled when she saw them approach.

"Thank you for accepting my invitation," she said, looking at the two as they took seats across the table from her. "David…" She returned her attention to the maître d'. "Would you mind bringing us a bottle of champagne – you know the one I like: *La Veuve Clicquot* – brut, won't you?"

"Certainly, Mrs. Palmer. Right away," David replied, trotting away.

"Don't be surprised," she said to Leon when she noted his frown. "I have some news for you two – for you in particular, Leon – which I think will be worth a little celebration."

"What sort of a surprise, Mrs. Palmer," Linda inquired. "When champagne is to be poured it usually means one has very good news to tell."

"Yes, my dear. You're perfectly correct. It is wonderful news for you both and for me personally."

As if on cue, David returned with an ice bucket and a bottle of Betty's favorite champagne. "May I open it?" he asked her.

"Yes, yes, of course. I didn't ask for it to stand unopened. So, please, go ahead, David."

As the cork popped out, David was ready with Betty's glass in hand to pour the bubbly in it. He then poured a glass for each of her guests, replaced the bottle in the bucket, bowed and left the table.

Betty took her glass in a toasting gesture and said, "To our future!"

Exchanging a glance, Leon and Linda repeated the toast and sipped a bit of the excellent champagne. They were still far from guessing the reason why they were sitting at their "target's" table. But they didn't dare ask any questions.

"You see, Mr. Summerville, the toast was particularly meant for you..."

"For me?" Leon looked as baffled as he felt. "How do you mean? Without sounding rude, Mrs. Palmer, but what would my future have to do with you?"

"A great deal in fact."

Leon and Linda could hardly wait to hear the punch line to this one. They had absolutely no clue what the lady was talking about.

"You see," Betty went on, "when my husband passed away a few years back, I had to take over his affairs and had to learn how to become a business woman all at once. It wasn't simple, but thanks to trustworthy and astute business associates I managed to maintain my husband's many endeavors in good stead. On the other hand, when my husband was alive, I had no opportunity to fulfill my sister's dying wish: for me to find her son. She had apparently put her boy up for adoption and somehow the infant found its way to Senegal and The Gambia." She stopped her narrative and riveted her eyes on Leon. He looked down and shook his head. "Can you guess what I am about to tell you, Mr. Summerville?"

He remained silent for a moment. Linda's gaze didn't leave Betty's face. She didn't want to end the suspense although she knew what the woman sitting opposite her was about to tell them.

"Yes, I can make a fairly good guess," Leon finally replied. "But I'm not sure I am ready to believe you."

"Oh but you don't have to believe me, Mr. Summerville, you only need to review the evidence I have gleaned and accumulated during this journey. It is obvious. I had to come to the only plausible conclusion – you are my sister's son and your DNA proves it beyond all reasonable doubt."

Leon smiled. "You'll have to excuse my skepticism, Mrs. Palmer. I am no longer a young man and I have much to be grateful for in my life, but if I am in fact your nephew, what happens then?"

"Not much for the time being, Mr. Summerville. When we get

back to the States, it will be time to call an extraordinary meeting of the board of directors. I will advise them that you will now have a place on the board and that you will be my successor designate once you have proven your competency at the helm of my companies."

Linda was beyond words. She could not truly believe what she was hearing. Her husband was to become the sole heir of an immense fortune and the director and CEO of a number of flourishing companies.

"Don't that beat all!" she exclaimed. "I always knew you had it in you, honey, but this is more than I ever expected."

He turned to look at her. "I think you're right, doll. I don't know how I'm going to manage though," he added, returning his gaze to Betty.

"There is no doubt in my mind that you have a good head for business, Mr. Summerville…"

"Please, call me Leon. Since we're family, that's the least I could ask."

"Yes, well, Leon, as I was saying, I have no doubt that you'll fare very well. As I told you both before I gave you the news, I had to learn how to manage enterprises worth billions of dollars when my husband suddenly left me in charge. Besides, you will have ample assistance. There will be a bank of accountants and lawyers at your disposal. And anything you want or need will be handed to you the minute you ask for it."

"That's sounds great," Leon uttered, somehow unsure how he was going to fare in a world he could only admire from the outside until today."

"And what happens now, Mrs. Palmer – or should I call you Aunt Betty?" Leon asked, drinking a bit more champagne and smiling at the woman who had suddenly decided to make him a very wealthy man.

"Yes, you can call me Aunt Betty if you choose. I'll be flattered if you do, actually. But to answer your question as to what happens now; it's fairly simple, we are going to have dinner and discuss the many aspects of your new life. How does that sound?"

Linda and Leon exchanged a glance and a broad smile appeared across their lips.

"I think that sounds like a plan, Aunt Betty," Leon answered, squeezing Linda's hand in one of his own, while he grabbed the menu with the other.

Tonight was perhaps a night of celebration for many passengers. There was a breath of relief floating about the ship. The worst of the epidemic had passed and all of the members of the WHO team were glad to have been able to inoculate hundreds of men, women and children in the course of this mission.

As for the other passengers, most were glad to be leaving Sierra Leone in the morning. They had seen the best of what Freetown and environs had to offer, but now they were ready to explore some other, more salubrious parts of Africa. The next port of call being Abidjan, the capital of the Côte d'Ivoire. Practically everyone was looking forward to visit it at leisure.

That evening, the Promenade Bar was abuzz with excitement. People were ready to 'get on with it'.

Among them were Mack and Joe. These two had enjoyed their cruise and were looking forward to set foot in a city that wasn't under quarantine or plagued with poverty and misery. They wanted to have some laughter to be remembered. They sat on their favorite stools and asked Irvine, the bartender if he had any blueberry tea.

"Really?" Irvine asked incredulously. "What about your usual scotch and bourbon, aren't those good enough anymore?"

"Not that you understand, my good fellow," Mack said in his best British accent, "It's for my dear wife. She'll be along any minute and she'll order a blueberry tea. And if you don't have it, she'll walk out of here annoyed. Do you get my drift?"

Irvine wasn't too sure of what the gentleman meant, but he soon gathered that Mrs. Mack should not be staying long at the bar, according to her husband.

"Well, I can order some blueberries from the kitchen, and I can get a pot of tea going," Irvine answered concertedly, while wiping the counter in front of his two favorite patrons.

"That's a very good response, Irvine. You'll be sure to add a tenner to my tab tonight, won't you?"

"May I ask why you don't want Mrs. Mack to spend time with you here in the bar?"

"It's just that she won't understand our jokes"—Mack nodded to Joe—"and I would prefer that she spend more time with her friends."

Prying into the passengers' business wasn't Irvine style. If they wanted to talk; fine. But if they didn't, he wouldn't meddle.

Gladys came in and strode decisively to the bar, amply covered the stool beside her husband and said to Irvine: "Do you happen to serve blueberry tea in this place?"

Irvine exploded in laughter and so did Joe and Mack under Gladys's amazed gaze.

CHAPTER FORTY-FOUR

No ivory on the coast

ABIDJAN IS AS MODERN AS ANY metropolis in the western hemisphere. There's very little difference between the capital of the Cote d'Ivoire and say Miami, except for the indigent population whose background differs greatly from the people living in Florida. The office buildings shimmered in the morning sun when *The Contessa* made her way into port. The freshness of the morning air was brushing everyone's cheeks with renewed hope for a different type of adventure.

Babette and Betty were among those who were ready to visit the city and even take a trip inland to some wildlife reserve.

Betty said, "I finally told him." She was all smiles.

"Told him what? And who's him?" Babette queried, taken aback by this sudden and somewhat disjointed announcement.

"I told Leon Summerville that he is my nephew."

"Really?" Babette said, stepping on the gangway to start their descent toward the busy port facilities. "Wasn't that a little premature?"

"Yes, perhaps, but I couldn't wait. I was like a parent waiting to see a child's reaction on Christmas morning."

"And what was the fifty-year-old child's reaction?" Babette turned to smile at her friend.

"I don't think he believed me at first. But later, when I explained that he could go through all of the evidence I gathered thus far, he seemed to accept the news as fact."

"What about his wife? How did she react?"

"Differently. I mean, she sounded very happy and surprised, of course. Then when I started explaining that her husband, as a company director, would receive a generous salary, but that neither of them could touch any of the investments or monies used for the day-to-day running of the companies, Linda seemed to shrink back."

Babette and Betty arrived at the customs' wickets; they presented their ship passenger ID cards; showed their ground tour passes and proceeded to exit the port where a van was expecting them.

Once they were sitting in the back seat of the mini-bus, Betty asked, "What do you think she expected?"

"Oh, I'm sure she didn't expect her husband to earn a salary, which she would have to use reasonably for the first year or so."

"She probably thought she would be able to run out and buy the shops out of their most expensive goods while paying with an unlimited funds company credit card."

"Exactly. Their credit cards, same as mine actually, will have a reasonable limit. And most of what they spend will have to be paid from Leon's salary – not from the company's bank account."

"I bet Linda Summerville didn't like that at all, did she?"

"It didn't seem so, no. Yet, she appeared to relax when I told her that they would be able to buy a new house and decorate it as they saw fit – within reason, of course."

"She is a 'big spender', Betty," Babette said. "She'll probably be the one who ruins her husband."

"Of that I am not too sure, Babette. You see, Leon is made of the same cloth as his mother was. She's not the big spender in that family; I rather think he's the opposite. He's no miser, mind you, but he doesn't seem to enjoy frivolities like Linda does."

"What makes you say that?"

"Simply this: when I told him that he could choose a new car, he was quick to say that they both had nearly new vehicles sitting in their garages in New Orleans and that, as far as he was concerned, 'a new car is always a new hassle' – to use his words."

"And you think he'll be able to curb his wife's spending?"

"That I don't know, Babette. Time will tell, I suppose."

Originally a small fishing village on the south coast of the Cote d'Ivoire, today Abidjan is by far the largest city in West Africa, counting no less than 4.4 million inhabitants. Following a yellow fever epidemic in 1895, the French government decided to move from Bassam to Abidjan's current location. By 1903, Abidjan attained the status of township. Located on the edge of the Lagoon n'doupe (the lagoon in the hot water) which became known as the Ebrie Lagoon, Abidjan offered more space for long-term settlement and trade expansion. Port Bouet, south of the town quickly grew into an international port-of-call. Abidjan was only destined to expand. It soon became the main economic center of the colony and a prime location for the distribution of products and goods inland. The city was designed in a grid pattern, such as many colonial cities were at the time. The "Plateau" in Tchaman was mostly populated by European settlers while the north of the city was inhabited by the "Colons". The two "cities" were separated by the Gallieni Military Barracks, which were replaced by the current courthouse after the Cote d'Ivoire declaration of independence. In the 1940's the Plateau saw the establishment of several hotels and resorts, one of which was to become the well-known Bardon Park Hotel – the first air-conditioned hotel built in a French colony. In 1950 the Vridi canal was completed. It linked the lagoon to the sea.

Although it is still in need of dredging and regular maintenance, the lagoon is considered the main water expanse around which the wealthy inhabitants want their houses constructed.

By 1995 Abidjan was (and still is) the financial center of West Africa. Yet, it is also the capital of poverty. Where there is opulence, there is penury and corruption in Africa. Most people live (or try to subsist) on less than $1.50 a day. They sell their wares at the central market and even offer "transport" services – a wheelbarrel is all you need to transport anything anywhere. And then there are telephone services. They "lend" you their cell phones for a price so you can call anyone in town if need be; sort of a mobile telephone booth.

Alan and Tiffany were walking through the market when they saw a police officer arrest a man for wearing three pairs of pants.

"Why is he wearing all those trousers do you think, I know black men tend to wear several pairs of briefs, but trousers?" Tiffany asked Alan.

The latter smiled. "That's a way to camouflage himself. He's probably a thief. And when the police are busy chasing a man wearing jeans, he's wearing a jogging suit."

Tiffany giggled. "They're resourceful, you can certainly say that for them."

"Yes they are. But that's nothing to compare to what you can buy or exchange in this market. If you have an old cell-phone and you want a new one, it's simple, you exchange it. You place the old phone in a new box – at the shop – and the shop keeper asks you to pay the difference between your old phone and the new one in another box."

"But you can't tell if you're really getting a new phone, can you?"

"Exactly. Nine times out of ten, your "new" phone is as old or older than the one you just exchanged."

"And people fall for that?"

"Oh yes – who doesn't like to find out what's in the box?"

While the two of them continued their market exploration, the mini-bus had driven Betty and Babette to the Banco National Park, east of the lagoon. The park covers nearly 300 square kilometers of rainforest. The lush vegetation and fauna hides a shameful past of destruction and devastation. This is where the hunters came to kill the elephants for food and ivory. Practically extinct in the early days of colonization, the herds – what was left of them – migrated north or went to lie down in the elephant cemeteries littering the countries east and south of the Ivory Coast. Today, there are no more elephants roaming the Ivory Coast. Only monkeys and small animals populate the parks.

"Sad, isn't it?" Babette said to Betty when the guide finished explaining what happened to the elephants that used to live in the region.

"I think it's shameful, Babette. What we did for profit and gain throughout the centuries is shameful. We should hide from the sight of God. How can we ever hope to be saved when we continue to destroy the gifts He gave us so graciously?"

"Man has a choice, Betty," Babette remarked somberly. "And he often makes the wrong decision."

"You're right, of course. But these hunters originally didn't kill for the tusks alone, I suppose."

"No they didn't," they heard their guide say from behind them. "An elephant could feed an entire tribe for months, not to mention the skin and hair which they used in the fabrication of many items."

"What did they do with the ivory?" Babette asked.

"They mostly used it in the making of small tools. You see, ivory is very strong and quite resistant to many attacks, but if it dries it becomes brittle and cracks easily, like old bones. So, the objects they carved were small and used in cooking or delicate operations."

"That's interesting," Betty remarked, as they continued walking along the red-dirt path.

That night, when everyone was back on board, Alan spent a bit of time with Mr. Atkinson and checking on his patient. He didn't want anything to happen to him before he flew home upon arrival in Accra.

"Doctor Mayhew, so nice of you to drop by. I think you will be happy to learn that I am able to move my forearm a little."

"That is excellent news indeed, Mr. Atkinson. But you should be careful not to pull on the muscles around the wound – the sutures are still fragile. I should be able to take them out tomorrow actually," Alan added as he finished examining his patient's shoulder and healing wound.

"Do you think I will be able to visit Abidjan tomorrow then – if you're taking out the stitches?" Mr. Atkinson sounded impatient to get out of his cabin.

"Perhaps, you could take a tour with one of the guides if you accept having Alice come with you."

A broad smile appeared on the little jeweler's lips. "I'll go anywhere with the dear woman, Doctor. She's saved my life more than once. Maybe I should ask her to marry me. What do you think?"

Alan erupted in laughter. "You couldn't do any better when it comes to choosing a good woman, Mr. Atkinson, but I don't think Alice will be agreeable to your proposal. She's very happy traveling the world unattached, I believe."

"Yes, yes, of course." The little jeweler smiled. "That reminds me of a little joke." Alan was all ears. "A man was speaking to God: "God, why did you make women so beautiful?" he asked. God said: "I did that to make you love them". Then the man asked: "Well, God; why did you make them such good cooks?" God said: "I did that to make you love them". The man then asked: "But God, why did you make women so stupid?" God said: "I did that to make them love you!"

Alan laughed and shook his head. "I'll have to remember that, Mr. Atkinson, but I wouldn't repeat this in front of Alice if I were you."

"No-no, of course not. And I surely didn't mean any of this in seriousness. I am rather an old independent sort, you see. Company bores me easily. So, I wouldn't want a good friendship, such as the one I entertain with Miss Alice, to deteriorate into a tiresome union."

"Very wise, sir," Alan concluded, shutting his medical bag and getting ready to leave the jeweler's suite.

"So, at what time should I be at the medical center tomorrow?"

"Make it early – say 9:00 a.m. – so that you can leave with Alice for your outing right afterward."

Walking to the cabin's door with his guest, Mr. Atkinson said, "Thank you, Doctor, I'll be there on the dot at nine a.m."

CHAPTER FORTY-FIVE

The last of Constantine . . .

THE NEXT EVENING, MOST OF the passengers seemed tired or anxious to retire. The heat in Abidjan is unusually overwhelming. Although the city is located on the coastline, it seems to be continually enveloped in a malodorous steam emanating from the lagoon. Alan even noticed that some passengers suffered from mild diarrhea or nausea. A dose of Pepto-Bismol was enough to calm their discomfort. Most of them were anxious to have a nice meal and get to their cabin for a good-night's rest.

Thus it was a perfect night for Constantine to make an appearance. He had entertained the passengers throughout the cruise and this was to be his last show before *The Contessa* reached Accra in Ghana.

"Ladies and Gentlemen," he began at the dinner-show when everyone was busy eating their dessert, "I don't want you to start crying or sobbing or even whimpering when I tell you that it's my last night..." Applause interrupted him. "If you think I'm about to kick the bucket and leave you..." The giggles and chuckles continued. "You're wrong. The captain has just decided that he had enough of my bad jokes and that he didn't want to see my face in his nightmares anymore!" Everyone was laughing heartily by now. "Well, sorry about that, Captain"—he turned toward Hildebrandt's table—"but I have a couple more up my sleeve if you don't mind." He paused. "After that, I promise I will leave ... quietly..." He looked around him. "Okay, folks, let's see now…. Ah, yes…. at our last encounter we were talking about death. Well, it reminded me of the time I attended the funeral of one of my friends. What I saw during the wake really reaffirmed my admiration for the legal profession. But let me just tell you what happened: There was this Brooklyn lawyer, a used car salesman and a banker gathered by my friend's coffin. In his grief, one of the three said, "In my family, we have a custom of giving the dead some money, so they'll have something to spend over there." They all agreed that this was appropriate. The banker dropped a hundred dollar bill into the casket, and the car salesman did the same. But guess what the lawyer did: he took out the bills and wrote a check for $300." Amid the applause, Constantine added, "I'll be back a little later with a last bedtime story, but for now, it's *Good Night* to you all."

In the morning, Alan was ready and waiting for Mr. Atkinson when Gaston came in. He walked into Alan's office with a decisive manner about him.

"I'm sorry, Dr. Mayhew, but I just wanted to know if we could meet later on today? At the Promenade Bar maybe?"

"We sure can do that, Gaston, but could you give me a hint as to what this is about?"

"It's about Mrs. Summerville, Doctor. If she does come and see you, please beware – she's really "unstable" right now."

Alan affixed a puzzled look on his face. "Can you tell me what you mean by "unstable"?"

"Sure; she's just gone crazy since she's learned that Leon is Mrs. Palmer's nephew."

"But I should have thought the news would have made her happy…"

"Well, I guess it did at first, but when she learned that neither she nor Leon could put their paws on Mrs. Palmer's dough immediately and that he would have to 'work' for the money, she went berserk."

"Okay," Alan replied, nodding. "Why don't I have a talk with her before we meet around one o'clock? If that's okay with you."

"Sure is, Doctor. In the meantime, I think I'll have a bit of a tour of Abidjan. I'm told it's a very interesting city."

"Maybe have a walk through the central market – that's a very "interesting" place to visit."

"Okay, I think I'll do that – without camera, cell phone or wallet, I gather?"

"Precisely. You get the picture."

Once Mr. Atkinson had his sutures removed and Alice had gone with him for a visit of the city and wilderness park, Alan decided it was about time to have a bit of a chat with Mrs. Summerville – before she went on a rampage.

When he knocked at the Summerville's door, he heard a shout in response: "Yes! Who is it?"

"Doctor Mayhew. May I have a word?"

"Sure, why not," she uttered, opening the door wide, "everybody seems to think I need a good talking-to." She stared at Alan before adding, "Sorry, Doctor, please come in." She extended an arm toward the small sofa in their mini-salon.

"Thanks," Alan replied, going to the indicated seat.

"Do you want a drink," she asked, going to the liquor cabinet.

"No thanks, Mrs. Summerville. I'm fine," he replied, taking a seat.

"I'll have one if you don't mind." Linda poured several fingers of cognac in a snifter, added a couple of ice cubes and some water before sitting herself down across from Alan. "Now, you said you wanted to have a word with me; what about?"

"Well, first I wanted to ask you if you had a chance to go shopping at the malls in Abidjan. I am told it's a fascinating city."

"Come, come, Doctor. I'm no fool. You didn't come here to talk about my shopping spree, did you?"

"No, not really, but it is indeed an experience in itself." He paused. "You're right, I came up to see you, because Gaston came to see me. He's very concerned."

"Concerned about what?" Linda snapped. "Well, I suppose he should be. When we go back to the States, we won't need his services, since my dear husband will now be a salaried employee of Palmer Industries – like the damned peon he is. Didn't have the backbone to tell the old witch where to get off, did he?"

Alan had seen and heard many irate women and angry ladies in his long career, but he would have to say Linda would probably top the list of "enraged" women. "But I thought Mr. Summerville was the sole heir of Mrs. Palmer's estate, isn't he?"

"Exactly my point, Doctor. Yet, the bitch has only seen fit to give him a salaried position on her board of directors and a title of CEO in the major enterprise. And that's it. Until the woman kicks the bucket, we'll have to live the life of salaried peons."

"But I suppose the salary is considerable, isn't it?"

"How ever much it is, Doctor Mayhew, it's not a fortune and it certainly does not give us the freedom to live or travel the in a manner to which we've been accustomed."

"You mean you won't have the freedom to spend as much as you want whenever you want, is that it?"

"You got it, Doc. But that's not really what bugs me; it's the fact that we have to live according to the imposed rules of the company. It almost feels as if we'll be set under a microscope and everything we'll do will be checked and rechecked."

"I gather you don't like to live by someone else's rules, do you, Mrs. Summerville?"

"You're darn right, I don't," Linda replied, swallowing a big gulp of her drink. "I hate gossipy wives. I don't want to be a member of the Country Club. I don't want to organize the kids' barbecue on Sunday. I don't want to go to these people's Christmas Party. I can't see myself "doing" lunch with any of these women. No, Doctor, I can't even contemplate living such a life."

"And what does Leon say about all this?"

"Oh, he's looking at the big picture and at our future, as he says. He's happy enough to take the deal. He won't have to worry about where his next paycheck is coming from..."

"But don't you two have several investments and growing concerns in New Orleans. Isn't he going to look after these?"

"No, Doctor. And that's just it. He plans to sell our property, *our house*, and put the proceeds into his aunt's company. Can you imagine that? Everything we've ever worked for going to the bitch?"

"Perhaps you should express your concerns to Mrs. Palmer and maybe come to an understanding whereby you stay in New Orleans to look after your estate (maybe even with Gaston's assistance) and keep it as your growing concern. Leon could 'commute' to Palmer Industries' board meetings when appropriate."

Mrs. Summerville put the snifter down on the coffee table and stared at Alan for a moment. "Yes, that's an excellent idea, Doctor. So I wouldn't be subjected to live the life of a CEO's wife, but be independent and have my own money, like I did before. I have heard of many modern couples that maintain two homes and lives and get together for trips et al."

When Alan reached the Promenade Bar it was about twelve-fifty. He spotted Gaston sitting at the counter in front of a tall glass of beer. Alan sat down on the stool next to him.

"Hi, Doc. I just got here myself. So, don't worry, you're not late."

"I didn't think I would be." He attracted the bartender's attention and ordered an orange juice. "How was your market stroll?"

"Ah, that was most interesting indeed," Gaston replied all smiles. "Thanks for the recommendation."

"Did you find something worth a couple of pennies?"

"Better than that, Doc. I think I swindled the swindler." He pulled a brand new Galaxy phone out of his pocket. "How's that for a find?"

Alan laughed outright. "You found the "right box", didn't you?"

Gaston nodded. "See, my old phone was insured against loss and damages, but not for being outdated and practically useless. So, and against your advice, I took it with me. When I got to the cell-phone vendors; I looked for one who could give me a good deal. None had any better deal than what I could find in the States. Yet, this last one made it a game – you put your phone in a box and you pay him fifty bucks to choose another box. Of course it was a gamble, but I got lucky I guess."

Looking down at the expensive smart phone, Alan said, "It does look like it." He looked up. "Have you checked that it works?"

"Oh that was the funny part. I scrolled down to find a number – it hadn't been erased from the memory – and called it. And I got a very angry woman at the other end of the line, saying something about being a cheat, or something of the sort. My African French is not the best. Anyway, it works."

"That's great, Gaston." Alan drank a long gulp of his juice. "Talking about angry women. I went to visit our friend, Mrs. Summerville. You were right, the woman is truly angry. It's as if you had thrown her in a cage and left her there to brew her discontent."

"What is she going to do now – apart from firing me – did she tell you?"

"No. But I suggested something to her that could solve her problem. I think she'll talk to you before she talks to Leon about it. But it involves you working with her again. Do you think you would want to do that?"

"I don't know, Doc. It depends on what she (or you) had in mind."

"Well, it's fairly simple really. Instead of selling the New Orleans business, maybe the two of you could run it?"

Gaston shook his head. "I don't know, Doc. The woman is all about money. She could care less how she gets it or how much she spends in one afternoon. What you're proposing would certainly solve her problem if she could keep her fingers out of the till, so to speak."

That night, Alan and Tiffany arrived at the cabaret restaurant when Constantine was delivering one of his serial jokes.

"I thought last night was his last?" Alan queried in a whisper as they took their seats at a table at the back of the cabaret.

"So did I, but the captain didn't want to let him off the hook yet."

Constantine was saying: "So I got home, and the phone was ringing. I picked it up, and said 'Who's speaking please?' And a voice said 'You are'."

"So I rang up my local swimming pool. I said 'Is that the local swimming pool?" He said, 'It depends where you're calling from'."

"So I rang up a local building firm, I said, 'I want a balcony outside my house.' He said, 'I'm not stopping you.' The applause and laughter interrupted him, but only for a few seconds.

He went on: "So I was in my car, and I was driving along, and my boss rang up, and he said "You've been promoted." And I swerved. And then he rang up a second time and said "You've been promoted again." And I swerved again. He rang up a third time and said "You're managing director." And I went into a tree. The policeman came up and said "What happened to you?" And I said "I *careered* off the road." When the applause and whistles died down, Constantine concluded, "I promise you: you won't see me in this cabaret again this trip. Have a fantastic night and a terribly boring trip home! Thank you!"

CHAPTER FORTY-SIX

Accra

ACCRA IS THE ELEVENT LARGEST city in Africa. With a population of over two million people, the metropolitan district extends northward from the port into the hills. Greater Accra is said to count a large cosmopolitan population of over four million. Accra was originally the capital of the British Gold Coast from 1877 to 1957. Today the capital is considered one of the most modern and comfortable cities on the West Coast of Africa. The city's architecture reflects its British history. These luxuriously restored buildings are next door to skyscrapers, office towers, shopping malls, and apartment blocks. Accra is the city of administrators, organizers and hostelry specialists. Novotel has establish a center of administration in the capital. The city's National Theater was built in 2010 with Chinese assistance. Apart from these eye-catching structures, Accra has been the host of numerous profitable and growing enterprises such as food processing, lumber, textile, chemicals and clothing. Accra and "its administrators" should be congratulated for the growing economy of their country.

When Babette finished reading the pamphlet, she shrugged her shoulders. Edmund was observing her, unobtrusively perched atop the liquor cabinet.

"Is there something bothering you, milady," he asked as he

floated down to sit across from his friend.

"Truly, Edmund, I don't know what to do. I should be glad to go home, yet I am not. I have been so thrilled to visit this continent, I wish I could spend several months here – I don't mean in Accra per se – but to visit the many places I haven't seen yet. I still want to climb the pyramid of Cheops, visit the diamond mines in Botswana, trek the trails of Kilimanjaro…"

Edmund's eyebrows rose significantly. "Are you sure you have not taken an extra dose of my grandson's vitamins?"

"Why? Do you think me incapable of exercising these old gams of mine?"

"I didn't say that, Babette, but in the list you just enumerated, there isn't one place where one could rest comfortably in front of a tall drink."

"You know I am not into lazing on a beach in the middle of the Pacific; a journey has to be interesting and educational for me to enjoy it. Tomorrow, we will be in Accra. It sounds like a most fascinating city, yet it is not an *interesting* place to visit. I would prefer to return to the desert and have another camel ride, or take a trip through the Sahel again – if it were safe to do so, of course, rather than visiting another city with skyscrapers."

"Well then, why don't you book yourself on a British Airways' flight to Cape Town or Cairo perhaps and visit those places…"

"You mean there's no time like the present, is that it?"

"Exactly, milady. I can assure you if I had the chance to return to some of the places I visited in my past, I certainly would. As it is though, I am happy that my great-grandson has allowed me to live a second life with my beautiful friend."

"You're such a romantic – always been – haven't you?"

"Of course, Babette. Romance is the pulse of life. Love is the only one of God's gifts that you cannot deny. You cannot push it away. Once it settles on your heart, it won't budge."

"How very well put, Edmund." Babette got up from the sofa. "And now I think I will find Mr. Atkinson and have a chat with the dear man. It's been such an ordeal for him. He deserves to spend his last night aboard in good company!"

Edmund burst out laughing. "You mean you, of course?"

"Is there anyone else in this room?"

Edmund returned to laughing.

Babette and a much restored Isaac Atkinson were seated at the terrace restaurant on the upper deck when their conversation veered to the subject of American politics.

"I am not really *au fait* with any of these political figureheads, Isaac," Babette said. "They always seem to try to do their best for the country and end up doing their worst I find."

"That's perhaps because of our failure in educating our children. We don't seem to understand that teaching history in our schools will assist our children in growing towards a brighter future."

"You mean learning from the past?"

"Yes, Miss Babette. That is exactly what I mean. But let me tell you a little story that I think you will appreciate." Babette loved the way Isaac always illustrated his opinions with a colorful story. He made her laugh.

Isaac smiled before he began, "Einstein dies and goes to heaven. At the Pearly Gates, Saint Peter tells him, "You look like Einstein, but you have no idea what some people will do to sneak into Heaven. Can you prove who you really are?" Einstein ponders for a few seconds and asks, "Could I have a blackboard and some chalk?" Saint Peter snaps his fingers and a blackboard and chalk instantly appear. Einstein proceeds to describe with arcane mathematics and symbols his theory of relativity. Saint Peter is suitably impressed. "You really ARE Einstein!" he says. "Welcome to heaven!" The next to arrive is Picasso. Once again, Saint Peter asks for credentials. Picasso asks, "Mind if I use that blackboard and chalk?" Saint Peter says, "Go ahead." Picasso erases Einstein's equations and sketches a truly stunning mural with just a few strokes of chalk. Saint Peter claps. "Surely you are the great artist you claim to be!" he says. "Come on in!" Then Saint Peter looks up and sees George W. Bush. Saint Peter scratches his head and says, "Einstein and Picasso both managed to prove their identity. How can you prove yours?" George W. looks bewildered and says, "Who are Einstein and Picasso?" Saint Peter sighs and says, "Come on in, George."

Laughing with Isaac, Babette nodded. "Well said, Isaac. I couldn't have described the American political situation better." She tittered some more.

"But let me ask you, Miss Babette; do you travel on these cruises very often?"

"Oh no… Well, I should say that I do as often as I can. You see, I am very lucky. I can work anywhere these days. As long as I can take my laptop with me, I can sit at a desk and work on my next play whether I am in my flat in Paris or in my suite aboard one of these ships."

"But aren't you supposed to be present at the rehearsal of your productions?"

"Of course. Yet, many of my plays – once produced – do not need my constant attention. Besides, I am only the writer and sometimes the director"—she giggled—"and the producer has the last word when it comes to the final product to be presented to the audience."

Isaac drank a little more of his papaya juice. He nodded. "You see, I have always admired people who can pack their bags on a whim and board a plane or a ship for some exotic destination. To me, it's like reliving the *Exodus* all over again."

"What is so scary about traveling?" Babette asked.

"Oh it's not the traveling itself that worries me, it's the people I leave behind."

"You mean your family?"

"Yes, but also the people who have worked with me for years. I wonder how they would feel if I stepped out on the spur of the moment only to come back after several weeks of absence."

"What about your wife or children, wouldn't they want to travel with you?"

Isaac smiled. "Unfortunately, I'm a widower, my dear Miss Babette. And as for my children, their lives take them to Europe occasionally or even back to Israel on holidays, so traveling with their granddad is not in their cards."

"Well, let me suggest something then: why not choose a destination every year and make a point of traveling to that spot for a couple of weeks' break?"

"That is a very good idea. But you see, I know myself. I will think of a spot and soon forget about it. Unless of course, I have to meet someone in that place."

"Well… In that case, my dear Isaac, if that's all that's stopping you from traveling, let me invite you to visit me in Paris. I have an opening Premiere next month and I think you would enjoy it."

Isaac peered in Babette's eyes. "Are you really inviting me to visit you in Paris?"

"Yes, Isaac, I am really inviting you to visit me in Paris."

"But why?"

"Don't you start asking questions, Isaac. Just be a gentleman and accept the gesture of friendship."

"Alright then," Isaac blurted, visibly taken aback and a bit flustered. "This is unexpected. But, I will make plans with my staff, I do accept, yes. Yes, my dear Babette, I accept your invitation. Thank you."

As Isaac and Babette were making plans to meet in Paris in a not too distant future, Alan and Tiffany were making plans for their upcoming holidays. Same as the playwright and the little jeweler, they were planning to take their vacations in the south of France.

"Driving along the *Corniche* and the Riviera and on to Italy sounds delightful," Tiffany said. "Do you think we'll have enough time to visit all the X's on your map?" she asked, looking down at the map of Europe laid out on their table.

"If we stick to some sort of schedule, we should be able to do it."

Tiffany shook her head. "No! I'm following a schedule every day of my working life; I have to plan my arrival and departure at every port of call, and you want me to do the same on my vacation? No! is the answer, Alan."

Oops, Alan thought, *let's put on the brakes right here, otherwise we'll have a head-on collision.*

"No problem, sweetie. We'll play it by ear then. I can understand what you're saying about schedules, and planning a holiday with timing and itinerary in mind – maybe we should just stay on the ship and return to Boston with it."

"No way! I've had enough of cruising for a while. It's the Riviera and Italy with you – or by myself if you wish to go back to Boston on your own!" Tiffany had a teasing smile on her lovely lips. She leaned to the back of the chair. Alan nodded. "But, you know, you just made me think of something."

"Oh, what's that?" Alan queried.

"Well, I met a lady the other day, she's a 'return cruiser' as she calls it. She takes cruises that are actually repositioning the vessel. She says that she's been on all sorts of cruises like that."

"But there's only a skeleton crew on board... Are you sure?"

"I can't say, Alan. But from what she said, she books her passage starting on the day the cruise lands in its last port of call and travels back to where ever the ship is going next. In this instance she would board in Accra and travel with *The Contessa* to Southampton and onto Boston."

"Do you know who she is? Did she give you a name?"

"Yes, I think she said her name was Mrs. Edith Galbraith. Why?"

"Because, you just gave me an idea, Tiff."

"Oh-no. I don't like to hear that – it usually means trouble. What's that idea of yours?"

"Let me ask you another question: Did you ask her why she traveled on this cruise then?"

"You mean why not wait until Accra?"

"Exactly. What is she doing aboard *The Contessa* right now?"

"Why don't we ask her? Or better, why don't I check her passenger details with Gilbert?"

"You do that while I contact Daniel Crosby. Maybe he could give us information as to who the lady really is."

"You think she's an impostor?"

"Not only that, but I think she's a diamond thief."

Tiffany opened her eyes wide. "Don't tell me: she's the one who stole the Star during the reception."

"Before I answer that question, let's just check who the lady really is, shall we?"

As soon as Gilbert and Daniel had been alerted of Alan's suspicion, Daniel asked for a background check to be done on Mrs. Galbraith. When Daniel's draconian boss replied that Mrs. Galbraith was in fact Mr. Eddy Albright, Daniel swore under his breath. He was an international diamond and jewelry thief with a long rap sheet. He was always difficult to locate, probably because by the time the authorities were about to nab him, he had disappeared into thin air. In reality the guy was escaping in drag aboard a ship returning to its port of origin.

"But why would she talk to me about these "repositioning cruises" and the fact that she…"

"He…" Daniel corrected.

"Yeah, well, that this person was traveling all over the world like that?" Tiffany said.

"Perhaps he is tired of running?" Gilbert suggested.

"Or maybe, he's already moved the Star to the next owner," Daniel said.

"And if we don't find the stone on her… I mean on him…" Gilbert added, "We can't arrest the guy."

"Exactly, Gilbert." Daniel nodded. "We can always spend the last few hours we have on this ship questioning the guy, but since we can't arrest him for felony thefts that have occurred five years ago or beyond, we'll have to let him be."

"You mean we can't touch the guy if he's not made a move in the past five years; is that it?" Gilbert sounded more than annoyed now. "Ridiculous! So, the Star of Sierra Leone is again lost forever if he doesn't have it on him!"

"And I hope it will stay that way," Tiffany said pensively.

Dr. Paul Davis trained in mainstream western medicine in Canada, the United States and England (Family Medicine, Occupational Medicine and Emergency Medicine). During his 35-year career, he has spent extended periods of time doing volunteer work and being a consultant in Asia, India, South & Central America and the Middle East. Dr. Davis uses his insider knowledge, as his novels are based on his ten-year career as a cruise ship doctor. He currently lives in Canada and is the director of a medical specialty group.

Other books by the author:

CRUISE SHIP CRIME MYSTERIES
A Medical Murder Mystery
The Curious Cargo of Bones
The German Intrigue
Murder in the Northwest Passage
The Ghost of Dr. Edmund Netter

NON-FICTION
Baby Boomer Longevity:
Strategies to Transform Your Health

Visit his websites at:
http://www.cruiseshipcrimesite.com
http://cruiseshipcrime.wordpress.com

Dr. Paul Davis is available for lectures and readings. For information regarding his availability, please contact Skye Wentworth, Publicist: skyewentworth@gmail.com.